EVERYMAN, I will go with thee,

and be thy guide,

In thy most need to go by thy side

THOMAS CARLYLE

Born in 1795 at Ecclefechan, the son of a stone-mason. Educated at Edinburgh University. Schoolmaster for a short time, but decided on a literary career, visiting Paris and London. Retired in 1828 to Dumfriesshire to write. In 1834 moved to Cheyne Row, Chelsea, and died there in 1881.

THOMAS CARLYLE

Selected Essays

INTRODUCTION BY

IAN CAMPBELL

*Lecturer in the Department of English
at the University of Edinburgh*

DENT: LONDON

EVERYMAN'S LIBRARY

DUTTON: NEW YORK

All rights reserved
Made in Great Britain
at the
Aldine Press · Letchworth · Herts
for
J. M. DENT & SONS LTD
Aldine House · Bedford Street · London
First included in Everyman's Library 1915
Last reprinted 1972

No. 704   ISBN (if a hardback) 0 460 00704 1
No. 1704   ISBN (if a paperback) 0 460 01704 7

INTRODUCTION

THE earliest of these essays dates from the beginning of the 1830s, when Carlyle was facing a crisis in his life's work. He had established himself as a scholar of some reputation, particularly as translator and interpreter of German writers, and since 1826 he had been happily married to Jane Welsh. Together they spent two pleasant years in Edinburgh, playing an active part in the city's literary and intellectual life, but in 1828 want of money forced them to move to Craigenputtoch, their isolated hill farm in Dumfriesshire. It was here that Carlyle spent some of the most productive years of his life, before moving in 1834 to London; Craigenputtoch saw the production of *Sartor Resartus*, and of many of the remarkable *Critical and Miscellaneous Essays* from which this volume is largely a selection. The Carlyle who appeared in Chelsea was quite well known, not yet for *Sartor*, but for these essays; many of the ideas of 1834 were to be characteristic of his work throughout his writing career, and so these essays form a major guide to Carlyle's thought and writing.

In 1831 the crisis which Carlyle faced was a change of direction, as old subjects palled. The translations of Goethe and the essays on German writers had given him a public reputation, and also enabled him largely to reconstruct the lost religious faith of his childhood, but now he moved on to wider issues. This was a healthy mode of proceeding, for the isolation of Craigenputtoch easily led to an unhealthy self-absorption and, in turn, to a coarsening of conversational powers, a tendency to monologue, which was unfavourably noted by Carlyle's friends in his rare city holidays during these years. Yet his interest in the world at large was intense, his passion for books, and for up-to-date news from the larger world, insatiable. The letters written at Craigenputtoch amply testify to this.[1] The times he clearly felt to be out of joint,

[1] In course of publication as vols. V–VII of the Duke-Edinburgh edition of the *Collected Letters of Thomas and Jane Welsh Carlyle*, ed. C. R. Sanders *et al.* (Durham, N.C.).

. . . times so stupid and prosaic as these; times of monotony and safety, and matter of fact, where affections are measured by the tale of guineas, where people's fortunes are exalted, and their purposes achieved by the force, not of the arm or the heart, but of the spinning-jenny and the steam-engine.[1]

These are ideas implicit in *Hard Times* and *Mary Barton*, but here written as early as 1831, and in the Dumfriesshire moor, not from the London metropolis. The essays of this period have a twofold character, self-aware yet sensitive to the world at large, insecure (in the sense that Carlyle's finances and reputation were alike insecure), yet animated by a passionate conviction in the writer's vision being correct, and justified. Refuge from doubt, and from appalling bleakness and loneliness, lay in application to writing.

We were not unhappy at Craigenputtoch: perhaps these were our happiest days. Useful, continual labour, essentially successful; that makes even the moor green. I found I could do fully *twice* as much work in a given time there, as with my best effort was possible in London—such the interruptions etc. . . .[2]

Craigenputtoch, and the essays written in this period, gave Carlyle a purposefulness and a self-assurance which animate all the writing in this volume. He became sure of himself, and less worried about the outside world, as he admitted to Emerson when he left for London in 1834. 'I care not for Toryism, for Church, Tithes, or the "Confusion" of Useful Knowledge:[3] much as I can speak and hear, I am alone, alone. . . .'[4]

'Boswell's Life of Johnson' and 'On History' exemplify the best writing of this period; alert, occasionally abrasive essays which are well constructed despite what seems today an over-generous amount of quotation. Carlyle stands revealed as a writer dominated by an interest in people, in those he considers admirable men, and in facts concerning these people.

---

[1] This quotation comes from one of Carlyle's minor essays, 'Cruthers and Jonson', published in *Fraser's Magazine* in January, 1831, but not included in the *Critical and Miscellaneous Essays*.

[2] T. Carlyle, *Reminiscences* (London, 1972), 58. [Everyman's University Library No. 1875].

[3] A satirical reference to Brougham's 'Society for the Diffusion of Useful Knowledge'.

[4] Carlyle to Emerson, 12th August 1834. *The Correspondence of Carlyle and Emerson*, ed. J. Slater (New York, 1964), 104–5.

Introduction

Scholarship, and bibliography, count for little—it is Johnson, not Boswell's *Life*, which interests our author. Boswell is admired for 'Loyalty, Discipleship, all that was ever meant by *Hero-worship*' (p. 11), but not much for the *Life*. Johnson, the great and serious man, his life and his struggles to literary success, are what count in this essay, focused on his 'high, keen-visioned, almost poetic soul' (p. 26), not on the ostensible title of the essay. The methodology of Carlyle's criticism is shown, and he expects other authors to abide by the same, or else to show in their works 'nothing but a pitiful Image of their own pitiful Self' ('On Biography,' p. 77) rather than the truth for which Carlyle restlessly seeks. The same search underlies his insistent dismissal of too-facile searches for a 'philosophy of history', in place of a recognition of history as a 'real Prophetic Manuscript, [which] can be fully interpreted by no man' ('On History,' p. 86). While the whole shape of history may be hidden, vignettes of the lives and characters of individuals are always available, and this biographical interest colours all Carlyle's historical writings, from the full-scale studies of Friedrich of Prussia, and Cromwell, to such occasional pieces as 'An Election to the Long Parliament'.

An interest in people is the key to the understanding of the two other main parts of this selection, 'Chartism' and 'The Nigger Question'. Even from the isolation of Craigenputtoch, Carlyle would appreciate the growing misery of the poor in the 1830s, and his articulate protest swelled throughout the 1830s and 1840s. Everyone was swept into this protest: 'All true men, high and low, each in his sphere, are consciously or unconsciously bringing it [a just society] to pass; all false and half-true men are fruitlessly spending themselves to hinder it from coming to pass' (p. 196). Carlyle did not spare himself in writing with scorn of a decayed ruling class, of the blighting 'cash-nexus' which reduced what should be a human society to a mechanical, utilitarian, indifferent arrangement. Profit and loss was no guide to treatment of human beings. Yet his scorn is more effective than his constructive suggestions, and the vague talk of emigration and education in the tenth chapter is much less memorable than the passionate concern with the plight of the poor which pulses through this important and seminal essay.

The same concern is seen in Carlyle's most abused and unpopular 'The Nigger Question', to many an objectionable early fascist document by a slaver, a heartless exploiter of unemancipated black labour. The reality of the situation is a lot more complex than this; [1] Carlyle's thinking is conditioned not by early fascism so much as by a serious attempt to reconcile present conditions with the early conditioning (and religious education) of his childhood. Further, he is not condemning the blacks out of hand, so much as condemning weak philanthropists who, Mrs Jellyby-like, see only their 'Benevolence' and 'Christian Philanthropy' (p. 305) for others at a distance, and ignore the fearful suffering on their doorsteps in England, in Ireland. In private life no one was more sympathetic to the plight of the poor, or more ready to alleviate suffering, than Carlyle, yet in 'The Nigger Question' he deliberately wrote from an extreme position, once more from an awareness of the plight of poor individuals, people he could see, and with whose plight he could sympathize. These essays all share this common concern, they are important landmarks in Carlyle's developing thought, and they show the developing conscience of the Victorian age.

Edinburgh, 1972.   IAN CAMPBELL.

[1] I have tried to argue this in 'Carlyle and the Negro Question Again' in *Criticism* XIII, 3 (Summer, 1971), 279–90.

SELECT BIBLIOGRAPHY

COLLECTED WORKS. 'Centenary' Edition (ed. H. D. Traill), 30 vols., New York, 1896–9; the standard edition. *Collectanea Thomas Carlyle 1821–1855*, 1903.

SEPARATE WORKS. *Wilhelm Meister's Apprenticeship. A Novel from the German of Goethe*, 3 vols., Edinburgh, 1824. *The Life of Schiller*, 1825. *German Romance* (including *Wilhelm Meister's Travels*), 4 vols., Edinburgh, 1827. *Sartor Resartus: the Life and Opinions of Herr Teufelsdröckh*, Boston, 1836. *The French Revolution. A History*, 3 vols., 1837. *Lectures on the History of Literature*, 1838. *Critical and Miscellaneous Essays*, 4 vols., Boston, 1838. *Chartism*, 1840. *On Heroes, Hero-Worship, and the Heroic in History*, 1841. *Past and Present*, 1843. *Oliver Cromwell's Letters and Speeches*, 2 vols., 1845. *Latter-Day Pamphlets*, 1850. *Life of John Starling*, 1851. *The History of Friedrich II of Prussia, called Frederick the Great*, 6 vols., 1858–65. *On the Choice of Books* [inaugural address at Edinburgh, 2nd April 1866], 1866. *The Early Kings of Norway: Also an Essay on the Portraits of John Knox*, 1875. *Reminiscences* (ed: J. A. Froude), 2 vols., 1881; (ed. C. E. Norton), 2 vols., 1887, 1932, 1972. *Reminiscences of my Irish Journey in 1849*, 1882. *Last Words of Thomas Carlyle*, 1892; reprinted 1972. *Lectures on the History of Literature*, 1892. *Montaigne and other Essays, Chiefly Biographical*, 1897. *Two Notebooks of Thomas Carlyle*, New York, 1898; reprinted part of Carlyle's voluminous diaries, still largely unprinted. *Journey to Germany, Autumn 1858*, New Haven, 1940. *Carlyle's Unfinished History of German Literature* (ed. H. Shine), Lexington, 1951.

BIOGRAPHY AND CRITICISM. J. A. Froude, *Thomas Carlyle*, 4 vols., 1882–4. F. W. Roe, *Thomas Carlyle as a Critic of Literature*, New York, 1910. D. A. Wilson, Life of Thomas Carlyle, 6 vols., 1923–34; sixth volume completed by D. W. MacArthur. Basil Willey, *Nineteenth Century Studies*, 1949. J. Holloway, *The Victorian Sage*, 1953. R. Wellek, *A History of Modern Criticism, 1750–1950*, 1955–66. G. B. Tennyson, *Sartor called Resartus*, Princeton, 1965. R. Wellek, *Confrontations*, Princeton, 1966. J. P. Siegel, ed., *Carlyle* (The Critical Heritage series), 1971.

BIBLIOGRAPHY. I. W. Dyer, *A Bibliography of Thomas Carlyle's Writings*, Portland, Maine, 1928; reprinted 1968.

The place of publication is London, unless otherwise stated.

CONTENTS

ENGLISH & OTHER
CRITICAL MISCELLANIES

BOSWELL'S LIFE OF JOHNSON [1]

[1832]

Æsop's Fly, sitting on the axle of the chariot, has been much laughed at for exclaiming: What a dust I do raise! Yet which of us, in his way, has not sometimes been guilty of the like? Nay, so foolish are men, they often, standing at ease and as spectators on the highway, will volunteer to exclaim of the Fly (not being tempted to it, as *he* was) exactly to the same purport: What a dust *thou* dost raise! Smallest of mortals, when mounted aloft by circumstances, come to seem great; smallest of phenomena connected with them are treated as important, and must be sedulously scanned, and commented upon with loud emphasis.

That Mr. Croker should undertake to edit *Boswell's Life of Johnson*, was a praiseworthy but no miraculous procedure: neither could the accomplishment of such undertaking be, in an epoch like ours, anywise regarded as an event in Universal History; the right or the wrong accomplishment thereof was, in very truth, one of the most insignificant of things. However, it sat in a great environment, on the axle of a high, fast-rolling, parliamentary chariot; and all the world has exclaimed over it, and the author of it: What a dust thou dost raise! List to the Reviews, and " Organs of Public Opinion," from the *National Omnibus* upwards: criticisms, vituperative and laudatory, stream from their thousand throats of brass and of leather; here chanting

[1] *Fraser's Magazine*, No. 28.—" The Life of Samuel Johnson, LL.D.; including a Tour to the Hebrides." By James Boswell, Esq.—A new Edition, with numerous Additions and Notes, by John Wilson Croker, LL.D., F.R.S. 5 vols. London, 1831.

Io-pæans; there grating harsh thunder or vehement shrew-
mouse squeaklets; till the general ear is filled, and nigh
deafened. Boswell's Book had a noiseless birth, compared
with this Edition of Boswell's Book. On the other hand,
consider with what degree of tumult *Paradise Lost* and the
Iliad were ushered in!

To swell such clamour, or prolong it beyond the time, seems
nowise our vocation here. At most, perhaps, we are bound
to inform simple readers, with all possible brevity, what
manner of performance and Edition this is; especially,
whether, in our poor judgment, it is worth laying out three
pounds sterling upon, yea or not. The whole business
belongs distinctly to the lower ranks of the trivial class.

Let us admit, then, with great readiness, that as Johnson
once said, and the Editor repeats, " all works which describe
manners require notes in sixty or seventy years, or less; "
that, accordingly, a new Edition of Boswell was desirable;
and that Mr. Croker has given one. For this task he had
various qualifications: his own voluntary resolution to do
it; his high place in society, unlocking all manner of archives
to him; not less, perhaps, a certain anecdotico-biographic
turn of mind, natural or acquired; we mean, a love for the
minuter events of History, and talent for investigating these.
Let us admit too, that he has been very diligent; seems to
have made inquiries perseveringly far and near; as well as
drawn freely from his own ample stores; and so tells us, to
appearance quite accurately, much that he has not found
lying on the highways, but has had to seek and dig for.
Numerous persons, chiefly of quality, rise to view in these
Notes; when and also where they came into this world,
received office or promotion, died and were buried (only
what they *did*, except digest, remaining often too mysterious),
—is faithfully enough set down. Whereby all that their
various and doubtless widely-scattered Tombstones could
have taught us, is here presented, at once, in a bound Book.
Thus is an indubitable conquest, though a small one, gained
over our great enemy, the all-destroyer Time; and as such
shall have welcome.

Nay, let us say that the spirit of Diligence, exhibited
in this department, seems to attend the Editor honestly
throughout: he keeps everywhere a watchful outlook on his
Text; reconciling the distant with the present, or at least

indicating and regretting their irreconcilability; elucidating, smoothing down; in all ways exercising, according to ability, a strict editorial superintendence. Any little Latin or even Greek phrase is rendered into English, in general with perfect accuracy; citations are verified, or else corrected. On all hands, moreover, there is a certain spirit of Decency maintained and insisted on: if not good morals, yet good manners, are rigidly inculcated; if not Religion, and a devout Christian heart, yet Orthodoxy, and a cleanly Shovel-hatted look,— which, as compared with flat Nothing, is something very considerable. Grant too, as no contemptible triumph of this latter spirit, that though the Editor is known as a decided Politician and Party-man, he has carefully subdued all temptations to transgress in that way: except by quite involuntary indications, and rather as it were the pervading temper of the whole, you could not discover on which side of the Political Warfare he is enlisted and fights. This, as we said, is a great triumph of the Decency-principle: for this, and for these other graces and performances, let the Editor have all praise.

Herewith, however, must the praise unfortunately terminate. Diligence, Fidelity, Decency, are good and indispensable: yet, without Faculty, without Light, they will not do the work. Along with that Tombstone-information, perhaps even without much of it, we could have liked to gain some answer, in one way or other, to this wide question: What and how was *English Life* in Johnson's time; wherein has ours grown to differ therefrom? In other words: What things have we to forget, what to fancy and remember, before we, from such distance, can put ourselves in Johnson's *place;* and so, in the full sense of the term, *understand* him, his sayings and his doings? This was indeed specially the problem which a Commentator and Editor had to solve: a complete solution of it should have lain in him, his whole mind should have been filled and prepared with perfect insight into it; then, whether in the way of express Dissertation, of incidental Exposition and Indication, opportunities enough would have occurred of bringing out the same: what was dark in the figure of the Past had thereby been enlightened; Boswell had, not in show and word only, but in very fact, been made *new* again, readable to us who are divided from him, even as he was to those close at hand. Of all which very little has been attempted here; accomplished, we should say, next to nothing, or altogether nothing.

Excuse, no doubt, is in readiness for such omission; and, indeed, for innumerable other failings;—as where, for example, the Editor will punctually explain what is already sun-clear; and then anon, not without frankness, declare frequently enough that " the Editor does not understand," that " the Editor cannot guess,"—while, for most part, the Reader cannot help both guessing and seeing. Thus, if Johnson say, in one sentence, that " English names should not be used in Latin verses; " and then, in the next sentence, speak blamingly of " Carteret being used as a dactyl," will the generality of mortals detect any puzzle there? Or again, where poor Boswell writes: " I always remember a remark made to me by a Turkish lady, educated in France: ' Ma foi, monsieur, notre bonheur dépend de la façon que notre sang circule;' " — though the Turkish lady here speaks English-French, where is the call for a Note like this: " Mr. Boswell no doubt fancied these words had some meaning, or he would hardly have quoted them: but what that meaning is, the Editor cannot guess "? The Editor is clearly no witch at a riddle.—For these and all kindred deficiencies the excuse, as we said, is at hand; but the fact of their existence is not the less certain and regrettable.

Indeed it, from a very early stage of the business, becomes afflictively apparent, how much the Editor, so well furnished with all external appliances and means, is from within unfurnished with means for forming to himself any just notion of Johnson, or of Johnson's Life; and therefore of speaking on that subject with much hope of edifying. Too lightly is it from the first taken for granted that *Hunger*, the great basis of our life, is also its apex and ultimate perfection; that as " Neediness and Greediness and Vainglory " are the chief qualities of most men, so no man, not even a Johnson, acts or can think of acting on any other principle. Whatsoever, therefore, cannot be referred to the two former categories (Need and Greed), is without scruple ranged under the latter. It is here properly that our Editor becomes burdensome; and, to the weaker sort, even a nuisance. " What good is it," will such cry, " when we had still some faint shadow of belief that man was better than a selfish Digesting-machine, what good is it to poke in, at every turn, and explain how this and that which we thought noble in old Samuel, was vulgar, base; that for him too there was no reality but in the Stomach; and except Pudding, and the finer species of pudding which is named Praise, life had no pabulum? Why, for instance, when we know that Johnson *loved* his good Wife, and says expressly that their marriage was ' a love-match on both sides,'—should two closed lips open to tell us only this: ' Is it not possible that the obvious advantage of having a woman of experience to superintend an establishment of this kind (the Edial School) may have contributed to a match so disproportionate in point of age? —ED.'? Or again when, in the Text, the honest cynic speaks freely of his former poverty, and it is known that he once lived on fourpence-halfpenny a-day,—need a Commentator advance, and comment thus: ' When we find Dr. Johnson tell unpleasant truths to, or of, other men, let us recollect that he does not appear to have spared himself, on occasions in which he might be forgiven for doing so ' ? Why in short," continues the exasperated Reader, " should Notes of this species stand affronting me, when there might have been no Note at all? "—Gentle Reader, we answer, Be not wroth. What other could an honest Commentator do, than give thee the best he had? Such was the picture and theorem he had fashioned for himself of the world and of man's doings therein: take it, and draw wise inferences from it. If there did exist a Leader of Public Opinion, and Champion of Orthodoxy in the Church of Jesus of Nazareth, who reckoned that man's glory consisted in not being poor; and that a Sage, and Prophet of his time, must needs blush because the world had paid him at that easy rate of fourpence-halfpenny *per diem*—was not the fact of such existence worth knowing, worth considering?

Of a much milder hue, yet to us practically of an all-defacing, and for the present enterprise quite ruinous character,— is another grand fundamental failing; the last we shall feel ourselves obliged to take the pain of specifying here. It is, that our Editor has fatally, and almost surprisingly, mistaken the limits of an Editor's function; and so, instead of working on the margin with his Pen, to elucidate as best might be, strikes boldly into the body of the page with his Scissors, and there clips at discretion! Four Books Mr. C. had by him, wherefrom to gather light for the fifth, which was Boswell's. What does he do but now, in the placidest manner,—slit the whole five into slips, and sew these together into a *sextum quid*, exactly at his own convenience; giving Boswell the credit of the whole! By what art-magic, our readers ask, has he united them? By the simplest of all: by Brackets. Never before was the full virtue of the Bracket made manifest. You begin a sentence under Boswell's guidance, thinking to be carried happily through it by the same: but no; in the middle, perhaps after your semicolon, and some consequent " for,"—starts up one of these Bracket-ligatures, and stitches you in from half a page to twenty or thirty pages of a Hawkins, Tyers, Murphy, Piozzi; so that often one must make the old sad reflection, Where we are, we know; whither we are going, no man knoweth! It is truly said also, There is much between the cup and the lip; but here the case is still sadder: for not till after consideration can you ascertain, now when the cup is *at* the lip, what liquor it is you are imbibing; whether Boswell's French wine which you began with, or some Piozzi's ginger-beer, or Hawkins's entire, or perhaps some other great Brewer's penny-swipes or even alegar, which has been surreptitiously substituted instead thereof. A situation almost original; not to be tried a second time! But, in fine, what ideas Mr. Croker entertains of a literary *whole* and the thing called *Book*, and how the very Printer's Devils did not rise in mutiny against such a conglomeration as this, and refuse to print it,—may remain a problem.

And now happily our say is said. All faults, the Moralists tell us, are properly *shortcomings*; crimes themselves are nothing other than a *not doing enough*; a *fighting*, but with defective vigour. How much more a mere insufficiency, and this after good efforts, in handicraft practice! Mr. Croker says: " The worst that can happen is that all the present Editor has contributed may, if the reader so pleases, be rejected as *surplusage*." It is our pleasant duty to take with hearty welcome what he has given; and render thanks even for what he meant to give. Next and finally, it is our painful duty to declare, aloud if that be necessary, that his gift, as weighed against the hard money which the Book-sellers demand for giving it you, is (in our judgment) very greatly the lighter. No portion, accordingly, of our small floating capital has been embarked in the business, or shall ever be; indeed, were we in the market for such a thing, there is simply *no* Edition of *Boswell* to which this last would seem preferable. And now enough, and more than enough!

We have next a word to say of James Boswell. Boswell has already been much commented upon; but rather in the way of censure and vituperation than of true recognition. He was a man that brought himself much before the world; confessed that he eagerly coveted fame, or if that were not possible, notoriety; of which latter as he gained far more than seemed his due, the public were incited, not only by their natural love of scandal, but by a special ground of envy, to say whatever ill of him could be said. Out of the fifteen millions that then lived, and had bed and board, in the British Islands, this man has provided us a greater *pleasure* than any other individual, at whose cost we now enjoy ourselves; perhaps has done us a greater *service* than can be specially attributed to more than two or three: yet, ungrateful that we are, no written or spoken eulogy of James Boswell anywhere exists; his recompense in solid pudding (so far as copyright went) was not excessive; and as for the empty praise, it has altogether been denied him. Men are unwiser than children; they do *not* know the hand that feeds them.

Boswell was a person whose mean or bad qualities lay open to the general eye; visible, palpable to the dullest. His good qualities, again, belonged not to the Time he lived in; were far from common then; indeed, in such a degree, were almost unexampled; not recognisable therefore by every one; nay, apt even (so strange had they grown) to be confounded with the very vices they lay contiguous to, and had sprung out of. That he was a wine-bibber and gross liver; gluttonously fond of whatever would yield him a little solacement, were it only of a stomachic character, is undeniable enough. That he was vain, heedless, a babbler; had much of the sycophant, alternating with the braggadocio, curiously spiced too with an all-pervading dash of the coxcomb; that he gloried much when the Tailor, by a court-suit, had made a new man of him; that he appeared at the Shakspeare Jubilee with a riband, imprinted " CORSICA BOSWELL," round his hat; and in short, if you will, lived no day of his life without doing and saying more than one pretentious ineptitude: all this unhappily is evident as the sun at noon.

The very look of Boswell seems to have signified so much.
In that cocked nose, cocked partly in triumph over his weaker
fellow-creatures, partly to snuff-up the smell of coming
pleasure, and scent it from afar; in those bag-cheeks, hanging like half-filled wine-skins, still able to contain more; in
that coarsely-protruded shelf-mouth, that fat dewlapped
chin; in all this, who sees not sensuality, pretension, bois-
terous imbecility enough; much that could not have been
ornamental in the temper of a great man's overfed great
man (what the Scotch name *flunky*), though it had been
more natural there? The under part of Boswell's face is of a
low, almost brutish character.

Unfortunately, on the other hand, what great and genuine
good lay in him was nowise so self-evident. That Boswell
was a hunter after spiritual Notabilities, that he loved such,
and longed, and even crept and crawled to be near them;
that he first (in old Touchwood Auchinleck's phraseology)
" took on with Paoli; " and then being off with " the Corsi-
can landlouper," took on with a schoolmaster, " ane that
keeped a schule, and ca'd it an academy: " that he did all
this, and could not help doing it, we account a very singular
merit. The man, once for all, had an " open sense," an
open loving heart, which so few have: where Excellence
existed, he was compelled to acknowledge it; was drawn
towards it, and (let the old sulphur-brand of a Laird say
what he liked) *could not but* walk with it,—if not as superior,
if not as equal, then as inferior and lackey, better so than not
at all. If we reflect now that his love of Excellence had not
only such an evil *nature* to triumph over; but also what an
education and social position withstood it and weighed it
down, its innate strength, victorious over all these things,
may astonish us. Consider what an inward impulse there
must have been, how many mountains of impediment hurled
aside, before the Scottish Laird could, as humble servant,
embrace the knees (the bosom was not permitted him) of the
English Dominie! Your Scottish Laird, says an English
naturalist of these days, may be defined as the hungriest
and vainest of all bipeds yet known. Boswell too was a
Tory; of quite peculiarly feudal, genealogical, pragmatical
temper; had been nurtured in an atmosphere of Heraldry,
at the feet of a very Gamaliel in that kind; within bare
walls, adorned only with pedigrees, amid serving-men in

threadbare livery; all things teaching him, from birth upwards, to remember that a Laird was a Laird. Perhaps there was a special vanity in his very blood: old Auchinleck had, if not the gay, tail-spreading, peacock vanity of his son, no little of the slow-stalking, contentious, hissing vanity of the gander; a still more fatal species. Scottish Advocates will yet tell you how the ancient man, having chanced to be the first sheriff appointed (after the abolition of " hereditary jurisdictions ") by royal authority, was wont, in dull-snuffing pompous tone, to preface many a deliverance from the bench with these words: " I, the first King's Sheriff in Scotland."

And now behold the worthy Bozzy, so prepossessed and held back by nature and by art, fly nevertheless like iron to its magnet, whither his better genius called! You may surround the iron and the magnet with what enclosures and encumbrances you please,—with wood, with rubbish, with brass: it matters not, the two feel each other, they struggle restlessly towards each other, they *will* be together. The iron may be a Scottish squirelet, full of gulosity and " gigmanity;" [1] the magnet an English plebeian, and moving rag-and-dust mountain, coarse, proud, irascible, imperious: nevertheless, behold how they embrace, and inseparably cleave to one another! It is one of the strangest phenomena of the past century, that at a time when the old reverent feeling of Discipleship (such as brought men from far countries, with rich gifts, and prostrate soul, to the feet of the Prophets) had passed utterly away from men's practical experience, and was no longer surmised to exist (as it does), perennial, indestructible, in man's inmost heart, — James Boswell should have been the individual, of all others, predestined to recall it, in such singular guise, to the wondering and, for a long while, laughing and unrecognising world. It has been commonly said, The man's vulgar vanity was all that attached him to Johnson; he delighted to be seen near him, to be thought connected with him. Now let it be at once granted that no consideration springing out of vulgar vanity could well be absent from the mind of James Boswell, in this his intercourse with Johnson, or in any considerable trans-

---

[1] " *Q.* What do you mean by ' respectable '?—*A.* He always kept a gig." (*Thurtell's Trial.*)—" Thus," it has been said, " does society naturally divide itself into four classes: Noblemen, Gentlemen, Gigmen and Men."

action of his life. At the same time, ask yourself: Whether
such vanity, and nothing else, actuated him therein; whether
this was the true essence and moving principle of the phenomenon, or not rather its outward vesture, and the accidental
environment (and defacement) in which it came to light?
The man was, by nature and habit, vain; a sycophant-
coxcomb, be it granted: but had there been nothing more
than vanity in him, was Samuel Johnson the man of men to
whom he must attach himself? At the date when Johnson
was a poor rusty-coated " scholar," dwelling in Temple-lane,
and indeed throughout their whole intercourse afterwards,
were there not chancellors and prime ministers enough;
graceful gentlemen, the glass of fashion; honour - giving
noblemen; dinner-giving rich men; renowned fire-eaters,
swordsmen, gownsmen; Quacks and Realities of all hues,—
any one of whom bulked much larger in the world's eye than
Johnson ever did? To any one of whom, by half that submissiveness and assiduity, our Bozzy might have recom-
mended himself; and sat there, the envy of surrounding
lickspittles; pocketing now solid emolument, swallowing
now well-cooked viands and wines of rich vintage; in each
case, also, shone-on by some glittering reflex of Renown or
Notoriety, so as to be the observed of innumerable observers.
To no one of whom, however, though otherwise a most
diligent solicitor and purveyor, did he so attach himself:
such vulgar courtierships were his paid drudgery, or leisure
amusement; the worship of Johnson was his grand, ideal,
voluntary business. Does not the frothy - hearted, yet
enthusiastic man, doffing his Advocate's-wig, regularly take
post, and hurry up to London, for the sake of his Sage chiefly;
as to a Feast of Tabernacles, the Sabbath of his whole year?
The plate-licker and wine-bibber dives into Bolt Court, to
sip muddy coffee with a cynical old man, and a sour-tempered
blind old woman (feeling the cups, whether they are full, with
her finger); and patiently endures contradictions without
end; too happy so he may but be allowed to listen and live.
Nay, it does not appear that vulgar vanity could ever have
been much flattered by Boswell's relation to Johnson. Mr.
Croker says, Johnson was, to the last, little regarded by the
great world; from which, for a vulgar vanity, all honour, as
from its fountain, descends. Bozzy, even among Johnson's
friends and special admirers, seems rather to have been

laughed at than envied: his officious, whisking, consequential ways, the daily reproofs and rebuffs he underwent, could gain from the world no golden but only leaden opinions. His devout Discipleship seemed nothing more than a mean Spanielship, in the general eye. His mighty "constellation," or sun, round whom he, as satellite, observantly gyrated, was, for the mass of men, but a huge ill-snuffed tallow-light, and he a weak night-moth, circling foolishly, dangerously about it, not knowing what he wanted. If he enjoyed Highland dinners and toasts, as henchman to a new sort of chieftain, Henry Erskine, in the domestic " Outer-House," could hand him a shilling " for the sight of his Bear." Doubtless the man was laughed at, and often heard himself laughed at for his Johnsonism. To be envied is the grand and sole aim of vulgar vanity; to be filled with good things is that of sensuality: for Johnson perhaps no man living *envied* poor Bozzy; and of good things (except himself paid for them) there was no vestige in that acquaintanceship. Had nothing other or better than vanity and sensuality been there, Johnson and Boswell had never come together, or had soon and finally separated again.

In fact, the so copious terrestrial dross that welters chaotically, as the outer sphere of this man's character, does but render for us more remarkable, more touching, the celestial spark of goodness, of light, and Reverence for Wisdom, which dwelt in the interior, and could struggle through such encumbrances, and in some degree illuminate and beautify them. There is much lying yet undeveloped in the love of Boswell for Johnson. A cheering proof, in a time which else utterly wanted and still wants such, that living Wisdom is quite *infinitely* precious to man, is the symbol of the Godlike to him, which even weak eyes may discern; that Loyalty, Discipleship, all that was ever meant by *Hero-worship*, lives perennially in the human bosom, and waits, even in these dead days, only for occasions to unfold it, and inspire all men with it, and again make the world alive! James Boswell we can regard as a practical witness, or real *martyr*, to this high everlasting truth. A wonderful martyr, if you will; and in a time which made such martyrdom doubly wonderful: yet the time and its martyr perhaps suited each other. For a decrepit, death-sick Era, when CANT had first decisively opened her poison-breathing lips to proclaim that God-

worship and Mammon-worship were one and the same, that
Life was a *Lie*, and the Earth Beelzebub's, which the *Supreme
Quack* should inherit; and so all things were fallen into the
yellow leaf, and fast hastening to noisome corruption: for
such an Era, perhaps no better Prophet than a parti-coloured
Zany-Prophet, concealing, from himself and others, his
prophetic significance in such unexpected vestures,—was
deserved, or would have been in place. A precious medicine
lay hidden in floods of coarsest, most composite treacle:
the world swallowed the treacle, for it suited the world's
palate; and now, after half a century, may the medicine
also begin to show itself! James Boswell belonged, in his
corruptible part, to the lowest classes of mankind; a foolish,
inflated creature, swimming in an element of self-conceit:
but in his corruptible there dwelt an incorruptible, all the
more impressive and indubitable for the strange lodging it
had taken.

Consider too, with what force, diligence and vivacity he
has rendered back all this which, in Johnson's neighbourhood,
his " open sense " had so eagerly and freely taken in. That
loose-flowing, careless-looking Work of his is as a picture by
one of Nature's own Artists; the best possible resemblance of
a Reality; like the very image thereof in a clear mirror.
Which indeed it was: let but the mirror be *clear*, this is the
great point; the picture must and will be genuine. How
the babbling Bozzy, inspired only by love, and the recognition and vision which love can lend, epitomises nightly the
words of Wisdom, the deeds and aspects of Wisdom, and so,
by little and little, unconsciously works together for us a
whole *Johnsoniad ;* a more free, perfect, sunlit and spirit-
speaking likeness than for many centuries had been drawn
by man of man! Scarcely since the days of Homer has the
feat been equalled; indeed, in many senses, this also is a
kind of Heroic Poem. The fit *Odyssey* of our unheroic age
was to be written, not sung; of a Thinker, not of a Fighter;
and (for want of a Homer) by the first open soul that might
offer,—looked such even through the organs of a Boswell.
We do the man's intellectual endowment great wrong, if
we measure it by its mere logical outcome; though here too,
there is not wanting a light ingenuity, a figurativeness and
fanciful sport, with glimpses of insight far deeper than the
common. But Boswell's grand intellectual talent was, as

such ever is, an *unconscious* one, of far higher reach and significance than Logic; and showed itself in the whole, not in parts. Here again we have that old saying verified, " The heart sees farther than the head."

Thus does poor Bozzy stand out to us as an ill-assorted, glaring mixture of the highest and the lowest. What, indeed, is man's life generally but a kind of beast-godhood; the god in us triumphing more and more over the beast; striving more and more to subdue it under his feet? Did not the Ancients, in their wise, perennially-significant way, figure Nature itself, their sacred ALL, or PAN, as a portentous commingling of these two discords; as musical, humane, oracular in its upper part, yet ending below in the cloven hairy feet of a goat? The union of melodious, celestial Freewill and Reason with foul Irrationality and Lust; in which, nevertheless, dwelt a mysterious unspeakable Fear and half-mad *panic* Awe; as for mortals there well might! And is not man a microcosm, or epitomised mirror of that same Universe; or rather, is not that Universe even Himself, the reflex of his own fearful and wonderful being, " the waste fantasy of his own dream "? No wonder that man, that each man, and James Boswell like the others, should resemble it! The peculiarity in his case was the unusual defect of amalgamation and subordination: the highest lay side by side with the lowest; not morally combined with it and spiritually transfiguring it, but tumbling in half-mechanical juxtaposition with it, and from time to time, as the mad alternation chanced, irradiating it, or eclipsed by it.

The world, as we said, has been but unjust to him; discerning only the outer terrestrial and often sordid mass; without eye, as it generally is, for his inner divine secret; and thus figuring him nowise as a god Pan, but simply of the bestial species, like the cattle on a thousand hills. Nay, sometimes a strange enough hypothesis has been started of him; as if it were in virtue even of these same bad qualities that he did his good work; as if it were the very fact of his being among the worst men in this world that had enabled him to write one of the best books therein! False hypothesis, we may venture to say, never rose in human soul. *Bad* is by its nature negative, and can do *nothing* ; whatsoever enabled us to *do* anything is by its very nature *good*. Alas, that there should be teachers in Israel, or even learners, to whom this

world-ancient fact is still problematical or even deniable!
Boswell wrote a good Book because he had a heart and an
eye to discern Wisdom, and an utterance to render it forth;
because of his free insight, his lively talent, above all, of his
Love and childlike Open-mindedness. His sneaking syco-
phancies, his greediness and forwardness, whatever was
bestial and earthy in him, are so many blemishes in his Book,
which still disturb us in its clearness; wholly hindrances,
not helps. Towards Johnson, however, his feeling was not
Sycophancy, which is the lowest, but Reverence, which is the
highest of human feelings. None but a *reverent* man (which
so unspeakably few are) could have found his way from
Boswell's environment to Johnson's: if such worship for
real God-made superiors showed itself also as worship for
apparent Tailor-made superiors, even as hollow interested
mouth-worship for such,—the case, in this composite human
nature of ours, was not miraculous, the more was the pity!
But for ourselves, let every one of us cling to this last article
of Faith, and know it as the beginning of all knowledge worth
the name: That neither James Boswell's good Book, nor any
other good thing, in any time or in any place, was, is or can
be performed by any man in virtue of his *badness*, but always
and solely in spite thereof.

As for the Book itself, questionless the universal favour
entertained for it is well merited. In worth as a Book we
have rated it beyond any other product of the eighteenth
century: all Johnson's own Writings, laborious and in their
kind genuine above most, stand on a quite inferior level to it;
already, indeed, they are becoming obsolete for this generation; and for some future generation may be valuable
chiefly as Prolegomena and expository Scholia to this
Johnsoniad of Boswell. Which of us remembers, as one of
the sunny spots of his existence, the day when he opened
these airy volumes, fascinating him by a true natural magic!
It was as if the curtains of the past were drawn aside, and
we looked mysteriously into a kindred country, where dwelt
our Fathers; inexpressibly dear to us, but which had seemed
forever hidden from our eyes. For the dead Night had
engulfed it; all was gone, vanished as if it had not been.
Nevertheless, wondrously given back to us, there once more
it lay; all bright, lucid, blooming; a little island of Creation
amid the circumambient Void. There it still lies; like a

thing stationary, imperishable, over which changeful Time were now accumulating itself in vain, and could not, any longer, harm it, or hide it.

If we examine by what charm it is that men are still held to this *Life of Johnson*, now when so much else has been forgotten, the main part of the answer will perhaps be found in that speculation " on the import of *Reality*," communicated to the world, last month, in this Magazine. The *Johnsoniad* of Boswell turns on objects that in very deed existed; it is all *true*. So far other in melodiousness of tone, it vies with the *Odyssey*, or surpasses it, in this one point: to us these read pages, as those chanted hexameters were to the first Greek hearers, are, in the fullest deepest sense, wholly *credible*. All the wit and wisdom lying embalmed in Boswell's Book, plenteous as these are, could not have saved it. Far more scientific *instruction* (mere excitement and enlightenment of the *thinking power*) can be found in twenty other works of that time, which make but a quite secondary impression on us. The other works of that time, however, fall under one of two classes: Either they are professedly Didactic; and, in that way, mere Abstractions, Philosophic Diagrams, incapable of interesting us much otherwise than as *Euclid's Elements* may do: Or else, with all their vivacity, and pictorial richness of colour, *they are Fictions and not Realities*. Deep truly, as Herr Sauerteig urges, is the force of this consideration: the thing here stated is a fact; those figures, that local habitation, are not shadow but substance. In virtue of such advantages, see how a very Boswell may become Poetical!

Critics insist much on the Poet that he should communicate an " Infinitude " to his delineation; that by intensity of conception, by that gift of " transcendental Thought," which is fitly named *genius*, and inspiration, he should *inform* the Finite with a certain Infinitude of significance; or as they sometimes say, ennoble the Actual into Idealness. They are right in their precept; they mean rightly. But in cases like this of the *Johnsoniad*, such is the dark grandeur of that " Time element," wherein man's soul here below lives imprisoned,—the Poet's task is, as it were, done to his hand: Time itself, which is the outer veil of Eternity, invests, of its own accord, with an authentic, felt " infinitude " whatsoever it has once embraced in its mysterious folds. Consider all that lies in that one word *Past !* What a pathetic, sacred, in every sense *poetic*, meaning is implied in it; a meaning growing ever the clearer, the farther we recede in Time,—the *more* of that same Past we have to look through!—On which ground indeed must Sauerteig have built, and not without plausibility, in that strange thesis of his: "That History, after all, is the true Poetry; that Reality, if rightly interpreted, is grander than Fiction; nay that even in the right interpretation of Reality and History does genuine Poetry consist."

Thus for *Boswell's Life of Johnson* has Time done, is Time still doing, what no ornament of Art or Artifice could have done for it. Rough Samuel and sleek wheedling James *were*, and *are not*. Their Life and whole personal Environment has melted into air. The Mitre Tavern still stands in Fleet Street: but where now is its scot-and-lot paying, beef-and-ale loving, cocked-hatted, pot-bellied Landlord; its rosy-faced assiduous Landlady, with all her shining brass-pans, waxed tables, well-filled larder-shelves; her cooks, and bootjacks, and errand-boys, and watery-mouthed hangers-on? Gone! Gone! The becking Waiter who, with wreathed smiles, was wont to spread for Samuel and Bozzy their supper of the gods, has long since pocketed his last sixpence; and vanished, sixpences and all, like a ghost at cock-crowing. The Bottles they drank out of are all broken, the Chairs they sat on all rotted and burnt; the very Knives and Forks they ate with have rusted to the heart, and become brown oxide of iron, and mingled with the indiscriminate clay. All, all has vanished; in every deed and truth, like that baseless fabric of Prospero's air-vision. Of the Mitre Tavern nothing but the bare walls remain there: of London, of England, of the World, nothing but the bare walls remain; and these also decaying (were they of adamant), only slower. The mysterious River of Existence rushes on: a new Billow thereof has arrived, and lashes wildly as ever round the old embankments; but the former Billow with *its* loud, mad eddyings, where is it?—Where!—Now this Book of Boswell's, this is precisely a revocation of the edict of Destiny; so that Time shall not utterly, not so soon by several centuries, have dominion over us. A little row of Naphtha-lamps, with its line of Naphtha-light, burns clear and holy through the dead Night of the Past: they who are gone are still here; though hidden they are revealed, though dead they yet speak. There it shines, that little miraculously lamplit Pathway; shedding its feebler and feebler twilight into the boundless dark Oblivion,—for all that our Johnson *touched* has become illuminated for us: on which miraculous little Pathway we can still travel, and see wonders.

It is not speaking with exaggeration, but with strict measured sobriety, to say that this Book of Boswell's will give us more real insight into the *History of England* during those days than twenty other Books, falsely entitled " Histories," which take to themselves that special aim. What good is it to me though innumerable Smolletts and Belshams keep dinning in my ears that a man named George the Third was born and bred up, and a man named George the Second died; that Walpole, and the Pelhams, and Chatham, and Rockingham, and Shelburne, and North, with their Coalition or their Separation Ministries, all ousted one another; and vehemently scrambled for " the thing they called the Rudder of Government, but which was in reality the Spigot of Taxation "? That debates were held, and infinite jarring and jargoning took place; and road-bills and enclosure-bills, and game-bills and India-bills, and Laws which no man can number, which happily few men needed to trouble their heads with beyond the passing moment, were enacted, and printed by the King's Stationer? That he who sat in Chancery, and rayed-out speculation from the Woolsack, was now a man that squinted, now a man that did not squint? To the hungry and thirsty mind all this avails next to nothing. These men and these things, we indeed know, did swim, by strength or by specific levity, as apples or as horse-dung, on the top of the current: but is it by painfully noting the courses, eddyings and bobbings hither and thither of such drift-articles, that you will unfold to me the nature of the current itself; of that mighty-rolling, loud-roaring Life-current, bottomless as the foundations of the Universe, mysterious as its Author? The thing I want to see is not Redbook Lists, and Court Calendars, and Parliamentary Registers, but the LIFE OF MAN in England: what men did, thought, suffered, enjoyed; the form, especially the spirit, of their terrestrial existence, its outward environment, its inward principle; *how* and *what* it was; whence it proceeded, whither it was tending.

Mournful, in truth, is it to behold what the business called

" History," in these so enlightened and illuminated times, still continues to be. Can you gather from it, read till your eyes go out, any dimmest shadow of an answer to that great question: How men lived and had their being; were it but economically, as, what wages they got, and what they bought with these? Unhappily you cannot. History will throw no light on any such matter. At the point where living memory fails, it is all darkness; Mr. Senior and Mr. Sadler must still debate this simplest of all elements in the condition of the Past: Whether men were better off, in their mere larders and pantries, or were worse off than now! History, as it stands all bound up in gilt volumes, is but a shade more instructive than the wooden volumes of a Backgammon-board. How my Prime Minister was appointed is of less moment to me than How my House Servant was hired. In these days, ten ordinary Histories of Kings and Courtiers were well exchanged against the tenth part of one good History of Booksellers.

For example, I would fain know the History of Scotland: who can tell it me? " Robertson," say innumerable voices; " Robertson against the world." I open Robertson; and find there, through long ages too confused for narrative, and fit only to be presented in the way of epitome and distilled essence, a cunning answer and hypothesis, not to this question: By whom, and by what means, when and how, was this fair broad Scotland, with its Arts and Manufactures, Temples, Schools, Institutions, Poetry, Spirit, National Character, created, and made arable, verdant, peculiar, great, here as I can see some fair section of it lying, kind and strong (like some Bacchus-tamed Lion), from the Castle-hill of Edinburgh? —but to this other question: How did the King keep himself alive in those old days; and restrain so many Butcher-Barons and ravenous Henchmen from utterly extirpating one another, so that killing went on in some sort of moderation? In the one little Letter of Æneas Sylvius, from old Scotland, there is more of History than in all this.—At length, however, we come to a luminous age, interesting enough; to the age of the Reformation. All Scotland is awakened to a second higher life: the Spirit of the Highest stirs in every bosom, agitates every bosom; Scotland is convulsed, fermenting, struggling to body itself forth anew. To the herdsman, among his cattle in remote woods; to the craftsman, in his rude, heath-thatched workshop, among his rude guild-brethren; to the great and to

the little, a new light has arisen: in town and hamlet groups
are gathered, with eloquent looks, and governed or ungovernable tongues; the great and the little go forth together to do
battle for the Lord against the mighty.   We ask, with breath-
less eagerness: How was it; how went it on?   Let us understand it, let us see it, and know it!—In reply, is handed us a
really graceful and most dainty little Scandalous Chronicle
(as for some Journal of Fashion) of two persons: Mary Stuart,
a Beauty, but over lightheaded; and Henry Darnley, a
Booby who had fine legs.   How these first courted, billed and
cooed, according to nature; then pouted, fretted, grew utterly
enraged, and blew one another up with gunpowder: this, and
not the History of Scotland, is what we good-naturedly read.
Nay, by other hands, something like a horse-load of other
Books have been written to prove that it was the Beauty who
blew up the Booby, and that it was not she.   Who or what
it was, the thing once for all *being* so effectually done, concerns
us little.   To know Scotland, at that great epoch, were a
valuable increase of knowledge: to know poor Darnley, and
see him with burning candle, from centre to skin, were no
increase of knowledge at all.—Thus is History written.

Hence, indeed, comes it that History, which should be
" the essence of innumerable Biographies," will tell us, question it as we like, less than one genuine Biography may do,
pleasantly and of its own accord!   The time is approaching
when History will be attempted on quite other principles;
when the Court, the Senate and the Battlefield, receding more
and more into the background, the Temple, the Workshop
and Social Hearth will advance more and more into the fore-
ground; and History will not content itself with shaping
some answer to that question: How were men *taxed* and *kept
quiet* then?   but will seek to answer this other infinitely wider
and higher question: How and what *were men* then?   Not
our Government only, or the " *House* wherein our life was
led," but the *Life* itself we led there, will be inquired into.
Of which latter it may be found that Government, in any
modern sense of the word, is after all but a secondary condition: in the mere sense of *Taxation* and *Keeping quiet*, a
small, almost a pitiful one.—Meanwhile let us welcome such
Boswells, each in his degree, as bring us any genuine contribution, were it never so inadequate, so inconsiderable.

An exception was early taken against this *Life of Johnson*, and all similar enterprises, which we here recommend; and has been transmitted from critic to critic, and repeated in their several dialects, uninterruptedly, ever since: That such jottings-down of careless conversation are an infringement of social privacy; a crime against our highest Freedom, the Freedom of man's intercourse with man. To this accusation, which we have read and heard oftener than enough, might it not be well for once to offer the flattest contradiction and plea of *Not at all guilty ?* Not that conversation is noted down, but that conversation should not deserve noting down, is the evil. Doubtless, if conversation be falsely recorded, then is it simply a Lie; and worthy of being swept, with all despatch, to the Father of Lies. But if, on the other hand, conversation can be authentically recorded, and any one is ready for the task, let him by all means proceed with it; let conversation be kept in remembrance to the latest date possible. Nay, should the consciousness that a man may be among us " taking notes " tend, in any measure, to restrict those floods of idle insincere *speech*, with which the *thought* of mankind is wellnigh drowned,—were it other than the most indubitable benefit? He who speaks honestly cares not, needs not care, though his words be preserved to remotest time: for him who speaks *dis*honestly, the fittest of all punishments seems to be this same, which the nature of the case provides. The dishonest speaker, not he only who purposely utters falsehoods, but he who does not purposely, and with sincere heart, utter Truth, and Truth alone; who babbles he knows not what, and has clapped no bridle on his tongue, but lets it run racket, ejecting chatter and futility, —is among the most indisputable malefactors omitted, or inserted, in the Criminal Calendar. To him that will well consider it, idle speaking is precisely the beginning of all Hollowness, Halfness, *Infidelity* (want of Faithfulness); the genial atmosphere in which rank weeds of every kind attain the mastery over noble fruits in man's life, and utterly choke them out: one of the most crying maladies of these days, and to be testified against, and in all ways to the uttermost withstood. Wise, of a wisdom far beyond our shallow depth, was that old precept: *Watch thy tongue ;* out of it are the issues of Life! " Man is properly an *incarnated word :* " the *word* that he speaks is the *man* himself. Were eyes put into our head, that we might *see ;* or only that we might fancy, and plausibly pretend, we had *seen* ? Was the tongue suspended there, that it might tell truly what we had seen, and make man the soul's-brother of man; or only that it might utter vain sounds, jargon, soul-confusing, and so *divide* man, as by enchanted walls of Darkness, from union with man? Thou who wearest that cunning, heaven-made organ, a Tongue, think well of this. Speak not, I passionately entreat thee, till thy thought hath silently matured itself, till thou have other than mad and mad-making noises to emit: *hold thy tongue* (thou hast it a-holding) till *some* meaning lie behind, to set it wagging. Consider the significance of SILENCE: it is boundless, never by meditating to be exhausted; unspeakably profitable to thee! Cease that chaotic hubbub, wherein thy own soul runs to waste, to confused suicidal dislocation and stupor: out of Silence comes thy strength. "Speech is silvern, Silence is golden; Speech is human, Silence is divine." Fool! thinkest thou that because no Boswell is there with ass-skin and blacklead to note thy jargon, it therefore dies and is harmless? Nothing dies, nothing can die. No idlest word thou speakest but is a seed cast into Time, and grows through all Eternity! The Recording Angel, consider it well, is no fable, but the truest of truths: the paper tablets thou canst burn; of the "iron leaf" there is no burning.—Truly, if we can permit God Almighty to note down our conversation, thinking it good enough for Him,—any poor Boswell need not scruple to work his will of it.

Leaving now this our English *Odyssey*, with its Singer and Scholiast, let us come to the *Ulysses ;* that great Samuel Johnson himself, the far-experienced, "much-enduring man," whose labours and pilgrimage are here sung. A full-length image of his Existence has been preserved for us: and he, perhaps of all living Englishmen, was the one who best deserved that honour. For if it is true, and now almost proverbial, that "the Life of the lowest mortal, if faithfully recorded, would be interesting to the highest;" how much more when the mortal in question was already distinguished in fortune and natural quality, so that his thinkings and doings were not significant of himself only, but of large masses of mankind! "There is not a man whom I meet on the streets," says one, "but I could like, were it otherwise convenient, to know his Biography: " nevertheless, could an enlightened curiosity be so far gratified, it must be owned the Biography of most ought to be, in an extreme degree, *summary*. In this world, there is so wonderfully little self-subsistence among men; next to no originality (though never absolutely *none*): one Life is too servilely the copy of another; and so in whole thousands of them you find little that is properly new; nothing but the old song sung by a new voice, with better or worse execution, here and there an ornamental quaver, and false notes enough: but the fundamental tune is ever the same; and for the *words*, these, all that they meant stands written generally on the Churchyard-stone: *Natus sum; esuriebam, quærebam; nunc repletus requiesco.* Mankind sail their Life-voyage in huge fleets, following some single whale-fishing or herring-fishing Commodore: the log-book of each differs not, in essential purport, from that of any other: nay the most have no legible log-book (reflection, observation not being among their talents); keep no reckoning, only *keep in sight* of the flagship,—and fish. Read the Commodore's Papers (know *his* Life); and even your lover of that street Biography will have learned the most of what he sought after.

Or, the servile *imitancy*, and yet also a nobler relationship and mysterious union to one another which lies in such imitancy, of Mankind might be illustrated under the different figure, itself nowise *original*, of a Flock of Sheep. Sheep go in flocks for three reasons: First, because they are of a gregarious temper, and *love* to be together: Secondly, because of their cowardice; they are afraid to be left alone: Thirdly, because the common run of them are dull of sight, to a proverb, and can have no choice in roads; sheep can in fact *see* nothing; in a celestial Luminary, and a scoured pewter Tankard, would discern only that both dazzled them, and were of unspeakable glory. How like their fellow-creatures of the human species! Men too, as was from the first maintained here, are gregarious; then surely faint - hearted enough, trembling to be left by themselves; above all, dull-sighted, down to the verge of utter blindness. Thus are we seen ever running in torrents, and mobs, if we run at all; and after what foolish scoured Tankards, mistaking them for Suns! Foolish Turnip-lanterns likewise, to all appearance supernatural, keep whole nations quaking, their hair on end.

Neither know we, except by blind habit, where the good pastures lie: solely when the sweet grass is between our teeth, we know it, and chew it; also when grass is bitter and scant, we know it,—and bleat and butt: these last two facts we know of a truth and in very deed. Thus do Men and Sheep play their parts on this Nether Earth; wandering restlessly in large masses, they know not whither; for most part, each following his neighbour, and his own nose.

Nevertheless, not always; look better, you shall find certain that do, in some small degree, *know whither*. Sheep have their Bell-wether; some ram of the folds, endued with more valour, with clearer vision than other sheep; he leads them through the wolds, by height and hollow, to the woods and water-courses, for covert or for pleasant provender; courageously marching, and if need be leaping, and with hoof and horn doing battle, in the van: him they courageously and with assured heart follow. Touching it is, as every herdsman will inform you, with what chivalrous devotedness these woolly Hosts adhere to their Wether; and rush after him, through good report and through bad report, were it into safe shelters and green thymy nooks, or into asphaltic lakes and the jaws of devouring lions. Ever also must we recall that fact which we owe Jean Paul's quick eye: " If you hold a stick before the Wether, so that he, by necessity, leaps in passing you, and then withdraw your stick, the Flock will nevertheless all leap as he did; and the thousandth sheep shall be found impetuously vaulting over air, as the first did over an otherwise impassable barrier." Reader, wouldst thou understand Society, ponder well those ovine proceedings; thou wilt find them all curiously significant.

Now if sheep always, how much more must men always, have their Chief, their Guide! Man too is by nature quite thoroughly *gregarious :* nay ever he struggles to be something more, to be *social ;* not even when Society has become impossible, does that deep-seated tendency and effort forsake him. Man, as if by miraculous magic, imparts his Thoughts, his Mood of mind to man; an unspeakable communion binds all past, present and future men into one indissoluble whole, almost into one living individual. Of which high, mysterious Truth, this disposition to *imitate*, to lead and be led, this impossibility *not* to imitate, is the most constant, and one of the simplest manifestations. To imitate! which of us all can measure the significance that lies in that one word? By virtue of which the infant Man, born at Woolsthorpe, grows up not to be a hairy Savage, and chewer of Acorns, but an Isaac Newton and Discoverer of Solar Systems!—Thus both in a celestial and terrestrial sense are we a *Flock*, such as there is no other: nay looking away from the base and ludicrous to the sublime and sacred side of the matter (since in every matter there are two sides), have not we also a SHEPHERD, " if we will but hear his voice "? Of those stupid multitudes there is no one but has an immortal Soul within him; a reflex and living image of God's whole Universe: strangely, from its dim environment, the light of the Highest looks through him;—for which reason, indeed, it is that we claim a brotherhood with him, and so love to know his History, and come into clearer and clearer union with all that he feels, and says, and does.

However, the chief thing to be noted was this: Amid those dull millions, who, as a dull flock, roll hither and thither, whithersoever they are led; and seem all sightless and slavish, accomplishing, attempting little save what the animal instinct in its somewhat higher kind might teach, To keep themselves and their young ones alive,—are scattered here and there superior natures, whose eye is not destitute of free vision, nor their heart of free volition. These latter, therefore, examine and determine, not what others do, but what it is right to do; towards which, and which only, will they, with such force as is given them, resolutely endeavour: for if the Machine, living or inanimate, is merely *fed*, or desires to be fed, and so *works ;* the Person can *will*, and so *do*. These are properly our Men, our Great Men; the guides of the dull host,—which follows them as by an irrevocable decree. They are the chosen of the world: they had this rare faculty not only of " supposing " and " inclining to think," but of *knowing* and *believing ;* the nature of their being was, that they lived not by Hearsay, but by clear Vision; while others hovered and swam along, in the grand Vanity-fair of the World, blinded by the mere Shows of things, these saw into the Things themselves, and could walk as men having an eternal loadstar, and with their feet on sure paths. Thus was there a *Reality* in their existence; something of a perennial character; in virtue of which indeed it is that the memory of them is perennial. Whoso belongs only to his own age, and reverences only *its* gilt Popinjays or soot-smeared Mumbojumbos, must needs die with it: though he have been crowned seven times in the capitol, or seventy-and-seven times, and Rumour have blown his praises to all the four winds, deafening every ear therewith,— it avails not; there was nothing universal, nothing eternal in him; he must fade away, even as the Popinjay-gildings and Scarecrow-apparel, which he could not see through. The great man does, in good truth, belong to his own age; nay more so than any other man; being properly the synopsis and epitome of such age with its interests and influences: but belongs likewise to all ages, otherwise he is not great. What was transitory in him passes away; and an immortal part remains, the significance of which is in strict speech inexhaustible,—as that of every *real* object is. Aloft, conspicuous, on his enduring basis, he stands there, serene, unaltering; silently addresses to every new generation a new lesson and monition. Well is his Life worth writing, worth interpreting; and ever, in the new dialect of new times, of re-writing and re-interpreting.

Of such chosen men was Samuel Johnson: not ranking among the highest, or even the high, yet distinctly admitted into that sacred band; whose existence was no idle Dream, but a Reality which he transacted *awake ;* nowise a Clothes-horse and Patent Digester, but a genuine Man. By nature he was gifted for the noblest of earthly tasks, that of Priesthood, and Guidance of mankind; by destiny, moreover, he was appointed to this task, and did actually, according to strength, fulfil the same: so that always the question, *How ; in what spirit ; under what shape ?* remains for us to be asked and answered concerning him. For as the highest Gospel was a Biography, so is the Life of every good man still an indubitable Gospel, and preaches to the eye and heart and whole man, so that Devils even must believe and tremble, these gladdest tidings: " Man is heaven-born; not the thrall of Circumstances, of Necessity, but the victorious subduer thereof: behold how he can become the ' Announcer of himself and of his Freedom;' and is ever what the Thinker has named him, ' the Messias of Nature.' "—Yes, Reader, all this that thou hast so often heard about " force of circumstances," " the creature of the time," " balancing of motives," and who knows what melancholy stuff to the like purport, wherein thou, as in a nightmare Dream, sittest paralysed, and hast no force left,—was in very truth, if Johnson and waking men are to be credited, little other than a hag-ridden vision of death-sleep; some *half*-fact, more fatal at times than a whole falsehood. Shake it off; awake; up and be doing, even as it is given thee!

The Contradiction which yawns wide enough in every Life, which it is the meaning and task of Life to reconcile, was in Johnson's wider than in most. Seldom, for any man, has the contrast between the ethereal heavenward side of things, and the dark sordid earthward, been more glaring: whether we look at Nature's work with him or Fortune's, from first to last, heterogeneity, as of sunbeams and miry clay, is on all hands manifest. Whereby indeed, only this was declared, That *much Life* had been given him; many things to triumph over, a great work to *do*. Happily also he did it; better than the most.

Nature had given him a high, keen-visioned, almost poetic soul; yet withal imprisoned it in an inert, unsightly body; he that could never rest had not limbs that would move with him, but only roll and waddle: the inward eye, all-penetrating, all-embracing, must look through bodily windows that were dim, half-blinded; he so loved men, and "never once *saw* the human face divine"! Not less did he prize the love of men; he was eminently social; the approbation of his fellows was dear to him, "valuable," as he owned, "if from the meanest of human beings:" yet the first impression he produced on every man was to be one of aversion, almost of disgust. By Nature it was farther ordered that the imperious Johnson should be born poor: the ruler-soul, strong in its native royalty, generous, uncontrollable, like the lion of the woods, was to be housed, then, in such a dwelling-place: of Disfigurement, Disease, and lastly of a Poverty which itself made him the servant of servants. Thus was the born king likewise a born slave: the divine spirit of Music must awake imprisoned amid dull-croaking universal Discords; the Ariel finds himself encased in the coarse hulls of a Caliban. So is it more or less, we know (and thou, O Reader, knowest and feelest even now), with all men: yet with the fewest men in any such degree as with Johnson.

Fortune, moreover, which had so managed his first appearance in the world, lets not her hand lie idle, or turn the other way, but works unweariedly in the same spirit, while he is journeying through the world. What such a mind, stamped of Nature's noblest metal, though in so ungainly a die, was specially and best of all fitted for, might still be a question. To none of the world's few Incorporated Guilds could he have adjusted himself without difficulty, without distortion; in none been a Guild-Brother well at ease. Perhaps, if we look to the strictly practical nature of his faculty, to the strength, decision, method that manifests itself in him, we may say that his calling was rather towards Active than Speculative life; that as Statesman (in the higher, now obsolete sense), Lawgiver, Ruler, in short as Doer of the Work, he had shone even more than as Speaker of the Word. His honesty of heart, his courageous temper, the value he set on things outward and material, might have made him a King among Kings. Had the golden age of those new French Prophets, when it shall be *à chacun selon sa capacité, à chaque capacité selon ses œuvres*, but arrived! Indeed even in our brazen and Birmingham-lacquer age, he himself regretted that he had not become a Lawyer, and risen to be Chancellor, which he might well have done. However, it was otherwise appointed. To no man does Fortune throw open all the kingdoms of this world, and say: It is thine; choose where thou wilt dwell! To the most she opens hardly the smallest cranny or doghutch, and says, not without asperity: There, that is thine while thou canst keep it; nestle thyself there, and bless Heaven! Alas, men must fit themselves into many things: some forty years ago, for instance, the noblest and ablest Man in all the British lands might be seen not swaying the royal sceptre, or the pontiff's censer, on the pinnacle of the World, but gauging ale-tubs in the little burgh of Dumfries! Johnson came a little nearer the mark than Burns: but with him too " Strength was mournfully denied its arena!" he too had to fight Fortune at strange odds, all his life long.

Johnson's disposition for *royalty* (had the Fates so ordered it) is well seen in early boyhood. " His favourites," says Boswell, " used to receive very liberal assistance from him; and such was the submission and deference with which he was treated, that three of the boys, of whom Mr. Hector was sometimes one, used to come in the morning as his humble attendants, and carry him to school. One in the middle stooped, while he sat upon his back, and one on each side support'ed him; and thus was he borne triumphant." The purfly, sand-blind lubber and blubber, with his open mouth, and face of bruised honeycomb; yet already dominant, imperial, irresistible! Not in the "King's-chair" (of human arms), as we see, do his three satellites carry him along: rather on the *Tyrant's-saddle*, the back of his fellow-creature, must he ride prosperous!—The child is father of the man. He who had seen fifty years into coming Time, would have felt that little spectacle of mischievous schoolboys to be a great one. For us, who look back on it, and what followed it, now from afar, there arise questions enough: How looked these urchins? What jackets and galligaskins had they; felt headgear, or of dogskin leather? What was old Lichfield doing then; what thinking?—and so on, through the whole series of Corporal Trim's "auxiliary verbs." A picture of it all fashions itself together;—only unhappily we have no brush and no fingers.

Boyhood is now past; the ferula of Pedagogue waves harmless, in the distance: Samuel has struggled up to uncouth bulk and youthhood, wrestling with Disease, and Poverty, all the way; which two continue still his companions. At College we see little of him; yet thus much, that things went not well. A rugged wildman of the desert, awakened to the feeling of himself; proud as the proudest, poor as the poorest; stoically shut up, silently enduring the incurable: what a world of blackest gloom, with sun-gleams and pale tearful moon-gleams, and flickerings of a celestial and an infernal splendour, was this that now opened for him! But the weather is wintry; and the toes of the man are looking through his shoes. His muddy features grow of a purple and sea-green colour; a flood of black indignation mantling beneath. A truculent, raw-boned figure! Meat he has probably little; hope he has less: his feet, as we said, have come into brotherhood with the cold mire.

"Shall I be particular," inquires Sir John Hawkins, " and relate a circumstance of his distress, that cannot be imputed to him as an effect of his own extravagance or irregularity, and consequently reflects no disgrace on his memory? He had scarce any change of raiment, and, in a short time after Corbet left him, but one pair of shoes, and those so old that his feet were seen through them: a gentleman of his college, the father of an eminent clergyman now living, directed a servitor one morning to place a new pair at the door of Johnson's chamber; who seeing them upon his first going out, so far forgot himself and the spirit which must have actuated his unknown benefactor, that, with all the indignation of an insulted man, he threw them away."

How exceedingly surprising!—The Rev. Dr. Hall remarks: " As far as we can judge from a cursory view of the weekly account in the buttery-books, Johnson appears to have lived as well as other commoners and scholars." Alas! such "cursory view of the buttery-books," now from the safe distance of a century, in the safe chair of a College Mastership, is one thing; the continual view of the empty or locked buttery itself was quite a different thing. But hear our Knight, how he farther discourses. " Johnson," quoth Sir John, could " not at this early period of his life divest himself of an idea that poverty was disgraceful; and was very severe in his censures of that economy in both our Universities, which exacted at meals the attendance of poor scholars, under the several denominations of Servitors in the one, and Sizers in the other: he thought that the scholar's, like the Christian life, levelled all distinctions of rank and worldly preëminence; but in this he was *mistaken:* civil polity " etc., etc.—Too true! It is man's lot to err.

However, Destiny, in all ways, means to prove the mistaken Samuel, and see what stuff is in him. He must leave these butteries of Oxford, Want like an armed man compelling him; retreat into his father's mean home; and there abandon himself for a season to inaction, disappointment, shame and nervous melancholy nigh run mad: he is probably the wretchedest man in wide England. In all ways he too must " become perfect through *suffering.*"—High thoughts have visited him; his College Exercises have been praised beyond the walls of College; Pope himself has seen that *Translation*, and approved of it: Samuel had whispered to himself: I too am " one and somewhat." False thoughts; that leave only misery behind! The fever-fire of Ambition is too painfully extinguished (but not cured) in the frost-bath of Poverty. Johnson has knocked at the gate, as one having a right; but there was no opening: the world lies all encircled as with brass; nowhere can he find or force the smallest entrance. An ushership at Market Bosworth, and " a disagreement between him and Sir Wolstan Dixie, the patron of the school," yields him bread of affliction and water of affliction; but so bitter, that unassisted human nature cannot swallow them. Young Samson will grind no more in the Philistine mill of

Bosworth; quits hold of Sir Wolstan, and the " domestic chaplaincy, so far at least as to say grace at table," and also to be " treated with what he represented as intolerable harshness; " and so, after " some months of such complicated misery," feeling doubtless that there are worse things in the world than quick death by Famine, " relinquishes a situation, which all his life afterwards he recollected with the strongest aversion, and even horror." Men like Johnson are properly called the Forlorn Hope of the World: judge whether his hope was forlorn or not, by this Letter to a dull oily Printer who called himself *Sylvanus Urban* :

" Sir,—As you appear no less sensible than your readers of the defect of your poetical article, you will not be displeased if (in order to the improvement of it) I communicate to you the sentiments of a person who will undertake, on reasonable terms, sometimes to fill a column.

" His opinion is, that the public would " etc., etc.

" If such a correspondence will be agreeable to you, be pleased to inform me in two posts, what the conditions are on which you shall expect it. Your late offer (for a Prize Poem) gives me no reason to distrust your generosity. If you engage in any literary projects besides this paper, I have other designs to impart."

Reader, the generous person, to whom this letter goes addressed, is " Mr. Edmund Cave, at St. John's Gate, London; " the addressor of it is Samuel Johnson, in Birmingham, Warwickshire.

Nevertheless, Life rallies in the man; reasserts its right to be *lived*, even to be enjoyed. " Better a small bush," say the Scotch, " than no shelter: " Johnson learns to be contented with humble human things; and is there not already an actual realised human Existence, all stirring and living on every hand of him? Go thou and do likewise! In Birmingham itself, with his own purchased goose-quill, he can earn " five guineas; " nay, finally, the choicest terrestrial good: a Friend, who will be Wife to him! Johnson's marriage with the good Widow Porter has been treated with ridicule by many mortals, who apparently had no understanding thereof. That the purblind, seamy-faced Wildman, stalking lonely, woe-stricken, like some Irish Gallowglass with peeled club, whose speech no man knew, whose look all men both laughed at and shuddered at, should find any brave female heart to acknowledge, at first sight and hearing of him, " This is the most sensible man I ever met with;" and then, with generous courage, to take him to itself, and say, Be thou mine; be thou warmed here, and thawed to life!—in all this, in the kind Widow's love and pity for him, in Johnson's love and gratitude, there is actually no matter for ridicule. Their wedded life, as is the common lot, was made up of drizzle and dry weather; but innocence and worth dwelt in it; and when death had ended it, a certain sacredness: Johnson's deathless affection for his Tetty was always venerable and noble.

However, be all this as it might, Johnson is now minded to wed; and will live by the trade of Pedagogy, for by this also may life be kept in. Let the world therefore take notice: "*At Edial near Lichfield, in Staffordshire, young gentlemen are boarded, and taught the Latin and Greek languages, by*—SAMUEL JOHNSON." Had this Edial enterprise prospered, how different might the issue have been! Johnson had lived a life of unnoticed nobleness, or swoln into some amorphous Dr. Parr, of no avail to us; Bozzy would have dwindled into official insignificance, or risen by some other elevation; old Auchinleck had never been afflicted with "ane that keeped a schule," or obliged to violate hospitality by a "Cromwell do? God, sir, he gart kings ken that there was a *lith* in their neck!"—But the Edial enterprise did not prosper; Destiny had other work appointed for Samuel Johnson; and young gentlemen got board where they could elsewhere find it. This man was to become a Teacher of grown gentlemen, in the most surprising way; a Man of Letters, and Ruler of the British Nation for some time,—not of their bodies merely but of their minds, not *over* them but *in* them.

The career of Literature could not, in Johnson's day, any more than now, be said to lie along the shores of a Pactolus: whatever else might be gathered there, gold-dust was nowise the chief produce. The world, from the times of Socrates, St. Paul, and far earlier, has always had its Teachers; and always treated them in a peculiar way. A shrewd Townclerk (not of Ephesus), once, in founding a Burgh-Seminary, when the question came, How the Schoolmasters should be maintained? delivered this brief counsel: " D—n them, keep them *poor !* " Considerable wisdom may lie in this aphorism. At all events, we see, the world has acted on it long, and indeed improved on it,—putting many a Schoolmaster of its

great Burgh-Seminary to a death which even *cost* it something.
The world, it is true, had for some time been too busy to go
out of its way, and *put* any author to death; however, the
old sentence pronounced against them was found to be pretty
sufficient. The first Writers, being Monks, were sworn to
a vow of Poverty; the modern Authors had no need to swear
to it. This was the epoch when an Otway could still die of
hunger; not to speak of your innumerable Scrogginses,
whom " the Muse found stretched beneath a rug," with
" rusty grate unconscious of a fire," stocking-nightcap,
sanded floor, and all the other escutcheons of the craft,
time out of mind the heirlooms of Authorship. Scroggins,
however, seems to have been but an idler; not at all so
diligent as worthy Mr. Boyce, whom we might have
seen *sitting up* in bed, with his wearing-apparel of Blanket
about him, and a hole slit in the same, that his hand might
be at liberty to work in its vocation. The worst was, that
too frequently a blackguard recklessness of temper ensued,
incapable of turning to account what good the gods even here
had provided: your Boyces acted on some stoico-epicurean
principle of *carpe diem*, as men do in bombarded towns, and
seasons of raging pestilence;—and so had lost not only their
life, and presence of mind, but their status as persons of
respectability. The trade of Author was at about one of its
lowest ebbs when Johnson embarked on it.

Accordingly we find no mention of Illuminations in the
city of London, when this same Ruler of the British Nation
arrived in it: no cannon-salvos are fired; no flourish of
drums and trumpets greets his appearance on the scene.
He enters quite quietly, with some copper halfpence in his
pocket; creeps into lodgings in Exeter Street, Strand; and
has a Coronation Pontiff also, of not less peculiar equipment,
whom, with all submissiveness, he must wait upon, in his
Vatican of St. John's Gate. This is the dull oily Printer
alluded to above.

" Cave's temper," says our Knight Hawkins, " was phlegmatic:
though he assumed, as the publisher of the Magazine, the name
of Sylvanus Urban, he had few of those qualities that constitute
urbanity. Judge of his want of them by this question, which he
once put to an author: ' Mr. ——, I hear you have just published
a pamphlet, and am told there is a very good paragraph in it upon
the subject of music: did you write that yourself? ' His discern-

ment was also slow; and as he had already at his command some writers of prose and verse, who, in the language of Booksellers, are called good hands, he was the backwarder in making advances, or courting an intimacy with Johnson. Upon the first approach of a stranger, his practice was to continue sitting; a posture in which he was ever to be found, and for a few minutes to continue silent: if at any time he was inclined to begin the discourse, it was generally by putting a leaf of the Magazine, then in the press, into the hand of his visitor, and asking his opinion of it. . . .

" He was so incompetent a judge of Johnson's abilities, that meaning at one time to dazzle him with the splendour of some of those luminaries in Literature, who favoured him with their correspondence, he told him that if he would, in the evening, be at a certain alehouse in the neighbourhood of Clerkenwell, he might have a chance of seeing Mr. Browne and another or two of those illustrious contributors: Johnson accepted the invitation; and being introduced by Cave, dressed in a loose horseman's coat, and such a great bushy wig as he constantly wore, to the sight of Mr. Browne, whom he found sitting at the upper end of a long table, in a cloud of tobacco-smoke, had his curiosity gratified." [1]

In fact, if we look seriously into the condition of Authorship at that period, we shall find that Johnson had undertaken one of the ruggedest of all possible enterprises; that here as elsewhere Fortune had given him unspeakable Contradictions to reconcile. For a man of Johnson's stamp, the Problem was twofold: *First*, not only as the humble but indispensable condition of all else, to keep himself, if so might be, *alive;* but *secondly*, to keep himself alive by speaking forth the *Truth* that was in him, and speaking it *truly*, that is, in the clearest and fittest utterance the Heavens had enabled him to give it, let the Earth say to this what she liked. Of which twofold Problem if it be hard to solve either member separately, how incalculably more so to solve it, when both are conjoined, and work with endless complication into one another! He that finds himself already *kept alive* can sometimes (unhappily not always) speak a little truth; he that finds himself able and willing, to all lengths, to *speak lies*, may, by watching how the wind sits, scrape together a livelihood, sometimes of great splendour: he, again, who finds himself provided with *neither* endowment, has but a ticklish game to play, and shall have praises if he win it. Let us look a little at both faces of the matter; and see what front they then offered our Adventurer, what front he offered them.

[1] Hawkins, pp. 46-50.

At the time of Johnson's appearance on the field, Literature, in many senses, was in a transitional state; chiefly in this sense, as respects the pecuniary subsistence of its cultivators. It was in the very act of passing from the protection of Patrons into that of the Public; no longer to supply its necessities by laudatory Dedications to the Great, but by judicious Bargains with the Booksellers. This happy change has been much sung and celebrated; many a "lord of the lion heart and eagle eye" looking back with scorn enough on the bygone system of Dependency: so that now it were perhaps well to consider, for a moment, what good might also be in it, what gratitude we owe it. That a good was in it, admits not of doubt. Whatsoever has existed has had its value: without some truth and worth lying in it, the thing could not have hung together, and been the organ and sustenance, and method of action, for men that reasoned and were alive. Translate a Falsehood which is wholly false into Practice, the result comes out *zero;* there is no fruit or issue to be derived from it. That in an age, when a Nobleman was still noble, still with his wealth the protector of worthy and humane things, and still venerated as such, a poor Man of Genius, his brother in nobleness, should, with unfeigned reverence, address him and say: "I have found Wisdom here, and would fain proclaim it abroad; wilt thou, of thy abundance, afford me the means?"—in all this there was no baseness; it was wholly an honest proposal, which a free man might make, and a free man listen to. So might a Tasso, with a *Gerusalemme* in his hand or in his head, speak to a Duke of Ferrara; so might a Shakspeare to his Southampton; and Continental Artists generally to their rich Protectors,—in some countries, down almost to these days. It was only when the reverence became *feigned,* that baseness entered into the transaction on both sides; and, indeed, flourished there with rapid luxuriance, till that became disgraceful for a Dryden, which a Shakspeare could once practise without offence.

Neither, it is very true, was the new way of Bookseller Mæcenasship worthless; which opened itself at this juncture, for the most important of all transport-trades, now when the old way had become too miry and impassable. Remark, moreover, how this second sort of Mæcenasship, after carrying us through nearly a century of Literary Time, appears now to have wellnigh discharged *its* function also; and to be working pretty rapidly towards some *third* method, the exact conditions of which are yet nowise visible. Thus all things have their end; and we should part with them all, not in anger, but in peace. The Bookseller-System, during its peculiar century, the whole of the eighteenth, did carry us handsomely along; and many good Works it has left us, and many good Men it maintained: if it is now expiring by PUFFERY, as the Patronage-System did by FLATTERY (for *Lying* is ever the forerunner of Death, nay is itself Death), let us not forget its benefits; how it nursed Literature through boyhood and school-years, as Patronage had wrapped it in soft swaddling-bands;—till now we see it about to put on the *toga virilis*, could it but *find* any such!

There is tolerable travelling on the beaten road, run how it may; only on the new road not yet levelled and paved, and on the old road all broken into ruts and quagmires, is the travelling bad or impracticable. The difficulty lies always in the *transition* from one method to another. In which state it was that Johnson now found Literature; and out of which, let us also say, he manfully carried it. What remarkable mortal *first paid copyright* in England we have not ascertained; perhaps, for almost a century before, some scarce visible or ponderable pittance of wages had occasionally been yielded by the Seller of Books to the Writer of them: the original Covenant, stipulating to produce *Paradise Lost* on the one hand, and *Five Pounds Sterling* on the other, still lies (we have been told) in black-on-white, for inspection and purchase by the curious, at a Bookshop in Chancery Lane. Thus had the matter gone on, in a mixed confused way, for some threescore years;—as ever, in such things, the old system *overlaps* the new, by some generation or two, and only dies quite out when the new has got a complete organisation and weather-worthy surface of its own. Among the first Authors, the very first of any significance, who lived by the day's wages of his craft, and composedly faced the world on that basis, was Samuel Johnson.

At the time of Johnson's appearance there were still two ways, on which an Author might attempt proceeding: there were the Mæcenases proper in the West End of London; and the Mæcenases virtual of St. John's Gate and Paternoster Row. To a considerate man it might seem uncertain which method were preferable: neither had very high attractions; the Patron's aid was now wellnigh *necessarily* polluted by sycophancy, before it could come to hand; the Bookseller's was deformed with greedy stupidity, not to say entire wooden-headedness and disgust (so that an Osborne even required to be knocked down, by an author of spirit), and could barely keep the thread of life together. The one was the wages of suffering and poverty; the other, unless you gave strict heed to it, the wages of sin. In time, Johnson had opportunity of looking into both methods, and ascertaining what they were; but found, at first trial, that the former would in nowise do for him. Listen, once again, to that far-famed Blast of Doom, proclaiming into the ear of Lord Chesterfield, and, through him, of the listening world, that patronage should be no more!

" Seven years, my Lord, have now past, since I waited in your outward rooms, or was repulsed from your door; during which time I have been pushing on my Work [1] through difficulties, of which it is useless to complain, and have brought it at last to the verge of publication, without one act of assistance,[2] one word of encouragement, or one smile of favour.

" The shepherd in Virgil grew at last acquainted with Love, and found him a native of the rocks.

" Is not a patron, my Lord, one who looks with unconcern on a man struggling for life in the water, and when he has reached ground, encumbers him with help? The notice which you have been pleased to take of my labours, had it been early, had been kind: but it has been delayed till I am indifferent and cannot enjoy it; till I am solitary and cannot impart it; till I am known and do not want it. I hope, it is no very cynical asperity, not to confess obligations where no benefit has been received; or to be unwilling that the public should consider me as owing that to a patron which Providence has enabled me to do for myself.

" Having carried on my Work thus far with so little obligation to any favourer of learning, I shall not be disappointed though I should conclude it, if less be possible, with less: for I have long been awakened from that dream of hope, in which I once boasted myself with so much exultation.

" My Lord, your Lordship's most humble, most obedient servant,   SAM. JOHNSON."

[1] The *English Dictionary*.

[2] Were time and printer's space of no value, it were easy to wash away certain foolish soot-stains dropped here as " Notes; " especially two: the one on this word, and on Boswell's Note to it; the other on the paragraph which follows. Let " ED." look a second time; he will find that Johnson's sacred regard for *Truth* is the only thing to be " noted " in the former case; also, in the latter, that this of " Love's being a native of the rocks" actually *has* a " meaning."

And thus must the rebellious " Sam. Johnson " turn him to the Bookselling guild, and the wondrous chaos of " Author by trade; " and, though ushered into it only by that dull oily Printer, " with loose horseman's coat and such a great bushy wig as he constantly wore," and only as subaltern to some commanding-officer " Browne, sitting amid tobacco-smoke at the head of a long table in the alehouse at Clerkenwell,"— gird himself together for the warfare; having no alternative!

Little less contradictory was that other branch of the two-fold Problem now set before Johnson: the speaking forth of *Truth*. Nay taken by itself, it had in those days become so complex as to puzzle strongest heads, with nothing else imposed on them for solution; and even to turn high heads of that sort into mere hollow *vizards*, speaking neither truth nor falsehood, nor anything but what the Prompter and Player (ὑποκριτὴς) put into them. Alas! for poor Johnson Contradiction abounded; in spirituals and in temporals, within and without. Born with the strongest unconquerable love of just Insight, he must begin to live and learn in a scene where Prejudice flourishes with rank luxuriance. England was all confused enough, sightless and yet restless, take it where you would; but figure the best intellect in England nursed up to manhood in the idol-cavern of a poor Tradesman's house, in the cathedral city of Lichfield! What is Truth? said jesting Pilate. What is Truth? might earnest Johnson much more emphatically say. Truth, no longer, like the Phœnix, in rainbow plumage, poured, from her glittering beak, such tones of sweetest melody as took captive every ear: the Phœnix (waxing old) had wellnigh ceased her singing, and empty wearisome Cuckoos, and doleful monotonous Owls, innumerable Jays also, and twittering Sparrows on the housetop, pretended they were repeating her.

It was wholly a divided age, that of Johnson; Unity existed nowhere, in its Heaven, or in its Earth. Society, through every fibre, was rent asunder: all things, it was then becoming visible, but could not then be understood, were moving onwards, with an impulse received ages before, yet now first with a decisive rapidity, towards that great chaotic gulf, where, whether in the shape of French Revolutions, Reform Bills, or what shape soever, bloody or bloodless, the descent and engulfment assume, we now see them weltering and boiling. Already Cant, as once before hinted, had begun

to play its wonderful part, for the hour was come: two
ghastly Apparitions, unreal *simulacra* both, HYPOCRISY and
ATHEISM are already, in silence, parting the world. Opinion
and Action, which should live together as wedded pair,
" one flesh," more properly as Soul and Body, have com-
menced their open quarrel, and are suing for a separate
maintenance,—as if they could exist separately. To the
earnest mind, in any position, firm footing and a life of Truth
was becoming daily more difficult: in Johnson's position
it was more difficult than in almost any other.

If, as for a devout nature was inevitable and indispensable,
he looked up to Religion, as to the polestar of his voyage,
already there was no *fixed* polestar any longer visible; but
two stars, a whole constellation of stars, each proclaiming
itself as the true. There was the red portentous comet-star
of Infidelity; the dim fixed-star, burning ever dimmer,
uncertain now whether not an atmospheric *meteor*, of Orthodoxy: which of these to choose? The keener intellects of
Europe had, almost without exception, ranged themselves
under the former: for some half century, it had been the
general effort of European speculation to proclaim that
Destruction of Falsehood was the only Truth; daily had
Denial waxed stronger and stronger, Belief sunk more and
more into decay. From our Bolingbrokes and Tolands
the sceptical fever had passed into France, into Scotland;
and already it smouldered, far and wide, secretly eating out
the heart of England. Bayle had played his part; Voltaire
on a wider theatre, was playing his,—Johnson's senior by
some fifteen years: Hume and Johnson were children almost
of the same year.[1] To this keener order of intellects did
Johnson's indisputably belong: was he to join them; was
he to oppose them? A complicated question: for, alas, the
Church itself is no longer, even to him, wholly of true adamant,
but of adamant and baked mud conjoined: the zealously
Devout has to find his Church tottering; and pause amazed
to see, instead of inspired Priest, many a swine-feeding
Trulliber ministering at her altar. It is not the least curious
of the incoherences which Johnson had to reconcile, that,
though by nature contemptuous and incredulous, he was,
at that time of day, to find his safety and glory in defending,
with his whole might, the traditions of the elders.

---

[1] Johnson, September 1709; Hume, April 1711.

Not less perplexingly intricate, and on both sides hollow or questionable, was the aspect of Politics. Whigs struggling blindly forward, Tories holding blindly back; each with some forecast of a half truth; neither with any forecast of the whole! Admire here this other Contradiction in the life of Johnson; that, though the most ungovernable, and in practice the most independent of men, he must be a Jacobite, and worshipper of the Divine Right. In Politics also there are Irreconcilables enough for him. As, indeed, how could it be otherwise? For when Religion is torn asunder, and the very heart of man's existence set against itself, then in all subordinate departments there must needs be hollowness, incoherence. The English Nation had rebelled against a Tyrant; and, by the hands of religious tyrannicides, exacted stern vengeance of him: Democracy had risen iron-sinewed, and, "like an infant Hercules, strangled serpents in its cradle." But as yet none knew the meaning or extent of the phenomenon: Europe was not ripe for it; not to be ripened for it but by the culture and various experience of another century and a half. And now, when the King-killers were all swept away, and a milder *second* picture was painted over the canvas of the *first*, and betitled "Glorious Revolution," who doubted but the catastrophe was over, the whole business finished, and Democracy gone to its long sleep? Yet was it like a business finished and not finished; a lingering uneasiness dwelt in all minds: the deep-lying, resistless Tendency, which had still to be *obeyed*, could no longer be *recognised*; thus was there halfness, insincerity, uncertainty in men's ways; instead of heroic Puritans and heroic Cavaliers, came now a dawdling set of argumentative Whigs, and a dawdling set of deaf-eared Tories; each half-foolish, each half-false. The Whigs were false and without basis; inasmuch as their whole object was Resistance, Criticism, Demolition,—they knew not why, or towards what issue. In Whiggism, ever since a Charles and his Jeffries had ceased to meddle with it, and to have any Russel or Sydney to meddle with, there could be no divineness of character; not till, in these latter days, it took the figure of a thorough-going, all-defying Radicalism, was there any solid footing for it to stand on. Of the like uncertain, half-hollow nature had Toryism become, in Johnson's time; preaching forth indeed an everlasting truth, the duty of Loyalty; yet now, ever since the final expulsion of the Stuarts, having no *Person*, but only an *Office* to be loyal to; no living *Soul* to worship, but only a dead velvet - cushioned *Chair*. Its attitude, therefore, was stiff-necked refusal to move; as that of Whiggism was clamorous command to move,—let rhyme and reason, on both hands, say to it what they might. The consequence was: Immeasurable floods of contentious jargon, tending nowhither; false conviction; false resistance to conviction; decay (ultimately to become decease) of whatsoever was once understood by the words, *Principle*, or *Honesty* of heart; the louder and louder triumph of *Half*ness and Plausibility over *Whole*ness and Truth;—at last, this all-overshadowing efflorescence of QUACKERY, which we now see, with all its deadening and killing fruits, in all its innumerable branches, down to the lowest. How, between these jarring extremes, wherein the rotten lay so inextricably intermingled with the sound, and as yet no eye could see through the ulterior meaning of the matter, was a faithful and true man to adjust himself?

That Johnson, in spite of all drawbacks, adopted the Conservative side; stationed himself as the unyielding opponent of Innovation, resolute to hold fast the form of sound words, could not but increase, in no small measure, the difficulties he had to strive with. We mean, the *moral* difficulties; for in *economical* respects, it might be pretty equally balanced; the Tory servant of the Public had perhaps about the same chance of promotion as the Whig: and all the promotion Johnson aimed at was the privilege *to live*. But, for what, though unavowed, was no less indispensable, for his peace of conscience, and the clear ascertainment and feeling of his Duty as an inhabitant of God's world, the case was hereby rendered much more complex. To resist Innovation is easy enough on one condition: that you resist Inquiry. This is, and was, the common expedient of your common Conservatives; but it would not do for Johnson: he was a zealous recommender and practiser of Inquiry; once for all, could not and would not believe, much less speak and act, a Falsehood: the *form* of sound words, which he held fast, must have a *meaning* in it. Here lay the difficulty: to behold a portentous mixture of True and False, and feel that he must dwell and fight there; yet to love and defend only the True. How worship, when you cannot and will not be an idolater; yet cannot help discerning that the Symbol of your Divinity has half become idolatrous? This was the question, which Johnson, the man both of clear eye and devout believing heart, must answer,—at peril of his life. The Whig or Sceptic, on the other hand, had a much simpler part to play. To him only the idolatrous side of things, nowise the divine one, lay visible: not *worship*, therefore, nay in the strict sense not heart-honesty, only at most lip- and hand-honesty, is required of him. What spiritual force is his, he can conscientiously employ in the work of cavilling, of pulling-down what is False. For the rest, that there is or can be any Truth of a higher than sensual nature, has not occurred to him. The utmost, therefore, that he as man has to aim at, is RE-SPECTABILITY, the suffrages of his fellow-men. Such suffrages he may weigh as well as count: or count only: according as he is a Burke or a Wilkes. But beyond these there lies nothing divine for him; these attained, all is attained. Thus is his whole world distinct and rounded-in; a clear goal is set before him; a firm path, rougher or smoother; at worst a firm region wherein to seek a path: let him gird-up his loins, and travel on without misgivings! For the honest Conservative, again, nothing is distinct, nothing rounded-in: RESPECTABILITY can nowise be his highest Godhead; not one aim, but two conflicting aims to be continually reconciled by him, has he to strive after. A difficult position, as we said; which accordingly the most did, even in those days, but half defend: by the surrender, namely, of their own too cumbersome *honesty* or even *understanding;* after which the completest defence was worth little. Into this difficult position Johnson, nevertheless, threw himself: found it indeed full of difficulties; yet held it out manfully, as an honest-hearted, open-sighted man, while life was in him.

Such was that same " twofold Problem " set before Samuel Johnson. Consider all these moral difficulties; and add to them the fearful aggravation, which lay in that other circumstance, that he needed a continual appeal to the Public, must continually produce a certain impression and conviction on the Public; that if he did not, he ceased to have " provision for the day that was passing over him," he could not any longer live! How a vulgar character, once launched into this wild element; driven onwards by Fear and Famine; without other aim than to clutch what Provender (of Enjoyment in

any kind) he could get, always if possible keeping *quite* clear
of the Gallows and Pillory, that is to say, minding heedfully
both " person " and " character,"—would have floated hither
and thither in it; and contrived to eat some three repasts
daily, and wear some three suits yearly, and then to depart
and disappear, having consumed his last ration: all this
might be worth knowing, but were in itself a trivial knowledge.
How a noble man, resolute for the Truth, to whom Shams
and Lies were once for all an abomination, was to act in it:
here lay the mystery. By what methods, by what gifts of
eye and hand, does a heroic Samuel Johnson, now when
cast forth into that waste Chaos of Authorship, maddest
of things, a mingled Phlegethon and Fleet-ditch, with its
floating lumber, and sea-krakens, and mud-spectres,—shape
himself a voyage; of the *transient* driftwood, and the *enduring*
iron, build him a sea-worthy Life-boat, and sail therein,
undrowned, unpolluted, through the roaring " mother of
dead dogs," onwards to an eternal Landmark, and City that
hath foundations? This high question is even the one
answered in Boswell's Book; which Book we therefore, not
so falsely, have named a *Heroic Poem ;* for in it there lies the
whole argument of such. Glory to our brave Samuel! He
accomplished this wonderful Problem; and now through long
generations we point to him, and say: Here also was a Man;
let the world once more have assurance of a Man!

Had there been in Johnson, now when afloat on that confusion worse confounded of grandeur and squalor, no light
but an earthly outward one, he too must have made ship-
wreck. With his diseased body and vehement voracious
heart, how easy for him to become a *carpe-diem* Philosopher,
like the rest, and live and die as miserably as any Boyce
of that Brotherhood! But happily there was a higher light
for him; shining as a lamp to his path; which, in all paths,
would teach him to act and walk not as a fool, but as wise,
and in those evil days too " redeeming the time." Under
dimmer or clearer manifestations, a Truth had been revealed
to him: I also am a Man; even in this unutterable element
of Authorship, I may live as beseems a man! That Wrong
is not only different from Right, but that it is in strict
scientific terms *infinitely* different; even as the gaining of
the whole world set against the losing of one's own soul, or
(as Johnson had it) a Heaven set against a Hell; that in all

situations out of the Pit of Tophet, wherein a living Man has stood or can stand, there is actually a Prize of quite *infinite* value placed within his reach, namely a *Duty* for him to do: this highest Gospel, which forms the basis and worth of all other Gospels whatsoever, had been revealed to Samuel Johnson; and the man had believed it, and laid it faithfully to heart. Such knowledge of the *transcendental*, immeasurable character of Duty we call the basis of all Gospels, the essence of all Religion: he who with his whole soul knows not this, as yet knows nothing, as yet *is* properly nothing.

This, happily for him, Johnson was one of those that knew: under a certain authentic Symbol it stood forever present to his eyes: a Symbol, indeed, waxing old as doth a garment; yet which had guided forward, as their Banner and celestial Pillar of Fire, innumerable saints and witnesses, the fathers of our modern world; and for him also had still a sacred significance. It does not appear that at any time Johnson was what we call irreligious: but in his sorrows and isolation, when hope died away, and only a long vista of suffering and toil lay before him to the end, then first did Religion shine forth in its meek, everlasting clearness; even as the stars do in black night, which in the daytime and dusk were hidden by inferior lights. How a true man, in the midst of errors and uncertainties, shall work out for himself a sure Life-truth; and adjusting the transient to the eternal, amid the fragments of ruined Temples build up, with toil and pain, a little Altar for himself, and worship there; how Samuel Johnson, in the era of Voltaire, can purify and fortify his soul, and hold real communion with the Highest, " in the Church of St. Clement Danes: " this too stands all unfolded in his Biography, and is among the most touching and memorable things there; a thing to be looked at with pity, admiration, awe. Johnson's Religion was as the light of life to him; without it his heart was all sick, dark and had no guidance left.

He is now enlisted, or impressed, into that unspeakable shoeblack-seraph Army of Authors; but can feel hereby that he fights under a celestial flag, and will quit him like a man. The first grand requisite, an assured heart, he therefore has: what his outward equipments and accoutrements are, is the next question; an important, though inferior one. His intellectual stock, intrinsically viewed, is perhaps inconsiderable:

the furnishings of an English School and English University; good knowledge of the Latin tongue, a more uncertain one of Greek: this is a rather slender stock of Education wherewith to front the world. But then it is to be remembered that his world was England; that such was the culture England commonly supplied and expected. Besides, Johnson has been a voracious reader, though a desultory one, and oftenest in strange scholastic, too obsolete Libraries; he has also rubbed shoulders with the press of Actual Life for some thirty years now: views or hallucinations of innumerable things are weltering to and fro in him. Above all, be his weapons what they may, he has an arm that can wield them. Nature has given him her choicest gift,—an open eye and heart. He will look on the world, wheresoever he can catch a glimpse of it, with eager curiosity: to the last, we find this a striking characteristic of him; for all human interests he has a sense; the meanest handicraftsman could interest him, even in extreme age, by speaking of his craft: the ways of men are all interesting to him; any human thing, that he did not know, he wished to know. Reflection, moreover, Meditation, was what he practised incessantly, with or without his will: for the mind of the man was earnest, deep as well as humane. Thus would the world, such fragments of it as he could survey, form itself, or continually tend to form itself, into a coherent Whole; on any and on all phases of which, his vote and voice must be well worth listening to. As a Speaker of the Word, he will speak real words; no idle jargon or hollow triviality will issue from him. His aim too is clear, attainable; that of *working for his wages :* let him *do* this honestly, and all else will follow of its own accord.

With such omens, into such a warfare, did Johnson go forth. A rugged hungry Kerne or Gallowglass, as we called him: yet indomitable; in whom lay the true spirit of a Soldier. With giant's force he toils, since such is his appointment, were it but at hewing of wood and drawing of water for old sedentary bushy-wigged Cave; distinguishes himself by mere quantity, if there is to be no other distinction. He can write all things; frosty Latin verses, if these are the saleable commodity; Book-prefaces, Political Philippics, Review Articles, Parliamentary Debates: all things he does rapidly; still more surprising, all things he does thoroughly and well. How he sits there, in his rough-hewn amorphous bulk, in that upper-room at St. John's Gate, and trundles-off sheet after sheet of those Senate-of-Lilliput Debates, to the clamorous Printer's Devils waiting for them with insatiable throat, down stairs; himself perhaps *impransus* all the while! Admire also the greatness of Literature; how a grain of mustard-seed cast into its Nile-waters, shall settle in the teeming mould, and be found, one day, as a Tree, in whose branches all the fowls of heaven may lodge. Was it not so with these Lilliput Debates? In that small project and act began the stupendous FOURTH ESTATE; whose wide world-embracing influences what eye can take in; in whose boughs are there not already fowls of strange feather lodged? Such things, and far stranger, were done in that wondrous old Portal, even in latter times. And then figure Samuel dining " behind the screen," from a trencher covertly handed-in to him, at a preconcerted nod from the " great bushy wig; " Samuel too ragged to show face, yet " made a happy man of " by hearing his praise spoken. If to Johnson himself, then much more to us, may that St. John's Gate be a place we can " never pass without veneration." [1]

[1] All Johnson's places of resort and abode are venerable, and now indeed to the many as well as to the few; for his name has become great; and, as we must often with a kind of sad admiration recognise, there is, even to the rudest man, no greatness so venerable as intellectual, as spiritual greatness; nay properly there is no other venerable at all. For example, what soul-subduing magic, for the very clown or craftsman of our England, lies in the word " Scholar "! " He is a Scholar: " he is a man *wiser* than we; of a wisdom to us *boundless*, infinite: who shall speak his worth! Such things, we say, fill us with a certain pathetic admiration of defaced and obstructed yet glorious man; archangel though in ruins,—or rather, though in *rubbish* of encumbrances and mud-incrustations, which also are not to be perpetual.

Nevertheless, in this mad-whirling all-forgetting London, the haunts of the mighty that were can seldom without a strange difficulty be discovered. Will any man, for instance, tell us which *bricks* it was in Lincoln's Inn Buildings that Ben Jonson's hand and trowel laid? No man, it is to be feared,—and also grumbled at. With Samuel Johnson may it prove otherwise! A Gentleman of the British Museum is said to have made drawings of all *his* residences: the blessing of Old Mortality be upon him! We ourselves, not without labour and risk, lately discovered GOUGH SQUARE, between Fleet Street and Holborn (adjoining both to BOLT COURT and to JOHNSON'S COURT); and on the second day of search, the very House there, wherein the *English Dictionary* was composed. It is the first or corner house on the right hand, as you enter through the arched way from the North-west. The actual occupant, an elderly, well-washed, decent-looking man, invited us to enter; and courteously undertook to be *cicerone ;* though in his memory lay nothing but the foolishest jumble and hallucination. It is a stout, old-fashioned, oak-balustraded house: " I have spent many a pound and penny on it since then," said the worthy Landlord: " here,

Poverty, Distress, and as yet Obscurity, are his companions:
so poor is he that his Wife must leave him, and seek shelter
among other relations; Johnson's household has accommoda-
tion for one inmate only. To all his ever-varying, ever-
recurring troubles, moreover, must be added this continual
one of ill-health, and its concomitant depressiveness: a
galling load, which would have crushed most common mortals
into desperation, is his appointed ballast and life-burden;
he "could not remember the day he had passed free from
pain." Nevertheless, Life, as we said before, is always Life:
a healthy soul, imprison it as you will, in squalid garrets,
shabby coat, bodily sickness, or whatever else, will assert
its heaven-granted indefeasible Freedom, its right to conquer
difficulties, to do work, even to feel gladness. Johnson does
not whine over his existence, but manfully makes the most
and best of it. "He said, a man might live in a garret at
eighteenpence a-week: few people would inquire where he
lodged; and if they did, it was easy to say, ' Sir, I am to be
found at such a place.' By spending threepence in a coffee-
house, he might be for some hours every day in very good
company; he might dine for sixpence, breakfast on bread-
and-milk for a penny, and do without supper. On *clean-
shirt day* he went abroad and paid visits." Think by whom
and of whom this was uttered, and ask then, Whether there
is more pathos in it than in a whole circulating-library of
Giaours and *Harolds*, or less pathos? On another occasion,
"when Dr. Johnson, one day, read his own Satire, in
which the life of a scholar is painted, with the various
obstructions thrown in his way to fortune and to fame, he
burst into a passion of tears: Mr. Thrale's family and Mr.
Scott only were present, who, in a jocose way, clapped him
on the back, and said, ' What's all this, my dear sir? Why,
you and I and *Hercules*, you know, were all troubled with
melancholy.' He was a very large man, and made-out the
triumvirate with Johnson and Hercules comically enough."

you see, this Bedroom was the Doctor's study; that was the garden "
(a plot of delved ground somewhat larger than a bed-quilt), " where
he walked for exercise; these three garret Bedrooms " (where his
three Copyists sat and wrote) " were the place he kept his—*Pupils* in! "
Tempus edax rerum ! Yet *ferax* also: for our friend now added, with
a wistful look, which strove to seem merely historical: " I let it all in
Lodgings, to respectable gentlemen; by the quarter or the month;
it's all one to me."—" To me also," whispered the Ghost of Samuel, as
we went pensively our ways.

These were sweet tears; the sweet victorious remembrance lay in them of toils indeed frightful, yet never flinched from, and now triumphed over. "One day it shall delight you also to remember labour done!"—Neither, though Johnson is obscure and poor, need the highest enjoyment of existence, that of heart freely communing with heart, be denied him. Savage and he wander homeless through the streets; without bed, yet not without friendly converse; such another conversation not, it is like, producible in the proudest drawing-room of London. Nor, under the void Night, upon the hard pavement, are their own woes the only topic: nowise; they "will stand by their country," they there, the two "Back-woodsmen" of the Brick Desert!

Of all outward evils Obscurity is perhaps in itself the least. To Johnson, as to a healthy-minded man, the fantastic article, sold or given under the title of *Fame*, had little or no value but its intrinsic one. He prized it as the means of getting him employment and good wages; scarcely as anything more. His light and guidance came from a loftier source; of which, in honest aversion to all hypocrisy or pretentious talk, he spoke not to men; nay perhaps, being of a *healthy* mind, had never spoken to himself. We reckon it a striking fact in Johnson's history, this carelessness of his to Fame. Most authors speak of their "Fame" as if it were a quite priceless matter; the grand ultimatum, and heavenly Constantine's - Banner they had to follow, and conquer under.—Thy "Fame"! Unhappy mortal, where will it and thou both be in some fifty years? Shakspeare himself has lasted but two hundred; Homer (partly by accident) three thousand: and does not already an ETERNITY encircle every *Me* and every *Thee?* Cease, then, to sit feverishly hatching on that "Fame" of thine; and flapping and shrieking with fierce hisses, like brood-goose on her last egg, if man shall or dare approach it! Quarrel not with me, hate me not, my Brother: make what thou canst of thy egg, and welcome: God knows, I will not steal it; I believe it to be *addle*.—Johnson, for his part, was no man to be killed by a review; concerning which matter, it was said by a benevolent person: If any author *can* be reviewed to death, let it be, with all convenient despatch, *done*. Johnson thankfully receives any word spoken in his favour; is nowise disobliged by a lampoon, but will look at it, if pointed out to him, and show how it might have been done better: the lampoon itself is indeed *nothing*, a soap-bubble that next moment will become a drop of sour suds; but in the meanwhile, if it do anything, it keeps him more in the world's eye, and the next *bargain* will be all the richer: " Sir, if they should cease to talk of me, I must starve." Sound heart and understanding head: these fail no man, not even a Man of Letters!

Obscurity, however, was, in Johnson's case, whether a light or heavy evil, likely to be no lasting one. He is animated by the spirit of a true *workman*, resolute to do his work well; and he *does* his work well; all his work, that of writing, that of living. A man of this stamp is unhappily not so common in the literary or in any other department of the world, that he can continue always unnoticed. By slow degrees, Johnson emerges; looming, at first, huge and dim in the eye of an observant few; at last disclosed, in his real proportions, to the eye of the whole world, and encircled with a " light-nimbus " of glory, so that whoso is not blind must and shall behold him. By slow degrees, we said; for this also is notable; slow but sure: as his fame waxes not by exaggerated clamour of what he *seems* to be, but by better and better insight of what he *is*, so it will last and stand wearing, being genuine. Thus indeed is it always, or nearly always, with true fame. The heavenly Luminary rises amid vapours; stargazers enough must scan it with critical telescopes; it makes no blazing, the world can either look at it, or forbear looking at it; not till after a time and times does its celestial eternal nature become indubitable. Pleasant, on the other hand, is the blazing of a Tarbarrel; the crowd dance merrily round it, with loud huzzaing, universal threetimes-three, and, like Homer's peasants, " bless the useful light: " but unhappily it so soon ends in darkness, foul choking smoke; and is kicked into the gutters, a nameless imbroglio of charred staves, pitch-cinders and *vomissement du diable* !

But indeed, from of old, Johnson has enjoyed all, or nearly all, that Fame can yield any man: the respect, the obedience of those that are about him and inferior to him; of those whose opinion alone can have any forcible impression on him. A little circle gathers round the Wise man; which gradually enlarges as the report thereof spreads, and more can come to see and to believe; for Wisdom is precious, and of irresistible attraction to all. "An inspired-idiot," Goldsmith, hangs strangely about him; though, as Hawkins says, "he loved not Johnson, but rather envied him for his parts; and once entreated a friend to desist from praising him, 'for in doing so,' said he, 'you harrow-up my very soul!'" Yet, on the whole, there is no evil in the "gooseberry-fool;" but rather much good; of a finer, if of a weaker, sort than Johnson's; and all the more genuine that he himself could never become *conscious* of it,—though unhappily never cease *attempting* to become so: the Author of the genuine *Vicar of Wakefield*, nill he, will he, must needs fly towards such a mass of genuine Manhood; and Dr. Minor keep gyrating round Dr. Major, alternately attracted and repelled. Then there is the chivalrous Topham Beauclerk, with his sharp wit, and gallant courtly ways: there is Bennet Langton, an orthodox gentleman, and worthy; though Johnson once laughed, louder almost than mortal, at his last will and testament; and "could not stop his merriment, but continued it all the way till he got without the Temple-gate; then burst into such a fit of laughter that he appeared to be almost in a convulsion; and, in order to support himself, laid hold of one of the posts at the side of the foot-pavement, and sent forth peals so loud that, in the silence of the night, his voice seemed to resound from Temple-bar to Fleet-ditch!" Lastly comes his solid-thinking, solid-feeding Thrale, the well-beloved man; with *Thralia*, a bright papilionaceous creature, whom the elephant loved to play with, and wave to and fro upon his trunk. Not to speak of a reverent Bozzy, for what need is there farther?—Or of the spiritual Luminaries, with tongue or pen, who made that age remarkable; or of Highland Lairds drinking, in fierce usquebaugh, "Your health, Toctor Shonson!"—Still less of many such as that poor "Mr. F. Lewis," older in date, of whose birth, death and whole terrestrial *res gestæ*, this only, and strange enough this actually, survives: "Sir, he lived in London, and hung loose upon society!" *Stat* PARVI *nominis umbra.*—

In his fifty-third year he is beneficed, by the royal bounty, with a Pension of three-hundred pounds. Loud clamour is always more or less insane: but probably the insanest of all loud clamours in the eighteenth century was this that was raised about Johnson's Pension. Men seem to be led by the noses: but in reality, it is by the ears,—as some ancient slaves were, who had their ears bored; or as some modern quadrupeds may be, whose ears are long. Very falsely was it said, "Names do not change Things." Names do change Things; nay for most part they are the only substance, which mankind can discern in Things. The whole sum that Johnson, during the remaining twenty-two years of his life, drew from the public funds of England, would have supported some Supreme Priest for about half as many weeks; it amounts very nearly to the revenue of our poorest Church-Overseer for one twelvemonth. Of secular Administrators of Provinces, and Horse-subduers, and Game-destroyers, we shall not so much as speak: but who were the Primates of England, and the Primates of All England, during Johnson's days? No man has remembered. Again, is the Primate of all England something, or is he nothing? If something, then what but the man who, in the supreme degree, teaches and spiritually edifies, and leads towards Heaven by guiding wisely through the Earth, the living souls that inhabit England? We touch here upon deep matters; which but remotely concern us, and might lead us into still deeper: clear, in the mean while, it is that the true Spiritual Edifier and Soul's-Father of all England was, and till very lately continued to be, the man named Samuel Johnson,—whom this scot-and-lot-paying world cackled reproachfully to see remunerated like a Supervisor of Excise!

If Destiny had beaten hard on poor Samuel, and did never cease to visit him too roughly, yet the last section of his Life might be pronounced victorious, and on the whole happy. He was not idle; but now no longer goaded-on by want; the light which had shone irradiating the dark haunts of Poverty, now illuminates the circles of Wealth, of a certain culture and elegant intelligence; he who had once been admitted to speak with Edmund Cave and Tobacco Browne, now admits a Reynolds and a Burke to speak with him. Loving friends are there; Listeners, even Answerers: the fruit of his long labours lies round him in fair legible Writings, of Philosophy, Eloquence, Morality, Philology; some excellent, all worthy and genuine Works; for which too, a deep, earnest murmur of thanks reaches him from all ends of his Fatherland. Nay there are works of Goodness, of undying Mercy, which even he has possessed the power to do: "What I gave I have;

what I spent I had!" Early friends had long sunk into the grave; yet in his soul they ever lived, fresh and clear, with soft pious breathings towards them, not without a still hope of one day meeting them again in purer union. Such was Johnson's Life: the victorious Battle of a free, true Man. Finally he died the death of the free and true: a dark cloud of Death, solemn and not untinged with haloes of immortal Hope, " took him away," and our eyes could no longer behold him; but can still behold the trace and impress of his courageous honest spirit, deep-legible in the World's Business, wheresoever he walked and was.

To estimate the quantity of Work that Johnson performed, how much poorer the World were had it wanted him, can, as in all such cases, never be accurately done; cannot, till after some longer space, be approximately done. All work is as seed sown; it grows and spreads, and sows itself anew, and so, in endless palingenesia, lives and works. To Johnson's Writings, good and solid, and still profitable as they are, we have already rated his Life and Conversation as superior. By the one and by the other, who shall compute what effects have been produced, and are still, and into deep Time, producing?

So much, however, we can already see: It is now some three quarters of a century that Johnson has been the Prophet of the English; the man by whose light the English people, in public and in private, more than by any other man's, have guided their existence. Higher light than that immediately *practical* one; higher virtue than an honest PRUDENCE, he could not then communicate; nor perhaps could they have received: such light, such virtue, however, he did communicate. How to thread this labyrinthic Time, the fallen and falling Ruin of Times; to silence vain Scruples, hold firm to the last the fragments of old Belief, and with earnest eye still discern some glimpses of a true path, and go forward thereon, " in a world where there is much to be done, and little to be known:" this is what Samuel Johnson, by act and word, taught his Nation; what his Nation received and learned of him, more than of any other. We can view him as the preserver and transmitter of whatsoever was genuine in the spirit of Toryism; which genuine spirit, it is now becoming manifest, must again embody itself in all new forms of Society, be what they may, that are to exist, and have continuance—elsewhere than on Paper. The *last* in many things, Johnson was the last genuine Tory; the last of Englishmen who, with strong voice and wholly-believing heart, preached the Doctrine of Standing still; who, without selfishness or slavishness, reverenced the existing Powers, and could assert the privileges of rank, though himself poor, neglected and plebeian; who had heart-devoutness with heart-hatred of cant, was orthodox-religious with his eyes open; and in all things and everywhere spoke out in plain English, from a soul wherein jesuitism could find no harbour, and with the front and tone not of a diplomatist but of a man.

The last of the Tories was Johnson: not Burke, as is often said; Burke was essentially a Whig, and only, on reaching the verge of the chasm towards which Whiggism from the first was inevitably leading, recoiled; and like a man vehement rather than earnest, a resplendent far-sighted Rhetorician rather than a deep sure Thinker, recoiled with no measure, convulsively, and damaging what he drove back with him.

In a world which exists by the balance of Antagonisms, the respective merit of the Conservator and the Innovator must ever remain debatable. Great, in the mean while, and undoubted for both sides, is the merit of him who, in a day of Change, walks wisely, honestly. Johnson's aim was in itself an impossible one: this of stemming the eternal Flood of Time; of clutching all things, and anchoring them down, and saying, Move not!—how could it or should it, ever have success? The strongest man can but retard the current partially and for a short hour. Yet even in such shortest retardation may not an inestimable value lie? If England has escaped the blood-bath of a French Revolution; and may yet, in virtue of this delay and of the experience it has given, work out her deliverance calmly into a new Era, let Samuel Johnson, beyond all contemporary or succeeding men, have the praise for it. We said above that he was appointed to be Ruler of the British Nation for a season: whoso will look beyond the surface, into the heart of the world's movements, may find that all Pitt Administrations, and Continental Subsidies, and Waterloo victories, rested on the possibility of making England, yet a little while, *Toryish*, Loyal to the Old; and this again on the anterior reality, that the Wise had found such Loyalty still practicable, and recommendable.

England had its Hume, as France had its Voltaires and Diderots; but the Johnson was peculiar to us.

If we ask now, by what endowment it mainly was that Johnson realised such a Life for himself and others; what quality of character the main phenomena of his Life may be most naturally deduced from, and his other qualities most naturally subordinated to, in our conception of him, perhaps the answer were: The quality of Courage, of Valour; that Johnson was a Brave Man. The Courage that can go forth, once and away, to Chalk-Farm, and have itself shot, and snuffed out, with decency, is nowise wholly what we mean here. Such courage we indeed esteem an exceeding small matter; capable of coexisting with a life full of falsehood, feebleness, poltroonery and despicability. Nay oftener it is Cowardice rather that produces the result: for consider, Is the Chalk-Farm Pistoleer inspired with any reasonable Belief and Determination; or is he hounded-on by haggard indefinable Fear,—how he will be *cut* at public places, and " plucked geese of the neighbourhood " will wag their tongues at him a plucked goose? If he go then, and be shot without shrieking or audible uproar, it is well for him: nevertheless there is nothing amazing in it. Courage to manage all this has not perhaps been denied to any man, or to any woman. Thus, do not recruiting sergeants drum through the streets of manufacturing towns, and collect ragged losels enough; every one of whom, if once dressed in red, and trained a little, will receive fire cheerfully for the small sum of one shilling *per diem*, and have the soul blown out of him at last, with perfect propriety? The Courage that dares only *die* is on the whole no sublime affair; necessary indeed, yet universal; pitiful when it begins to parade itself. On this Globe of ours there are some thirty-six persons that manifest it, seldom with the smallest failure, during every second of time. Nay look at Newgate: do not the offscourings of Creation, when condemned to the gallows as if they were not men but vermin, walk thither with decency, and even to the scowls and hootings of the whole Universe, give their stern good-night in silence? What is to be undergone only once, we may undergo; what must be, comes almost of its own accord. Considered as Duellist, what a poor figure does the fiercest Irish Whiskerando make in comparison with any English Game-cock, such as you may buy for fifteenpence!

The Courage we desire and prize is not the Courage to die decently, but to live manfully. This, when by God's grace it has been given, lies deep in the soul; like genial heat, fosters all other virtues and gifts; without it they could not live. In spite of our innumerable Waterloos and Peterloos, and such campaigning as there has been, this Courage we allude to, and call the only true one, is perhaps rarer in these last ages than it has been in any other since the Saxon Invasion under Hengist. Altogether extinct it can never be among men; otherwise the species Man were no longer for this world: here and there, in all times, under various guises, men are sent hither not only to demonstrate but exhibit it, and testify, as from heart to heart, that it is still possible, still practicable.

Johnson, in the eighteenth century, and as Man of Letters, was one of such; and, in good truth, "the bravest of the brave." What mortal could have more to war with? Yet, as we saw, he yielded not, faltered not; he fought, and even, such was his blessedness, prevailed. Whoso will understand what it is to have a man's heart may find that, since the time of John Milton, no braver heart had beat in any English bosom than Samuel Johnson now bore. Observe too that he never called himself brave, never felt himself to be so; the more completely *was* so. No Giant Despair, no Golgotha Death-dance or Sorcerer's-Sabbath of "Literary Life in London," appals this pilgrim; he works resolutely for deliverance; in still defiance steps stoutly along. The thing that is given him to do, he can make himself do; what is to be endured, he can endure in silence.

How the great soul of old Samuel, consuming daily his own bitter unalleviable allotment of misery and toil, shows beside the poor flimsy little soul of young Boswell; one day flaunting in the ring of vanity, tarrying by the wine-cup and crying, Aha, the wine is red; the next day deploring his downpressed, night-shaded, quite poor estate, and thinking it unkind that the whole movement of the Universe should go on, while *his* digestive-apparatus had stopped! We reckon Johnson's "talent of silence" to be among his great and too rare gifts. Where there is nothing farther to be done, there shall nothing farther be said: like his own poor blind Welshwoman, he accomplished somewhat, and also "endured fifty years of wretchedness with unshaken fortitude." How grim was

Life to him; a sick Prison-house and Doubting-castle! "His great business," he would profess, "was to escape from himself." Yet towards all this he has taken his position and resolution; can dismiss it all "with frigid indifference, having little to hope or to fear." Friends are stupid, and pusillanimous, and parsimonious; "wearied of his stay, yet offended at his departure:" it is the manner of the world. "By popular delusion," remarks he with a gigantic calmness, "illiterate writers will rise into renown:" it is portion of the History of English Literature; a perennial thing, this same popular delusion; and will—alter the character of the Language.

Closely connected with this quality of Valour, partly as springing from it, partly as protected by it, are the more recognisable qualities of Truthfulness in word and thought, and Honesty in action. There is a reciprocity of influence here: for as the realising of Truthfulness and Honesty is the lifelight and great aim of Valour, so without Valour they cannot, in anywise, be realised. Now, in spite of all practical shortcomings, no one that sees into the significance of Johnson will say that his prime object was not Truth. In conversation, doubtless, you may observe him, on occasion, fighting as if for victory;—and must pardon these ebulliences of a careless hour, which were not without temptation and provocation. Remark likewise two things: that such prize-arguings were ever on merely superficial debatable questions; and then that they were argued generally by the fair laws of battle and logic-fence, by one cunning in that same. If their purpose was excusable, their effect was harmless, perhaps beneficial: that of taming noisy mediocrity, and showing it another side of a debatable matter; to see *both* sides of which was, for the first time, to see the Truth of it. In his Writings themselves are errors enough, crabbed prepossessions enough; yet these also of a quite extraneous and accidental nature, nowhere a wilful shutting of the eyes to the Truth. Nay, is there not everywhere a heartfelt discernment, singular, almost admirable, if we consider through what confused conflicting lights and hallucinations it had to be attained, of the highest everlasting Truth, and beginning of all Truths: this namely, that man is ever, and even in the age of Wilkes and Whitefield, a Revelation of God to man; and lives, moves and has his being in Truth only; is either true, or, in strict speech, *is* not at all?

Quite spotless, on the other hand, is Johnson's love of Truth, if we look at it as expressed in Practice, as what we have named Honesty of action. " Clear your mind of Cant; " *clear* it, throw Cant utterly away: such was his emphatic, repeated precept; and did not he himself faithfully conform to it? The Life of this man has been, as it were, turned inside out, and examined with microscopes by friend and foe; yet was there no Lie found in him. His Doings and Writings are not *shows* but *performances:* you may weigh them in the balance, and they will stand weight. Not a line, not a sentence is dishonestly done, is other than it pretends to be. Alas! and he wrote not out of inward inspiration, but to earn his wages: and with that grand perennial tide of " popular delusion " flowing by; in whose waters he nevertheless refused to fish, to whose rich oyster-beds the dive was too muddy for him. Observe, again, with what innate hatred of Cant, he takes for himself, and offers to others, the lowest possible view of his business, which he followed with such nobleness. Motive for writing he had none, as he often said, but money; and yet he wrote *so*. Into the region of Poetic Art he indeed never rose; there was no *ideal* without him avowing itself in his work: the nobler was that unavowed *ideal* which lay within him, and commanded saying, Work out thy Artisanship in the spirit of an Artist! They who talk loudest about the dignity of Art, and fancy that they too are Artistic guild-brethren, and of the Celestials,—let them consider well what manner of man this was, who felt himself to be only a hired day - labourer. A labourer that was worthy of his hire; that has laboured not as an eye-servant, but as one found faithful! Neither was Johnson in those days perhaps wholly a unique. Time was when, for money, you might have ware: and needed not, in all departments, in that of the Epic Poem, in that of the Blacking-bottle, to rest content with the mere *persuasion* that you had ware. It was a happier time. But as yet the seventh Apocalyptic Bladder (of PUFFERY) had not been rent open,—to whirl and grind, as in a West-Indian Tornado, all earthly trades and things into wreck, and dust, and consummation,—and regeneration. Be it quickly, since it must be!—

That Mercy can dwell only with Valour, is an old sentiment or proposition; which in Johnson again receives confirmation. Few men on record have had a more merciful, tenderly affectionate nature than old Samuel. He was called the Bear; and did indeed too often look, and roar, like one; being forced to it in his own defence: yet within that shaggy exterior of his there beat a heart warm as a mother's, soft as a little child's. Nay generally, his very roaring was but the anger of affection: the rage of a Bear, if you will; but of a Bear bereaved of her whelps. Touch his Religion, glance at the Church of England, or the Divine Right; and he was upon you! These things were his Symbols of all that was good and precious for men; his very Ark of the Covenant: whoso laid hand on them tore asunder his heart of hearts. Not out of hatred to the opponent, but of love to the thing opposed, did Johnson grow cruel, fiercely contradictory: this is an important distinction; never to be forgotten in our censure of his conversational outrages. But observe also with what humanity, what openness of love, he can attach himself to all things: to a blind old woman, to a Doctor Levett, to a cat "Hodge." "His thoughts in the latter part of his life were frequently employed on his deceased friends; he often muttered these or suchlike sentences: ' Poor man! and then he died.' " How he patiently converts his poor home into a Lazaretto; endures, for long years, the contradiction of the miserable and unreasonable; with him unconnected, save that they had no other to yield them refuge! Generous old man! Worldly possession he has little; yet of this he gives freely; from his own hard-earned shilling, the halfpence for the poor, that "waited his coming out," are not withheld: the poor "waited the coming out" of one not quite so poor! A Sterne can write sentimentalities on Dead Asses: Johnson has a rough voice; but he finds the wretched Daughter of Vice fallen down in the streets; carries her home on his own shoulders, and like a good Samaritan gives help to the help-needing, worthy or unworthy. Ought not Charity, even in that sense, to cover a multitude of sins? No Penny-a-week Committee-Lady, no manager of Soup-Kitchens, dancer at Charity-Balls, was this rugged, stern-visaged man: but where, in all England, could there have been found another soul so full of Pity, a hand so heavenlike bounteous as his? The widow's mite, we know, was greater than all the other gifts.

Perhaps it is this divine feeling of Affection, throughout manifested, that principally attracts us towards Johnson. A true brother of men is he; and filial lover of the Earth; who, with little bright spots of Attachment, "where lives and works some loved one," has beautified "this rough solitary Earth into a peopled garden." Lichfield, with its mostly dull and limited inhabitants, is to the last one of the sunny islets for him: *Salve magna parens!* Or read those Letters on his Mother's death: what a genuine solemn grief and pity lies recorded there; a looking back into the Past, unspeakably mournful, unspeakably tender. And yet calm, sublime; for he must now act, not look: his venerated Mother has been taken from him; but he must now write a *Rasselas* to defray her funeral! Again in this little incident, recorded in his Book of Devotion, are not the tones of sacred Sorrow and Greatness deeper than in many a blank-verse Tragedy;—as, indeed, "the fifth act of a Tragedy," though unrhymed, does "lie in every death-bed, were it a peasant's, and of straw:"

"Sunday, October 18, 1767. Yesterday, at about ten in the morning, I took my leave forever of my dear old friend, Catherine Chambers, who came to live with my mother about 1724, and has been but little parted from us since. She buried my father, my brother and my mother. She is now fifty-eight years old.

"I desired all to withdraw; then told her that we were to part forever; that as Christians, we should part with prayer; and that I would, if she was willing, say a short prayer beside her. She expressed great desire to hear me; and held up her poor hands as she lay in bed, with great fervour, while I prayed kneeling by her. . . .

"I then kissed her. She told me that to part was the greatest pain she had ever felt, and that she hoped we should meet again in a better place. I expressed, with swelled eyes and great emotion of tenderness, the same hopes. We kissed and parted; I humbly hope, to meet again, and to part no more."

Tears trickling down the granite rock: a soft well of Pity springs within!—Still more tragical is this other scene: "Johnson mentioned that he could not in general accuse himself of having been an undutiful son. 'Once, indeed,' said he, 'I was disobedient: I refused to attend my father to Uttoxeter market. Pride was the source of that refusal, and the remembrance of it was painful. A few years ago I desired to atone for this fault.'"—But by what method?—What method was now possible? Hear it; the words are again given as his own, though here evidently by a less capable reporter:

" Madam, I beg your pardon for the abruptness of my departure in the morning, but I was compelled to it by conscience. Fifty years ago, Madam, on this day, I committed a breach of filial piety. My father had been in the habit of attending Uttoxeter market, and opening a stall there for the sale of his Books. Confined by indisposition, he desired me, that day, to go and attend the stall in his place. My pride prevented me; I gave my father a refusal.—And now to-day I have been at Uttoxeter; I went into the market at the time of business, uncovered my head, and stood with it bare, for an hour, on the spot where my father's stall used to stand. In contrition I stood, and I hope the penance was expiatory."

Who does not figure to himself this spectacle, amid the " rainy weather, and the sneers," or wonder, " of the by-standers " ? The memory of old Michael Johnson, rising from the far distance; sad-beckoning in the " moonlight of memory: " how he had toiled faithfully hither and thither; patiently among the lowest of the low; been buffeted and beaten down, yet ever risen again, ever tried it anew—And oh, when the wearied old man, as Bookseller, or Hawker, or Tinker, or whatsoever it was that Fate had reduced him to, begged help of *thee* for one day,—how savage, diabolic, was that mean Vanity, which answered, No! He sleeps now; after life's fitful fever, he sleeps well: but thou, O Merciless, how now wilt thou still the sting of that remembrance?— The picture of Samuel Johnson standing bareheaded in the market there, is one of the grandest and saddest we can paint. Repentance! Repentance! he proclaims, as with passionate sobs: but only to the ear of Heaven, if Heaven will give him audience: the earthly ear and heart, that should have heard it, are now closed, unresponsive forever.

That this so keen-loving, soft-trembling Affectionateness, the inmost essence of his being, must have looked forth, in one form or another, through Johnson's whole character, practical and intellectual, modifying both, is not to be doubted. Yet through what singular distortions and superstitions, moping melancholies, blind habits, whims about " entering with the right foot," and " touching every post as he walked along; " and all the other mad chaotic lumber of a brain that, with sun-clear intellect, hovered forever on the verge of insanity,—must that same inmost essence have looked forth; unrecognisable to all but the most observant! Accordingly it was not recognised; Johnson passed not for a fine nature, but for a dull, almost brutal one. Might not, for example, the first-fruit of such a Lovingness, coupled with his quick Insight, have been expected to be a peculiarly courteous demeanour as man among men? In Johnson's " Politeness," which he often, to the wonder of some, asserted to be great, there was indeed somewhat that needed explanation. Nevertheless, if he insisted always on handing lady-visitors to their carriage; though with the certainty of collecting a mob of gazers in Fleet Street,—as might well be, the beau having on, by way of court-dress, " his rusty brown morning suit, a pair of old shoes for slippers, a little shrivelled wig sticking on the top of his head, and the sleeves of his shirt and the knees of his breeches hanging loose: "—in all this we can see the spirit of true Politeness, only shining through a strange medium. Thus again, in his apartments, at one time, there were unfortunately no chairs. " A gentleman who frequently visited him whilst writing his *Idlers*, constantly found him at his desk, sitting on one with three legs; and on rising from it, he remarked that Johnson never forgot its defect; but would either hold it in his hand, or place it with great composure against some support; taking no notice of its imperfection to his visitor,"—who meanwhile, we suppose, sat upon folios, or in the sartorial fashion. " It was remarkable in Johnson," continues Miss Reynolds (*Renny dear*), " that no external circumstances ever prompted him to make any apology, or to seem even sensible of their existence. Whether this was the effect of philosophic pride, or of some partial notion of his respecting high-breeding, is doubtful." That it *was*, for one thing, the effect of genuine Politeness, is nowise doubtful. Not of the Pharisaical Brummellean Politeness, which would suffer crucifixion rather than ask twice for soup: but the noble universal Politeness of a man that knows the dignity of men, and feels his own; such as may be seen in the patriarchal bearing of an Indian Sachem; such as Johnson himself exhibited, when a sudden chance brought him into dialogue with his King. To us, with our view of the man, it nowise appears " strange " that he should have boasted himself cunning in the laws of Politeness; nor " stranger still," habitually attentive to practise them.

More legibly is this influence of the Loving heart to be traced in his intellectual character. What, indeed, is the beginning of intellect, the first inducement to the exercise thereof, but attraction towards somewhat, *affection* for it? Thus too, who ever saw, or will see, any true talent, not to speak of genius, the foundation of which is not goodness, love? From Johnson's strength of Affection, we deduce many of his intellectual peculiarities; especially that threatening array of perversions, known under the name of " Johnson's Prejudices." Looking well into the root from which these sprang, we have long ceased to view them with hostility, can pardon and reverently pity them. Consider with what force early-imbibed opinions must have clung to a soul of this Affection. Those evil-famed Prejudices of his, that Jacobitism, Church-of-Englandism, hatred of the Scotch, belief in Witches, and suchlike, what were they but the ordinary beliefs of well-doing, well-meaning provincial Englishmen in that day? First gathered by his Father's hearth; round the kind " country fires " of native Stafford-shire; they grew with his growth and strengthened with his strength: they were hallowed by fondest sacred recollections; to part with them was parting with his heart's blood. If the man who has no strength of Affection, strength of Belief, have no strength of Prejudice, let him thank Heaven for it, but to himself take small thanks.

Melancholy it was, indeed, that the noble Johnson could not work himself loose from these adhesions; that he could only purify them, and wear them with some nobleness. Yet let us understand how they grew out from the very centre of his being: nay moreover, how they came to cohere in him with what formed the business and worth of his Life, the sum of his whole Spiritual Endeavour. For it is on the same ground that he became throughout an Edifier and Repairer, not, as the others of his make were, a Puller-down; that in an age of universal Scepticism, England was still to produce its Believer. Mark too his candour even here; while a Dr. Adams, with placid surprise, asks, " Have we not evidence enough of the soul's immortality? " Johnson answers, " I wish for more."

But the truth is, in Prejudice, as in all things, Johnson was the product of England; one of those *good* yeomen whose limbs were made in England: alas, the last of *such* Invincibles, their day being now done! His culture is wholly English; that not of a Thinker but of a " Scholar: " his interests are wholly English; he sees and knows nothing but

England; he is the John Bull of Spiritual Europe: let him
live, love him, as he was and could not but be! Pitiable it
is, no doubt, that a Samuel Johnson must confute Hume's
irreligious Philosophy by some " story from a Clergyman of
the Bishoprick of Durham; " should see nothing in the great
Frederick but " Voltaire's lackey; " in Voltaire himself but
a man *acerrimi ingenii, paucarum literarum ;* in Rousseau
but one worthy to be hanged; and in the universal, long-
prepared, inevitable Tendency of European Thought but a
green-sick milkmaid's crotchet of, for variety's sake, " milk-
ing the Bull." Our good, dear John! Observe too what it
is that he sees in the city of Paris: no feeblest glimpse of
those D'Alemberts and Diderots, or of the strange questionable work they did; solely some Benedictine Priests, to talk
kitchen-latin with them about *Editiones Principes*. " *Monsheer
Nongtongpaw !* "—Our dear, foolish John: yet is there a
lion's heart within him!—Pitiable all these things were, we say;
yet nowise inexcusable; nay, as basis or as foil to much else
that was in Johnson, almost venerable. Ought we not, indeed, to honour England, and English Institutions and Way
of Life, that they could still equip such a man; could furnish
him in heart and head to be a Samuel Johnson, and yet to
love them, and unyieldingly fight for them? What truth
and living vigour must such Institutions once have had,
when, in the middle of the Eighteenth Century, there was
still enough left in them for this!

It is worthy of note that, in our little British Isle, the two
grand Antagonisms of Europe should have stood embodied,
under their very highest concentration, in two men produced
simultaneously among ourselves. Samuel Johnson and
David Hume, as was observed, were children nearly of the
same year: through life they were spectators of the same
Life-movement; often inhabitants of the same city. Greater
contrast, in all things, between two great men, could not be.
Hume, well-born, competently provided for, whole in body
and mind, of his own determination forces a way into Literature: Johnson, poor, moonstruck, diseased, forlorn, is forced
into it " with the bayonet of necessity at his back." And
what a part did they severally play there! As Johnson
became the father of all succeeding Tories; so was Hume the
father of all succeeding Whigs, for his own Jacobitism was
but an accident, as worthy to be named Prejudice as any of

Johnson's. Again, if Johnson's culture was exclusively English; Hume's, in Scotland, became European;—for which reason too we find his influence spread deeply over all quarters of Europe, traceable deeply in all speculation, French, German, as well as domestic; while Johnson's name, out of England, is hardly anywhere to be met with. In spiritual stature they are almost equal; both great, among the greatest: yet how unlike in likeness! Hume has the widest, methodising, comprehensive eye; Johnson the keenest for perspicacity and minute detail: so had, perhaps chiefly, their education ordered it. Neither of the two rose into Poetry; yet both to some approximation thereof: Hume to something of an Epic clearness and method, as in his delineation of the Commonwealth Wars; Johnson to many a deep Lyric tone of plaintiveness and impetuous graceful power, scattered over his fugitive compositions. Both, rather to the general surprise, had a certain rugged Humour shining through their earnestness: the indication, indeed, that they *were* earnest men, and had *subdued* their wild world into a kind of temporary home and safe dwelling. Both were, by principle and habit, Stoics: yet Johnson with the greater merit, for he alone had very much to triumph over; farther, he alone ennobled his Stoicism into Devotion. To Johnson Life was as a Prison, to be endured with heroic faith: to Hume it was little more than a foolish Bartholomew-Fair Show-booth, with the foolish crowdings and elbowings of which it was not worth while to quarrel; the whole would break up, and be at liberty, so *soon*. Both realised the highest task of Manhood, that of living like men; each died not unfitly, in his way: Hume as one, with factitious, half-false gaiety, taking leave of what was itself wholly but a Lie: Johnson as one, with awe-struck, yet resolute and piously expectant heart, taking leave of a Reality, to enter a Reality still higher. Johnson had the harder problem of it, from first to last: whether, with some hesitation, we can admit that he was intrinsically the better-gifted, may remain undecided.

These two men now rest; the one in Westminster Abbey here; the other in the Calton-Hill Churchyard of Edinburgh. Through Life they did not meet: as contrasts, " like in unlike," love each other; so might they two have loved, and communed kindly,—had not the terrestrial dross and darkness that was in them withstood! One day, their spirits, what Truth was in each, will be found working, living in harmony and free union, even here below. They were the two half-men of their time: whoso should combine the intrepid Candour and decisive scientific Clearness of Hume, with the Reverence, the Love and devout Humility of Johnson, were the whole man of a new time. Till such whole man arrive for us, and the distracted time admit of such, might the Heavens but bless poor England with half-men worthy to tie the shoe-latchets of these, resembling these even from afar! Be both attentively regarded, let the true Effort of both prosper;—and for the present, both take our affectionate farewell!

BIOGRAPHY [1]

[1832]

MAN'S sociality of nature evinces itself, in spite of all that
can be said, with abundant evidence by this one fact, were
there no other: the unspeakable delight he takes in Biography. It is written, "The proper study of mankind is
man;" to which study, let us candidly admit, he, by true or
by false methods, applies himself, nothing loath. "Man is
perennially interesting to man; nay, if we look strictly to it,
there is nothing else interesting." How inexpressibly comfortable to know our fellow-creature; to see into him, understand his goings-forth, decipher the whole heart of his
mystery: nay, not only to see into him, but even to see out
of him, to view the world altogether as he views it; so that
we can theoretically construe him, and could almost practically personate him; and do now thoroughly discern both
what manner of man he is, and what manner of thing he has
got to work on and live on!

A scientific interest and a poetic one alike inspire us in
this matter. A scientific: because every mortal has a
Problem of Existence set before him, which, were it only,
what for the most it is, the Problem of keeping soul and body
together, must be to a certain extent *original*, unlike every
other; and yet, at the same time, so *like* every other; like
our own, therefore; instructive, moreover, since we also are
indentured to *live*. A poetic interest still more: for precisely
this same struggle of human Freewill against material
Necessity, which every man's Life, by the mere circumstance
that the man continues alive, will more or less victoriously
exhibit,—is that which above all else, or rather inclusive
of all else, calls the Sympathy of mortal hearts into action;
and whether as acted, or as represented and written of, not

[1] *Fraser's Magazine*, No. 27 (for April).—"The Life of Samuel John-
son, LL.D.; including a Tour to the Hebrides." By James Boswell,
Esq.—A new Edition, with numerous Additions and Notes, by John
Wilson Croker, LL.D., F.R.S. 5 vols. London, 1831.

only is Poetry, but is the sole Poetry possible. Borne onwards by which two all-embracing interests, may the earnest Lover of Biography expand himself on all sides, and indefinitely enrich himself. Looking with the eyes of every new neighbour, he can discern a new world different for each: feeling with the heart of every neighbour, he lives with every neighbour's life, even as with his own. Of these millions of living men, each individual is a mirror to us; a mirror both scientific and poetic; or, if you will, both natural and magical; — from which one would so gladly draw aside the gauze veil; and, peering therein, discern the image of his own natural face, and the supernatural secrets that prophetically lie under the same!

Observe, accordingly, to what extent, in the actual course of things, this business of Biography is practised and relished. Define to thyself, judicious Reader, the real significance of these phenomena, named Gossip, Egoism, Personal Narrative (miraculous or not), Scandal, Raillery, Slander, and suchlike; the sum-total of which (with some fractional addition of a better ingredient, generally too small to be noticeable) constitutes that other grand phenomenon still called " Conversation." Do they not mean wholly: *Biography* and *Autobiography ?* Not only in the common Speech of men; but in all Art too, which is or should be the concentrated and conserved essence of what men can speak and show, Biography is almost the one thing needful.

Even in the highest works of Art, our interest, as the critics complain, is too apt to be strongly or even mainly of a Biographic sort. In the Art we can nowise forget the Artist: while looking on the *Transfiguration*, while studying the *Iliad*, we ever strive to figure to ourselves what spirit dwelt in Raphael; what a head was that of Homer, wherein, woven of Elysian light and Tartarean gloom, that old world fashioned itself together, of which these written Greek characters are but a feeble though perennial copy. The Painter and the Singer are present to us; we partially and for the time become the very Painter and the very Singer, while we enjoy the Picture and the Song. Perhaps too, let the critic say what he will, this is the highest enjoyment, the clearest recognition, we can have of these. Art indeed is Art; yet Man also is Man. Had the *Transfiguration* been painted without human hand; had it grown merely on the canvas, say by atmospheric influences, as lichen-pictures do on rocks,—it were a grand Picture doubtless; yet nothing like so grand as *the* Picture, which, on opening our eyes, we everywhere in Heaven and in Earth see painted; and everywhere pass over with indifference,—because the Painter was not a Man. Think of this; much lies in it. The Vatican is great; yet poor to Chimborazo or the Peak of Teneriffe: its dome is but a foolish Big-endian or Little-endian chip of an egg-shell, compared with that star-fretted Dome where Arcturus and Orion glance forever; which latter, notwithstanding, who looks at, save perhaps some necessitous stargazer bent to make Almanacs; some thick-quilted watchman, to see what weather it will prove? The Biographic interest is wanting: no Michael Angelo was He who built that "Temple of Immensity;" therefore do we, pitiful Littlenesses as we are, turn rather to wonder and to worship in the little toybox of a Temple built by our like.

Still more decisively, still more exclusively does the Biographic interest manifest itself, as we descend into lower regions of spiritual communication; through the whole range of what is called Literature. Of history, for example, the most honoured, if not honourable species of composition, is not the whole purport Biographic? "History," it has been said, "is the essence of innumerable Biographies." Such, at least, it should be: whether it is, might admit of question. But, in any case, what hope have we in turning over those old interminable Chronicles, with their garrulities and insipidities; or still worse, in patiently examining those modern Narrations, of the Philosophic kind, where "Philosophy, teaching by Experience," has to sit like owl on housetop, *seeing* nothing, *understanding* nothing, uttering only, with such solemnity, her perpetual most wearisome *hoo-hoo:* —what hope have we, except the for most part fallacious one of gaining some acquaintance with our fellow-creatures, though dead and vanished, yet dear to us; how they got along in those old days, suffering and doing; to what extent, and under what circumstances, they resisted the Devil and triumphed over him, or struck their colours to him, and were trodden under foot by him; how, in short, the perennial Battle went, which men name Life, which we also in these new days, with indifferent fortune, have to fight, and must bequeath to our sons and grandsons to go on fighting,—

till the Enemy one day be quite vanquished and abolished, or else the great Night sink and part the combatants; and thus, either by some Millennium or some new Noah's Deluge, the Volume of Universal History wind itself up! Other hope, in studying such Books, we have none: and that it is a deceitful hope, who that has tried knows not? A feast of widest Biographic insight is spread for us; we enter full of hungry anticipations: alas, like so many other feasts, which Life invites us to, a mere Ossian's " feast of *shells*,"—the food and liquor being all emptied out and clean gone, and only the vacant dishes and deceitful emblems thereof left! Your modern Historical Restaurateurs are indeed little better than high-priests of Famine; that keep choicest china dinner-sets, only no dinner to serve therein. Yet such is our Biographic appetite, we run trying from shop to shop, with ever new hope; and, unless we could eat the wind, with ever new disappointment.

Again, consider the whole class of Fictitious Narratives; from the highest category of epic or dramatic Poetry, in Shakspeare and Homer, down to the lowest of froth Prose in the Fashionable Novel. What are all these but so many mimic Biographies? Attempts, here by an inspired Speaker, there by an uninspired Babbler, to deliver himself, more or less ineffectually, of the grand secret wherewith all hearts labour oppressed: The significance of Man's Life;—which deliverance, even as traced in the unfurnished head, and printed at the Minerva Press, finds readers. For, observe, though there is *a* greatest Fool, as a superlative in every kind; and *the* most Foolish man in the Earth is now indubitably living and breathing, and did this morning or lately eat breakfast, and is even now digesting the same; and looks out on the world with his dim horn-eyes, and inwardly forms some unspeakable theory thereof: yet where shall the authentically Existing be personally met with! Can one of us, otherwise than by guess, know that we have got sight of him, have orally communed with him? To take even the narrower sphere of this our English Metropolis, can any one confidently say to himself, that he has conversed with the identical, individual Stupidest man now extant in London? No one. Deep as we dive in the Profound, there is ever a new depth opens: where the ultimate bottom may lie, through what new scenes of being we must pass before reaching it (except that we know it does lie somewhere, and might by human faculty and opportunity be reached), is altogether a mystery to us. Strange, tantalising pursuit! We have the fullest assurance, not only that there is a Stupidest of London men actually resident, with bed and board of some kind, in London; but that several persons have been or perhaps are now speaking face to face with him: while for us, chase it as we may, such scientific blessedness will too probably be forever denied!—But the thing we meant to enforce was this comfortable fact, that no known Head was so wooden, but there might be other heads to which it were a genius and Friar Bacon's Oracle. Of no given Book, not even of a Fashionable Novel, can you predicate with certainty that its vacuity is absolute; that there are not other vacuities which shall partially replenish themselves therefrom, and esteem it a *plenum*. How knowest thou, may the distressed Novelwright exclaim, that I, here where I sit, am the Foolishest of existing mortals; that this my Long-ear of a Fictitious Biography shall not find one and the other, into whose still longer ears it may be the means, under Providence, of instilling somewhat? We answer, None knows, none can certainly know: therefore, write on, worthy Brother, even as thou canst, even as it has been given thee.

Here, however, in regard to " Fictitious Biographies," and much other matter of like sort, which the greener mind in these days inditeth, we may as well insert some singular sentences on the importance and significance of *Reality*, as they stand written for us in Professor Gottfried Sauerteig's *Æsthetische Springwurzeln ;* a Work, perhaps, as yet new to most English readers. The Professor and Doctor is not a man whom we can praise without reservation; neither shall we say that his *Springwurzeln* (a sort of magical picklocks, as he affectedly names them) are adequate to " *start* " every *bolt* that locks-up an æsthetic mystery: nevertheless, in his crabbed, one-sided way, he sometimes hits masses of the truth. We endeavour to translate faithfully, and trust the reader will find it worth serious perusal:

" The significance, even for poetic purposes," says Sauerteig, " that lies in REALITY is too apt to escape us; is perhaps only now beginning to be discerned. When we named *Rousseau's Confessions* an elegiaco-didactic Poem, we meant more than an empty figure of speech; we meant a historical scientific fact.

" Fiction, while the feigner of it knows that he is feigning, partakes, more than we suspect, of the nature of *lying ;* and has ever an, in some degree, unsatisfactory character. All Mythologies were once Philosophies; were *believed :* the Epic Poems of old time, so long as they continued *epic,* and had any complete impressiveness, were Histories, and understood to be narratives of *facts.* In so far as Homer employed his gods as mere ornamental fringes, and had not himself, or at least did not expect his hearers to have, a belief that they were real agents in those antique doings; so far did he fail to be *genuine ;* so far was he a partially *hollow* and false singer; and sang to please only a portion of man's mind, not the whole thereof.

" Imagination is, after all, but a poor matter when it has to part company with Understanding, and even front it hostilely in flat contradiction. Our mind is divided in twain: there is contest; wherein that which is weaker must needs come to the worse. Now of all feelings, states, principles, call it what you will, in man's mind, is not Belief the clearest, strongest; against which all others contend in vain? Belief is, indeed, the beginning and first condition of all spiritual Force whatsoever: only in so far as Imagination, were it but momentarily, is *believed,* can there be any use or meaning in it, any enjoyment of it. And what is momentary Belief? The enjoyment of a moment. Whereas a perennial Belief were enjoyment perennially, and with the whole united soul.

" It is thus that I judge of the Supernatural in an Epic Poem; and would say, the instant it has ceased to be authentically supernatural, and become what you call ' Machinery: ' sweep it out of sight (*schaff' es mir vom Halse*)! Of a truth, that same ' Machinery,' about which the critics make such hubbub, was well named *Machinery ;* for it is in very deed mechanical, nowise inspired or poetical. Neither for us is there the smallest æsthetic enjoyment in it; save only in this way; that we believe it *to have been believed,*—by the Singer or his Hearers; into whose case we now laboriously struggle to transport ourselves; and so, with stinted enough result, catch some reflex of the Reality, which for them was wholly real, and visible face to face. Whenever it has come so far

that your ' Machinery ' is avowedly mechanical and unbe-
lieved,—what is it else, if we dare tell ourselves the truth, but
a miserable, meaningless Deception, kept-up by old use and
wont alone? If the gods of an *Iliad* are to us no longer
authentic Shapes of Terror, heart-stirring, heart-appalling,
but only vague-glittering Shadows,—what must the dead
Pagan gods of an *Epigoniad* be, the dead-living Pagan-
Christian gods of a *Lusiad*, the concrete-abstract, evangelical-
metaphysical gods of a *Paradise Lost ?* Superannuated
lumber! Cast raiment, at best; in which some poor mime,
strutting and swaggering, may or may not set forth new
noble Human Feelings (again a Reality), and so secure, or
not secure, our pardon of such hoydenish masking; for which,
in any case, he has a pardon to *ask*.

" True enough, none but the earliest Epic Poems can claim
this distinction of entire credibility, of Reality: after an *Iliad*,
a *Shaster*, a *Koran*, and other the like primitive performances,
the rest seem, by this rule of mine, to be altogether excluded
from the list. Accordingly, what *are* all the rest, from
Virgil's *Æneid* downwards, in comparison? Frosty, artificial,
heterogeneous things; more of gumflowers than of roses;
at the best, of the two mixed incoherently together: to some
of which, indeed, it were hard to deny the title of Poems;
yet to no one of which can that title belong in any sense even
resembling the old high one it, in those old days, conveyed,—
when the epithet ' divine ' or ' sacred ' as applied to the
uttered Word of man, was not a vain metaphor, a vain sound,
but a real name with meaning. Thus, too, the farther we
recede from those early days, when Poetry, as true Poetry is
always, was still sacred or divine, and inspired (what ours,
in great part, only pretends to be),—the more impossible
becomes it to produce any, we say not true Poetry, but
tolerable semblance of such; the hollower, in particular,
grow all manner of Epics; till at length, as in this generation,
the very name of Epic sets men a-yawning, the announcement
of a new Epic is received as a public calamity.

" But what if the *impossible* being once for all quite dis-
carded, the *probable* be well adhered to: how stands it with
fiction *then ?* Why, then, I would say, the evil is much
mended, but nowise completely cured. We have then, in
place of the wholly dead modern Epic, the partially living
modern Novel; to which latter it is much easier to lend that

above-mentioned, so essential 'momentary credence' than
to the former: indeed, infinitely easier; for the former being
flatly incredible, no mortal *can* for a moment credit it, for a
moment enjoy it. Thus, here and there, a *Tom Jones*, a
Meister, a *Crusoe*, will yield no little solacement to the minds
of men; though still immeasurably less than a *Reality* would,
were the significance thereof as impressively unfolded, were
the genius that could so unfold it once given us by the kind
Heavens. Neither say thou that proper Realities are wanting: for Man's Life, now, as of old, is the genuine work of
God; wherever there is a Man, a God also is revealed, and
all that is Godlike: a whole epitome of the Infinite, with its
meanings, lies enfolded in the Life of every Man. Only,
alas, that the Seer to discern this same Godlike, and with fit
utterance *un*fold it for us, is wanting, and may long be
wanting!

"Nay, a question arises on us here, wherein the whole
German reading-world will eagerly join: Whether man *can*
any longer be so interested by the spoken Word, as he often
was in those primeval days, when rapt away by its inscrutable power, he pronounced it, in such dialect as he had, to
be *transcendental* (to *transcend* all measure), to be sacred,
prophetic and the inspiration of a god? For myself, I (*ich
meines Ortes*), by faith or by insight, do heartily understand
that the answer to such question will be, Yea! For never
that I could in searching find out, has Man been, by Time
which devours so much, deprivated of any faculty whatsoever
that he in any era was possessed of. To my seeming, the
babe born yesterday has all the organs of Body, Soul and
Spirit, and in exactly the same combination and entireness,
that the oldest Pelasgic Greek, or Mesopotamian Patriarch,
or Father Adam himself could boast of. Ten fingers, one
heart with venous and arterial blood therein, still belong to
man that is born of woman: when did he lose any of his
spiritual Endowments either; above all, his highest spiritual
Endowment, that of revealing Poetic Beauty, and of adequately receiving the same? Not the material, not the
susceptibility is wanting; only the Poet, or long series of
Poets, to work on these. True, alas too true, the Poet *is*
still utterly wanting, or all but utterly: nevertheless have
we not centuries enough before us to produce him in? Him
and much else!—I, for the present, will but predict that chiefly

by working more and more on REALITY, and evolving more and more wisely *its* inexhaustible meanings; and, in brief, speaking forth in fit utterance whatsoever our whole soul *believes*, and ceasing to speak forth what thing soever our whole soul does not believe,—will this high emprise be accomplished, or approximated to."

These notable, and not unfounded, though partial and *deep*-seeing rather than *wide*-seeing observations on the great import of REALITY, considered even as a poetic material, we have inserted the more willingly, because a transient feeling to the same purpose may often have suggested itself to many readers; and, on the whole, it is good that every reader and every writer understand, with all intensity of conviction, what quite infinite worth lies in *Truth :* how all-pervading, omnipotent, in man's mind, is the thing we name *Belief.* For the rest, Herr Sauerteig, though one-sided, on this matter of Reality, seems heartily persuaded, and is not perhaps so ignorant as he looks. It cannot be unknown to him, for example, what noise is made about " Invention; " what a supreme rank this faculty is reckoned to hold in the poetic endowment. Great truly is Invention: nevertheless, that is but a poor exercise of it with which Belief is not concerned. " An Irishman with whisky in his head," as poor Byron said, will invent you, in this kind, till there is enough and to spare. Nay, perhaps, if we consider well, the highest exercise of Invention has, in very deed, nothing to do with Fiction; but is an invention of new Truth, what we can call a Revelation; which last does undoubtedly transcend all other poetic efforts, nor can Herr Sauerteig be too loud in its praises. But, on the other hand, whether such effort is still possible for man, Herr Sauerteig and the bulk of the world are probably at issue!—and will probably continue so till that same " Revelation," or new " Invention of Reality," of the sort he desiderates, shall itself make its appearance.

Meanwhile, quitting these airy regions, let any one bethink him how impressive the smallest historical *fact* may become, as contrasted with the grandest *fictitious event ;* what an incalculable force lies for us in this consideration: The Thing which I here hold imaged in my mind did actually occur; was, in very truth, an element in the system of the All, whereof I too form part; had therefore, and has, through all time, an authentic being; is not a dream, but a reality! We ourselves can remember reading, in *Lord Clarendon*,[1] with feelings perhaps somehow accidentally opened to it,—certainly with a depth of impression strange to us then and now,—that insignificant-looking passage, where Charles, after the battle of Worcester, glides down, with Squire Careless, from the Royal Oak, at nightfall, being hungry: how, " making a shift to get over hedges and ditches, after walking at least eight or nine miles, which were the more grievous to the King by the weight of his boots (for he could not put *them* off when he cut off his hair, for want of shoes), before morning they came to *a poor cottage, the owner whereof, being a Roman Catholic, was known to Careless.*" How this poor drudge, being knocked-up from his snoring, " carried them into a little barn full of hay, which was a better lodging than he had for himself; " and by and by, not without difficulty, brought his Majesty " a piece of bread and a great pot of buttermilk," saying candidly that " he himself lived by his daily labour, and that what he had brought him was the fare he and his wife had: " on which nourishing diet his Majesty, " staying upon the haymow," feeds thankfully for two days; and then departs, under new guidance, having first changed clothes, down to the very shirt and " old pair of shoes," with his landlord; and so, as worthy Bunyan has it, " goes on his way, and sees him no more." Singular enough, if we will think of it! This, then, was a genuine flesh-and-blood Rustic of the year 1651: he did actually swallow bread and buttermilk (not having ale and bacon), and do field-labour: with these hobnailed " shoes " has sprawled through mud-roads in winter, and, jocund or not, driven his team a-field in summer: he made bargains; had chafferings and higglings, now a sore heart, now a glad one; was born; was a son, was a father; toiled in many ways, being forced to it, till the strength was all worn out of him; and then—lay down " to rest his galled back," and sleep there till the long-distant morning!—How comes it, that he alone of all the British rustics who tilled and lived along with him, on whom the blessed sun on that same " fifth day of September " was shining, should have chanced to rise on us; that this poor pair of clouted Shoes, out of the million million hides that have been tanned, and cut, and worn, should still subsist, and hang visibly together? We see him but for a moment;

[1] *History of the Rebellion*, iii. 625.

for one moment, the blanket of the Night is rent asunder, so that we behold and see, and then closes over him—forever.

So too, in some *Boswell's Life of Johnson*, how indelible and magically bright does many a little *Reality* dwell in our remembrance! There is no need that the personages on the scene be a King and Clown; that the scene be the Forest of the Royal Oak, " on the borders of Staffordshire;" need only that the scene lie on this old firm Earth of ours, where we also have so surprisingly arrived; that the personages be *men*, and *seen* with the eyes of a man. Foolish enough, how some slight, perhaps mean and even ugly incident, if *real* and well presented, will fix itself in a susceptive memory, and lie ennobled there; silvered over with the pale cast of thought, with the pathos which belongs only to the Dead. For the Past is all holy to us; the Dead are all holy, even they that were base and wicked while alive. Their baseness and wickedness was not *They*, was but the heavy and unmanageable Environment that lay round them, with which they fought unprevailing: *they* (the ethereal god-given Force that dwelt in them, and was their *Self*) have now shuffled-off that heavy Environment, and are free and pure: their life-long Battle, go how it might, is all ended, with many wounds or with fewer; they have been recalled from it, and the once harsh-jarring battlefield has become a silent awe-inspiring Golgotha, and *Gottesacker* (Field of God)!—Boswell relates this in itself smallest and poorest of occurrences: " As we walked along the Strand to-night, arm in arm, a woman of the town accosted us in the usual enticing manner. ' No, no, my girl,' said Johnson; ' it won't do.' He, however, did not treat her with harshness; and we talked of the wretched life of such women." Strange power of *Reality !* Not even this poorest of occurrences, but now, after seventy years are come and gone, has a meaning for us. Do but consider that it is *true ;* that it did in very deed occur ! That unhappy Outcast, with all her sins and woes, her lawless desires, too complex mischances, her wailings and her riotings, has departed utterly; alas! her siren finery has got all besmutched, ground, generations since, into dust and smoke; of her degraded body, and whole miserable earthly existence, all is away: *she* is no longer here, but far from us, in the bosom of Eternity,—whence we too came, whither we too are bound ! Johnson said, " No, no, my girl; it won't do;" and then

" we talked ; "—and herewith the wretched one, seen but
for the twinkling of an eye, passes on into the utter Darkness.
No high Calista, that ever issued from Story-teller's brain,
will impress us more deeply than this meanest of the mean;
and for a good reason: That *she* issued from the Maker of
Men.

It is well worth the Artist's while to examine for himself
what it is that gives such pitiable incidents their memorable-
ness; his aim likewise is, above all things, to be *memorable*.
Half the effect, we already perceive, depends on the object;
on its being *real*, on its being really *seen*. The other half will
depend on the observer; and the question now is: How are
real objects to be *so* seen; on what quality of observing, or
of style in describing, does this so intense pictorial power
depend? Often a slight circumstance contributes curiously
to the result: some little, and perhaps to appearance accidental, feature is presented; a light-gleam, which instantaneously
excites the mind, and urges it to complete the picture, and
evolve the meaning thereof for itself. By critics, such light-
gleams and their almost magical influence have frequently
been noted: but the power to produce such, to select such
features as will produce them, is generally treated as a knack,
or trick of the trade, a secret for being " graphic ; " whereas
these magical feats are, in truth, rather inspirations; and the
gift of performing them, which acts unconsciously, without
forethought, and as if by nature alone, is properly a *genius*
for description.

One grand, invaluable secret there is, however, which includes all the rest, and, what is comfortable, lies clearly in
every man's power: *To have an open loving heart, and what
follows from the possession of such*. Truly, it has been said,
emphatically in these days ought it to be repeated: A loving
Heart is the beginning of all Knowledge. This it is that opens
the whole mind, quickens every faculty of the intellect to do
its fit work, that of *knowing ;* and therefrom, by sure consequence, of *vividly uttering-forth*. Other secret for being
" graphic " is there none, worth having: but this is an all-
sufficient one. See, for example, what a small Boswell can
do! Hereby, indeed, is the whole man made a living mirror,
wherein the wonders of this ever-wonderful Universe are, in
their true light (which is ever a magical, miraculous one)
represented, and reflected back on us. It has been said,

"the heart sees farther than the head:" but, indeed, without the seeing heart, there is no true seeing for the head so much as possible; all is mere *oversight*, hallucination and vain superficial phantasmagoria, which can permanently profit no one.

Here, too, may we not pause for an instant, and make a practical reflection? Considering the multitude of mortals that handle the Pen in these days, and can mostly spell, and write without glaring violations of grammar, the question naturally arises: How is it, then, that no Work proceeds from them, bearing any stamp of authenticity and permanence; of worth for more than one day? Ship-loads of Fashionable Novels, Sentimental Rhymes, Tragedies, Farces, Diaries of Travel, Tales by flood and field, are swallowed monthly into the bottomless Pool: still does the Press toil; innumerable Paper-makers, Compositors, Printers' Devils, Book-binders, and Hawkers grown hoarse with loud proclaiming, rest not from their labour; and still, in torrents, rushes on the great array of Publications, unpausing, to their final home; and still Oblivion, like the Grave, cries, Give! Give! How is it that of all these countless multitudes, no one can attain to the smallest mark of excellence, or produce aught that shall endure longer than "snow-flake on the river," or the foam of penny-beer? We answer: Because they *are* foam; because there is no *Reality* in them. These Three Thousand men, women and children, that make up the army of British Authors, do not, if we will well consider it, *see* anything whatever; consequently *have* nothing that they can record and utter, only more or fewer things that they can plausibly pretend to record. The Universe, of Man and Nature, is still quite shut-up from them; the "open secret" still utterly a secret; because no sympathy with Man or Nature, no love and free simplicity of heart has yet unfolded the same. Nothing but a pitiful Image of their own pitiful Self, with its vanities, and grudgings, and ravenous hunger of all kinds, hangs forever painted in the retina of these unfortunate persons; so that the starry ALL, with whatsoever it embraces, does but appear as some expanded magic-lantern shadow of that same Image,—and naturally looks pitiful enough.

It is vain for these persons to allege that they are naturally without gift, naturally stupid and sightless, and so *can* attain to no knowledge of anything; therefore, in writing of anything, must needs write falsehoods of it, there being in it no truth for them. Not so, good Friends. The stupidest of you has a certain faculty; were it but that of articulate speech (say, in the Scottish, the Irish, the Cockney dialect, or even in "Governess-English"), and of physically discerning what lies under your nose. The stupidest of you would perhaps grudge to be compared in faculty with James Boswell; yet see what he has produced! You do not use your faculty honestly; your heart is shut up; full of greediness, malice, discontent; so your intellectual sense cannot be open. It is vain also to urge that James Boswell had opportunities; saw great men and great things, such as you can never hope to look on. What make ye of Parson White in Selborne? He had not only no great men to look on, but not even men; merely sparrows and cock-chafers: yet has he left us a *Biography* of these; which, under its title *Natural History of Selborne*, still remains valuable to us; which has copied a little sentence or two *faithfully* from the Inspired Volume of Nature, and so is itself not without inspiration. Go ye and do likewise. Sweep away utterly all frothiness and falsehood from your heart; struggle unweariedly to acquire, what is possible for every god-created Man, a free, open, humble soul: *speak not at all, in any wise, till you have somewhat to speak ;* care not for the *reward* of your speaking, but simply and with undivided mind for the *truth* of your speaking: then be placed in what section of Space and of Time soever, do but open your eyes, and they shall actually *see*, and bring you real *knowledge*, wondrous, worthy of *belief ;* and instead of one Boswell and one White, the world will rejoice in a thousand,—stationed on their thousand several watch-towers, to instruct us by indubitable documents, of whatsoever in our so stupendous World comes to light and *is !* O, had the Editor of this Magazine but a magic rod to turn all that not inconsiderable Intellect, which now deluges us with artificial fictitious soap-lather, and mere Lying, into the faithful study of Reality,—what knowledge of great, everlasting Nature, and of Man's ways and doings therein, would not every year bring us in! Can we but change one single soap-latherer and mountebank Juggler, into a true Thinker and Doer, who even *tries* honestly to think and do,—great will be our reward.

But to return; or rather from this point to begin our journey! If now, what with Herr Sauerteig's *Springwurzeln*, what with so much lucubration of our own, it have become apparent how deep, immeasurable is the "worth that lies in *Reality*," and farther, how exclusive the interest which man takes in Histories of Man,—may it not seem lamentable, that so few genuinely good *Biographies* have yet been accumulated in Literature; that in the whole world, one cannot find, going strictly to work, above some dozen, or baker's dozen, and those chiefly of very ancient date? Lamentable; yet, after what we have just seen, accountable. Another question might be asked: How comes it that in England we have simply one good Biography, this *Boswell's Johnson;* and of good, indifferent, or even bad attempts at Biography, fewer than any civilised people? Consider the French and Germans, with their Moreris, Bayles, Jördenses, Jöchers, their innumerable *Mémoires,* and *Schilderungen,* and *Biographies Universelles;* not to speak of Rousseaus, Goethes, Schubarts, Jung-Stillings: and then contrast with these our poor Birches and Kippises and Pecks; the whole breed of whom, moreover, is now extinct!

With this question, as the answer might lead us far, and come out unflattering to patriotic sentiment, we shall not intermeddle; but turn rather, with great pleasure, to the fact, that one excellent Biography *is* actually English;—and even now lies, in Five new Volumes, at our hand, soliciting a new consideration from us; such as, age after age (the Perennial showing ever new phases as *our* position alters), it may long be profitable to bestow on it;—to which task we here, in this position, in this age, gladly address ourselves.

First, however, let the foolish April-fool Day pass by; and our Reader, during these twenty-nine days of uncertain weather that will follow, keep pondering, according to convenience, the purport of BIOGRAPHY in general: then, with the blessed dew of May-day, and in unlimited convenience of space, shall all that we have written on *Johnson* and *Boswell's Johnson* and *Croker's Boswell's Johnson* be faithfully laid before him.

ON HISTORY [1]

[1830]

CLIO was figured by the ancients as the eldest daughter of
Memory, and chief of the Muses; which dignity, whether we
regard the essential qualities of her art, or its practice and
acceptance among men, we shall still find to have been fitly
bestowed. History, as it lies at the root of all science, is also
the first distinct product of man's spiritual nature; his
earliest expression of what can be called Thought. It is a
looking both before and after; as, indeed, the coming Time
already waits, unseen, yet definitely shaped, predetermined
and inevitable, in the Time come; and only by the combination of both is the meaning of either completed. The Sibyl-
line Books, though old, are not the oldest. Some nations
have prophecy, some have not: but of all mankind, there is
no tribe so rude that it has not attempted History, though
several have not arithmetic enough to count Five. History
has been written with quipo-threads, with feather-pictures,
with wampum-belts; still oftener with earth-mounds and
monumental stone-heaps, whether as pyramid or cairn; for
the Celt and the Copt, the Red man as well as the White, lives
between two eternities, and warring against Oblivion, he
would fain unite himself in clear conscious relation, as in dim
unconscious relation he is already united, with the whole
Future and the whole Past.

A talent for History may be said to be born with us, as our
chief inheritance. In a certain sense all men are historians.
Is not every memory written quite full with Annals, wherein
joy and mourning, conquest and loss manifoldly alternate;
and, with or without philosophy, the whole fortunes of one
little inward Kingdom, and all its politics, foreign and domestic, stand ineffaceably recorded? Our very speech is curiously
historical. Most men, you may observe, speak only to
narrate; not in imparting what they have thought, which
indeed were often a very small matter, but in exhibiting what

[1] *Fraser's Magazine*, No. 10.

they have undergone or seen, which is a quite unlimited one, do talkers dilate. Cut us off from Narrative, how would the stream of conversation, even among the wisest, languish into detached handfuls, and among the foolish utterly evaporate! Thus, as we do nothing but enact History, we say little but recite it: nay rather, in that widest sense, our whole spiritual life is built thereon. For, strictly considered, what is all Knowledge too but recorded Experience, and a product of History; of which, therefore, Reasoning and Belief, no less than Action and Passion, are essential materials?

Under a limited, and the only practicable shape, History proper, that part of History which treats of remarkable action, has, in all modern as well as ancient times, ranked among the highest arts, and perhaps never stood higher than in these times of ours. For whereas, of old, the charm of History lay chiefly in gratifying our common appetite for the wonderful, for the unknown; and her office was but as that of a Minstrel and Storyteller, she has now farther become a Schoolmistress, and professes to instruct in gratifying. Whether, with the stateliness of that venerable character, she may not have taken up something of its austerity and frigidity; whether in the logical terseness of a Hume or Robertson, the graceful ease and gay pictorial heartiness of a Herodotus or Froissart may not be wanting, is not the question for us here. Enough that all learners, all inquiring minds of every order, are gathered round her footstool, and reverently pondering her lessons, as the true basis of Wisdom. Poetry, Divinity, Politics, Physics, have each their adherents and adversaries; each little guild supporting a defensive and offensive war for its own special domain; while the domain of History is as a Free Emporium, where all these belligerents peaceably meet and furnish themselves; and Sentimentalist and Utilitarian, Sceptic and Theologian, with one voice advise us: Examine History, for it is " Philosophy teaching by Experience."

Far be it from us to disparage such teaching, the very attempt at which must be precious. Neither shall we too rigidly inquire: How much it has hitherto profited? Whether most of what little practical wisdom men have, has come from study of professed History, or from other less boasted sources, whereby, as matters now stand, a Marlborough may become great in the world's business, with no History save what he derives from Shakspeare's Plays? Nay, whether in that same teaching by Experience, historical Philosophy has yet properly deciphered the first element of all science in this kind: What the aim and significance of that wondrous changeful Life it investigates and paints may be? Whence the course of man's destinies in this Earth originated, and whither they are tending? Or, indeed, if they have any course and tendency, are really guided forward by an unseen mysterious Wisdom, or only circle in blind mazes without recognisable guidance? Which questions, altogether fundamental, one might think, in any Philosophy of History, have since the era when Monkish Annalists were wont to answer them by the long-ago extinguished light of their Missal and Breviary, been by most philosophical Historians only glanced at dubiously and from afar; by many, not so much as glanced at.

The truth is, two difficulties, never wholly surmountable, lie in the way. Before Philosophy can teach by Experience, the Philosophy has to be in readiness, the Experience must be gathered and intelligibly recorded. Now, overlooking the former consideration, and with regard only to the latter, let any one who has examined the current of human affairs, and how intricate, perplexed, unfathomable, even when seen into with our own eyes, are their thousandfold blending movements, say whether the true representing of it is easy or impossible. Social Life is the aggregate of all the individual men's Lives who constitute society; History is the essence of innumerable Biographies. But if one Biography, nay our own Biography, study and recapitulate it as we may, remains in so many points unintelligible to us; how much more must these million, the very facts of which, to say nothing of the purport of them, we know not, and cannot know!

Neither will it adequately avail us to assert that the general inward condition of Life is the same in all ages; and that only the remarkable deviations from the common endowment and common lot, and the more important variations which the outward figure of Life has from time to time undergone, deserve memory and record. The inward condition of Life, it may rather be affirmed, the conscious or half-conscious aim of mankind, so far as men are not mere digesting-machines, is the same in no two ages; neither are the more important outward variations easy to fix on, or always well capable of representation. Which was the greatest

innovator, which was the more important personage in man's
history, he who first led armies over the Alps, and gained the
victories of Cannæ and Thrasymene; or the nameless boor
who first hammered out for himself an iron spade? When the
oak-tree is felled, the whole forest echoes with it; but a
hundred acorns are planted silently by some unnoticed breeze.
Battles and war-tumults, which for the time din every ear,
and with joy or terror intoxicate every heart, pass away like
tavern-brawls; and, except some few Marathons and Mor-
gartens, are remembered by accident, not by desert. Laws
themselves, political Constitutions, are not our Life, but only
the house wherein our Life is led: nay they are but the bare
walls of the house; all whose essential furniture, the inventions and traditions, and daily habits that regulate and support our existence, are the work not of Dracos and Hampdens,
but of Phœnician mariners, of Italian masons and Saxon
metallurgists, of philosophers, alchymists, prophets, and all
the long-forgotten train of artists and artisans; who from
the first have been jointly teaching us how to think and how
to act, how to rule over spiritual and over physical Nature.
Well may we say that of our History the more important part
is lost without recovery; and,—as thanksgivings were once
wont to be offered " for unrecognised mercies,"—look with
reverence into the dark untenanted places of the Past, where,
in formless oblivion, our chief benefactors, with all their
sedulous endeavours, but not with the fruit of these, lie
entombed.

So imperfect is that same Experience, by which Philosophy
is to teach. Nay, even with regard to those occurrences which
do stand recorded, which, at their origin have seemed worthy
of record, and the summary of which constitutes what we now
call History, is not our understanding of them altogether
incomplete; is it even possible to represent them as they
were? The old story of Sir Walter Raleigh's looking from
his prison-window, on some street tumult, which afterwards
three witnesses reported in three different ways, himself
differing from them all, is still a true lesson for us. Consider
how it is that historical documents and records originate;
even honest records, where the reporters were unbiased by
personal regard; a case which, were nothing more wanted,
must ever be among the rarest. The real leading features of
a historical Transaction, those movements that essentially

characterise it, and alone deserve to be recorded, are nowise the foremost to be noted. At first, among the various witnesses, who are also parties interested, there is only vague wonder, and fear or hope, and the noise of Rumour's thousand tongues; till, after a season, the conflict of testimonies has subsided into some general issue; and then it is settled by majority of votes, that such and such a "Crossing of the Rubicon," an "Impeachment of Strafford," a "Convocation of the Notables," are epochs in the world's history, cardinal points on which grand world-revolutions have hinged. Suppose, however, that the majority of votes was all wrong; that the real cardinal points lay far deeper; and had been passed over unnoticed, because no Seer, but only mere Onlookers, chanced to be there! Our clock strikes when there is a change from hour to hour; but no hammer in the Horologe of Time peals through the universe when there is a change from Era to Era. Men understand not what is among their hands: as calmness is the characteristic of strength, so the weightiest causes may be most silent. It is, in no case, the real historical Transaction, but only some more or less plausible scheme and theory of the Transaction, or the harmonised result of many such schemes, each varying from the other and all varying from truth, that we can ever hope to behold.

Nay, were our faculty of insight into passing things never so complete, there is still a fatal discrepancy between our manner of observing these, and their manner of occurring. The most gifted man can observe, still more can record, only the *series* of his own impressions: his observation, therefore, to say nothing of its other imperfections, must be *successive*, while the things done were often *simultaneous*; the things done were not a series, but a group. It is not in acted, as it is in written History: actual events are nowise so simply related to each other as parent and offspring are; every single event is the offspring not of one, but of all other events, prior or contemporaneous, and will in its turn combine with all others to give birth to new: it is an ever-living, ever-working Chaos of Being, wherein shape after shape bodies itself forth from innumerable elements. And this Chaos, boundless as the habitation and duration of man, unfathomable as the soul and destiny of man, is what the historian will depict, and scientifically gauge, we may say, by threading it with single lines of a few ells in length! For as all Action is, by its nature, to be figured as extended in breadth and in depth, as well as in length; that is to say, is based on Passion and Mystery, if we investigate its origin; and spreads abroad on all hands, modifying and modified; as well as advances towards completion,—so all Narrative is, by its nature, of only one dimension; only travels forward towards one, or towards successive points: Narrative is *linear*, Action is *solid*. Alas for our " chains," or chainlets, of " causes and effects," which we so assiduously track through certain hand-breadths of years and square miles, when the whole is a broad, deep Immensity, and each atom is " chained " and com-plected with all! Truly, if History is Philosophy teaching by Experience, the writer fitted to compose History is hitherto an unknown man. The Experience itself would require All-knowledge to record it,—were the All-wisdom needful for such Philosophy as would interpret it, to be had for asking. Better were it that mere earthly Historians should lower such pretensions, more suitable for Omniscience than for human science; and aiming only at some picture of the things acted, which picture itself will at best be a poor approximation, leave the inscrutable purport of them an acknowledged secret; or at most, in reverent Faith, far different from that teaching of Philosophy, pause over the mysterious vestiges of Him, whose path is in the great deep of Time, whom History indeed reveals, but only all History, and in Eternity, will clearly reveal.

Such considerations truly were of small profit, did they, instead of teaching us vigilance and reverent humility in our inquiries into History, abate our esteem for them, or dis-courage us from unweariedly prosecuting them. Let us search more and more into the Past; let all men explore it, as the true fountain of knowledge; by whose light alone, consciously or unconsciously employed, can the Present and the Future be interpreted or guessed at. For though the whole meaning lies far beyond our ken; yet in that complex Manuscript, covered over with formless inextricably-en-tangled unknown characters,—nay which is a *Palimpsest*, and had once prophetic writing, still dimly legible there,—some letters, some words, may be deciphered; and if no complete Philosophy, here and there an intelligible precept, available in practice, be gathered: well understanding, in the meanwhile, that it is only a little portion we have deciphered; that much still remains to be interpreted; that History is a real Prophetic Manuscript, and can be fully interpreted by no man.

But the Artist in History may be distinguished from the Artisan in History; for here, as in all other provinces, there are Artists and Artisans; men who labour mechanically in a department, without eye for the Whole, not feeling that there is a Whole; and men who inform and ennoble the humblest department with an Idea of the Whole, and habitually know that only in the Whole is the Partial to be truly discerned. The proceedings and the duties of these two, in regard to History, must be altogether different. Not, indeed, that each has not a real worth, in his several degree. The simple husbandman can till his field, and by knowledge he has gained of its soil, sow it with the fit grain, though the deep rocks and central fires are unknown to him: his little crop hangs under and over the firmament of stars, and sails through whole untracked celestial spaces, between Aries and Libra; nevertheless it ripens for him in due season, and he gathers it safe into his barn. As a husbandman he is blameless in disregarding those higher wonders; but as a thinker, and faithful inquirer into Nature, he were wrong. So likewise is it with the Historian, who examines some special aspect of History; and from this or that combination of circumstances, political, moral, economical, and the issues it has led to, infers that such and such properties belong to human society, and that the like circumstances will produce the like issue; which inference, if other trials confirm it, must be held true and practically valuable. He is wrong only, and an artisan, when he fancies that these properties, discovered or discoverable, exhaust the matter; and sees not, at every step, that it is inexhaustible.

However, that class of cause-and-effect speculators, with whom no wonder would remain wonderful, but all things in Heaven and Earth must be computed and " accounted for; " and even the Unknown, the Infinite in man's Life, had under the words *enthusiasm, superstition, spirit of the age* and so forth, obtained, as it were, an algebraical symbol and given value,—have now wellnigh played their part in European culture; and may be considered, as in most countries, even in England itself where they linger the latest, verging towards extinction. He who reads the inscrutable Book of Nature as if it were a Merchant's Ledger, is justly suspected of having never seen that Book, but only some school Synopsis thereof; from which, if taken for the real Book, more error than insight is to be derived.

Doubtless also, it is with a growing feeling of the infinite nature of History, that in these times, the old principle, division of labour, has been so widely applied to it. The Political Historian, once almost the sole cultivator of History, has now found various associates, who strive to elucidate other phases of human Life; of which, as hinted above, the political conditions it is passed under are but one, and though the primary, perhaps not the most important, of the many outward arrangements. Of this Historian himself, moreover, in his own special department, new and higher things are beginning to be expected. From of old, it was too often to be reproachfully observed of him, that he dwelt with disproportionate fondness in Senate-houses, in Battle-fields, nay even in Kings' Antechambers; forgetting, that far away from such scenes, the mighty tide of Thought and Action was still rolling on its wondrous course, in gloom and brightness; and in its thousand remote valleys, a whole world of Existence, with or without an earthly sun of Happiness to warm it, with or without a heavenly sun of Holiness to purify and sanctify it, was blossoming and fading, whether the " famous victory " were won or lost. The time seems coming when much of this must be amended; and he who sees no world but that of courts and camps; and writes only how soldiers were drilled and shot, and how this ministerial conjuror out-conjured that other, and then guided, or at least held, something which he called the rudder of Government, but which was rather the spigot of Taxation, wherewith, in place of steering, he could tap, and the more cunningly the nearer the lees,—will pass for a more or less instructive Gazetteer, but will no longer be called a Historian.

However, the Political Historian, were his work performed with all conceivable perfection, can accomplish but a part, and still leaves room for numerous fellow-labourers. Foremost among these comes the Ecclesiastical Historian; endeavouring, with catholic or sectarian view, to trace the progress of the Church; of that portion of the social establishments, which respects our religious condition; as the other portion does our civil, or rather, in the long-run, our economical condition. Rightly conducted, this department were undoubtedly the more important of the two; inasmuch as it concerns us more to understand how man's moral well-being had been and might be promoted, than to understand in the like sort his physical well-being; which latter is ultimately the aim of all Political arrangements. For the physically happiest is simply the safest, the strongest; and, in all conditions of Government, Power (whether of wealth as in these days, or of arms and adherents as in old days) is the only outward emblem and purchase-money of Good. True Good, however, unless we reckon Pleasure synonymous with it, is said to be rarely, or rather never, offered for sale in the market where that coin passes current. So that, for man's true advantage, not the outward condition of his life, but the inward and spiritual, is of prime influence; not the form of Government he lives under, and the power he can accumulate there, but the Church he is a member of, and the degree of moral elevation he can acquire by means of its instruction. Church History, then, did it speak wisely, would have momentous secrets to teach us: nay, in its highest degree, it were a sort of continued Holy Writ; our Sacred Books being, indeed, only a History of the primeval Church, as it first arose in man's soul, and symbolically embodied itself in his external life. How far our actual Church Historians fall below such unattainable standards, nay below quite attainable approximations thereto, we need not point out. Of the Ecclesiastical Historian we have to complain, as we did of his Political fellow-craftsman, that his inquiries turn rather on the outward mechanism, the mere hulls and superficial accidents of the object, than on the object itself: as if the Church lay in Bishops' Chapter-houses, and Ecumenic Council-halls, and Cardinals' Conclaves, and not far more in the hearts of Believing Men; in whose walk and conversation, as influenced thereby, its chief manifestations were to be looked for, and its progress or decline ascertained. The History of the Church is a History of the Invisible as well as of the Visible Church; which latter, if disjoined from the former, is but a vacant edifice; gilded, it may be, and overhung with old votive gifts, yet useless, nay pestilentially unclean; to write whose history is less important than to forward its downfall.

Of a less ambitious character are the Histories that relate
to special separate provinces of human Action; to Sciences,
Practical Arts, Institutions and the like; matters which do
not imply an epitome of man's whole interest and form of
life; but wherein, though each is still connected with all,
the spirit of each, at least its material results, may be in some
degree evolved without so strict a reference to that of the
others. Highest in dignity and difficulty, under this head,
would be our histories of Philosophy, of man's opinions and
theories respecting the nature of his Being, and relations to
the Universe Visible and Invisible: which History, indeed,
were it fitly treated, or fit for right treatment, would be a
province of Church History; the logical or dogmatical
province thereof; for Philosophy, in its true sense, is or
should be the soul, of which Religion, Worship is the body;
in the healthy state of things the Philosopher and Priest
were one and the same. But Philosophy itself is far enough
from wearing this character; neither have its Historians
been men, generally speaking, that could in the smallest
degree approximate it thereto. Scarcely since the rude era
of the Magi and Druids has that same healthy identification
of Priest and Philosopher had place in any country: but
rather the worship of divine things, and the scientific investigation of divine things, have been in quite different hands,
their relations not friendly but hostile. Neither have the
Brückers and Bühles, to say nothing of the many unhappy
Enfields who have treated of that latter department, been
more than barren reporters, often unintelligent and unintelligible reporters, of the doctrine uttered; without force
to discover how the doctrine originated, or what reference
it bore to its time and country, to the spiritual position of
mankind there and then. Nay, such a task did not perhaps
lie before them, as a thing to be attempted.

Art also and Literature are intimately blended with
Religion; as it were, outworks and abutments, by which
that highest pinnacle in our inward world gradually connects
itself with the general level, and becomes accessible therefrom.
He who should write a proper History of Poetry, would
depict for us the successive Revelations which man had
obtained of the Spirit of Nature; under what aspects he had
caught and endeavoured to body forth some glimpse of that
unspeakable Beauty, which in its highest clearness is Religion,

is the inspiration of a Prophet, yet in one or the other degree must inspire every true Singer, were his theme never so humble. We should see by what steps men had ascended to the Temple; how near they had approached; by what ill hap they had, for long periods, turned away from it, and grovelled on the plain with no music in the air, or blindly struggled towards other heights. That among all our Eichhorns and Wartons there is no such Historian, must be too clear to every one. Nevertheless let us not despair of far nearer approaches to that excellence. Above all, let us keep the Ideal of it ever in our eye; for thereby alone have we even a chance to reach it.

Our histories of Laws and Constitutions, wherein many a Montesquieu and Hallam has laboured with acceptance, are of a much simpler nature; yet deep enough if thoroughly investigated; and useful, when authentic, even with little depth. Then we have Histories of Medicine, of Mathematics, of Astronomy, Commerce, Chivalry, Monkery; and Goguets and Beckmanns have come forward with what might be the most bountiful contribution of all, a History of Inventions. Of all which sorts, and many more not here enumerated, not yet devised, and put in practice, the merit and the proper scheme may, in our present limits, require no exposition.

In this manner, though, as above remarked, all Action is extended three ways, and the general sum of human Action is a whole Universe, with all limits of it unknown, does History strive by running path after path, through the Impassable, in manifold directions and intersections, to secure for us some oversight of the Whole; in which endeavour, if each Historian look well around him from his path, tracking it out with the *eye*, not, as is more common, with the *nose*, she may at last prove not altogether unsuccessful. Praying only that increased division of labour do not here, as elsewhere, aggravate our already strong Mechanical tendencies, so that in the manual dexterity for parts we lose all command over the whole, and the hope of any Philosophy of History be farther off than ever,—let us all wish her great and greater success.

ON HISTORY AGAIN [1]

[1833]

[The following singular Fragment on *History* forms part, as may be recognised, of the Inaugural Discourse delivered by our assiduous " D. T." at the opening of the *Society for the Diffusion of Common Honesty.* The Discourse, if one may credit the Morning Papers, " touched in the most wonderful manner, didactically, poetically, almost prophetically, on all things in this world and the next, in a strain of sustained or rather of suppressed passionate eloquence rarely witnessed in Parliament or out of it: the chief bursts were received with profound silence,"—interrupted, we fear, by snuff-taking. As will be seen, it is one of the didactic passages that we introduce here. The Editor of this Magazine is responsible for its accuracy, and publishes, if not with leave given, then with leave taken.—O. Y.]

. . . HISTORY recommends itself as the most profitable of all studies: and truly, for such a being as Man, who is born, and has to learn and work, and then after a measured term of years to depart, leaving descendants and performances, and so, in all ways, to vindicate himself as vital portion of a Mankind, no study could be fitter. History is the Letter of Instructions, which the old generations write and posthumously transmit to the new; nay it may be called, more generally still, the Message, verbal or written, which all Mankind delivers to every man; it is the only *articulate* communication (when the inarticulate and mute, intelligible or not, lie round us and in us, so strangely through every fibre of our being, every step of our activity) which the Past can have with the Present, the Distant with what is Here. All Books, therefore, were they but Song-books or treatises on Mathematics, are in the long-run historical documents— as indeed all Speech itself is: thus might we say, History is not only the fittest study, but the only study, and includes all others whatsoever. The Perfect in History, he who understood, and saw and knew within himself, *all* that the whole Family of Adam had hitherto *been* and hitherto *done,* were perfect in all learning extant or possible; needed not thenceforth to *study* any more; had thenceforth nothing left but to *be* and to *do* something himself, that others might make History of it, and learn of *him*.

Perfection in any kind is well known not to be the lot of man: but of all supernatural perfect-characters this of the Perfect in History (so easily conceivable, too) were perhaps the most miraculous. Clearly a faultless monster which the world is not to see, not even on paper. Had the Wandering Jew, indeed, begun to wander at Eden, and with a Fortunatus's Hat on his head! Nanac Shah too, we remember, steeped himself three days in some sacred Well; and there learnt all things: Nanac's was a far easier method; but unhappily not practicable—in this climate. Consider, however, at what immeasurable distance from this perfect Nanac your highest imperfect Gibbons play their part! Were there no brave men, thinkest thou, before Agamemnon? Beyond the Thracian Bosphorus, was all dead and void; from Cape Horn to Nova Zembla, round the whole habitable Globe, not a mouse stirring? Or, again, in reference to Time:—the Creation of the World is indeed old, compare it to the Year One; yet young, of yesterday, compare it to Eternity! Alas, all Universal History is but a sort of Parish History; which the " P. P. Clerk of this Parish," member of " our Alehouse Club " (instituted for what " Psalmody " is in request there) puts together,—in such sort as his fellow-members will praise. Of the *thing* now gone silent, named Past, which was once Present, and loud enough, how much do we know? Our " Letter of Instructions " comes to us in the saddest state; falsified, blotted out, torn, lost and but a shred of it in existence; this too so difficult to read or spell.

Unspeakably precious meanwhile is our shred of a Letter, is our written or spoken Message, such as we have it. Only he who understands what has been, can know what should be and will be. It is of the last importance that the individual have ascertained his relation to the whole; " an individual helps not," it has been written; " only he who unites with many at the proper hour." How easy, in a sense, for your all-instructed Nanac to work without waste or force (or what we call fault); and, in practice, act new History, as perfectly as, in theory, he knew the old! Comprehending what the given world was, what it had and what it wanted, how might his clear effort strike-in at the right time and the right point; wholly increasing the true current and tendency, nowhere cancelling itself in opposition thereto! Unhappily, such smooth-running, ever-accelerated course is nowise the one appointed us; cross-currents we have, perplexed back-floods; innumerable efforts (every new man is a new effort) consume themselves in aimless eddies: thus is the River of Existence so wild-flowing, wasteful; and whole multitudes, and whole generations, in painful unreason, spend and are spent on what can never profit. Of all which, does not one-half originate in this which we have named want of Perfection in History;—the other half, indeed, in another want still deeper, still more irremediable?

Here, however, let us grant that Nature, in regard to such historic want, is nowise blamable: taking up the other face of the matter, let us rather admire the pains she has been at, the truly magnificent provision she has made, that this same Message of Instructions might reach us in boundless plenitude. Endowments, faculties enough, we have: it is her wise will too that no faculty of Speech, once given, becomes not more a gift than a necessity; the Tongue, with or without much meaning, will keep in motion; and only in some La Trappe by unspeakable self-restraint forbear wagging. As little can the fingers that have learned the miracle of Writing lie idle; if there is a rage of speaking, we know also there is a rage of writing, perhaps the more furious of the two. It is said, "so eager are men to speak, they will not let one another get to speech;" but, on the other hand, writing is usually transacted in private, and every man has his own desk and inkstand, and sits independent and unrestrainable there. Lastly, multiply this power of the Pen some ten-thousandfold: that is to say, invent the Printing-Press, with its Printer's Devils, with its Editors, Contributors, Book-sellers, Billstickers, and see what it will do! Such are the means wherewith Nature, and Art the daughter of Nature, have equipped their favourite Man, for publishing himself to man.

Consider, now, two things: first, that one Tongue, of average velocity, will publish at the rate of a thick octavo volume per day; and then how many nimble-enough Tongues may be supposed to be at work on this Planet Earth, in this

City London, at this hour! Secondly, that a Literary Contributor, if in good heart and urged by hunger, will many times, as we are credibly informed, accomplish his two Magazine sheets within the four-and-twenty hours; such Contributors being now numerable not by the thousand, but by the million. Nay, taking History, in its narrower, vulgar sense, as the mere chronicle of " occurrences," of things that can be, as we say, " narrated," our calculation is still but a little altered. Simple Narrative, it will be observed, is the grand staple of Speech; " the common man," says Jean Paul, " is copious in Narrative, exiguous in Reflection; only with the cultivated man is it otherwise, reversewise." Allow even the thousandth part of human publishing for the emission of Thought, though perhaps the millionth were enough, we have still the nine hundred and ninety-nine employed in History proper, in relating occurrences, or conjecturing probabilities of such; that is to say, either in History or Prophecy, which is a new form of History:—and so the reader can judge with what abundance this life-breath of the human intellect is furnished in our world; whether Nature has been stingy to him or munificent. Courage, reader! Never can the historical inquirer want pabulum, better or worse: are there not forty-eight longitudinal feet of small-printed History in thy Daily Newspaper?

The truth is, if Universal History is such a miserable defective " shred " as we have named it, the fault lies not in our historic organs, but wholly in our misuse of these; say rather, in so many wants and obstructions, varying with the various age, that pervert our right use of them; especially two wants that press heavily in all ages: want of Honesty, want of Understanding. If the thing published is not true, is only a supposition, or even a wilful invention, what can be done with it, except abolish it and annihilate it? But again, Truth, says Horne Tooke, means simply the thing *trowed*, the thing believed; and now, from this to the thing *itself*, what a new fatal deduction have we to suffer! Without Understanding, Belief itself will profit little: and how can your publishing avail, when there was no vision in it, but mere blindness? For as in political appointments, the man you appoint is not he who was ablest to discharge the duty, but only he who was ablest to be appointed; so too, in all historic elections and selections, the maddest work goes on. The event worthiest to be known is perhaps of all others the least spoken of: nay, some say, it lies in the very nature of such events to be so. Thus, in those same forty-eight longitudinal feet of History, or even when they have stretched out into forty-eight longitudinal miles, of the like quality, there may not be the forty-eighth part of a hairsbreadth that will turn to anything. Truly, in these times, the quantity of printed Publication that will need to be consumed with fire, before the smallest permanent advantage can be drawn from it, might fill us with astonishment, almost with apprehension. Where, alas, is the intrepid Herculean Dr. Wagtail, that will reduce all these paper-mountains into tinder, and extract therefrom the three drops of Tinder-water Elixir?

For indeed, looking at the activity of the historic Pen and Press through this last half-century, and what bulk of History it yields for that period alone, and how it is henceforth like to increase in decimal or vigesimal geometric progression, —one might feel as if a day were not distant, when perceiving that the whole Earth would not now contain those writings of what was done in the Earth, the human memory must needs sink confounded, and cease remembering!—To some the reflection may be new and consolatory, that this state of ours is not so unexampled as it seems; that with memory and things memorable the case was always intrinsically similar. The Life of Nero occupies some diamond pages of our Tacitus: but in the parchment and papyrus archives of Nero's generation how many did it fill? The author of the *Vie de Sénèque*, at this distance, picking-up a few residuary snips, has with ease made two octavos of it. On the other hand, were the contents of the then extant Roman memories, or, going to the utmost length, were all that was then *spoken* on it, put in types, how many " longitudinal feet " of small-pica had we, —in belts that would go round the Globe!

History, then, before it can become Universal History, needs of all things to be compressed. Were there no epitomising of History, one could not remember beyond a week. Nay, go to that with it, and exclude compression altogether, we could not remember an hour, or at all: for Time, like Space, is *infinitely* divisible; and an hour with its events, with its sensations and emotions, might be diffused to such expansion as should cover the whole field of memory, and push all else over the limits. Habit, however, and the natural constitution of man, do themselves prescribe service-able rules for remembering; and keep at a safe distance from us all such fantastic possibilities;—into which only some foolish Mahomedan Caliph, ducking his head in a bucket of enchanted water, and so beating-out one wet minute into seven long years of servitude and hardship, could fall. The rudest peasant has his complete set of Annual Registers legibly printed in his brain; and, without the smallest train-ing in Mnemonics, the proper pauses, subdivisions and sub-ordinations of the little to the great, all introduced there. Memory and Oblivion, like Day and Night, and indeed like all other Contradictions in this strange dualistic Life of ours, are necessary for each other's existence: Oblivion is the dark page, whereon Memory writes her light-beam characters, and makes them legible; were it all light, nothing could be read there, any more than if it were all darkness.

As with man and these autobiographic Annual-Registers of his, so goes it with Mankind and its Universal History, which also is *its* Autobiography: a like unconscious talent of remembering and of forgetting again does the work here. The transactions of the day, were they never so noisy, cannot remain loud forever; the morrow comes with its new noises, claiming also to be registered: in the im-measurable conflict and concert of this chaos of existence, figure after figure sinks, as *all* that has emerged must one day sink: what cannot be kept in mind will even go out of mind; History contracts itself into readable extent; and at last, in the hands of some Bossuet or Müller, the whole printed History of the World, from the Creation downwards, has grown shorter than that of the Ward of Portsoken for one solar day.

Whether such contraction and epitome is always wisely formed, might admit of question; or rather, as we say, admits of no question. Scandalous Cleopatras and Messalinas, Cali-gulas and Commoduses, in unprofitable proportion, survive for memory; while a scientific Pancirollus has to write his Book of Arts Lost; and a moral Pancirollus, were the vision lent him, might write a still more mournful Book of Virtues Lost; of noble men, doing and daring and enduring, whose heroic life, as a new revelation and development of Life itself, were a possession for all, but is now lost and forgotten, History having otherwise filled her page. In fact, here as elsewhere, what we call Accident governs much; in any case, History must come together not as it should, but as it can and will.

Remark nevertheless how, by natural tendency alone, and as it were without man's forethought, a certain fitness of selection, and this even to a high degree, becomes inevitable. Wholly worthless the selection could not be, were there no better rule than this to guide it: that men permanently speak only of what is extant and actively alive beside them. Thus do the things that have produced fruit, nay whose fruit still grows, turn out to be the things chosen for record and writing of; which things alone were great, and worth recording. The Battle of Châlons, where Hunland met Rome, and the Earth was played for, at sword-fence, by two earth-bestriding giants, the sweep of whose swords cut kingdoms in pieces, hovers dim in the languid remembrance of a few; while the poor police-court Treachery of a wretched Iscariot, transacted in the wretched land of Palestine, centuries earlier, for " thirty pieces of silver," lives clear in the heads, in the hearts of all men. Nay moreover, as only that which bore fruit was great; so of all things, that whose fruit is still here and growing must be the greatest, the best worth remembering; which again, as we see, by the very nature of the case, is mainly the thing remembered. Observe, too, how this " mainly " tends always to become a " solely," and the approximate continually approaches nearer: for triviality after triviality, as it perishes from the living activity of men, drops away from their speech and memory, and the great and vital more and more exclusively survive there. Thus does Accident correct Accident; and in the wondrous boundless jostle of things (an aimful POWER presiding over it, say rather, dwelling *in* it), a result comes out that may be put-up with.

Curious, at all events, and worth looking at once in our life, is this same compressure of History, be the process thereof what it may. How the " forty-eight longitudinal feet " have shrunk together after a century, after ten centuries! Look back from end to beginning, over any History; over our own *England :* how, in rapidest law of perspective, it dwindles from the canvas! An unhappy Sybarite, if we stand within two centuries of him and name him Charles Second, shall have twelve times the space of a heroic Alfred;

two or three thousand times, if we name him George the
Fourth. The whole Saxon Heptarchy, though events, to
which Magna Charta, and the world-famous Third Reading,
are as dust in the balance, took place then,—for did not
England, to mention nothing else, get itself, if not represented
in Parliament, yet converted to Christianity?—the whole
Saxon Heptarchy, I say, is summed-up practically in that
one sentence of Milton's, the only one succeeding writers
have copied, or readers remembered, of the "fighting and
flocking of kites and crows." Neither was that an unim-
portant wassail-night, when the two black-browed Brothers,
strongheaded, headstrong, Hengst and Horsa (*Stallion* and
Horse), determined on a man-hunt in Britain, the boar-
hunt at home having got overcrowded; and so, of a few
hungry Angles made an English Nation, and planted it here,
and—produced *thee*, O Reader! Of Hengst's campaignings
scarcely half a page of good Narrative can now be written;
the *Lord Mayor's Visit to Oxford* standing, meanwhile,
revealed to mankind in a respectable volume. Nay what of
this? Does not the Destruction of a Brunswick Theatre
take above a million times as much telling as the Creation of
a World?

To use a ready-made similitude, we might liken Universal
History to a magic web; and consider with astonishment
how, by philosophic insight and indolent neglect, the ever-
growing fabric wove itself forward, out of that ravelled
immeasurable mass of threads and thrums, which we name
Memoirs; nay, at each new lengthening, at each new *epoch*,
changed its whole proportions, its hue and structure to the
very origin. Thus, do not the records of a Tacitus acquire
new meaning, after seventeen hundred years, in the hands
of a Montesquieu? Niebuhr has to reinterpret for us, at
a still greater distance, the writings of a Titus Livius: nay,
the religious archaic chronicles of a Hebrew Prophet and
Lawgiver escape not the like fortune; and many a ponderous
Eichhorn scans, with new-ground philosophic spectacles,
the revelation of a Moses, and strives to reproduce for this
century what, thirty centuries ago, was of plainly infinite
significance to all. Consider History with the beginnings of
it stretching dimly into the remote Time; emerging darkly
out of the mysterious Eternity: the ends of it enveloping *us*
at this hour, whereof we at this hour, both as actors and

relators, form part! In shape we might mathematically name it *Hyperbolic-Asymptotic*; ever of *infinite* breadth around us; soon shrinking within narrow limits: ever narrowing more and more into the infinite depth behind us. In essence and significance it has been called " the true Epic Poem, and universal Divine Scripture, *whose* ' plenary inspiration ' no man, out of Bedlam or in it, shall bring in question."

AN ELECTION TO THE LONG
PARLIAMENT [1]

[1844]

ANTHONY WOOD, a man to be depended on for accuracy, states as a fact that John Pym, Clerk of the Exchequer, and others, did, during the autumn of 1640, ride to and fro over England, inciting the people to choose members of their faction. Pym and others. Pym "rode about the country to promote elections of the Puritanical brethren to serve in Parliament; wasted his body much in carrying-on the cause, and was himself," as we well know, "elected a Burgess." As for Hampden, he had long been accustomed to ride: "being a person of antimonarchical principles," says Anthony, "he did not only ride, for several years before the Grand Rebellion broke out, into Scotland, to keep consults with the Covenanting brethren there; but kept his circuits to several Puritanical houses in England; particularly to that of Knightley in Northamptonshire," to Fawsley Park, then and now the house of the Knightleys, "and also to that of William Lord Say at Broughton near Banbury in Oxfordshire:" [2]— Mr. Hampden might well be on horseback in election-time. These Pyms, these Hampdens, Knightleys were busy riding over England in those months: it is a little fact which Anthony Wood has seen fit to preserve for us.

A little fact, which, if we meditate it, and picture in any measure the general humour and condition of the England that then was, will spread itself into great expanse in our imagination! What did they say, do, think, these patriotic missionaries, "as they rode about the country"? What did they propose, advise, in the successive Townhalls, Country-houses, and "Places of Consult"? John Pym, Clerk of the Exchequer, Mr. Hampden of Great Hampden,

---

[1] *Fraser's Magazine*, No. 178.
[2] Wood's *Athenæ* (Bliss's edition), iii. 73, 59; Nugent's *Hampden*, i. 327.

riding to and fro, lodging with the Puritan Squires of this English Nation, must have had notable colloquies! What did the Townspeople say in reply to them? We have a great curiosity to know about it: how this momentous General Election, of autumn 1640, went on; what the physiognomy or figure of it was; how "the remarkablest Parliament that ever sat, the father of all Free British Parliaments, American Congresses and French Conventions, that have sat since in this world," was got together!

To all which curiosities and inquiries, meanwhile, there is as good as no answer whatever. Wood's fact, such as it is, has to twinkle for us like one star in a heaven otherwise all dark, and shed what light it can. There is nothing known of this great business, what it was, what it seemed to be, how in the least it transacted itself, in any town, or county, or locality. James Heath, "Carrion Heath" as Smelfungus calls him, does, in his *Flagellum* (or *Flagitium*[1] as it properly is), write some stuff about Oliver Cromwell and Cambridge Election; concerning which latter and Cleaveland the Poet there is also another blockheadism on record:—but these, and the like, mere blockheadisms, pitch-dark stupidities and palpable falsities,—what can we do with these? Forget them, as soon as possible, to all eternity;—that is the evident rule: Admit that we do honestly know nothing, instead of misknowing several things, and in some sense all things, which is a great misfortune in comparison!

Contemporary men had no notion, as indeed they seldom have in such cases, what an enormous work they were going-on with; and nobody took note of this election more than any former one. Besides, if they had known, they had other business than to write accounts of it for *us*. But how could anybody know that this was to be the *Long* Parliament, and to cut his Majesty's head off, among other feats? A very "spirited election," I dare believe:—but there had been another election that same year, equally spirited, which had issued in a *Short* Parliament, and mere "second Episcopal War." There had been three prior elections, sufficiently spirited; and had issued, each of them, in what we may call a futile shriek; their Parliaments swiftly vanishing again.

[1] Or, *Life of Oliver Cromwell* (London, 1663): probably, all things considered, the brutalest Platitude this English Nation has to show for itself in writing.

Sure enough, from whatever cause it be, the world, as we said, knows not anywhere of the smallest authentic notice concerning this matter, which is now so curious to us, and is partly becoming ever more curious. In the old Memoirs, not entirely so dull when once we understand them; in the multitudinous rubbish-mountains of old Civil-War Pamphlets (some thirty or fifty thousand of them in the British Museum alone, unread, unsorted, unappointed, unannealed!), which will continue dull till, by real labour and insight, of which there is at present little hope, the ten-thousandth part of them be extracted; and the nine-thousand nine-hundred and ninety-nine parts of them be eaten by moths, or employed in domestic cookery when fuel grows scarce;—in these chaotic masses of old dull printing there is not to be met with, in long years of manipulation, one solitary trait of any election, in any point of English land, to this same Long Parliament, the remarkablest that ever sat in the world. England was clearly all alive then,—with a moderate crop of corn just reaped from it; and other things not just ready for reaping yet. In Newcastle, in "the Bishoprick" and that region, a Scotch Army, bristling with pike and musket, sonorous with drum and psalm-book, all snugly garrisoned and billeted "with £850 a-day;" over in Yorkshire an English Army, not quite so snugly; and a "Treaty of Ripon" going on; and immense things in the wind, and Pym and Hampden riding to and fro to hold "consults:" it must have been an election worth looking at! But none of us will see it; the Opacities have been pleased to suppress this election, considering *it* of no interest. It is erased from English and from human Memory, or was never recorded there,—(owing to the stupor and dark nature of that faculty, we may well say). It is a lost election; swallowed in the dark deeps: *premit atra Nox.* Black Night; and this one fact of Anthony Wood's more or less faintly twinkling there!

In such entire darkness, it was a welcome discovery which the present Editor made, of certain official or semi-official Documents, legal testimonies and signed affidavits, relative to the Election for Suffolk, such as it actually showed itself to men's observation in the Town of Ipswich on that occasion: Documents drawn-up under the exact eye of Sir Simonds D'Ewes, High-Sheriff of Suffolk; all carefully preserved these two centuries, and still lying safe for the inspection of the curious among the *Harley Manuscripts* in the British Museum. Sir Simonds, as will be gradually seen, had his reasons for getting these Documents drawn-up; and luckily, when the main use of them was over, his thrifty historical turn of mind induced him to preserve them for us. A man of sublime Antiquarian researches, Law-learning, human and divine accomplishments, and generally somewhat Grandisonian in his ways; a man of scrupulous Puritan integrity, of high-flown conscientiousness, exactitude and distinguished perfection; ambitious to be the pink of Christian country-gentlemen and magistrates of counties; really a most spotless man and High-Sheriff: how shall he suffer, in Parliament or out of it, to the latest posterity, any shadow from election-brabbles or the like indecorous confusion to rest on his clear-polished character? Hence these Documents;—for there had an unseemly brabble, and altercation from unreasonable persons, fallen-out at this Election, which " might have ended in blood," from the nose or much deeper, had Sir Simonds been a less perfect High-Sheriff! Hence these Documents, we say; and they are preserved to us.

The Documents, it must be at once owned, are somewhat of the wateriest: but the reader may assure himself they are of a condensed, emphatic, and very potent nature, in comparison with the generality of Civil-War documents and records! Of which latter indeed, and what quality they are of, the human mind, till once it has earnestly tried them, can form no manner of idea. We had long heard of Dulness, and thought we knew it a little; but here first *is* the right dead Dulness, Dulness its very self! Ditch-water, fetid bilge-water, ponds of it and oceans of it; wide-spread genuine Dulness, without parallel in this world: such is the element in which that history of our Heroic Seventeenth Century as yet rots and swims! The hapless inquirer swashes to and fro, in the sorrow of his heart: if in an acre of stagnant water he can pick-up half a peascod, let him thank his stars!

This Editor, in such circumstances, read the D'Ewes Documents, and re-read them, not without some feeling of satisfaction. Such as they are, they bring one face to face with an actual election, at Ipswich, " in Mr. Hambie's field, on Monday the 19th of October 1640, an extreme windy day." There is the concrete figure of that extreme windy Monday,

Monday gone Two-hundred and odd years: the express image of Old Ipswich, and Old England, and that Day; exact to Nature herself,—though in a most dark glass, the more is the pity! But it is a glass; it is the authentic *mind*, namely, or *seeing-faculty*, of Sir Simonds D'Ewes and his Affidavit-makers, who did look on the thing with eyes and minds, and got a real picture of it for themselves. Alas, we too could see *it*, the very thing as it then and there was, through these men's poor limited authentic picture of it here preserved for us, had we eyesight *enough* ;—a consideration almost of a desperate nature! Eyesight *enough*, O reader: a man in that case were a god, and could do various things!—

We will not overload these poor Documents with commentary. Let the public, as we have done, look with its own eyes. To the commonest eyesight a markworthy old fact or two may visibly disclose itself; and in shadowy outline and sequence, to the interior regions of the seeing-faculty, if the eyesight be beyond common, a whole world of old facts,—an old contemporary England at large, as it stood and lived, on that " extreme windy day,"—may more or less dimly suggest themselves. The reader is to transport himself to Ipswich; and, remembering always that it is two centuries and four years ago, look about him there as he can. Some opportunity for getting these poor old Documents copied into modern hand has chanced to arise; and here, with an entire welcome to all faithful persons who are sufficiently patient of dulness for the sake of direct historical knowledge, they are given forth in print.

It is to be premised that the Candidates in this Election are Three: Sir Nathaniel Barnardiston and Sir Philip Parker on the Puritan side; and Mr. Henry North, son of Sir Roger North, on the Court or Royalist side. Sir Roger is himself already elected, or about to be elected, for the borough of Eye;—and now Mr. Henry, heir-apparent, is ambitious to be Knight of the Shire. He, if he can, will oust one of the two Puritans, he cares little which, and it shall be tried on Monday.

To most readers these Candidates are dark and inane, mere Outlines of Candidates: but Suffolk readers, in a certain dim way, recognise something of them. " The Parkers still continue in due brilliancy, in that shire: a fine old place, at Long Melford, near Bury:—but this Parker," says our

Suffolk monitor,[1] " is of another family, the family of Lord Morley-and-Monteagle, otherwise not unknown in English History.[2] The Barnardistons too," it would appear, " had a noble mansion in the east side of the county, though it has quite vanished now, and corn is growing on the site of it," and the family is somewhat eclipsed. The Norths are from Mildenhall, from Finborough, Laxfield; the whole world knows the North kindred, Lord Keeper Norths, Lord Guildford Norths, of which these Norths of ours are a junior twig. Six lines are devoted by Collins Dryasdust[3] to our Candidate Mr. Henry, of Mildenhall, and to our Candidate's Father and Uncle; testifying indisputably that they lived, and that they died.

Let the reader look in the dim faces, Royalist and Puritan, of these respectable Vanished Gentlemen; let him fancy their old Great Houses, in this side of the county or that other, standing all young, firm, fresh-pargeted, and warm with breakfast-fire, on that " extreme windy morning," which have fallen into such a state of dimness now! Let the reader, we say, look about him in that old Ipswich; in that old vanished population: perhaps he may recognise a thing or two. There is the old " Market Cross," for one thing; " an old Grecian circular building, of considerable diameter; a dome raised on distinct pillars, so that you could go freely in and out between them; a figure of Justice on the top; " which the elderly men in Ipswich can still recollect, for it did not vanish till some thirty years ago. The " Corn Hill " again, being better rooted, has not vanished hitherto, but is still extant as a Street and Hill; and the Townhall stands on one side of it.

Samuel Duncon, the Town-constable, shall speak first. " The Duncons were a leading family in the Corporation of Ipswich; Robert Duncon was patron of the," etc. etc.: so it would appear; but this Samuel, Town-constable, must have been of the more decayed branches, poor fellow! What most concerns us is, that he seems to do his constabling in a really

---

[1] D. E. Davy, Esq., of Ufford, in that County, whose learning in Suffolk History is understood to be supreme, and whose obliging disposition we have ourselves experienced.

[2] " It was to William Parker, Lord Monteagle, ancestor of this Sir Philip, that the Letter was addressed which saved the King and Parliament from the Gunpowder Plot. Sir Philip had been High-Sheriff in 1637; he died in 1675."—*Dryasdust MSS.*

[3] *Peerage*, iv. 62, 63 (London, 1741).

judicious manner, with unspeakable reverence to the High-Sheriff; that he expresses himself like a veracious person, and writes a remarkably distinct hand. We have sometimes, for light's sake, slightly modified Mr. Duncon's punctuation; but have respected his and the High - Sheriff's spelling, though it deserves little respect,—and have in no case, never so slightly, meddled with his sense. The questionable *italic letters in brackets* are evident interpolations;—omissible, if need be.

SUFFOLKE ELECTION [1]

No. I

[*Samuel Duncon testifieth*]

"Memorandum, That upon Monday the 19th day of October this present year 1640, the election of two Knights for the Shire was at Ipswich in Suffolke; the Writt being read about eight of the clocke in the morning; and in the Markett Crosse where the County Court is generally kept, Mr. Henry North sonne of Sir Roger North was there at the reading of the said Writt. All this time the other two, namely, Sir Nathaniel Barnardiston and Sir Philip Parker, were at the King's Head; and Mr. North was carried about neare halfe an houre before the other two came [*Carried about in his chair by the jubilant people : Let all men see, and come and vote for him. The chairing was then the first step, it would seem*]; and after the other two were taken there, Mr. North was carried into the field neare the said towne, called Mr. Hambie's feild: [2] and the said High-Sherriffe was there polling, about halfe an houre before the other twc Knights knewe either of his being polling, or of the High-Sherriff's intention to take the Poll in that place. But at length the two Knights were carried into the said feild; and before they came there, the tables which were sett for them, the said Sir Nathaniel and Sir Philip, were thrust downe, and troaden under foot [*Such a pressure and crowding was there !*]; and they both caused but one table to bee sett there,—till about

---

[1] From *Harleian MSS.*, British Museum (Parliamentary Affairs collected by Sir S. D'Ewes), No. 165, fol. 5-8.

[2] Or, " Hanbie's field," as the Duncon *MS*. has it: he probably means Hamby. " A family of the latter name had property at Ipswich and about it, in those times."—*Dryasdust MSS.*

three of the clocke of the afternoone, the said day, about which time Sir Nathaniel had another table sett there, a little remote from the other. And when they went about to poll, they wanted a clarke. I, Samuel! Duncon, standing by, some requested mee; and upon the Under-Sherriff's allowance, I did take names, and one Mr. Fishar with mee, he for Sir Nathaniel, and myselfe for Sir Philip; although many that came for the one, came for the other; and if any came for Mr. North (as there did some), wee tooke them like-wise for him. And Mr. John Clinch of Creting,[1] Sir Roger North's brother-in-law, or some other of Mr. North his ['*North his*' means North's] friends, stoode by all the time. And after the space of one quarter of an houre, came Sir Robert Crane,[2] and did oppose against Mr. Fishar; and then came the said High-Sherriffe himselfe to the table, wheere wee weere writing, and discharged Mr. Fishar, and tooke his papers of him; and at the request of Sir Roger North did appoint one Mr. John Sheppard to write in his place, who then tooke names for Sir Nathaniel, and myselfe for Sir Philip. About one houre after, Sir Robert Crane and the rest of Mr. North his friends moved Sir Nathaniel that wee might leave off polling for him and Sir Philip, and take the Poll only for Mr. North; for, they said, Mr. North's table was much pestred, and many of his men would be gone out of towne, being neare night,—and the like reasons. Which reasons might as well have been alledged in the behalfe of Sir Nathaniel and Sir Philip: but without reasoning, Sir Nathaniel did grant them their desire; and presently Sir Robert Crane went and called all that were for Mr. North to come to that table; and soe Mr. Sheppard and myselfe tooke for Mr. North as long as wee could well see; which I think was about one houre. Having done, wee gave upp our Bookes, and did goe to Mrs. Penning's house in Ipswich, where Sir Roger North was then with the said High-Sherriffe: and I heard no oppositions at that time taken against any thing

---

[1] " The family of Clinch, or Clench as it should be spelt, were of note in Suffolk. They descended from John Clench of," etc. etc., " buried in 1607, with a handsome monument to his memory. He was one of the Justices of the King's Bench. His Grandson, John Clench, Esq., was High-Sheriff of the County in 1639."—*Dryasdust MSS*. This, I think, is our and Samuel Duncon's Clench.

[2] " Sir Robert Crane was descended from a Norfolk family, which migrated," etc. " He was created a Baronet in May 1627. He was of Chilton Hall, near Sudbury; he died in 1642."—*Ibid.*

that had passed that Monday at the taking of the said Poll; but Sir Roger North and the said High-Sherriffe did part very courteously and friendly, each from the other.

" But by the next morning it was generally thought, that Sir Nathaniel and Sir Philip had outstripped Mr. North, about 500 voices apiece, at the Poll taken on the Monday foregoing; soe as the said Sir Roger being, it seemes, much vexed thereat, came to the said High-Sherriffe's lodging about eight of the clocke, the same Teuesday morning, and begann to make cavills against what had passed at the taking of the Poll the day past. And then they went to the Poll againe; and two tables were sett in the Markett Crosse,[1] whereat the Poll was taken for Mr. North by four clarkes on oath, two writing the same names. About 12 of the clocke, the same forenoone, the Court was adjourned to two of the clocke in the afternoone. About which time the said High-Sherriffe repairing thither againe, did with much patience attend the same Mr. North's Poll, sitting sometimes about a quarter of an houre before any came in to give their voice, for the said Mr. North. And as the said High-Sheriffe was soe attending his [*Sir Roger North's*] said sonne's Poll, about three of the clocke the same afternoone, came Sir Roger North, accompanied with divers gentlemen, most of them armed with swords or rapiers [*Lo, there !*], into the said Mearkett Crosse; and the said High-Sherriffe very respectfully attending with silence to what the said Sir Roger North had to say, he fell into most outrageous, unjust and scandalous criminations against the said High-Sherriffe; charging him to have dealt partiallie and unjustlie, and to have wronged his said sonne. To all which violent accusations, the said High-Sherriffe, having desired silence, did answeare soe fully and readily, as it gave all unpartiall and honest men full satisfaction. A while after the said High-Sherriffe's speech was ended, the said Sir Roger North with divers others went upp and downe in such a manner on the said Corne Hill, as I, the said Samuell Duncon, fearing that much danger and bloudshedd might ensue, and being one of the constables of Ipswich, did in the King's Majestie's name charge some of the said company to desist [*Highly proper, in such a place as the Corne Hill !*]. SAMUEL DUNCON."

---

[1] " A spacious place; there was room enough in it: see the old copperplate of 1780."—*Drvasdust MSS.*

No. II

[Samuel Duncon testifieth for the second time]

" *Monday, the* 19*th of October* 1640

" When I came into the field where the Polling was for the Knights of the Shire, the first place I settled at was an Elm [*Nota bene*] in the middle of the feild, where there were polling for Sir Nathaniel Barnardiston and Sir Philip Parker: and there was a long table, at one end whereof was Mr. Robert Dowe, clerke; and he did write for both the foresaid knights; and Mr. Farran, Under-Sherriffe,[1] did sweare the people; and at the other end of the same table did Mr. Robert Clarke write for Sir Philip, and Mr. Peter Fisher wrot for Sir Nathaniel; and sometimes Mr. Chopping [2] did sweare the people at that end, and sometimes Mr. Robert Clerke did sweare them.

" After I had stood there one houre or thereabout, Mr. Robert Clerke his nose did bleede [*Ominous ?*], so as he coulde not write, and then he called mee to write in his stead, and the Under-Sherriffe required me so to doe; which I did till his nose left bleeding, and then he tooke the Booke again and wrot himselfe. Then I stood by againe about another houre, and then with the violent presse of the people, the tressolls brake, and the table fell downe to the ground [*Aha !*]. There was a cessation of writing until the table was set up againe. In that interim, Peter Fisher and Samuel Duncon went to the Conduit-head [*Mark !*]; and having a table sett up there, they did write there for the two foresaid Knights: and then, at the former place [*Beside the big Elm, namely, under its creaking boughs, and brown leaves dropping*], when the table was up againe, Mr. Dowe wrot still for the two Knights, and then [' *Then*' *signifies* ' *meanwhile*'] at the other end of the table was Mr. Robert Clarke writing for Sir Philip. And then there was no man at that end writing for Sir Nathaniel; which presently bred this confusion inevitable, viz. when men had with much trouble pressed to the

---

[1] " Under-Sheriff," so Duncon calls him; but the real Under-Sheriff was Mr. Choppine, to whom this Mr. Farran must have been assistant or temporary substitute.

[2] " A.D. 1640. John Choppine, Gent., Under-Sheriff; Tallemach Choppine of Coddenham's brother."—*Harleian MSS.* No. 99, fol. 7.

end of the table (where Mr. Clarke did only take for Sir
Philip), and desired to be sworne and entered for both, Mr.
Clerke would sweare and take them onely for Sir Philip;
and would send them to the place where Mr. Fisher was
writing for Sir Nathaniel [*And I for Sir Philip still ? No,
I had ceased ; the official nose having done bleeding : see
presently*], at the foresaid Conduit-head: whereupon men,
being unwilling to endure so much trouble as to presse twice
into such great crowdes, began to murmure and complaine
[*Very naturally I*], saying they would not endure this, but
desired they might be discharged at one place; also Mr. Fisher
came to Mr. Clerke, and demanded the reason Why there was
no one to take for Sir Nathaniel at that end of the table, where
the said Clerke did take names for Sir Philip? and Mr.
Fisher said that men complained because they were not
despatched for both at once; and said also they would goe
away, and not endure this crowding twice.   When I [*Having
now quitted the Conduit-head, and come to the Elm again*] saw
no clerke to write for Sir Nathaniel, I desired this inconveni-
ence aforesaid might be prevented; and seeing a Paper
Booke in Mr. Farran his hands, I sayd to him, ' Mr. Farran,
you see there wants a clerke at the other end of the table to
write for Sir Nathaniel; ' and then Mr. Farran gave me the
Paper Booke in his hands, and sayd to mee, ' Write you, for
Sir Nathaniel at that end of the table,' where Mr. Clerke did
write for Sir Philip. And then I, having the Booke, did
write for Sir Nathaniel till the evening.   And at that end of
the table where [' *table where*,' not ' *end where* '] Mr. Robert
Dowe did write at one end, and Mr. Clerke and myselfe at
the other end, there were present two or three knightes or
gentlemen, all the whole time, of Mr. North's partie: sometimes Sir Robert Crane, and Mr. — Waldegrave, and Mr.
John Smith,[1] and Mr. Henry North sen. [*This is the Candidate's Uncle, come over from Laxfield, I think, to see fair play*.]
No man, all that time, made any observation against mee;
and yet they stoode, some of these and sometimes some others

---

[1] Smith is undecipherable; being " very frequent " in Suffolk, as
elsewhere. Of Waldegrave, the Monitor says, " There being no Christian name mentioned, it is hard to say what individual is meant.
Doubtless he was one of the Waldegraves of Smallbridge. Wm. Waldegrave, Esq., son of Sir Wm. Waldegrave, Knight, of Smallbridge in
Bures, Suffolk, would be about forty years of age about this time: "—
let us fancy it was he.

of that side, all the afternoone, and did supravise all the clerkes. Also, at night, when wee were breaking up, Mr. Clerke demanded of Mr. Clinch [*Clinch of Creting,—whom we saw above*] if he could find any fault with us in doing any wrong? To which he answered, ' He could not as yet, if there were no other carriage than there had yet beene,' or to that effect. Neither was there any, that day, who did find fault with the clerkes, in my hearing; but sometimes some muttering and complaining about some particular questions in the oaths, which (as soon as they came to the High-Sherriffe his intelligence) were rectified and settled.

" And at night, when wee broke up, I gave my Booke that I wrott in, unto the Under-Sheriffe, Mr. Farran, before I stirred from the table where I wrott; and then wee came home with the High-Sheriffe to Mrs. Penning's howse [*Did she keep the King's Head ?*]; and there did the High-Sheriffe call for all the Bookes from the Under-Sheriffe, and in the presence of Sir Roger North, and Mr. North his brother, and more other gentlemen, locke up all the Bookes in a little truncke; and sett that truncke in his owne lodging-chamber; and gave the key thereof to his Under-Sheriffe, who lodged not in that howse where the Bookes were.

" *Tuesday, the 20th of October* 1640

" In the morning Mr. High-Sheriffe came into the Corne Hill at Ipswich and the Knights, to make an end of polling. Whereupon the clerkes who wrot the day before appeared, and wrot againe as before. But Mr. High-Sheriffe commanded that wee should all of us make new Bookes to write in; for he would not stirr those that were wrot-in the day before: and so wee did, and wrot in new Bookes.

" And all that day also while wee wrot, there were divers supravisors; but they found no fault with the clerkes in my hearing; and at noone, when wee brake upp, I gave my Booke againe into Mr. Farran, before I stirred from the table where I wrot. And in the afternoone, wee came together againe, and made an end of polling; and towards the end of polling, before wee had done polling at the table where I sat to write, Sir Roger with the rest of the knights and gentlemen went about the Corne Hill, swinging their caps and hats crying, ' A North! A North!' [*Questionable*]; which caused me to admire; because I knew the Bookes were not cast up [*And nobody could yet tell who was to win*].

" Then after that, Mr. High-Sheriffe went to Mrs. Penning's, and the Knights followed him, and the clerkes to summe up the Bookes.   But the night grew on so fast, that they could not be ended that night: then Mr. High-Sheriffe did againe locke up the Bookes in the same truncke they were in before, and gave the key to Mr. — North, and sett the truncke into his chamber, and appointed to meete the next day upon [*Means, in it, not on the roof of it; the figure of Justice stands on the roof*] the Townhall."

[Samuel Duncon still testifieth]

" Memorandum, That on Tuesday October 20, in the afternoone, this present year 1640, the High-Sherriffe of the county of Suffolk, sitting in the Markett Crosse [*Note him !*], in Ipswich, where hee kept his County Court, and had that afternoone taken the poll of divers that came to give their voices for Mr. Henry North, sonne of Sir Roger North [*Grammar fails a little*].   And when it appeared, after some stay, that noe more weere likely to come, and Mr. Gardener Webb [1] speaking concerning the said election averred That the said High-Sherriffe had been damnably base in all his carriage.   Whereupon I, Samuel Duncon, hearing the same, did [*As an enemy of blasphemy, and Constable of this Borough*] enforme the said High-Sheriffe of that outrageous and scandalous speeche; who thereupon asking the said Webb, Whether hee had spoken the said wordes or not? he answered, with much impudence and earnestness, That he had said soe, and would maintain it.   And did thereupon in the presence of the said High-Sherriffe call mee, the said Samuel Duncon, base rascall and rogue [*He shall answer it !*] because I had acquainted the said High-Sherriffe with his said injurious speeches.   SAMUEL DUNCON."

---

[1] " Gardiner Webb was the son of William Webb of Ixworth in Suffolk, attorney-at-law.   He became heir, in right of his mother (who was one of the Gardiners of Elmswell), to considerable landed property " (*Dryasdust MSS.*); and seems to have been a hot-tempered loose-spoken individual.

No. III

[Samuel Duncon still testifieth, though without signature]

"Wednesday the 21st October 1640

"The truncke was brought up into the Townhall, and the High-Sherriffe and the rest of the knights and gentlemen came up together to make end of their Bookes: and they passed quietly untill my Booke was produced; and then Mr. North protested against my Booke, and Sir Roger came up and exclaimed at mee, and said I was no fitt clerke, neyther authorised to write. Then was Mr. Farran called, and asked How I came to write? Which he answered, 'He never saw mee before Monday in all his life, but wanting one to write, and I standing by, he requested mee to write.' The High-Sherriffe told Sir Roger, 'He could not but accept of my Booke, and would doe so if I had wrot for his own sonne;' and for myselfe, as I then testified, so am I ready to make oath, being lawfully called, That my Booke was just and right, and that I did not write one name that was not sworne for Sir Nathaniel; and notwithstanding Sir Roger and other knights did speake their large pleasures of mee and charged me with direct and manifest outrage [*Maltreating the honest Town-constable : shameful !*].

"In conclusion, the High-Sherriffe finished the Bookes, and soe we brake up that night, and the next day we proclaymed Sir Nathaniel Barnardiston and Sir Philip Parker Knights of the Shire for the ensuing Parliament."

[SAMUEL DUNCON: signature not given.]

"To all these Three Pages I am ready to give testimony; and to the whole substance thereof. EDW. BESTWALL." [1]

No. IV

[Samuel Duncon still testifieth]

"Memorandum, Upon Tuesday morning some women [*Puritan women ; zealous beyond discretion !*] came to be

---

[1] Bestwall is not known to Dryasdust. An impartial onlooker, and presumably nothing more. The "Three Pages" he vouches for are all these testimonies of Duncon's from beginning to end,—*nearly eight* pages as printed here.

sworne for the two foresaid Knights; and Mr. Robert Clerke did suddenly take some of them; but as soone as Mr. High-Sherriffe had intelligence of it, wee had worde brought to the table where Mr. Clerke and myselfe wrot, that Mr. Sheriffe would have us take no women's oaths; and both the Knights desired that those that were taken might be put out, and that we should take no more: and so we refused the rest of the women after that notice from Mr. High-Sherriffe; and when Mr. High-Sherriffe cast up the Bookes, he cast out the women out of the generall summe."

[SAMUEL DUNCON: signature not given.]

These transactions are of " so high a nature," it is probable a Parliamentary Committee will have to sit upon them: justice between the vociferous irrational Sir Roger and the discreet unspotted Sir Simonds will then be done. Duncon backed by Bestwall, in writing, and by the Under-Sheriffs Farran and Choppin *vivâ voce* if needful, and indeed by the whole town of Ipswich if needful,—may sufficiently evince that Mr. High-Sheriff's carriage in the business was perfection or nearly so. The accurate Magistrate meanwhile thinks good to subjoin a succinct Narrative of his own, which he is ready to sign when required; every word of which can be proved by the oath of witnesses. No. V. is clearly by D'Ewes himself; there are even some directions to his clerk about writing it fair.

No. V

A short and true relation of the carriage of the Election of the Knights for the Countie of Suffolke at Ipswich, which beganne there upon Monday morning, October 19, this present Year 1640, and ended upon the Thursday morning then next ensuing.[1]

" The Under-Sherriffe having had order from the High-Sheriffe of the same Countie to provide honest and able men to take the Poll, and to looke to gett ready materialls for the Election, went to Ipswich on Friday night: and the said High-Sherriffe was purposed to have gone thither the next day, but that hee understood the small-pox [*Nota bene*] was

[1] From *Harleian MSS*. British Museum, collected by Sir S. D'Ewes, No. 158, p. 275.

exceeding spread in the said towne. Sir Nathaniel Barnardiston and Sir Philip Parker joined together, and Henry North stood singlie, for the place of Knights of the Shire.

"The said High-Sherriffe came to Ipswich about eight of the clocke of the said Monday morning.[1] To whom Sir Roger North, father of the said Mr. Henry North, and divers other gentlemen repairing, hee yeilded to them to have the Poll taken in a feild neare the towne; and soe, after a little discourse without further stay, went to the Markett Crosse, and caused the King's Majestie's Writt to bee published; by which meanes the said Mr. North was carried about a good while before the other Knights [*Yes !*] had notice that the said Writt was published. And this the said High-Sherriffe did about an houre and halfe sooner than he was by law compelled to; that there might be noe just ground of cavill, as if he had delaied the business [*Sir Simonds is himself known to be a Puritan ; already elected, or about to be elected, for the town of Sudbury. So high stood Sudbury then ; sunk now so low !*].

"After the publication of which, the said High-Sherriffe withdrew himselfe to make haste into the said feild [*Mr. Hambie's field ; with the Conduit-head and big Elms in it*] to take the Poll. But before hee got thither, or any place was made readie for the clerkes to write, the said Mr. North was brought into the feild [*Triumphantly in his chair*]; and many of the gentrie as well as others that were of his partie pressed soe upon the place where the planks and boards were setting upp, as they could not be fastened or finished. All this time the other two Knights knew yett nothing that the said Poll was begunn in the said feild: soe as [*So that*] the said High-Sherriffe begann Mr. North's poll alone, and admitted a clerke. The said Sir Roger North proffered to write the names, with the clerke his [*The High-Sheriff's*] Under-Sherriffe had before appointed, which hee [*The High-Sheriff*] conceived hee was not in law bound unto.

"Having then taken the Poll a while, in the said Sir Roger North's presence and his said sonne's, the companie did tread upon the said planks with such extreme violence, as having divers times borne them downe upon the said High-Sherriffe; and hee having used all meanes of entreatie and perswasion to desire them to beare off, as did the said Sir

[1] He lived at Stow Hall (*Autobiography of D'Ewes*); he must have started early.

Roger North also,—the said High-Sherriffe was at the last forced to give over; and soe gave speedie order, by the advice of the said Sir Roger North and others, To have three severall tables ['*Three:*' *Duncon notices only two of them; one under the Elm, one at the Conduit-head, where the Puritan Knights were polling; Sir Simonds himself superintends the Norths' table :—*' *three several tables* '] sett upp against trees or other places wheere they might not bee borne downe by violence. Which being verie speedilie performed, the said High-Sherriffe went in person and assisted at the said table wheere Mr. North's poll was taking, leaving his Under-Sherriffe and sworne deputies to attend the other tables, and to administer the oath, where the said Sir Roger and his sonne did appoint their kindred and friends to overview all that was done.

"The said High-Sherriffe did there, without eating or drinking, assist the said Mr. North, from about nine of the clocke in the morning till it grew just upon night, notwith-standing it was in the open feild, and a verie cold and windie day: and did in his owne person take much paines to dispatch the said Poll; which had been much better advanced, if such as came to the same had not treaded with such extreme violence one upon another. And whereas the said Sir Nathaniel Barnardiston came, about twelve of the clocke that forenoone, to the said High-Sherriffe, desiring him that all the companie might dissolve to goe to dinner, and that in respect of the great winde, the Poll in the afternoone might be taken in the said towne of Ipswich [*A very reasonable motion*]: The said High-Sherriffe, upon the said Mr. North's request to the contrarie, staide in the said feild till the shutting upp of the said day, as is aforesaid.

"What was done at the other tables the said High-Sherriffe knew not; but twice, upon complaint to him made, repaired thither, and certified and reconciled all matters. And during the same day alsoe the said High-Sherriffe did desire the said Sir Roger North to sende for another table to the place wheere he sate, being willing by all meanes to expedite the said Poll. And though there were not one man sworne for the other two Knights at the said Mr. North's table,—yet were there divers sworne at one of the other two tables for the said Mr. North; soe as, by this and the early beginning of the said Mr. North's poll, he had neare upon

Two-hundred voices advantage of the other two Knights, had they come single; but they having manie hundreds that gave voices for them jointly, did before night outstrippe his votes by about Fowre-hundred apiece.

" At the said High-Sherriffe's rising from the said Poll on the said Monday night, hee tooke the Bookes from the said clerkes; and though by lawe he was tied to call noe partie to assist him in the laying them upp, yet to take away all possible cause of cavill, and to showe his integritie in the whole proceedings, hee called the said Sir Roger North to him, and desired him to accompanie him not only to the places wheere he received all the other Bookes or Papers from his said Under-Sherriffe, or the other clarkes that wrote them, but to his lodging also [*Mrs. Penning's*]; wheere hee bound and sealed upp the said Bookes and Papers, in the presence of the said Sir Roger North and the said Under-Sherriffe; then locking them upp, gave the key to his said Under-Sherriffe to keepe; having first asked the said Sir Roger, If hee were not a person fitte to be trusted with it? And soe the said Sir Roger North departed, in a verie friendly and amicable manner, from the said High-Sherriffe, without so much as moving the least complaint against any of the said proceedings of that day.

" But it seemes, after his departure, having that night learned that the other Knights' polls outstripped his said sonne's by divers hundreds,—he came the next morning to the said High-Sherriffe's lodging; and beganne, in violent and passionate termes, to charge him That hee had dealt unjustlie and partiallie in taking the Poll the day past [*Behold* /]: which at the present caused the said High-Sherriffe to wonder at that sudden and unexpected change; in respect the same Sir Roger parted in soe friendlie a manner from him the night foregoing, and that his indefatigable paines the day past deserved rather just acknowledgment than such unjust expostulation [*Certainly* /].

' The said High-Sherriffe therefore, having received the said key from his said Under-Sherriffe, in the presence of the said Sir Roger North, departed to the finishing of the said Poll. And whereas the other two Knights had but each of them one table allowed at which two clerkes only wrote; the said High-Sherriffe allowed the said Mr. North two tables and four clerkes: and at noone when the said Court was adjourned to two of the clocke of the same afternoone, the said High-Sherriffe having taken all the Bookes and Papers touching the same Poll from his Under-Sherriffe, or the clerkes which wrot them, desired the said Mr. North himselfe to accompanie him to his said lodging; which he did, and sawe them sealed and locked upp, and then had himselfe the key along with him.

"But all these testimonies of the said High-Sherriffe's impartialitie, and integritie in his proceedings, did in noe way mitigate the passion and indignation of the said Sir Roger North and some others, who now beganne to give the cause upp as conclamated [1] and lost; and therefore, though the said High-Sherriffe afterwardes in his numbering the votes of the said Poll did proceed with it in publike view, which hee might have done privately with his own clerkes, yet all the time after hee was often interrupted by most unjust and outrageous accusations and criminations; and by that meanes was almost as long, within an houre or two, in numbering the names of the said Poll, as hee was in taking the Poll itselfe. And in all differences that emergently fell out in numbering the said names, wheere there was but any equalitie of doubt, the said High-Sherriffe prevailed with the other two Knights to let the advantage rest on the said Mr. North's side.

"And though the said Sir Roger North came, on the said Tuesday in the afternoone, October 20th, into the Countie Court whilst the said High-Sherriff sate taking the Poll for his said sonne, and there used most outrageous and violent speeches against the said High-Sherriffe [*Hear Duncon too*], and told him 'Hee would make it good with his bloud;' yet the said High-Sherriffe, seeing him accompanied with many young gentlemen and others, all or most of them armed with their swords and their rapiers [*Questionable !*], and fearing if he had made use of his just power to punish such an affront, much bloudshedd would have ensued, hee rather passed it over with an invincible patience; and only stoode upp, and desired silence to cleare himselfe from these unjust assertions and criminations which had been laid upon him; and resolved to expect redresse of his enemies from the High Court of Parliament [*Far the better plan, Mr. High-Sheriff !—which,*

---

[1] *Conclamatum est;*—summoned nine times, and making no answer, is now to be held for *dead.*

among other good effects, has yielded us these present Documents withal].

" Yet the said Sir Roger, not satisfied herewith, did, a little after, with the said companie of young gentlemen, and others that followed him, armed as aforesaid, or the greater part of them, go about the Corne Hill in Ipswich, where the Crosse stands, and cried, ' A North! a North!' calling the saylers Water-dogges [*Puritan sailors ;—mark it ; had voted for the Gospel Candidates : ' Water-dogs*'], and otherwise provoking them: one also of the companie drewe out his sword [*Lo, there !*], and brandished it about, nor did they give over till one of the Constables of Ipswich [*Sam Duncon ; we saw him doing it*], being a sworne officer, charged them In the King's name to desist. The other two Knights, then sitting at the Poll, were fain at the instant to withdraw themselves in at the next windowe of the house wheere they stoode; having first besought the people and saylers to bee quiet, and not to answer violence with violence. For it is too apparent what was sought for in that dangerous action; and that if the said High-Sherriffe had, at that present, made use of his power to vindicate his owne affronts and sufferings, much bloudshedde might have ensued. Nor did the said High-Sherriffe suffer only from the violent language of the said Sir Roger North and some others of qualitie, but from two of the Webbes alsoe, whose Christian names were Roger and Gardiner [*The intemperate Webbes of Ixworth*], and suchlike persons of inferiour rank. The said High-Sherriffe having sate out all Wednesday October 21, from morning till night, in the West Hall or Court House in Ipswich aforesaid, without dining, did at last, notwithstanding the violent interruptions of the said Sir Roger North and others, finish the numbring of the said votes that day; and found that the said Sir Nathaniel Barnardiston had 2140 voices, and Sir Philip Parker 2240 at the least,—besides the voices of all such persons as had been admitted without the said High-Sherriffe's knowledge, and were by him, upon numbring the same, disallowed and cast out. And the said Mr. Henry North had 1422.

" The next morning, October 22, the said High-Sherriffe made open publication of the said votes; and pronounced the said Sir Nathaniel Barnardiston and Sir Philip Parker the due elected Knights for the said Countie of Suffolke.

And then caused the indentures witnessing the same election to be there ensealed and loyallie [*Lawfully*] executed.

" 'Tis true that, by the ignorance of some of the clerkes at the other tables, the oaths of some single women [*We saw it with Duncon*] that were freeholders were taken, without the knowledge of the said High-Sherriffe; who, as soon as he had notice thereof, instantlie sent to forbidd the same, conceiving it a matter verie unworthy of anie gentleman, and most dishonourable in such an election, to make use of their voices, although they might in law have been allowed; nor did the said High-Sherriffe allow of the said votes upon his numbring the said Poll, but with the allowance and consent of the said two Knights themselves discount them and cast them out.

" Now, though all the frivolous cavills, exceptions and protestations which were made against the foresaid Election by the said Sir Roger North or others did only concerne the Poll which was taken on the said Monday October 19; and are sufficiently answered with the verie preceding bare Narration of the true carriage thereof; and the rather, because himselfe accompanying the said High-Sherriffe the same evening when he received all the said Bookes and Papers from his said Under-Sherriffe, or such persons who had written them, did except against noe person, nor noe booke or paper, but consented to the sealing and locking them upp as Acts by which the matter in question was to be decided: Yet to satisfy all the world, such exceptions shall be heare set down, and clearly elevated or wiped away, which on the Tuesday and Wednesday following were pressed at Ipswich upon the said High-Sherriffe, with soe much outrageous passion as he could be scarce permitted to make answer to the same, by reason of the vociferation and clamours of the other partie.

" It was objected, That the said High-Sherriffe made delaies on purpose to hinder the said Mr. North. This is so frivolous as 'tis not worth the answering; for the hindrance must have been equallie prejudiciale to the other two Knights as well as to him. Nay, on the contrarie, if any had wrong, they had; for the said High-Sherriffe soe hastened both the reading of the Writt, and goeing to the Poll as hee could not in time give the other two Knights notice of it. Soe as if the said Mr. North's companie had not by their overpressing violence throwne downe the boards and planks, wheere the said High-Sherriffe begann his the said Mr. North's poll alone, hee had gained neare upon an houre's advantage of the other two.

" Another objection, That the said High-Sherriffe refused such clerkes as the said Sir Roger North offered him; telling him hee was provided. This is a shamefull objection: as if the adverse partie were to provide men to take the poll. In this matter the said High-Sherriffe committed all to the trust and care of his Under-Sherriffe, who assured him hee had provided able and sufficient writers; yet did the said High-Sherriffe admitt a clarke, at the said Mr. North's poll, to write with the clerke his said Under-Sherriffe had provided, upon the motion of the said Sir Roger North.

" A third objection, That the said Mr. North lost many voices that were forced to goe out of towne the same Monday, because they could not be sworne. And soe doubtless did the other two likewise. And this was an invincible or remediless mischief on all sides. And 'tis evident the extreame pressing of the said Mr. North's votes hindred some hundreds from being dispatched. Besides, the said High-Sherriffe, at his entreatie, forebore his dinner [*The high-spirited immaculate man*], to sitt it out with him in the winde and cold till night; which deserved acknowledgment, and not rage and furie. Besides, he made the said Sir Roger North once or twice to send for another table to the same place; which courtesie the said High-Sherriffe afforded the said Mr. North the next morning, more than was allowed the other two Knights. And had the said Mr. North lost the place by one or two hundred voices, there might indeed be some colour that hee had miscarried because the Poll could not be finished on the said Monday night; which notwithstanding that it had been soe, yet the said High-Sherriffe was noe ways the cause thereof. But it is noe ways probable that the said Mr. North should be so ill-beloved or lightlie esteemed by such as appeared for him, that Seven-hundred persons would all depart and desert his cause, rather than abide and stay one night in Ipswich to assist him with their votes. For by so many at the least did either of the other two Knights carrie it from him.

" Lastly, for conclusion of the whole. There is not a word or sillible sett down here, which is not notoriously known to manie, or which the said High-Sherriffe himself will not make good by his corporall oath, being loyallie thereunto called, as also by the Bookes and Papers taken at the said Poll. Soe as never was innocency oppressed more by violence and fury; nor did his royall Majestie's Authoritie ever suffer more in the person of his Minister, than by the outrageous affronts offered unto, and unjust criminations heaped upon, the said High-Sherriffe at the said Election."

Such is the account High-Sheriff D'Ewes has to give of himself, concerning his carriage in the Election of Knights of the Shire for Suffolk on this memorable occasion. He has written it down in an exact manner, to be ready for the Parliament, or for any and all persons interested; his clerks can now make copies of it as many as wanted. In the same Volume, No. 158 of the *Harley Collection*, there is another copy of this " short and true relation," with slight changes, principally in the punctuation; doubtless the immaculate Magistrate saw good to revise his Narrative more than once, and bring it still nearer perfection: he adds always this direction for the amanuenses: " They are desired who take a coppie of this to compare it with the originall after they have transcribed it,"—to be sure that they are exact. The original, which, at any rate, in D'Ewes's hand, few persons could have read, is happily lost.

No notice in the *Commons Journals*, or elsewhere, indicates at all whether this case ever came before the Election Committee of the Long Parliament. But if it did, as is probable enough, we put it to the commonest sense of mankind, whether on Sir Roger North's side it could have a leg to stand on! No Election Committee can have difficulty here. Accordingly our Puritan Knights Sir Philip Parker and Sir Nathaniel Barnardiston sat indisputable as County Members for Suffolk, Mr. Henry North consoling himself as he could. Sir Simonds the High-Sheriff had another case before the Parliament; this namely, that he being High-Sheriff had returned *himself* for Sudbury as duly elected there, which was thought informal by some: but in this too he prospered, and sat for that Borough. The intemperate Sir Roger, as we said, was admitted Member for Eye: but in the second year, mingling with " Commission of Array " and other Royalist concerns, to small purpose as is likely, he, like many others, was "disabled,"—cast forth, to Oxford, to "malignancy," disaster, and a fate that has not been inquired into.

Sir Simonds sat spotless for Sudbury; made occasional fantastic Speeches; and what is far more important for us, took exact Notes. Several of his Speeches he has preserved in writing; one, probably the most fantastic and pedantic of all, he sent forth in print: it relates to a dispute for seniority that had arisen between Oxford University and Cambridge; proves by unheard-of arguments and erudition, obsolete now to all mortals, that Cambridge, which was his own University, is by far the older,—older than Alfred himself, old as the very hills in a manner. Sir Simonds had the happiness to "shake hands with Mr. Prynne," when he came to the Parliament Committee on his deliverance from prison, and to congratulate Mr. Prynne on the changed aspects that then were. He wrote frequent letters to "Abraham Wheloc" and many others. Far better, he almost daily dictated to his secretary, or jotted-down for him on scraps of paper, Notes of the Proceedings of the Long Parliament; which Notes still exist, safe in the British Museum; unknown seemingly to all the learned. He was a thin high-flown character, of eminent perfection and exactitude, little fit for any solid business in this world, yet by no means without his uses there.

This one use, had there been no other, That he took Notes of the Long Parliament! Probably there is much light waiting us in these Notes of his, were they once disimprisoned into general legibility. They extend, in various forms, in various degrees of completeness, to the year 1645: but in that year, after the victory of Naseby, the questionable course things were taking gave offence to our Presbyterian Grandison; he sat mostly silent, with many thoughts, and forbore jotting any farther. Two of his written Speeches relate to the confused negotiations with King Charles in the Isle of Wight; and are strong in the Royalist-Presbyterian direction. Colonel Pride, in the end, purged him out altogether, on the memorable 6th December 1648; sent him, with four or five score others, "over to the Tavern called Hell, kept by Mr. Duke, near Palaceyard,"—in the most unheard-of manner! For, on questioning Mr. Hugh Peters, who had come across to them, By what law? By what shadow or vestige of any law, common or statutory, human or divine, is this unheard-of thing done?—the candid Mr. Peters, a man of good insight and considerable humour of character, answered these much-injured honourable gentlemen, " By the law of Necessity; truly by the power of the sword! " And they remained in a nearly rabid state; evidently purged out, without reason and without remedy; and had to retire to their respective countries, and there rhyme the matter for themselves as they could.

Our poor Knight, Sir Simonds, soon after died; leaving an unspotted pedant character, and innumerable Manuscripts behind him. Besides his *History of the Parliaments of Queen Elizabeth*, a laborious compilation, which has since been printed, long ago, and still enjoys a good reputation of its sort, there are, as we count, some Ninety and odd Volumes of his Papers still extant in the British Museum: very worthless some of them, very curious others;—among which latter, certain portions of his *Autobiography*, already known in print,[1] are well worth reading; and these his *Notes of the Long Parliament* are perhaps, to us English, the most interesting of all the Manuscripts that exist there. Pury's Notes of the Long Parliament [2] appear to be irretrievably lost; Varney's, which also have never yet been made accessible,[3] extend over only a short early period of the business: it is on these Notes of D'Ewes's, principally, that some chance of understanding the procedure and real character of the

---

[1] *Bibliotheca Topographica*, No. 6.

[2] " Mr. Robinson asked me this morning," Monday, 12 Jan., 1656-7, " before the Speaker came, If I took Notes at Scot's Committee? I said, Yea. He told me He had much ado to forbear moving against my taking Notes, for it was expressly against the Orders of the House. I told him how *Mr. Davy* took Notes all the Long Parliament, and that Sir Symons D'Ewes wrote great volumes " of the like. *Burton's Diary* (London, 1828), i. 341.

Of Sir Simonds's " great volumes " we are here speaking: but who the " Mr. Davy " is? No person of the name of *Davy* sat in the Long Parliament at all; or could by possibility have taken Notes! After multifarious examination, and bootless trial of various names more or less resembling *Davy*, a sight of the original MS. of the thing called *Burton's Diary* was procured; and the name " Davy " then straightway turned out to be *Pury*. Pury, or Purry, perhaps now written *Perry*, Alderman of Gloucester, and once well known as Member for that City. But of him or of his *Notes*, on repeated application there, no trace could now be found. If, as is possible, they still exist, in the buried state, in those regions,—to resuscitate and print them were very meritorious.

[3] Edited now (London, 1845) by Mr. Bruce.

Long Parliament appears still to depend for us. At present, after shiploads of historical printing, it is and remains mere darkness visible; if in these Notes by an accurate eye-witness there be no chance of light, then is light anywhere hopeless, and this remarkablest Parliament that ever sat will continue an enigma forever. In such circumstances, we call these Notes the most interesting of all Manuscripts. To an English soul who would understand what was really memorable and godlike in the History of his Country, distinguishing the same from what was at bottom *un*memorable and devil-like; who would bear in everlasting remembrance the doings of our noble heroic men, and sink into everlasting oblivion the doings of our loud ignoble quacks and sham-heroes,—what other record can be so precious? If English History have nothing to afford us concerning the Puritan Parliament but vague incoherencies, inconceivabilities and darkness visible,—English History, in this Editor's opinion, must be in a poor way!

It has often been a question, Why none of the Dryasdust Publishing Societies, the *Camden* or some other, has gone into these D'Ewes's *MSS.* in an efficient spirit, and fished-up somewhat of them? Surely it is the office of such Publishing Societies. Now when Booksellers are falling irrecoverably into the hand-to-mouth system, unable to publish anything that will not repay them on the morrow morning; and in Printed Literature, as elsewhere, matters seem hastening pretty fast towards strange consummations: who else but the Printing Societies is to do it? They should lay aside vain Twaddle and Dilettantism, and address themselves to their function by real Labour and Insight, as above hinted,—of which, alas, there is at present little hope!

Unhappily the Publishing Societies, generally speaking, are hitherto " Dryasdust " ones; almost a fresh nuisance rather than otherwise. They rarely spend labour on a business, rarely insight; they consider that sham-labour, and a twilight of ignorance and buzzard stupidity, backed by prurient desire for distinction, with the subscription of a guinea a year, will do the turn. It is a fatal mistake! Accordingly the Books they print, intending them apparently to be read by some class of human creatures, are wonderful. Alas, they have not the slightest talent for knowing, first of all, what *not* to print; what, as a thing dead, and incapable of ever interesting or profiting a human creature more, ought not to be printed again, to steal away the valuable cash, and the invaluable time and patience of any man again! It is too bad. How sorrowful to see a mass of printed Publishings and Republishings, all in clear white paper, bound in cloth and gold lettered; concerning which you have to acknowledge that there should *another* artist be appointed to go in the rear of them, to fork them swiftly into the oven, and save all men's resources from one kind of waste at least. Mr. Chadwick proposes that sweepers shall go in the rear of all horses in London, and instantly sweep-up their offal, before it be trampled abroad over the pavement to general offence. Yes; but what sweeper shall follow the Dryasdust Printing Societies, the Authors, Publishers, and other Prurient-Stupids of this intellectual Metropolis, who are rising to a great height at present! Horse-offal, say Chadwick and the Philanthropists very justly, if not at once swept-up, is trampled abroad over the pavements, into the sewers, into the atmosphere, into the very lungs and hearts of the citizens: Good Heavens, and to think of Author-offal, and how *it* is trampled into the very souls of men; and how the rains and the trunkmakers do not get it abolished for years on years, in some instances!

TWO HUNDRED AND FIFTY YEARS AGO[1]

DUELLING

[1850]

DUELLING, in Queen Elizabeth's reign, was very prevalent; nor has it abated in King James's. It is one of the sincerities of Human Life, which bursts through the thickest-quilted formulas; and in Norse-Pagan, in Christian, New-Christian, and all manner of ages, will, one way or the other, contrive to show itself.

A background of wrath, which can be stirred-up to the murderous infernal pitch, does lie in every man, in every creature; this is a fact which cannot be contradicted;— which indeed is but another phasis of the more general fact, that every one of us is a *Self*, that every one of us calls himself *I*. How can you be a Self, and not have tendencies to self-defence! This background of wrath,—which surely ought to blaze-out as seldom as possible, and then as nobly as possible, —may be defined as no other than the general radical fire, in its least-elaborated shape, whereof Life itself is composed. Its least-elaborated shape, this flash of accursed murderous rage;—as the glance of mother's-love, and all intermediate warmths and energies and genialities, are the same element *better* elaborated. Certainly the elaboration is an immense matter,—indeed, is the whole matter! But the figure, moreover, under which your infernal element itself shall make its appearance, nobly or else ignobly, is very significant. From Indian Tomahawks, from Irish Shillelahs, from Arkansas Bowie-knives, up to a deliberate Norse *Holmgang*, to any civilised Wager of Battle, the distance is great.

[1] Found recently in *Leigh Hunt's Journal*, Nos. 1, 3, 6 (Saturday 7th December 1850 *et seqq*.). Said there to be " from a Waste-paper Bag" of mine. Apparently some fraction of a certain *History* (Failure of a History) *of James I.*, of which I have indistinct recollections. (*Note of* 1857.)

Certain small fractions of events in this kind, which give us a direct glance into Human Existence in those days, are perhaps, in the dim scarcity of all events that are not dead and torpid, worth snatching from the general leaden haze of my erudite friend, and saving from bottomless Nox for a while.

No. I

HOLLES OF HAUGHTON

John Holles, Esquire, or, to speak properly, Sir John Holles, of Haughton, in Notts; the same Sir John whom we saw lately made Comptroller of the Prince's Household;—an indignant man, not without some relation to us here: John Holles indignantly called it "political simony" this selling of honours; which indeed it was: but what then? It was doable, it was done for others; it was desirable to John also, who possessed the requisite cash. He was come of London citizens, had got broad lands and manors, Haughton, Erby and others; had wealth in abundance,—"his father used to keep a troop of players;" he now, in this epoch, for a consideration of £10,000, gets himself made Earl of Clare. We invite our readers to look back some two-score years upon his history, and notice slightly the following circumstances there.

John Holles, Esquire, of Haughton, in Notts, a youth of fortune, spirit and accomplishment, who had already seen service under the Veres, the Frobishers, by land and sea, did in 1591, in his twenty-sixth year, marry his fair neighbour, Anne Stanhope;—Mistress Anne Stanhope, daughter of Sir Thomas Stanhope, in those parts, from whom innumerable Chesterfields, Harringtons and other Stanhopes extant to this very day descend. This fair Anne Stanhope, beautiful in her fardingales and antiquarian headgear, had been the lady of John Holles's heart in those old times; and he married her, thinking it no harm. But the Shrewsburys, of Worksop, took offence at it. In his father's time, who kept the troop of players and did other things, John Holles had been bespoken for a daughter of the Shrewsburys; and now here has he gone over to the Stanhopes, enemies of the house of Shrewsbury. Ill blood in consequence; ferment of high humours; a Montague-and-Capulet business; the very retainers, on both sides, biting thumbs at one another.

Pudsey, a retainer on the Shrewsbury Worksop side, bit his thumb at Orme, a retainer on the Holles Haughton side; was called-out with drawn rapier; was slain on the spot, like fiery Tybalt, and never bit his thumb more. Orme, poor man, was tried for murder; but of course the Holleses and the Stanhopes could not let him be hanged; they made interest, they fee'd law-counsel,—they smuggled him away to Ireland, and he could not be hanged. Whereupon Gervase Markham, a passably loose-tongued, loose-living gentleman, sworn squire-of-dames to the Dowager of Shrewsbury, took upon himself to say publicly, "That John Holles was himself privy to Pudsey's murder; that John Holles himself, if justice were done——!" And thereupon John Holles, at Haughton, in Notts, special date not given, presumable date 1594 or '95, indited this emphatic Note, already known to some readers:

"For Gervase Markham

"Whereas you have said that I was guilty of that villany of Orme in the death of Pudsey, I affirm that you lie, and lie like a villain; which I shall be ready to make good upon yourself, or upon any gentleman my equal living.—JOHN HOLLES."

Gervase Markham, called upon in this emphatic way, answered, "Yes, he would fight; certainly;—and it should be in Worksop Park, on such a day as would suit Holles best." Worksop Park; locked Park of the Shrewsburys! Holles, being in his sound wits, cannot consent to fight there; and Markham and the world silently insinuate, "Are you subject to niceties in your fighting, then? Readier, after all, with your tongue than with your rapier?" These new intolerabilities John Holles had to pocket as he could, to keep close in the scabbard, beside his rapier, till perhaps a day would come.

Time went on: John Holles had a son; then, in 1579, a second son, Denzil by name. Denzil Holles, Oliver Cromwell's Denzil: yes, reader, this is he; come into the world not without omens! For at his christening, Lady Stanhope, glad matron, came as grandmother and godmother; and Holles, like a dutiful son-in-law, escorted her homewards through the Forest again. Forest of merry Sherwood, where Robin Hood and others used to inhabit; that way lies their road. And now, riding so toward Shelton House, through the glades of Sherwood, whom should they chance to meet but Gervase Markham also ambling along, with some few in his company! Here, then, had the hour arrived.

With slight salutation and time of day, the two parties passed on: but Holles, with convenient celerity, took leave of his mother-in-law: " Adieu, noble Madam, it is all straight road now!" Waving a fond adieu, Holles gallops back through Sherwood glades; overtakes Markham; with brief emphasis, bids him dismount, and stand upon his guard. And so the rapiers are flashing and jingling in the Forest of Sherwood; and two men are flourishing and fencing, their intents deadly and not charitable. " Markham," cried Holles, " guard yourself better, or I shall spoil you presently;" for Markham, thrown into a flurry, fences ill; in fact, rather capers and flourishes than fences; his antagonist standing steady in his place the while, supple as an eel, alert as a serpent, and with a sting in him too. See, in few passes, our alert Holles has ended the capering of Markham; has pierced and spitted him through the lower abdominal regions, in very important quarters of the body, " coming out at the small of the back " ! That, apparently, will do for Markham; loose-tongued, loose-living Gervase Markham lies low, having got enough. Visible to us there, in the glades of ancient Sherwood, in the depths of long-vanished years! O Dryasdust, was there not a Human Existence going-on there too; of hues other than the leaden-hazy? The fruit-trees looked all leafy, blossomy, my erudite friend, and the Life-tree Igdrasil which fills this Universe; and they had not yet rotted to brown peat! Torpid events shall be simply damnable, and continually claim oblivion from all souls; but the smallest fractions of events not torpid shall be welcome. John Holles, " with his man Acton," leaving Markham in this sated condition, ride home to Haughton with questionable thoughts.

Nevertheless Markham did not die. He was carried home to Worksop, pale, hopeless; pierced in important quarters of the body: and the Earl of Shrewsbury " gathered a hundred retainers to apprehend Holles; " and contrariwise the Earl of Sheffield came to Haughton with fifty retainers to protect Holles;—and in the mean while Markham began to show symptoms of recovering, and the retainers dispersed themselves again. The Doctor declared that Markham would live; but that,—but that——Here, we will suppose, the Doctor tragi-comically shook his head, pleading the imperfections of language! Markham did live long after; breaking several of the commandments, but keeping one of them it is charitably believed. For the rest, having " vowed never to eat supper nor to take the sacrament " till he was revenged on Holles, he did not enjoy either of those consolations in this world.[1]

Such doings went forward in Sherwood Forest and in our English Life-arena elsewhere; the trees being as yet all green and leafy.

No. II

CROYDON RACES

Sardanapalus Hay, and other Scotch favourites of King James, have transiently gleamed athwart us; their number is in excess, not in defect. These hungry magnificent individuals, of whom Sardanapalus Hay is one, and supreme Car another, are an eye-sorrow to English subjects; and sour looks, bitter gibes, followed by duels within and without the verge, keep his Majesty's pacificatory hand in use. How many duels has he soldered-up, with difficulty: for the English are of a grim humour when soured; and the Scotch too are fierce and proud; and it is a truculent swashbuckler age, ready with its stroke, in whatever else it may be wanting.

Scotch Maxwell, James Maxwell, Usher of the Black or some kind of Rod, did he not, in his insolent sardonic way, of which he is capable, take a certain young tastefully dizened English gentleman by the bandstring, nay perhaps by the earring and its appendage, by some black ribbon in or about the ear; and so, by the ribbon, *lead* him out from the Royal Presence,—as if he had been a nondescript in Natural History; some tame rabbit, of unusual size and aspect, with ribbon in its ear! Such touches of sardonic humour please me little. The Four Inns of Court were in deadly emotion; and fashionable Young England in general demanded satisfaction, with a growl that was tremendous enough. Sardonic Maxwell had to apologise in the completest manner,—and be more wary in future how he led-out fashionable young gentlemen.

[1] The above facts are given in Gervase Holles's Manuscript *Memoirs of the Family of Holles* (in *Biographia Britannica*, § Holles); a Manuscript which some of our Dryasdust Societies ought to print.

" *Beati pacifici*, Happy are the peacemakers," said his
Majesty always. Good Majesty; shining examples of justice too he is prepared to afford; and has a snarl in him
which can occasionally bite. Of Crichton Lord Sanquhar,
from the pleasant valley of Nith,—how the Fencing-master
accidentally pricked an eye out of him, and he forgave it;
how, much wrought-upon afterwards, he was at last induced
to have the Fencing-master assassinated;—and to have himself executed in Palace Yard in consequence, and his two
assassin servants hanged in Fleet Street; rough Border serving-men of all work, too unregardful of the gallows: of this
unadmirable Crichton the whole world heard, not without
pity, and can still hear.[1]

This of Croydon Races, too, if we read old *Osborne* with
reflection, will become significant of many things. How the
races were going on, a new delightful invention of that age;
and Croydon Heath was populous with multitudes come to
see; and between James Ramsay of the Dalhousie Ramsays,
and Philip Herbert of the Montgomery Herberts, there rose
sudden strife; sharp passages of wit,—ending in a sharp
stroke of Ramsay's switch over the crown and face of my
Lord Montgomery, the great Earl of Pembroke's brother,
and himself capable to be Earl Pembroke! It is a fact of the
most astonishing description: undeniable,—though the exact
date and circumstances will now never be discovered in this
world. It is all vague as cloud, in old *Osborne ;* lies off or on,
within sight of Prince Henry's Pageant; exact date of it never
to be known. Yet is it well recognisable as distant ill-defined
land, and no cloud; not dream but astonishing fact. Can the
reader sufficiently admire at it? The honourable Philip
Herbert, of the best blood of England, here is he switched over
the crown by an accursed Scotch Ramsay! We hear the
swift-stinging descent of the ignominious horse-switch; we
see the swift-blazing countenances of gods and men.

Instantaneous shriek, as was inevitable, rises near and far:
The Scotch insolence, Scotch pride and hunger, Scotch
damnability! And " a cripple man, with only the use of
three fingers," crooked of shape, hot of temper, rode about
the field with drawn dagger; urging in a shrill manner, that
we should prick every Scotch lown of them home to their own
beggarly country again, or to the Devil,—off Croydon Heath,

[1] *State Trials.*

at least. The name of this shrill individual, with dagger grasped between two fingers and a thumb, was " John Pinchback " or Pinchbeck; and appears here in History, with something like golden lustre, for one moment and no more. " Let us breakfast on them at Croydon," cries Pinchbeck, in a shrill, inspired manner; "and sup on them at London! " The hour was really ominous. But Philip Herbert, beautiful young man, himself of infirm temper and given to strokes, stood firmly dissuasive: he is in the King's service, how shall he answer it; he was himself to blame withal. And young Edward Sackville is, with his young friend Bruce of Kinloss, firmly dissuasive; it is the Bruce whom we saw at the chapel-door, stepping-out a new-made knight, now here with Sackville; dear friends these, not always to be friends! But for the present they are firmly dissuasive; all considerate persons are dissuasive. Pinchbeck's dagger brandishes itself in vain.

Sits the wind so, O Pinchbeck? Sidney's sister, Pembroke's mother: this is her son, and he stands a switch?—Yes, my shrill crookbacked friend, to avoid huge riot and calamity, he does so: and I see a massive nobleness in the man, which thou, egregious cock of bantam, wilt never in this world comprehend, but only crow over in thy shrill way. Ramsay and the Scots, and all persons, rode home unharmed that night; and my shrill friend gradually composed himself again. Philip Herbert may expect knighthoods, lordhoods, court-promotions: neither did his heroic mother " tear her hair," I think, to any great extent,—except in the imagination of Osborne, Pinchbeck and suchlike.

This was the scene of Croydon Races; a fact, and significant of many facts, that hangs-out for us like a cloud-island, and is not cloud.[1]

No. III

SIR THOMAS DUTTON AND SIR HATTON CHEEK

His Majesty, as I perceive in spite of calumnies, was not a " coward; " see how he behaved in the Gowrie Conspiracy and elsewhere. But he knew the value, to all persons, and to all interests of persons, of a whole skin; how unthrifty every-

---

[1] Francis Osborne's *Traditional Memorials on the Reign of James the First* (Reprinted in Sir Walter Scott's *History of the Court of James I.* Edinburgh, 1811), pp. 220-227.

where is any solution of continuity, if it can be avoided! He struggled to preside pacifically over an age of some ferocity much given to wrangling. Peace here, if possible; skins were not made for mere slitting and slashing! You that are for war, cannot you go abroad, and fight the Papist Spaniards? Over in the Netherlands there is always fighting enough. You that are of ruffling humour, gather your truculent ruffians together; make yourselves colonels over them; go to the Netherlands, and fight your bellyful!

Which accordingly many do, earning deathless war-laurels for the moment; and have done, and will continue doing, in those generations. Our gallant Veres, Earl of Oxford and the others, it has long been their way: gallant Cecil, to be called Earl of Wimbledon; gallant Sir John Burroughs, gallant Sir Hatton Cheek,—it is still their way. Deathless military renowns are gathered there in this manner; deathless for the moment. Did not Ben Jonson, in his young hard days, bear arms very manfully as a private soldado there? Ben, who now writes learned plays and court-masks as Poet Laureate, served manfully with pike and sword there for his groat a day with rations. And once when a Spanish soldier came strutting forward between the lines, flourishing his weapon, and defying all persons in general,—Ben stept forth, as I hear; [1] fenced that braggart Spaniard, since no other would do it; and ended by soon slitting him in two, and so silencing him! Ben's war-tuck, to judge by the flourish of his pen, must have had a very dangerous stroke in it.

"Swashbuckler age," we said; but the expression was incorrect, except as a figure. Bucklers went out fifty years ago, " about the twentieth of Queen Elizabeth; " men do not now swash with them, or fight in that way. Iron armour has mostly gone out, except in mere pictures of soldiers: King James said, It was an excellent invention; you could get no harm in it, and neither could you do any. Bucklers, either for horse or foot, are quite gone. Yet old Mr. Stowe, good chronicler, can recollect when every gentleman had his buckler: and at length every serving-man and City dandy. Smithfield,—still a waste field, full of puddles in wet weather, —was in those days full of buckler-duels, every Sunday and holiday in the dry season; and was called Ruffian's Rig, or some such name.

[1] *Life of Ben Jonson.*

A man, in those days, bought his buckler, of gilt leather and wood, at the haberdasher's; "hung it over his back, by a strap fastened to the pommel of his sword in front." Elegant men showed what taste, or sense of poetic beauty, was in them, by the fashion of their buckler. With Spanish beaver, with starched ruff, and elegant Spanish cloak, with elegant buckler hanging at his back, a man, if his moustachios and boots were in good order, stepped forth with some satisfaction. Full of strange oaths, and bearded like the pard; a decidedly truculent-looking figure. Jostle him in the street thoroughfares, accidentally splash his boots as you pass,—by Heaven, the buckler gets upon his arm, the sword flashes in his fist, with oaths enough; and you too being ready, there is a noise! Clink, clank, death and fury; all persons gathering round, and new quarrels springing from this one! And Dogberry comes up with the town-guard? And the shopkeepers hastily close their shops? Nay, it is hardly necessary, says Mr. Howe: these buckler-fights amount only to noise, for most part; the jingle of iron against tin and painted leather. Ruffling swashers strutting along, with big oaths and whiskers, delight to pick a quarrel; but the rule is, you do not thrust, you do not strike below the waist; and it was oftenest a dry duel—mere noise, as of working tinsmiths, with profane swearing! Empty vapouring bullyrooks and braggarts, they encumber the thoroughfares mainly. Dogberry and Verges ought to apprehend them. I have seen, in Smithfield on a dry holiday, "thirty of them on a side," fighting and hammering as if for life; and was not at the pains [1] to look at them, the blockheads; their noise as the mere beating of old kettles to me!

The truth is, serving-men themselves, and City apprentices, had got bucklers; and the duels, no death following, ceased to be sublime. About fifty years ago, serious men took to fighting with rapiers, and the buckler fell away. Holles in Sherwood, as we saw, fought with rapier, and he soon spoiled Markham. Rapier and dagger especially; that is a more silent duel, but a terribly serious one! Perhaps the reader will like to take a view of one such serious duel in those days, and therewith close this desultory chapter.

It was at the siege of Juliers, in the Netherlands wars, of

[1] Stowe's *Chronicle*, and Howe's *Continuation*, 1024, etc.

the year 1610;[1] we give the date, for wars are perpetual, or nearly so, in the Netherlands. At one of the storm-parties of the siege of Juliers, the gallant Sir Hatton Cheek, above alluded to, a superior officer of the English force which fights there under my Lord Cecil, that shall be Wimbledon; the gallant Sir Hatton, I say, being of hot temper, superior officer, and the service a storm-party on some bastion or demilune, speaks sharp word of command to Sir Thomas Dutton, the officer under him, who also is probably of hot temper in this hot moment. Sharp word of command to Dutton; and the movement not proceeding rightly, sharp word of rebuke. To which Dutton, with kindled voice, answers something sharp; is answered still more sharply with voice high-flaming;— whereat Dutton suddenly holds in; says merely, "He is under military duty here, but perhaps will not always be so;" and rushing forward, does his order silently, the best he can. His order done, Dutton straightway lays down his commission; packs up, that night, and returns to England.

Sir Hatton Cheek prosecutes his work at the siege of Juliers; gallantly assists at the taking of Juliers, triumphant over all the bastions and half-moons there; but hears withal that Dutton is, at home in England, defaming him as a choleric tyrant and so forth. Dreadful news; which brings some biliary attack on the gallant man, and reduces him to a bed of sickness. Hardly recovered, he despatches message to Dutton, That he will request to have the pleasure of his company, with arms and seconds ready, on some neutral ground,—Calais sands for instance,—at an early day, if convenient. Convenient; yes, as dinner to the hungry! answers Dutton; and time, place and circumstances are rapidly enough agreed upon.

And so, on Calais sands, in a winter morning of the year 1610, this is what we see, most authentically, through the

[1] Siege began in the latter end of July 1610; ended victoriously, 4th September following: principal assaults were, 10th August and 14th August; in one of which this affair of ours must have taken rise. Siege commanded by Christian of Anhalt, a famed Protestant Captain of those times. Henri IV. of France was assassinated while setting-out for this siege; Prince Maurice of Nassau was there; "Dutch troops, French, English and German" (Brandenburgers and Pfalz-Neuburgers chiefly, *versus* Kaiser Rodolf II. and his unjust seizure of the Town) "fought with the greatest unity." Prelude to the Thirty-Years' War, and one of the principal sources of it, this Controversy about Juliers. (Carl Friedrich Pauli: *Allgemeine Preussische Staats-Geschichte*, 4to, Halle, 1762 iii. 502-527.)

lapse of dim Time. Two gentlemen stript to the shirt and waistband; in the two hands of each a rapier and dagger clutched; their looks sufficiently serious! The seconds, having stript, equipt, and fairly overhauled and certified them, are just about retiring from the measured fate-circle, not without indignation that *they* are forbidden to fight. Two gentlemen in this alarming posture; of whom the Universe knows, has known, and will know nothing, except that they were of choleric humour, and assisted in the Netherlands wars! They are evidently English human creatures, in the height of silent fury, and measured circuit of fate; whom we here audibly name once more, Sir Hatton Cheek, Sir Thomas Dutton, knights both, soldadoes both. Ill-fated English human creatures, what horrible confusion of the Pit is this?

Dutton, though in suppressed rage, the seconds about to withdraw, will explain some things if a word were granted. "No words," says the other; "stand on your guard!" brandishing his rapier, grasping harder his dagger. Dutton, now silent too, is on his guard. Good Heavens: after some brief flourishing and flashing,—the gleam of the swift clear steel playing madly in one's eyes,—they, at the first pass, plunge home on one another; home, with beak and claws; home to the very heart! Cheek's rapier is through Dutton's throat from before, and his dagger is through it from behind,—the windpipe miraculously missed; and, in the same instant, Dutton's rapier is through Cheek's body from before, his dagger through his back from behind,—lungs and life *not* missed; and the seconds have to advance, "pull out the four bloody weapons," disengage that hell-embrace of theirs. This is serious enough! Cheek reels, his life fast flowing; but still rushes rabid on Dutton, who merely parries, skips; till Cheek reels down, dead in his rage. "He had a bloody burial there that morning," says my ancient friend.[1] He will assist no more in the Netherlands or other wars.

Such scene does History disclose, as in sunbeams, as in blazing hell-fire, on Calais sands, in the raw winter morning; then drops the blanket of centuries, of everlasting Night, over it, and passes on elsewhither. Gallant Sir Hatton Cheek lies buried there, and Cecil of Wimbledon, son of Burleigh, will have to seek another superior officer. What became of the living Dutton afterwards, I have never to this moment had the least hint.

[1] Wilson (in Kennet), ii. 684.

CORN-LAW RHYMES [1]

[1832]

SMELFUNGUS REDIVIVUS, throwing down his critical assaying balance some years ago, and taking leave of the Belles-Lettres function, expressed himself in this abrupt way: "The end having come, it is fit that we end. Poetry having ceased to be read, or published, or written, how can it continue to be reviewed? With your Lake Schools, and Border-Thief Schools, and Cockney and Satanic Schools, there has been enough to do; and now, all these Schools having burnt or smouldered themselves out, and left nothing but a wide-spread wreck of ashes, dust and cinders,—or perhaps dying embers, kicked to and fro under the feet of innumerable women and children in the Magazines, and at best blown here and there into transient sputters, with vapour enough, so as to form what you might name a boundless Green-sick, or New-Sentimental, or Sleep-Awake School,—what remains but to adjust ourselves to circumstances? Urge me not," continues the able Editor, suddenly changing his figure, "with considerations that Poetry, as the inward voice of Life, must be perennial, only dead in one form to become alive in another; that this still abundant deluge of Metre, seeing there must needs be fractions of Poetry floating scattered in it, ought still to be net-fished, at all events surveyed and taken note of: the survey of English Metre, at this epoch, perhaps transcends the human faculties; to hire-out the reading of it, by estimate, at a remunerative rate per page, would, in few Quarters, reduce the cash-box of any extant Review to the verge of insolvency."

What our distinguished contemporary has said remains said. Far be it from us to censure or counsel any able

---

[1] *Edinburgh Review*, No. 110. — 1. "Corn-Law Rhymes." Third Edition. 8vo. London, 1831.
2. "Love ; a Poem." By the Author of "Corn-Law Rhymes." Third Edition. 8vo. London, 1831.
3. "The Village Patriarch ; a Poem." By the Author of "Corn-Law Rhymes." 12mo. London, 1831.

Editor; to draw aside the Editorial veil, and, officiously prying into his interior mysteries, impugn the laws he walks by! For Editors, as for others, there are times of perplexity, wherein the cunning of the wisest will scantily suffice his own wants, to say nothing of his neighbour's.

To us, on our side, meanwhile, it remains clear that Poetry, or were it but Metre, should nowise be altogether neglected. Surely it is the Reviewer's trade to sit watching not only the tillage, crop-rotation, marketings and good or evil husbandry of the Economic Earth, but also the weather-symptoms of the Literary Heaven, on which those former so much depend: if any promising or threatening meteoric phenomenon make its appearance, and he proclaim not tidings thereof, it is at his peril. Farther, be it considered how, in this singular poetic epoch, a small matter constitutes a novelty. If the whole welkin hang overcast in drizzly dinginess, the feeblest light-gleam, or speck of blue, cannot pass unheeded.

The Works of this Corn-Law Rhymer we might liken rather to some little fraction of a rainbow: hues of joy and harmony, painted out of troublous tears. No round full bow, indeed; gloriously spanning the heavens; shone on by the full sun; and, with seven-striped, gold-crimson border (as is in some sort the office of Poetry) dividing Black from Brilliant: not such; alas, still far from it! Yet, in very truth, a little prismatic blush, glowing genuine among the wet clouds; which proceeds, if you will, from a sun cloud-hidden, yet indicates that a sun does shine, and above those vapours, a whole azure vault and celestial firmament stretch serene.

Strange as it may seem, it is nevertheless true, that here we have once more got sight of a Book calling itself Poetry, yet which actually is a kind of Book, and no empty paste-board Case, and simulacrum or " ghost-defunct " of a Book, such as is too often palmed on the world, and handed over Booksellers' counters, with a demand of real money for it, as if it too were a reality. The speaker here is of that singular class who have something to say; whereby, though delivering himself in verse, and in these days, he does not deliver himself wholly in jargon, but articulately, and with a certain degree of meaning, that has been *believed*, and therefore is again believable.

To some the wonder and interest will be heightened by another circumstance: that the speaker in question is not

school-learned, or even furnished with pecuniary capital;
is, indeed, a quite unmoneyed, russet-coated speaker; nothing
or little other than a Sheffield worker in brass and iron, who
describes himself as "one of the lower, little removed above
the lowest class." Be of what class he may, the man is
provided, as we can perceive, with a rational god-created
soul; which too has fashioned itself into some clearness,
some self-subsistence, and can actually see and know with
its own organs; and in rugged substantial English, nay with
tones of poetic melody, utter forth what it has seen.

It used to be said that lions do not paint, that poor men
do not write; but the case is altering now. Here is a voice
coming from the deep Cyclopean forges, where Labour, in
real soot and sweat, beats with his thousand hammers "the
red son of the furnace;" doing personal battle with Necessity,
and her dark brute Powers, to make them reasonable and
serviceable; an intelligible voice from the hitherto Mute and
Irrational, to tell us at first-hand how it is with him, what in
very deed is the theorem of the world and of himself, which
he, in those dim depths of his, in that wearied head of his,
has put together. To which voice, in several respects
significant enough, let good ear be given.

Here too be it premised, that nowise under the category
of "Uneducated Poets," or in any fashion of dilettante
patronage, can our Sheffield friend be produced. His position
is unsuitable for that: so is ours. Genius, which the French
lady declared to be of no sex, is much more certainly of no
rank; neither when "the spark of Nature's fire" has been
imparted, should Education take high airs in her artificial
light,—which is too often but phosphorescence and putrescence. In fact, it now begins to be suspected here and there,
that this same aristocratic recognition, which looks down
with an obliging smile from its throne, of bound Volumes and
gold Ingots, and admits that it is wonderfully well for one of
the uneducated classes, may be getting out of place. There
are unhappy times in the world's history, when he that is the
least educated will chiefly have to say that he is the least perverted; and with the multitude of false eye-glasses, convex,
concave, green, even yellow, has not lost the natural use of
his eyes. For a generation that reads Cobbett's Prose, and
Burns's Poetry, it need be no miracle that here also is a man
who can handle both pen and hammer like a man.

Nevertheless, this serene-highness attitude and temper is so frequent, perhaps it were good to turn the tables for a moment, and see what look it has under that reverse aspect. How were it if we surmised, that for a man gifted with natural vigour, with a man's character to be developed in him, more especially if in the way of Literature, as Thinker and Writer, it is actually, in these strange days, no special misfortune to be trained up among the Uneducated classes, and not among the Educated; but rather of two misfortunes the smaller?

For all men, doubtless, obstructions abound; spiritual growth must be hampered and stunted, and has to struggle through with difficulty, if it do not wholly stop. We may grant, too, that, for a mediocre character, the continual training and tutoring, from language-masters, dancing-masters, posture-masters of all sorts, hired and volunteer, which a high rank in any time and country assures, there will be produced a certain superiority, or at worst, air of superiority, over the corresponding mediocre character of low rank: thus we perceive the vulgar Do-nothing, as contrasted with the vulgar Drudge, is in general a much prettier man; with a wider, perhaps clearer outlook into the distance; in innumerable superficial matters, however it may be when we go deeper, he has a manifest advantage. But with the man of uncommon character, again, in whom a germ of irrepressible Force has been implanted, and *will* unfold itself into some sort of freedom, altogether the reverse may hold. For such germs too, there is, undoubtedly enough, a proper soil where they will grow best, and an improper one where they will grow worst. True also, where there is a will, there is a way; where a genius has been given, a possibility, a certainty of its growing is also given. Yet often it seems as if the injudicious gardening and manuring were worse than none at all; and killed what the inclemencies of blind chance would have spared. We find accordingly that few Fredericks or Napoleons, indeed none since the Great Alexander, who unfortunately drank himself to death too soon for proving what lay in him, were nursed up with an eye to their vocation: mostly with an eye quite the other way, in the midst of isolation and pain, destitution and contradiction. Nay in our own times, have we not seen two men of genius, a Byron and a Burns; they both, by mandate of Nature, struggle and must struggle towards clear Manhood, stormfully enough, for the space of six-and-thirty years; yet only the gifted Ploughman can partially prevail therein: the gifted Peer must toil and strive, and shoot-out in wild efforts, yet die at last in Boyhood, with the promise of his Manhood still but announcing itself in the distance. Truly, as was once written, "it is only the artichoke that will not grow except in gardens; the acorn is cast carelessly abroad into the wilderness, yet on the wild soil it nourishes itself, and rises to be an oak." All woodmen, moreover, will tell you that fat manure is the ruin of your oak; likewise that the thinner and wilder your soil, the tougher, more iron-textured is your timber,—though unhappily also the smaller. So too with the spirits of men: they become pure from their errors by suffering for them; he who has battled, were it only with Poverty and hard toil, will be found stronger, more expert, than he who could stay at home from the battle, concealed among the Provision-waggons, or even not unwatchfully "abiding by the stuff." In which sense, an observer, not without experience of our time, has said: Had I a man of clearly developed character (clear, sincere within its limits), of insight, courage and real applicable force of head and of heart, to search for; and not a man of luxuriously distorted character, with haughtiness for courage, and for insight and applicable force, speculation and plausible show of force,—it were rather among the lower than among the higher classes that I should look for him.

A hard saying, indeed, seems this same: that he, whose other wants were all beforehand supplied; to whose capabilities no problem was presented except even this, How to cultivate them to best advantage, should attain less real culture than he whose first grand problem and obligation was nowise spiritual culture, but hard labour for his daily bread! Sad enough must the perversion be, where preparations of such magnitude issue in abortion; and so sumptuous an Art with all its appliances can accomplish nothing, not so much as necessitous Nature would of herself have supplied! Nevertheless, so pregnant is Life with evil as with good; to such height in an age rich, plethorically overgrown with means, can means be accumulated in the wrong place, and immeasurably aggravate wrong tendencies, instead of righting them, this sad and strange result may actually turn out to have been realised.

But what, after all, is meant by *uneducated*, in a time when Books have come into the world; come to be household furniture in every habitation of the civilised world? In the poorest cottage are Books; is one Book, wherein for several thousands of years the spirit of man has found light, and nourishment, and an interpreting response to whatever is Deepest in him; wherein still, to this day, for the eye that will look well, the Mystery of Existence reflects itself, if not resolved, yet revealed, and prophetically emblemed; if not to the satisfying of the outward sense, yet to the opening of the inward sense, which is the far grander result. " In Books lie the creative phœnix-ashes of the whole Past." All that men have devised, discovered, done, felt or imagined, lies recorded in Books; wherein whoso has learned the mystery of spelling printed letters may find it, and appropriate it.

Nay, what indeed is all this? As if it were by universities and libraries and lecture-rooms, that man's Education, what we can call Education, were accomplished; solely, or mainly, by instilling the dead letter and record of other men's Force, that the living Force of a new man were to be awakened, enkindled and purified into victorious clearness! Foolish Pedant, that sittest there compassionately descanting on the Learning of Shakspeare! Shakspeare had penetrated into innumerable things; far into Nature with her divine Splendours and infernal Terrors, her Ariel Melodies, and mystic mandragora Moans; far into man's workings with Nature, into man's Art and Artifice; Shakspeare knew (*kenned*, which in those days still partially meant *can-ned*) innumerable things; what men are, and what the world is, and how and what men aim at there, from the Dame Quickly of modern Eastcheap to the Cæsar of ancient Rome, over many countries, over many centuries: of all this he had the clearest understanding and constructive comprehension; all this was his Learning and Insight; what now is thine? Insight into none of those things; perhaps, strictly considered, into no thing whatever: solely into thy own sheepskin diplomas, fat academic honours, into vocables and alphabetic letters, and but a little way into these!—The grand result of schooling is a mind with just vision to discern, with free force to do: the grand schoolmaster is Practice.

And now, when *kenning* and *can-ning* have become two altogether different words; and this, the first principle of human culture, the foundation-stone of all but false imaginary culture, that men must, before every other thing, be trained to *do* somewhat, has been, for some generations, laid quietly on the shelf, with such result as we see,—consider what advantage those same uneducated Working classes have over the educated Unworking classes, in one particular; herein, namely, that they must *work*. To work! What incalculable sources of cultivation lie in that process, in that attempt; how it lays hold of the whole man, not of a small theoretical calculating fraction of him, but of the whole practical, doing and daring and enduring man; thereby to awaken dormant faculties, root-out old errors, at every step! He that has done nothing has known nothing. Vain is it to sit scheming and plausibly discoursing: up and be doing! If thy knowledge be real, put it forth from thee: grapple with real Nature; try thy theories there, and see how they hold out. *Do* one thing, for the first time in thy life do a thing; a new light will rise to thee on the doing of all things whatsoever. Truly, a boundless significance lies in work; whereby the humblest craftsman comes to attain much, which is of indispensable use, but which he who is of no craft, were he never so high, runs the risk of missing. Once turn to Practice, Error and Truth will no longer consort together: the result of Error involves you in the square-root of a negative quantity; try to *extract* that, to extract any earthly substance or sustenance from that! The honourable Member can discover that " there is a reaction," and believe it, and wearisomely reason on it, in spite of all men, while he so pleases, for still his wine and his oil will not fail him: but the sooty Brazier, who discovered that brass was green-cheese, has to act on his discovery; finds therefore, that, singular as it may seem, brass cannot be masticated for dinner, green-cheese will not beat into fire-proof dishes; that such discovery, therefore, has no legs to stand on, and must even be let fall. Now, take this principle of difference through the entire lives of two men, and calculate what it will amount to! Necessity, moreover, which we here see as the mother of Accuracy, is well known as the mother of Invention. He who wants everything must know many things, do many things, to procure even a few: different enough with him, whose indispensable knowledge is this only, that a finger will pull the bell!

So that, for all men who live, we may conclude, this Life of Man is a school, wherein the naturally foolish will continue foolish though you bray him in a mortar, but the naturally wise will gather wisdom under every disadvantage. What, meanwhile, must be the condition of an Era, when the highest advantages there become perverted into drawbacks; when, if you take two men of genius, and put the one between the handles of a plough, and mount the other between the painted coronets of a coach-and-four, and bid them both move along, the former shall arrive a Burns, the latter a Byron: two men of talent, and put the one into a Printer's chapel, full of lamp-black, tyrannous usage, hard toil, and the other into Oxford universities, with lexicons and libraries, and hired expositors and sumptuous endowments, the former shall come out a Dr. Franklin, the latter a Dr. Parr!—

However, we are not here to write an Essay on Education, or sing *misereres* over a " world in its dotage; " but simply to say that our Corn-Law Rhymer, educated or uneducated as Nature and Art have made him, asks not the smallest patronage or compassion for his rhymes, professes not the smallest contrition for them. Nowise in such attitude does he present himself; not supplicatory, deprecatory, but sturdy, defiant, almost menacing. Wherefore, indeed, should he supplicate or deprecate? It is out of the abundance of the heart that he has spoken: praise or blame cannot make it truer or falser than it already is. By the grace of God this man is sufficient for himself; by his skill in metallurgy can beat out a toilsome but a manful living, go how it may; has arrived too at that singular audacity of believing what he knows, and acting on it, or writing on it, or thinking on it, without leave asked of any one: there shall he stand, and work, with head and with hand, for himself and the world; blown about by no wind of doctrine; frightened at no Reviewer's shadow; having, in his time, looked substances enough in the face, and remained unfrightened.

What is left, therefore, but to take what he brings, and as he brings it? Let us be thankful, were it only for the day of small things. Something it is that we have lived to welcome once more a sweet Singer wearing the likeness of a Man. In humble guise, it is true, and of stature more or less marred in its development; yet not without a genial robustness, strength and valour built on honesty and love; on the whole, a genuine man, with somewhat of the eye and speech and bearing that beseems a man. To whom all other genuine men, how different soever in subordinate particulars, can gladly hold out the right hand of fellowship.

The great excellence of our Rhymer, be it understood, then, we take to consist even in this, often hinted at already, that he is *genuine*. Here is an earnest truth-speaking man; no theoriser, sentimentaliser, but a practical man of work and endeavour, man of sufferance and endurance. The thing that he speaks is not a hearsay, but a thing which he has himself known, and by experience become assured of. He has used his eyes for seeing; uses his tongue for declaring what he has seen. His voice, therefore, among the many noises of our Planet, will deserve its place better than the most; will be well worth some attention. Whom else should we attend to but such? The man who speaks with some half shadow of a Belief, and supposes, and inclines to think; and considers not with undivided soul, what is true, but only what is plausible, and will find audience and recompense: do we not meet him at every street-turning, on all highways and byways; is he not stale, unprofitable, ineffectual, wholly grown a weariness of the flesh? So rare is his opposite in any rank of Literature or of Life, so very rare, that even in the lowest he is precious. The authentic insight and experience of any human soul, were it but insight and experience in hewing of wood and drawing of water, is real knowledge, a real possession and acquirement, how small soever: *palabra*, again, were it a supreme pontiff's, is wind merely, and nothing, or less than nothing. To a considerable degree, this man, we say, has worked himself loose from cant and conjectural halfness, idle pretences and hallucinations, into a condition of Sincerity. Wherein, perhaps, as above argued, his hard social environment, and fortune to be " a workman born," which brought so many other retardations with it, may have forwarded and accelerated him.

That a man, Workman or Idleman, encompassed, as in these days, with persons in a state of willing or unwilling Insincerity, and necessitated, as man is, to learn whatever he does traditionally learn by *imitating* these, should nevertheless shake off Insincerity, and struggle out from that dim pestiferous marsh-atmosphere, into a clearer and purer height,—betokens in him a certain Originality; in which rare gift, force of all kinds is presupposed. To our Rhymer, accordingly, as hinted more than once, vision and determination have not been denied: a rugged, homegrown understanding is in him; whereby, in his own way, he has mastered this and that, and looked into various things, in general honestly and to purpose, sometimes deeply, piercingly and with a Seer's eye. Strong thoughts are not wanting, beautiful thoughts; strong and beautiful expressions of thought. As traceable, for instance, in this new illustration of an old argument, the mischief of Commercial Restrictions:

> These, O ye quacks, these are your remedies:
> Alms for the Rich, a bread-tax for the Poor!
> Soul-purchased harvests on the indigent moor!—
> Thus the winged victor of a hundred fights,
> The warrior Ship, bows low her banner'd head,
> When through her planks the seaborn reptile bites
> Its deadly way;—and sinks in Ocean's bed,
> Vanquish'd by worms. What then? The worms were fed.
> Will not God smite thee back, thou whited wall?
> Thy life is lawless, and thy law a lie,
> Or Nature is a dream unnatural:
> Look on the clouds, the streams, the earth, the sky;
> Lo, all is interchange and harmony!
> Where is the gorgeous pomp which, yester morn,
> Curtained yon Orb with amber, fold on fold?
> Behold it in the blue of Rivelin, borne
> To feed the all-feeding sea! The molten gold
> Is flowing pale in Loxley's waters cold,
> To kindle into beauty tree and flower,
> And wake to verdant life hill, vale and plain.
> Cloud trades with river, and exchange is power:
> But should the clouds, the streams, the winds disdain
> Harmonious intercourse, nor dew nor rain
> Would forest-crown the mountains: airless day
> Would blast on Kinderscout the heathy glow;
> No purply green would meeken into gray
> O'er Don at eve; no sound of river's flow
> Disturb the Sepulchre of all below.

Nature and the doings of men have not passed by this man unheeded, like the endless cloud-rack in dull weather; or lightly heeded, like a theatric phantasmagoria; but earnestly inquired into, like a thing of reality; reverently loved and worshipped, as a thing with divine significance in its reality, glimpses of which divineness he has caught and laid to heart. For his vision, as was said, partakes of the genuinely Poetical;

he is not a Rhymer and Speaker only, but, in some genuine sense, something of a Poet.

Farther, we must admit him, what indeed is already herein admitted, to be, if clear-sighted, also brave-hearted. A troublous element is his; a Life of painfulness, toil, insecurity, scarcity; yet he fronts it like a man; yields not to it, tames it into some subjection, some order; its wild fearful dinning and tumult, as of a devouring Chaos, becomes a sort of wild war-music for him; wherein too are passages of beauty, of melodious melting softness, of lightness and briskness, even of joy. The stout heart is also a warm and kind one; Affection dwells with Danger, all the holier and the lovelier for such stern environment. A working man is this; yet, as we said, a man: in his sort, a courageous, much-loving, faithfully enduring and endeavouring man.

What such a one, so gifted and so placed, shall say to a Time like ours; how he will fashion himself into peace, or war, or armed neutrality, with the world and his fellow-men; and work out his course in joy and grief, in victory and defeat, is a question worth asking: which in these three little Volumes partly receives answer. He has turned, as all thinkers up to a very high and rare order in these days must do, into Politics; is a Reformer, at least a stern Complainer, Radical to the core: his poetic melody takes an elegiaco-tragical character; much of him is converted into hostility, and grim, hardly-suppressed indignation, such as right long denied, hope long deferred, may awaken in the kindliest heart. Not yet as a rebel against anything does he stand; but as a free man, and the spokesman of free men, not far from rebelling against much; with sorrowful appealing dew, yet also with incipient lightning, in his eyes; whom it were not desirable to provoke into rebellion. He says in Vulcanic dialect, his feelings have been *hammered* till they are *cold-short ;* so they will no longer bend; " they snap, and fly off,"—in the face of the hammerer. Not unnatural, though lamentable! Nevertheless, under all disguises of the Radical, the Poet is still recognisable: a certain music breathes through all dissonances, as the prophecy and ground-tone of returning harmony; the man, as we said, is of a poetical nature.

To his Political Philosophy there is perhaps no great importance attachable. He feels, as all men that live must do, the disorganisation, and hard-grinding, unequal pressure of our Social Affairs; but sees into it only a very little farther than far inferior men do. The frightful condition of a Time, when public and private Principle, as the word was once understood, having gone out of sight, and Self-interest being left to plot, and struggle, and scramble, as it could and would, Difficulties had accumulated till they were no longer to be borne, and the spirit that should have fronted and conquered them seemed to have forsaken the world;—when the Rich, as the utmost they could resolve on, had ceased to govern, and the Poor, in their fast-accumulating numbers, and ever-widening complexities, had ceased to be able to do without governing; and now the plan of " Competition " and " *Laissez-faire* " was, on every side, approaching its consummation; and each, bound-up in the circle of his own wants and perils, stood grimly distrustful of his neighbour, and the distracted Common-weal was a Common-woe, and to all men it became apparent that the end was drawing nigh:—all this black aspect of Ruin and Decay, visible enough, experimentally known to our Sheffield friend, he calls by the name of " Corn-Law," and expects to be in good part delivered from, were the accursed Bread-tax repealed.

In this system of political Doctrine, even as here so emphatically set forth, there is not much of novelty. Radicals we have many; loud enough on this and other grievances; the removal of which is to be the one thing needful. The deep, wide flood of bitterness, and hope becoming hopeless, lies acrid, corrosive in every bosom; and flows fiercely enough through any orifice Accident may open: through Law-Reform, Legislative Reform, Poor-Laws, want of Poor-Laws, Tithes, Game-Laws, or, as we see here, Corn-Laws. Whereby indeed only this becomes clear, that a deep wide flood of evil does exist and corrode; from which, in all ways, blindly and seeingly, men seek deliverance, and cannot rest till they find it; least of all till they know what part and proportion of it is to *be* found. But with us foolish sons of Adam this is ever the way: some evil that lies nearest us, be it a chronic sickness, or but a smoky chimney, is ever the acme and sum-total of all evil; the black hydra that shuts us out from a Promised Land; and so, in poor Mr. Shandy's fashion, must we " shift from trouble to trouble, and from side to side; button-up one cause of vexation, and unbutton another."

Thus for our keen-hearted singer, and sufferer, has the

" Bread-tax," in itself a considerable but no immeasurable
smoke-pillar, swoln out to be a world-embracing Darkness,
that darkens and suffocates the whole earth, and has blotted
out the heavenly stars. Into the merit of the Corn-Laws,
which has often been discussed, in fit season, by competent
hands, we do not enter here; least of all in the way of argument, in the way of blame, towards one who, if he read such
merit with some emphasis " on the scantier trenchers of his
children," may well be pardoned. That the " Bread-tax,"
with various other taxes, may ere long be altered and abrogated, and the Corn-Trade become as free as the poorest
" bread-taxed drudge " could wish it, or the richest " satrap
bread-tax-fed " could fear it, seems no extravagant hypothesis: would that the mad Time could, by such simple
hellebore-dose, be healed! Alas for the diseases of a world
lying in wickedness, in heart-sickness and atrophy, quite
another alcahest is needed;—a long, painful course of medicine and regimen, surgery and physic, not yet specified or
indicated in the Royal-College Books!

But if there is little novelty in our friend's Political Philosophy, there is some in his political Feeling and Poetry. The
peculiarity of this Radical is, that with all his stormful de-
structiveness he combines a decided loyalty and faith. If he
despise and trample under foot on the one hand, he exalts
and reverences on the other; the " landed pauper in his
coach-and-four " rolls all the more glaringly, contrasted with
the " Rockinghams and Savilles " of the past, with the
" Lansdowns and Fitzwilliams," many a " Wentworth's
lord," still " a blessing " to the present. This man, indeed,
has in him the root of all reverence,—a principle of Religion.
He believes in a Godhead, not with the lips only, but apparently with the heart; who, as has been written, and often
felt, " reveals Himself in Parents, in all true Teachers and
Rulers,"—as in false Teachers and Rulers quite Another
may be revealed! Our Rhymer, it would seem, is no Metho-
dist: far enough from it. He makes " the Ranter," in his
hot-headed way, exclaim over

The Hundred Popes of England's Jesuistry;

and adds, by way of note, in his own person, some still
stronger sayings: How " this baneful corporation, dismal as
its Reign of Terror is, and long-armed its Holy Inquisition,

must condescend to learn and teach what is useful, or go where all nuisances go." As little perhaps is he a Church-man; the "Cadi-Dervish" seems nowise to his mind. Scarcely, however, if at all, does he show aversion to the Church as Church; or, among his many griefs, touch upon Tithes as one. But, in any case, the black colours of Life, even as here painted, and brooded over, do not hide from him that a God is the Author and Sustainer thereof; that God's world, if made a House of Imprisonment, can also be a House of Prayer; wherein for the weary and heavy-laden pity and hope are not altogether cut away.

It is chiefly in virtue of this inward temper of heart, with the clear disposition and adjustment which for all else results therefrom, that our Radical attains to be Poetical; that the harsh groanings, contentions, upbraidings, of one who unhappily has felt constrained to adopt such mode of utter-ance, become ennobled into something of music. If a land of bondage, this is still his Father's land, and the bondage endures not forever. As worshipper and believer, the captive can look with seeing eye: the aspect of the Infinite Universe still fills him with an Infinite feeling; his chains, were it but for moments, fall away; he soars free aloft, and the sunny regions of Poesy and Freedom gleam golden afar on the widened horizon. Gleamings we say, prophetic dawnings from those far regions, spring up for him; nay, beams of actual radiance. In his ruggedness, and dim contractedness (rather of place than of organ), he is not without touches of a feeling and vision, which, even in the stricter sense, is to be named poetical.

One deeply poetical idea, above all others, seems to have taken hold of him: the idea of TIME. As was natural to a poetic soul, with few objects of Art in its environment, and driven inward, rather than invited outward, for occupation. This deep mystery of ever-flowing Time; bringing forth, and as the Ancients wisely fabled, devouring what it has brought forth; rushing on, *in* us, yet above us, all uncontrol-lable by us; and under it, dimly visible athwart it, the bottomless Eternal;—this is, indeed, what we may call the primary idea of Poetry; the first that introduces itself into the poetic mind. As here:

> The bee shall seek to settle on his hand,
> But from the vacant bench haste to the moor,

Mourning the last of England's high-soul'd Poor,
And bid the mountains weep for Enoch Wray.
And for themselves,—albeit of things that last
Unalter'd most; for they shall pass away
Like Enoch, though their iron roots seem fast,
Bound to the eternal future as the past:
The Patriarch died; and they shall be no more!
Yes, and the sailless worlds, which navigate
The unutterable Deep that hath no shore,
Will lose their starry splendour soon or late,
Like tapers, quench'd by Him, whose will is fate!
Yes, and the Angel of Eternity,
Who numbers worlds and writes their names in light,
One day, O Earth, will look in vain for thee,
And start and stop in his unerring flight,
And with his wings of sorrow and affright
Veil his impassion'd brow and heavenly tears!

And not the first idea only, but the greatest, properly the parent of all others. For if it can rise in the remotest ages, in the rudest states of culture, wherever an " inspired thinker " happens to exist, it connects itself still with all great things; with the highest results of new Philosophy, as of primeval Theology; and for the Poet, in particular, is as the life-element, wherein alone his conceptions can take poetic form and the whole world become miraculous and magical.

> We *are such stuff*
> As Dreams are made of: and our little life
> Is rounded with a Sleep!

Figure that, believe that, O Reader; then say whether the *Arabian Tales* seem wonderful!—" Rounded with a sleep (*mit Schlaf umgeben*)! " says Jean Paul; " these three words created whole volumes in me."

To turn now on our worthy Rhymer, who has brought us so much, and stingily insist on his errors and shortcomings, were no honest procedure. We should have the whole poetical encyclopædia to draw upon, and say commodiously, such and such an item is *not* here; of which encyclopædia the highest genius can fill but a portion. With much merit, far from common in his time, he is not without something of the faults of his time. We praised him for originality; yet is there a certain remainder of imitation in him; a tang of the Circulating Libraries; as in Sancho's wine, with its key and thong, there was a tang of iron and leather. To be reminded of Crabbe, with his truthful severity of style, in such a place, we cannot object; but what if there were a slight bravura dash of the fair tuneful Hemans? Still more, what have we to do with Byron, and his fierce vociferous mouthings, whether " passionate," or not passionate and only theatrical? King Cambyses' vein is, after all, but a worthless one; no vein for a wise man. Strength, if that be the thing aimed at, does not manifest itself in spasms, but in stout bearing of burdens. Our Author says, " It is too bad to exalt into a hero the coxcomb who would have gone into hysterics if a tailor had laughed at him." Walk not in his footsteps, then, we say, whether as hero or as singer; repent a little, for example, over somewhat in that fuliginous, blue-flaming, pitch-and-sulphur " Dream of Enoch Wray," and write the next otherwise.

We mean no imitation in a bad palpable sense; only that there is a tone of such occasionally audible, which ought to be removed;—of which, in any case, we make not much. Imitation is a leaning on something foreign; incompleteness of individual development, defect of free utterance. From the same source spring most of our Author's faults; in particular, his worst, which, after all, is intrinsically a defect of manner. He has little or no Humour. Without Humour of character he cannot well be; but it has not yet got to utterance. Thus, where he has mean things to deal with, he knows not how to deal with them; oftenest deals with them more or less meanly. In his vituperative prose Notes, he seems embarrassed; and but ill hides his embarrassment, under an air of predetermined sarcasm, of knowing briskness, almost of vulgar pertness. He says, he cannot help it; he is poor, hard-worked, and " soot is soot." True, indeed; yet there is no connexion between Poverty and Discourtesy; which latter originates in Dulness alone. Courtesy is the due of man to man; not of suit-of-clothes to suit-of-clothes. He who could master so many things, and make even Corn-Laws rhyme, we require of him this farther thing: a bearing worthy of himself, and of the order he belongs to,—the highest and most ancient of all orders, that of Manhood. A pert snappishness is no manner for a brave man; and then the manner so soon influences the matter: a far worse result. Let him speak wise things, and speak them wisely; which latter may be done in many dialects, grave and gay, only in the snappish dialect seldom or never.

The truth is, as might have been expected, there is still much lying in him to be developed; the hope of which development it were rather sad to abandon. Why, for example, should not his view of the world, his knowledge of what is and has been in the world, indefinitely extend itself? Were he merely the " uneducated Poet," we should say, he had read largely; as he is not such, we say, Read still more, much more largely. Books enough there are in England, and of quite another weight and worth than that circulating-library sort; may be procured too, may be read, even by a hard-worked man; for what man (either in God's service or the Devil's, as himself chooses it) is not hard-worked? But here again, where there is a will there is a way. True, our friend is no longer in his teens; yet still, as would seem, in the vigour of his years: we hope too that his mind is not finally shut-in, but of the improvable and enlargeable sort. If Alfieri (also kept busy enough, with horse-breaking and what not) learned Greek after he was fifty, why is the Corn-Law Rhymer too old to learn?

However, be in the future what there may, our Rhymer has already done what was much more difficult, and better than reading printed books;—looked into the great prophetic manuscript Book of Existence, and read little passages there. Here, for example, is a sentence tolerably spelled:

> Where toils the Mill by ancient woods embraced,
> Hark, how the cold steel screams in hissing fire!
> Blind Enoch sees the Grinder's wheel no more,
> Couch'd beneath rocks and forests, that admire
> Their beauty in the waters, ere they roar
> Dash'd in white foam the swift circumference o'er.
> There draws the Grinder his laborious breath;
> There coughing at his deadly trade he bends:
> Born to die young, he fears nor man nor death;
> Scorning the future, what he earns he spends;
> Debauch and riot are his bosom friends.
>
> .   .   .   .   .
>
> Behold his failings! Hath he virtues too?
> He is no Pauper, blackguard though he be:
> Full well he knows what minds combined can do.
> Full well maintains his birthright: he is free,
> And, frown for frown, outstares monopoly.
> Yet Abraham and Elliot both in vain

> Bid science on his cheek prolong the bloom:
> He *will* not live!   He seems in haste to gain
> The undisturb'd asylum of the tomb,
> And, old at two-and-thirty, meets his doom!

Or this, " of Jem, the rogue avowed,"

> Whose trade is Poaching!   Honest Jem works not,
> Begs not, but thrives by plundering beggars here.
> Wise as a lord, and quite as good a shot,
> He, like his betters, lives in hate and fear,
> And feeds on partridge because bread is dear.
> Sire of six sons apprenticed to the jail,
> He prowls in arms, the Tory of the night;
> With them he shares his battles and his ale,
> With him they feel the majesty of might,
> No Despot better knows that Power is Right.
> Mark his unpaidish sneer, his lordly frown;
> Hark how he calls the beadle and flunky liars;
> See how magnificently he breaks down
> His neighbour's fence, if so his will requires,
> And how his struttle emulates the squire's!
>
> .   .   .   .   .   .
>
> Jem rises with the Moon; but when she sinks,
> Homeward with sack-like pockets, and quick heels,
> Hungry as boroughmongering gowl, he slinks.
> *He* reads not, writes not, thinks not, scarcely feels;
> Steals all he gets; serves Hell with all he steals!

It is rustic, rude existence; barren moors, with the smoke of Forges rising over the waste expanse.   Alas, no Arcadia; but the actual dwelling-place of actual toil-grimed sons of Tubalcain: yet are there blossoms, and the wild natural fragrance of gorse and broom; yet has the Craftsman pauses in his toil; the Craftsman too has an inheritance in Earth, and even in Heaven:

> Light!   All is not corrupt, for thou art pure,
> Unchanged and changeless.   Though frail man is vile,
> Thou look'st on him; serene, sublime, secure,
> Yet, like thy Father, with a pitying smile.
> Even on this wintry day, as marble cold,
> Angels might quit their home to visit thee,
> And match their plumage with thy mantle roll'd
> Beneath God's Throne, o'er billows of a sea
> Whose isles are Worlds, whose bounds Infinity.
> Why, then, is Enoch absent from my side?
> I miss the rustle of his silver hair;
> A guide no more, I seem to want a guide,
> While Enoch journeys to the house of prayer;

Ah, ne'er came Sabbath-day but he was there!
Lo how, like him, erect and strong though gray,
Yon village-tower time-touch'd to God appeals!
And hark! the chimes of morning die away:
Hark! to the heart the solemn sweetness steals,
Like the heart's voice, unfelt by none who feels
That God is Love, that Man is living Dust;
Unfelt by none whom ties of brotherhood
Link to his kind; by none who puts his trust
In nought of Earth that hath survived the Flood,
Save those mute charities, by which the good
Strengthen poor worms, and serve their Maker best.
Hail, Sabbath! Day of mercy, peace and rest!
Thou o'er loud cities throw'st a noiseless spell;
The hammer there, the wheel, the saw molest
Pale Thought no more: o'er Trade's contentious hell
Meek Quiet spreads her wings invisible.
And when thou com'st, less silent are the fields,
Through whose sweet paths the toil-freed townsman steals.
To him the very air a banquet yields.
Envious he watches the poised hawk that wheels
His flight on chainless winds. Each cloud reveals
A paradise of beauty to his eye.
His little Boys are with him, seeking flowers,
Or chasing the too-venturous gilded fly.
So by the daisy's side he spends the hours,
Renewing friendship with the budding bowers:
And while might, beauty, good without alloy,
Are mirror'd in his children's happy eyes,—
In His great Temple offering thankful joy
To Him, the infinitely Great and Wise,
With soul attuned to Nature's harmonies,
Serene and cheerful as a sporting child,—
His *heart* refuses to believe that man
Could turn into a hell the blooming wild,
The blissful country where his childhood ran
A race with infant rivers, ere began—

—" king-humbling " Bread-tax, " blind Misrule," and several
other crabbed things!

And so our Corn-Law Rhymer plays his part. In this wise
does he indite and act his Drama of Life, which for him is all-
too Domestic-Tragical. It is said, " the good actor soon
makes us forget the bad theatre, were it but a barn; while,
again, nothing renders so apparent the badness of the bad
actor as a theatre of peculiar excellence." How much more
in a theatre and drama such as these of Life itself! One
other item, however, we must note in that ill-decorated

Sheffield theatre: the back-scene and bottom-decoration of it all; which is no other than a Workhouse. Alas, the Workhouse is the bourne whither all these actors and workers are bound; whence none that has once passed it returns! A bodeful sound, like the rustle of approaching world-devouring tornadoes, quivers through their whole existence; and the voice of it is, Pauperism! The thanksgiving they offer up to Heaven is, that they are not yet Paupers; the earnest cry of their prayer is, that " God would shield them from the bitterness of Parish Pay."

Mournful enough, that a white European Man must pray wistfully for what the horse he drives is sure of,—That the strain of his whole faculties may not fail to earn him food and lodging. Mournful that a gallant manly spirit, with an eye to discern the world, a heart to reverence it, a hand cunning and willing to labour in it, must be haunted with such a fear. The grim end of it all, Beggary! A soul loathing, what true souls ever loath, Dependence, help from the unworthy to help; yet sucked into the world-whirlpool,—able to do no other: the highest in man's heart struggling vainly against the lowest in man's destiny! In good truth, if many a sickly and sulky Byron, or Byronlet, glooming over the woes of existence, and how unworthy God's Universe is to have so distinguished a resident, could transport himself into the patched coat and sooty apron of a Sheffield Blacksmith, made with as strange faculties and feelings as he, made by God Almighty all one as he was,—it would throw a light on much for him.

Meanwhile, is it not frightful as well as mournful to consider how the wide-spread evil is spreading wider and wider? Most persons, who have had eyes to look with, may have verified, in their own circle, the statement of this Sheffield Eyewitness, and " from their own knowledge and observation fearlessly declare that the little master-manufacturer, that the working man generally, is in a much worse condition than he was twenty-five years ago." Unhappily, the fact is too plain; the reason and scientific necessity of it is too plain. In this mad state of things, every new man is a new misfortune; every new market a new complexity; the chapter of chances grows ever more incalculable; the hungry gamesters (whose stake is their life) are ever increasing in numbers; the world-movement rolls on: by what method shall the weak and help-needing, who has none to help him, withstand it? Alas, how many brave hearts, ground to pieces in that unequal battle, have already sunk; in every sinking heart, a Tragedy, less famous than that of the Sons of Atreus; wherein, however, if no " kingly house," yet a manly house went to the dust, and a whole manly lineage was swept away! Must it grow worse and worse, till the last brave heart is broken in England; and this same " brave Peasantry " has become a kennel of wild-howling ravenous Paupers? God be thanked! there is some feeble shadow of hope that the change may have begun while it was yet time. You may lift the pressure from the free man's shoulders, and bid him go forth rejoicing; but lift the slave's burden, he will only wallow the more composedly in his sloth: a nation of degraded men cannot be raised up, except by what we rightly name a miracle.

Under which point of view also, these little Volumes, indicating such a character in such a place, are not without significance. One faint symptom, perhaps, that clearness will return, that there is a possibility of its return. It is as if from that Gehenna of Manufacturing Radicalism, from amid its loud roaring and cursing, whereby nothing became feasible, nothing knowable, except this only, that misery and malady existed there, we heard now some manful tone of reason and determination, wherein alone can there be profit, or promise of deliverance. In this Corn-Law Rhymer we seem to trace something of the antique spirit; a spirit which had long become invisible among our working as among other classes; which here, perhaps almost for the first time, reveals itself in an altogether modern political vesture. " The Pariahs of the Isle of Woe," as he passionately names them, are no longer Pariahs if they have become Men. Here is one man of their tribe; in several respects a true man; who has abjured Hypocrisy and Servility, yet not therewith trodden Religion and Loyalty under foot; not without justness of insight, devoutness, peaceable heroism of resolve; who, in all circumstances, even in these strange ones, will be found quitting himself like a man. One such that has found a voice: who knows how many mute but not inactive brethren he may have, in his own and in all other ranks? Seven thousand that have not bowed the knee to Baal! These are the men, wheresoever found, who are to stand forth in England's evil day, on whom the hope of England rests.

For it has been often said, and must often be said again, that all Reform except a moral one will prove unavailing. Political Reform, pressingly enough wanted, can indeed root-out the weeds (gross deep-fixed lazy dock-weeds, poisonous obscene hemlocks, ineffectual spurry in abundance); but it leaves the ground *empty*, — ready either for noble fruits, or for new worse tares! And how else is a Moral Reform to be looked for but in this way, that more and more Good Men are, by a bountiful Providence, sent hither to disseminate Goodness; literally to *sow* it, as in seeds shaken abroad by the living tree? For such, in all ages and places, is the nature of a Good Man; he is ever a mystic creative centre of Goodness: his influence, if we consider it, is not to be measured; for his works do not die, but being of Eternity, are eternal; and in new transformation, and ever-wider diffusion, endure, living and life-giving. Thou who exclaimest over the horrors and baseness of the Time, and how Diogenes would now need *two* lanterns in daylight, think of this: over the Time thou hast no power; to redeem a World sunk in dishonesty has not been given thee: solely over one man therein thou hast a quite absolute uncontrollable power; him redeem, him make honest; it will be something, it will be much, and thy life and labour not in vain.

We have given no epitomised abstract of these little Books, such as is the Reviewer's wont: we would gladly persuade many a reader, high and low, who takes interest not in rhyme only, but in reason, and the condition of his fellow-man, to purchase and peruse them for himself. It is proof of an innate love of worth, and how willingly the Public, did not thousand-voiced Puffery so confuse it, would have to do with substances, and not with deceptive shadows, that these Volumes carry "Third Edition" marked on them,—on all of them but the newest, whose fate with the reading world we yet know not; which, however, seems to deserve not worse but better than either of its forerunners.

Nay, it appears to us as if in this humble Chant of the *Village Patriarch* might be traced rudiments of a truly great idea; great though all undeveloped. The Rhapsody of "Enoch Wray" is, in its nature and unconscious tendency,

Epic; a whole world lies shadowed in it. What we might
call an inarticulate, half-audible Epic! The main figure is
a blind aged man; himself a ruin, and encircled with the ruin
of a whole Era. Sad and great does that image of a universal
Dissolution hover visible as a poetic background. Good old
Enoch! He could *do* so much; was so wise, so valiant. No
Ilion had he destroyed; yet somewhat he had built up:
where the Mill stands noisy by its cataract, making corn into
bread for men, it was Enoch that reared it, and made the rude
rocks send it water; where the mountain Torrent now boils
in vain, and is mere passing music to the traveller, it was
Enoch's cunning that spanned it with that strong Arch, grim,
time-defying. Where Enoch's hand or mind has been,
Disorder has become Order; Chaos has receded some little
handbreadth, had to give up some new handbreadth of his
ancient realm. Enoch too has seen his followers fall round
him (by stress of hardship, and the arrows of the gods), has
performed funeral games for them, and raised sandstone
memorials, and carved his *Abiit ad Plures* thereon, with his
own hand. The living chronicle and epitome of a whole
century; when he departs, a whole century will become dead,
historical.

Rudiments of an Epic, we say; and of the true Epic of our
Time,—were the genius but arrived that could sing it! Not
" Arms and the Man; " " Tools and the Man," that were
now our Epic. What indeed are Tools, from the Hammer and
Plummet of Enoch Wray to this Pen we now write with, but
Arms, wherewith to do battle against UNREASON without or
within, and smite in pieces not miserable fellow-men, but
the Arch-Enemy that makes us all miserable; henceforth
the only legitimate battle!

Which Epic, as we granted, is here altogether imperfectly
sung; scarcely a few notes thereof brought freely out: nevertheless with indication, with prediction that it will be sung.
Such is the purport and merit of the *Village Patriarch;* it
struggles towards a noble utterance, which however it can
nowise find. Old Enoch is from the first speechless, heard
of rather than heard or seen; at best, mute, motionless like
a stone pillar of his own carving. Indeed, to find fit utterance
for such meaning as lies struggling here, is a problem, to
which the highest poetic minds may long be content to
accomplish only approximate solutions. Meanwhile, our

honest Rhymer, with no guide but the instinct of a clear
natural talent, has created and adjusted somewhat, not without vitality of union; has avoided somewhat, the road to
which lay open enough. His *Village Patriarch*, for example,
though of an elegiac strain, is not wholly lachrymose, not
without touches of rugged gaiety;—is like Life itself, with
tears and toil, with laughter and rude play, such as metallurgic
Yorkshire sees it: in which sense, that wondrous Courtship
of the sharp-tempered, oft-widowed Alice Green may pass,
questionable, yet with a certain air of soot-stained genuineness. And so has, not a Picture, indeed, yet a sort of genial
Study or Cartoon come together for him: and may endure
there, after some flary oil-daubings, which we have seen
framed with gilding, and hung-up in proud galleries, have
become rags and rubbish.

To one class of readers especially, such Books as these
ought to be interesting: to the highest, that is to say, the
richest class. Among our Aristocracy, there are men, we
trust there are many men, who feel that they also are workmen, born to toil, ever in their great Taskmaster's eye,
faithfully with heart and head for those that with heart and
hand do, under the same great Taskmaster, toil for them;—
who have even this noblest and hardest work set before them:
To deliver out of that Egyptian bondage to Wretchedness,
and Ignorance, and Sin, the hardhanded millions; of whom
this hardhanded earnest witness and writer is here representative. To such men his writing will be as a Document,
which they will lovingly interpret: what is dark and
exasperated and acrid, in their humble Brother, they for
themselves will enlighten and sweeten; taking thankfully
what is the real purport of his message, and laying it earnestly
to heart. Might an instructive relation and interchange
between High and Low at length ground itself, and more and
more perfect itself,—to the unspeakable profit of all parties;
for if all parties are to love and help one another, the first
step towards this is, that all thoroughly understand one
another! To such rich men an authentic message from the
hearts of poor men, from the heart of one poor man, will be
welcome.

To another class of our Aristocracy, again, who unhappily
feel rather that they are *not* workmen; and profess not so
much to bear any burden, as to be themselves, with utmost

attainable *steadiness*, and if possible *gracefulness*, borne,—such a phenomenon as this of the Sheffield Corn-Law Rhymer, with a Manchester Detrosier, and much else, pointing the same way, will be quite unwelcome; indeed, to the clearer-sighted, astonishing and alarming. It indicates that they find themselves, as Napoleon was wont to say, " in a new position;"—a position wonderful enough; of extreme singularity, to which, in the whole course of History, there is perhaps but one case in some measure parallel. The case alluded to stands recorded in the *Book of Numbers :* the case of Balaam the son of Beor.

Truly, if we consider it, there are few passages more notable and pregnant in their way, than this of Balaam. The Midianitish Soothsayer (Truth-speaker, or as we should now say, Counsel-giver and Senator) is journeying forth, as he has from of old quite prosperously done, in the way of his vocation; not so much to " curse the people of the Lord," as to earn for himself a comfortable penny by such means as are possible and expedient; something, it is hoped, midway between cursing and blessing; which shall not, except in case of necessity, be either a curse or a blessing, or indeed be anything so much as a Nothing that will look like a Something and bring wages in. For the man is not dishonest; far from it: still less is he honest; but above all things, he is, has been and will be, respectable. Did calumny ever dare to fasten itself on the fair fame of Balaam? In his whole walk and conversation, has he not shown consistency enough; ever doing and speaking the thing that was decent; with proper spirit maintaining his status; so that friend and opponent held him in respect, and he could defy the spiteful world to say on any occasion, *Herein* art thou a knave? And now as he jogs along, in official comfort, with brave official retinue, his heart filled with good things, his head with schemes for the Preservation of Game, the Suppression of Vice, and the Cause of Civil and Religious Liberty all over the World;—consider what a spasm, and life-clutching ice-taloned pang, must have shot through the brain and pericardium of Balaam, when his Ass not only on the sudden stood stock-still, defying spur and cudgel, but—*began to talk*, and that in a reasonable manner! Did not his face, elongating, collapse, and tremour occupy his joints? For the thin crust of Respectability has cracked asunder; and a bottomless preternatural Inane yawns under him instead. Farewell, a long farewell to all my greatness: the spirit-stirring Vote, ear-piercing Hear; the big Speech that makes ambition virtue; soft Palm-greasing first of raptures, and Cheers that emulate sphere-music: Balaam's occupation's gone!—

As for our stout Corn-Law Rhymer, what can we say by way of valediction but this, " Well done; come again, doing better "? Advices enough there were; but all lie included under one: To keep his eyes open, and do honestly whatsoever his hand shall find to do. We have praised him for sincerity: let him become more and more sincere; casting out all remnants of Hearsay, Imitation, ephemeral Speculation; resolutely " *clearing* his mind of Cant." We advised a wider course of reading: would he forgive us if we now suggested the question, Whether Rhyme is the only dialect he can write in; whether Rhyme is, after all, the natural or fittest dialect for him? In good Prose, which differs inconceivably from bad Prose, what may not be written, what may not be read; from a Waverley Novel to an Arabic Koran, to an English Bible! Rhyme has plain advantages; which, however, are often purchased too dear. If the inward thought *can* speak itself, instead of sing itself, let it, especially in these quite unmusical days, do the former! In any case, if the inward Thought do not sing itself, that singing of the outward Phrase is a timber-toned false matter we could well dispense with. Will our Rhymer consider himself, then; and decide for what is actually best? Rhyme, up to this hour, never seems altogether obedient to him; and disobedient Rhyme, —who would ride on *it* that had once learned walking!

He takes amiss that some friends have admonished him to quit Politics: we will not repeat that admonition. Let him, on this as on all other matters, take solemn counsel with his own Socrates'-Demon; such as dwells in every mortal; such as he is a happy mortal who can hear the voice of, follow the behests of, like an unalterable law. At the same time, we could truly wish to see such a mind as his engaged rather in considering what, in his own sphere, could be *done*, than what, in his own or other spheres, ought to be *destroyed ;* rather in producing or preserving the True, than in mangling and slashing asunder the False. Let him be at ease: the False is already dead, or lives only with a mock life. The death-sentence of the False was of old, from the first beginning of it, written in Heaven; and is now proclaimed in the Earth, and read aloud at all market-crosses; nor are innumerable volunteer tipstaves and headsmen wanting, to execute the same: for which needful service men inferior to him may suffice. Why should the heart of the Corn-Law Rhymer be troubled? Spite of "Bread-tax," he and his brave children, who will emulate their sire, have yet bread: the Workhouse, as we rejoice to fancy, has receded into the safe distance; and is now quite shut-out from his poetic pleasure-ground. Why should he afflict himself with devices of "Boroughmongering gowls," or the rage of the Heathen imagining a vain thing? This matter, which he calls Corn-Law, will not have completed itself, adjusted itself into clearness, for the space of a century or two: nay after twenty centuries, what will there, or can there be for the son of Adam but Work, Work, two hands quite *full* of Work! Meanwhile, is not the Corn-Law Rhymer already a king, though a belligerent one; king of his own mind and faculty; and what man in the long-run is king of more? Not one in the thousand, even among sceptred kings, is king of so much. Be diligent in business, then; fervent in spirit. Above all things, lay aside anger, uncharitableness, hatred, noisy tumult; avoid them, as worse than Pestilence, worse than "Bread-tax" itself:

> For it well beseemeth kings, all mortals it beseemeth well,
> To possess their souls in patience, and await what can betide.

CHARTISM

" It never smokes but there is fire."—Old Proverb.

[1839]

CHAPTER I

CONDITION-OF-ENGLAND QUESTION

A FEELING very generally exists that the condition and
disposition of the Working Classes is a rather ominous matter
at present; that something ought to be said, something ought
to be done, in regard to it. And surely, at an epoch of history
when the " National Petition " carts itself in wagons along
the streets, and is presented " bound with iron hoops, four
men bearing it," to a Reformed House of Commons; and
Chartism numbered by the million and half, taking nothing
by its iron-hooped Petition, breaks out into brickbats, cheap
pikes, and even into sputterings of conflagration, such very
general feeling cannot be considered unnatural! To us
individually this matter appears, and has for many years
appeared, to be the most ominous of all practical matters
whatever; a matter in regard to which if something be not
done, something will *do* itself one day, and in a fashion that
will please nobody. The time is verily come for acting in it;
how much more for consultation about acting in it, for
speech and articulate inquiry about it!

We are aware that, according to the newspapers, Chartism
is extinct; that a Reform Ministry has " put down the chimera
of Chartism " in the most felicitous effectual manner. So
say the newspapers;—and yet, alas, most readers of newspapers know withal that it is indeed the " chimera " of
Chartism, not the reality, which has been put down. The
distracted incoherent embodiment of Chartism, whereby in
late months it took shape and became visible, this has been
put down; or rather has fallen down and gone asunder by
gravitation and law of nature: but the living essence of
Chartism has not been put down. Chartism means the bitter

discontent grown fierce and mad, the wrong condition therefore or the wrong disposition, of the Working Classes of
England. It is a new name for a thing which has had many
names, which will yet have many. The matter of Chartism
is weighty, deep-rooted, far-extending; did not begin yesterday; will by no means end this day or to-morrow. Reform
Ministry, constabulary rural police, new levy of soldiers,
grants of money to Birmingham; all this is well, or is not
well; all this will put down only the embodiment or
" chimera " of Chartism. The essence continuing, new and
ever new embodiments, chimeras madder or less mad, have
to continue. The melancholy fact remains, that this thing
known at present by the name of Chartism does exist; has
existed; and, either " put down," into secret treason, with
rusty pistols, vitriol-bottle and match-box, or openly brandishing pike and torch (one knows not in which case *more*
fatal-looking), is like to exist till quite other methods have
been tried with it. What means this bitter discontent of
the Working Classes? Whence comes it, whither goes it?
Above all, at what price, on what terms, will it probably
consent to depart from us and die into rest? These are
questions.

To say that it is mad, incendiary, nefarious, is no answer.
To say all this, in never so many dialects, is saying little.
" Glasgow Thuggery," " Glasgow Thugs; " it is a witty
nickname: the practice of " Number 60 " entering his dark
room, to contract for and settle the price of blood with
operative assassins, in a Christian city, once distinguished
by its rigorous Christianism, is doubtless a fact worthy of all
horror: but what will horror do for it? What will execration;
nay at bottom, what will condemnation and banishment to
Botany Bay do for it? Glasgow Thuggery, Chartist torch-
meetings, Birmingham riots, Swing conflagrations, are so
many symptoms on the surface; you abolish the symptom to
no purpose, if the disease is left untouched. Boils on the
surface are curable or incurable,—small matter which, while
the virulent humour festers deep within; poisoning the
sources of life; and certain enough to find for itself ever new
boils and sore issues; ways of announcing that it continues
there, that it would fain not continue there.

Delirious Chartism will not have raged entirely to no purpose, as indeed no earthly thing does so, if it have forced all

thinking men of the community to think of this vital matter, too apt to be overlooked otherwise. Is the condition of the English working people wrong; so wrong that rational working men cannot, will not, and even should not rest quiet under it? A most grave case, complex beyond all others in the world; a case wherein Botany Bay, constabulary rural police, and suchlike, will avail but little. Or is the discontent itself mad, like the shape it took? Not the condition of the working people that is wrong; but their disposition, their own thoughts, beliefs and feelings that are wrong? This too were a most grave case, little less alarming, little less complex than the former one. In this case too, where constabulary police and mere rigour of coercion seems more at home, coercion will by no means do all, coercion by itself will not even do much. If there do exist general madness of discontent, then sanity and some measure of content must be brought about again,—not by constabulary police alone. When the thoughts of a people, in the great mass of it, have grown mad, the combined issue of that people's workings will be a madness, an incoherency and ruin! Sanity will have to be recovered for the general mass; coercion itself will otherwise cease to be able to coerce.

We have heard it asked, Why Parliament throws no light on this question of the Working Classes, and the condition or disposition they are in? Truly to a remote observer of Parliamentary procedure it seems surprising, especially in late Reformed times, to see what space this question occupies in the Debates of the Nation. Can any other business whatsoever be so pressing on legislators? A Reformed Parliament, one would think, should inquire into popular discontents *before* they get the length of pikes and torches! For what end at all are men, Honourable Members and Reform Members, sent to St. Stephen's with clamour and effort; kept talking, struggling, motioning and counter-motioning? The condition of the great body of people in a country is the condition of the country itself: this you would say is a truism in all times; a truism rather pressing to get recognised as a truth now, and be acted upon, in these times. Yet read Hansard's Debates, or the Morning Papers, if you have nothing to do! The old grand question, whether A is to be in office or B, with the innumerable subsidiary questions growing out of that, courting paragraphs and suffrages for

a blessed solution of that: Canada question, Irish Appropria-
tion question, West-India question, Queen's Bedchamber
question; Game Laws, Usury Laws; African Blacks, Hill
Coolies, Smithfield cattle, and Dog-carts,—all manner of
questions and subjects, except simply this the alpha and
omega of all! Surely Honourable Members ought to speak
of the Condition-of-England question too. Radical Members,
above all; friends of the people; chosen with effort, by the
people, to interpret and articulate the dumb deep want
of the people! To a remote observer they seem oblivious of
their duty. Are they not there, by trade, mission, and express
appointment of themselves and others, to speak for the good
of the British Nation? Whatsoever great British interest
can the least speak for itself, for that beyond all they are
called to speak. They are either speakers for that great
dumb toiling class which cannot speak, or they are nothing
that one can well specify.

Alas, the remote observer knows not the nature of Parliaments: how Parliaments, extant there for the British Nation's
sake, find that they are extant withal for their own sake;
how Parliaments travel so naturally in their deep-rutted
routine, commonplace worn into ruts axle-deep, from which
only strength, insight and courageous generous exertion can
lift any Parliament or vehicle; how in Parliaments, Reformed
or Unreformed, there may chance to be a strong man, an
original, clear-sighted, great-hearted, patient and valiant
man, or to be none such;—how, on the whole, Parliaments,
lumbering along in their deep ruts of commonplace, find, as
so many of us otherwise do, that the ruts *are* axle-deep, and
the travelling very toilsome of itself, and for the day the evil
thereof sufficient! What Parliaments ought to have done
in this business, what they will, can or cannot yet do, and
where the limits of their faculty and culpability may lie, in
regard to it, were a long investigation; into which we need
not enter at this moment. What they have done is unhappily
plain enough. Hitherto, on this most national of questions,
the Collective Wisdom of the Nation has availed us as good
as nothing whatever.

And yet, as we say, it is a question which cannot be left
to the Collective Folly of the Nation! In or out of Parliament, darkness, neglect, hallucination must contrive to
cease in regard to it; true insight into it must be had. How

inexpressibly useful were true insight into it; a genuine understanding by the upper classes of society what it is that the under classes intrinsically mean; a clear interpretation of the thought which at heart torments these wild inarticulate souls, struggling there, with inarticulate uproar, like dumb creatures in pain, unable to speak what is in them! Something they do mean; some true thing withal, in the centre of their confused hearts,—for they are hearts created by Heaven too: to the Heaven it is clear what thing; to us not clear. Would that it were! Perfect clearness on it were equivalent to remedy of it. For, as is well said, all battle is misunderstanding; did the parties know one another, the battle would cease. No man at bottom means injustice; it is always for some obscure distorted image of a right that he contends: an obscure image diffracted, exaggerated, in the wonderfulest way, by natural dimness and selfishness; getting tenfold more diffracted by exasperation of contest, till at length it become all but irrecognisable; yet still the image of a right. Could a man own to himself that the thing he fought for was wrong, contrary to fairness and the law of reason, he would own also that it thereby stood condemned and hopeless; he could fight for it no longer. Nay independently of right, could the contending parties get but accurately to discern one another's might and strength to contend, the one would peaceably yield to the other and to Necessity; the contest in this case too were over. No African expedition now, as in the days of Herodotus, is fitted out *against the South-wind*. One expedition was satisfactory in that department. The South-wind Simoom continues blowing occasionally, hateful as ever, maddening as ever; but one expedition was enough. Do we not all submit to Death? The highest sentence of the law, sentence of death, is passed on all of us by the fact of birth; yet we live patiently under it, patiently undergo it when the hour comes. Clear undeniable right, clear undeniable might: either of these once ascertained puts an end to battle. All battle is a confused experiment to ascertain one and both of these.

What are the rights, what are the mights of the discontented Working Classes in England at this epoch? He were an Œdipus, and deliverer from sad social pestilence, who could resolve us fully! For we may say beforehand, The struggle that divides the upper and lower in society over Europe, and more painfully and notably in England than elsewhere, this too is a struggle which will end and adjust itself as all other struggles do and have done, by making the right clear and the might clear; not otherwise than by that. Meantime, the questions, Why are the Working Classes discontented; what is their condition, economical, moral, in their houses and their hearts, as it is in reality and as they figure it to themselves to be; what do they complain of; what ought they, and ought they not to complain of?—these are measurable questions; on some of these any common mortal, did he but turn his eyes to them, might throw some light. Certain researches and considerations of ours on the matter, since no one else will undertake it, are now to be made public. The researches have yielded us little, almost nothing; but the considerations are of old date, and press to have utterance. We are not without hope that our general notion of the business, if we can get it uttered at all, will meet some assent from many candid men.

CHAPTER II

STATISTICS

A WITTY statesman said, you might prove anything by figures. We have looked into various statistic works, Statistic-Society Reports, Poor-Law Reports, Reports and Pamphlets not a few, with a sedulous eye to this question of the Working Classes and their general condition in England; we grieve to say, with as good as no result whatever. Assertion swallows assertion; according to the old Proverb, " as the *statist* thinks, the bell clinks "! Tables are like cobwebs, like the sieve of the Danaides; beautifully reticulated, orderly to look upon, but which will hold no conclusion. Tables are abstractions, and the object a most concrete one, so difficult to read the essence of. There are innumerable circumstances; and one circumstance left out may be the vital one on which all turned. Statistics is a science which ought to be honourable, the basis of many most important sciences; but it is not to be carried on by steam, this science, any more than others are; a wise head is requisite for carrying it on. Conclusive facts are inseparable from inconclusive except by a head that already understands and knows. Vain to send the purblind and blind to the shore of a Pactolus never so golden: these find only gravel; the seer and finder alone picks up gold grains there. And now the purblind offering you, with asseveration and protrusive importunity, his basket of gravel as gold, what steps are to be taken with him?—Statistics, one may hope, will improve gradually, and become good for something. Meanwhile, it is to be feared the crabbed satirist was partly right, as things go: "A judicious man," says he, "looks at Statistics, not to get knowledge, but to save himself from having ignorance foisted on him." With what serene conclusiveness a member of some Useful-Knowledge Society stops your mouth with a figure of arithmetic! To him it seems he has there extracted the elixir of the matter, on which now nothing more can be said. It is needful that you look into his said extracted elixir; and ascertain, alas, too probably, not without a sigh, that it is wash and vapidity, good only for the gutters.

Twice or three times have we heard the lamentations and prophecies of a humane Jeremiah, mourner for the poor, cut short by a statistic fact of the most decisive nature: How can the condition of the poor be other than good, be other than better; has not the average duration of life in England, and therefore among the most numerous class in England, been proved to have increased? Our Jeremiah had to admit that, if so, it was an astounding fact; whereby all that ever he, for his part, had observed on other sides of the matter, was overset without remedy. If life last longer, life must be less worn upon, by outward suffering, by inward discontent, by hardship of any kind; the general condition of the poor must be bettering instead of worsening. So was our Jeremiah cut short. And now for the " proof "? Readers who are curious in statistic proofs may see it drawn out with all solemnity, in a Pamphlet " published by Charles Knight and Company," [1]—and perhaps himself draw inferences from it. Northampton Tables, compiled by Dr. Price " from registers of the Parish of All Saints from 1735 to 1780; " Carlisle Tables, collected by Dr. Heysham from observation of Carlisle City for eight years, " the calculations founded on them " conducted by another Doctor; incredible " document considered satisfactory by men of science in France: "—alas,

---

[1] *An Essay on the Means of Insurance against the Casualties of,* etc., etc. London, Charles Knight and Company, 1836. Price 2s.

is it not as if some zealous scientific son of Adam had proved the deepening of the Ocean, by survey, accurate or cursory, of two mud-plashes on the coast of the Isle of Dogs? " Not to get knowledge, but to save yourself from having ignorance foisted on you " !

The condition of the working-man in this country, what it is and has been, whether it is improving or retrograding,— is a question to which from statistics hitherto no solution can be got. Hitherto, after many tables and statements, one is still left mainly to what he can ascertain by his own eyes, looking at the concrete phenomenon for himself. There is no other method; and yet it is a most imperfect method. Each man expands his own hand-breadth of observation to the limits of the general whole; more or less, each man must take what he himself has seen and ascertained for a sample of all that is seeable and ascertainable. Hence discrepancies, controversies wide-spread, long-continued; which there is at present no means or hope of satisfactorily ending. When Parliament takes up " the Condition-of-England question," as it will have to do one day, then indeed much may be amended! Inquiries wisely gone into, even on this most complex matter, will yield results worth something, not nothing. But it is a most complex matter; on which, whether for the past or the present, Statistic Inquiry, with its limited means, with its short vision and headlong extensive dogmatism, as yet too often throws not light, but error worse than darkness.

What constitutes the well-being of a man? Many things; of which the wages he gets, and the bread he buys with them, are but one preliminary item. Grant, however, that the wages were the whole; that once knowing the wages and the price of bread, we know all; then what are the wages? Statistic Inquiry, in its present unguided condition, cannot tell. The average rate of day's wages is not correctly ascertained for any portion of this country; not only not for half-centuries, it is not even ascertained anywhere for decades or years: far from instituting comparisons with the past, the present itself is unknown to us. And then, given the average of wages, what is the constancy of employment; what is the difficulty of finding employment; the fluctuation from season to season, from year to year? Is it constant, calculable wages; or fluctuating, incalculable, more or less of the nature of gambling? This secondary circumstance, of quality in wages, is perhaps even more important than the primary one of quantity. Farther we ask, Can the labourer, by thrift and industry, hope to rise to mastership; or is such hope cut off from him? How is he related to his employer; by bonds of friendliness and mutual help; or by hostility, opposition, and chains of mutual necessity alone? In a word, what degree of contentment can a human creature be supposed to enjoy in that position? With hunger preying on him, his contentment is likely to be small! But even with abundance, his discontent, his real misery may be great. The labourer's feelings, his notion of being justly dealt with or unjustly; his wholesome composure, frugality, prosperity in the one case, his acrid unrest, recklessness, gin-drinking, and gradual ruin in the other,—how shall figures of arithmetic represent all this? So much is still to be ascertained; much of it by no means easy to ascertain! Till, among the "Hill Cooly" and "Dog-cart" questions, there arise in Parliament and extensively out of it "a Condition-of-England question," and quite a new set of inquirers and methods, little of it is likely to be ascertained.

One fact on this subject, a fact which arithmetic *is* capable of representing, we have often considered would be worth all the rest: Whether the labourer, whatever his wages are, is saving money? Laying up money, he proves that his condition, painful as it may be without and within, is not yet desperate; that he looks forward to a better day coming, and is still resolutely steering towards the same; that all the lights and darknesses of his lot are united under a blessed radiance of hope,—the last, first, nay one may say the sole blessedness of man. Is the habit of saving increased and increasing, or the contrary? Where the present writer has been able to look with his own eyes, it is decreasing, and in many quarters all but disappearing. Statistic science turns up her Savings-Bank Accounts, and answers, "Increasing rapidly." Would that one could believe it! But the Danaides'-sieve character of such statistic reticulated documents is too manifest. A few years ago, in regions where thrift, to one's own knowledge, still was, Savings-Banks were not; the labourer lent his money to some farmer, of capital, or supposed to be of capital,—and has too often lost it since; or he bought a cow with it, bought a cottage with it; nay hid it under his thatch: the Savings-Banks books then exhibited mere blank and zero. That they swell yearly now, if such be the fact, indicates that what thrift exists does gradually resort more and more thither rather than else-whither; but the question, Is thrift increasing? runs through the reticulation, and is as water spilt on the ground, not to be gathered here.

These are inquiries on which, had there been a proper " Condition-of-England question," some light would have been thrown, before " torch-meetings " arose to illustrate them! Far as they lie out of the course of Parliamentary routine, they should have been gone into, should have been glanced at, in one or the other fashion. A Legislature making laws for the Working Classes, in total uncertainty as to these things, is legislating in the dark; not wisely, nor to good issues. The simple fundamental question, Can the labouring man in this England of ours, who is willing to labour, find work, and subsistence by his work? is matter of mere conjecture and assertion hitherto; not ascertainable by authentic evidence: the Legislature, satisfied to legislate in the dark, has not yet sought any evidence on it. They pass their New Poor-Law Bill, without evidence as to all this. Perhaps their New Poor-Law Bill is itself only intended as an *experimentum crucis* to ascertain all this? Chartism is an answer, seemingly not in the affirmative.

CHAPTER III

NEW POOR-LAW

To read the Reports of the Poor-Law Commissioners, if one had faith enough, would be a pleasure to the friend of humanity. One sole recipe seems to have been needful for the woes of England: " refusal of out-door relief." England lay in sick discontent, writhing powerless on its fever-bed, dark, nigh desperate, in wastefulness, want, improvidence, and eating care, till like Hyperion down the eastern steeps, the Poor-Law Commissioners arose, and said, Let there be workhouses, and bread of affliction and water of affliction there! It was a simple invention; as all truly great inventions are. And see, in any quarter, instantly as the walls of the workhouse arise, misery and necessity fly away, out of sight,—out of being, as is fondly hoped, and dissolve into the inane; industry, frugality, fertility, rise of wages, peace on earth and goodwill towards men do,—in the Poor-Law Commissioners' Reports,—infallibly, rapidly or not so rapidly, to the joy of all parties, supervene. It was a consummation devoutly to be wished. We have looked over these four annual Poor-Law Reports with a variety of reflections; with no thought that our Poor-Law Commissioners are the inhuman men their enemies accuse them of being; with a feeling of thankfulness rather that there do exist men of that structure too; with a persuasion deeper and deeper that Nature, who makes nothing to no purpose, has not made either them or their Poor-Law Amendment Act in vain. We hope to prove that they and it were an indispensable element, harsh but salutary, in the progress of things.

That this Poor-law Amendment Act meanwhile should be, as we sometimes hear it named, the " chief glory " of a Reform Cabinet, betokens, one would imagine, rather a scarcity of glory there. To say to the poor, Ye shall eat the bread of affliction and drink the water of affliction, and be very miserable while here, required not so much a stretch of heroic faculty in any sense, as due toughness of bowels. If paupers are made miserable, paupers will needs decline in multitude. It is a secret known to all rat-catchers: stop up the granary-crevices, afflict with continual mewing, alarm, and going-off of traps, your " chargeable labourers " disappear, and cease from the establishment. A still briefer method is that of arsenic; perhaps even a milder, where otherwise permissible. Rats and paupers can be abolished; the human faculty was from of old adequate to grind them down, slowly or at once, and needed no ghost or Reform Ministry to teach it. Furthermore when one hears of " all the labour of the country being absorbed into employment " by this new system of affliction, when labour complaining of want can find no audience, one cannot but pause. That misery and unemployed labour should " disappear " in that case is natural enough; should go out of sight,—but out of existence? What we do know is, that " the rates are diminished," as they cannot well help being; that no statistic tables as yet report much increase of deaths by starvation: this we do know, and not very conclusively anything more than this. If this be absorption of all the labour of the country, then all the labour of the country is absorbed.

To believe practically that the poor and luckless are here only as a nuisance to be abraded and abated, and in some permissible manner made away with, and swept out of sight, is not an amiable faith. That the arrangements of good and ill success in this perplexed scramble of a world, which a blind goddess was always thought to preside over, are in fact the work of a seeing goddess or god, and require only not to be meddled with: what stretch of heroic faculty or inspiration of genius was needed to teach one that? To button your pockets and stand still, is no complex recipe. *Laissez faire, laissez passer!* Whatever goes on, ought it not to go on; " the widow picking nettles for her children's dinner; and the perfumed seigneur delicately lounging in the Œil-de-Bœuf, who has an alchemy whereby he will extract from her the third nettle, and name it rent and law "? What is written and enacted, has it not black-on-white to show for itself? Justice is justice; but all attorney's parchment is of the nature of Targum or sacred-parchment. In brief, ours is a world requiring only to be well let alone. Scramble along, thou insane scramble of a world, with thy pope's tiaras, king's mantles and beggar's gabardines, chivalry-ribbons and plebeian gallows-ropes, where a Paul shall die on the gibbet and a Nero sit fiddling as imperial Cæsar; *thou* art all right, and shalt scramble even so; and whoever in the press is trodden down, has only to lie there and be trampled broad:—Such at bottom seems to be the chief social principle, if principle it have, which the Poor-Law Amendment Act has the merit of courageously asserting, in opposition to many things. A chief social principle which this present writer, for one, will by no manner of means believe in, but pronounce at all fit times to be false, heretical and damnable, if ever aught was!

And yet, as we said, Nature makes nothing in vain; not even a Poor-Law Amendment Act. For withal we are far from joining in the outcry raised against these poor Poor-Law Commissioners, as if they were tigers in men's shape; as if their Amendment Act were a mere monstrosity and horror, deserving instant abrogation. They are not tigers; they are men filled with an idea of a theory: their Amendment Act, heretical and damnable as a whole truth, is orthodox and laudable as a *half*-truth; and was imperatively required to be put in practice. To create men filled with a

theory, that refusal of outdoor relief was the
Nature had no readier way of getting out-o
In fact, if we look at the old Poor-Law, in i
opposite social principle, that Fortune's aw
of Justice, we shall find it to have become
portable, demanding, if England was not d
anarchy, to be done away with.

Any law, however well meant as a law, which has become
a bounty on unthrift, idleness, bastardy and beer-drinking,
must be put an end to. In all ways it needs, especially in
these times, to be proclaimed aloud that for the idle man
there is no place in this England of ours. He that will not
work, and save according to his means, let him go elsewhither; let him know that for *him* the law has made no soft
provision, but a hard and stern one; that by the Law of Nature,
which the Law of England would vainly contend against
in the long-run, *he* is doomed either to quit these habits, or
miserably be extruded from this Earth, which is made on
principles different from these. He that will not work
according to his faculty, let him perish according to his
necessity: there is no law juster than that. Would to Heaven
one could preach it abroad into the hearts of all sons and
daughters of Adam, for it is a law applicable to all; and
bring it to bear, with practical obligation strict as the Poor-
Law Bastille, on all! We had then, in good truth, a " perfect
constitution of society; " and " God's fair Earth and Task-
garden, where whosoever is not working must be begging or
stealing," were then actually what always, through so many
changes and struggles, it is endeavouring to become.

That this law of " No work no recompense " should first
of all be enforced on the *manual* worker, and brought strin-
gently home to him and his numerous class, while so many
other classes and persons still go loose from it, was natural to
the case. Let it be enforced there, and rigidly made good.
It behoves to be enforced everywhere, and rigidly made good;
—alas, not by such simple methods as "refusal of out-door
relief," but by far other and costlier ones; which too, however,
a bountiful Providence is not unfurnished with, nor, in these
latter generations (if we will understand their convulsions and
confusions), sparing to apply. Work is the mission of man
in this Earth. A day is ever struggling forward, a day will
arrive in some approximate degree, when he who has no work

o, by whatever name he may be named, will not find it
ood to show himself in our quarter of the Solar System; but
may go and look out elsewhere, If there be any *Idle* Planet
discoverable?—Let the honest working man rejoice that such
law, the first of Nature, has been made good on him; and
hope that, by and by, all else will be made good. It is the
beginning of all. We define the harsh New Poor-Law to *be*
withal a " protection of the thrifty labourer against the
thriftless and dissolute; " a thing inexpressibly important;
a *half*-result, detestable, if you will, when looked upon as
the whole result; yet without which the whole result is forever unattainable. Let wastefulness, idleness, drunkenness,
improvidence take the fate which God has appointed them;
that their opposites may also have a chance for *their* fate.
Let the Poor-Law Administrators be considered as useful
labourers whom Nature has furnished with a whole theory
of the universe, that they might accomplish an indispensable
fractional practice there, and prosper in it in spite of much
contradiction.

We will praise the New Poor-Law, farther, as the probable
preliminary of *some* general charge to be taken of the lowest
classes by the higher. Any general charge whatsoever,
rather than a conflict of charges, varying from parish to
parish; the emblem of darkness, of unreadable confusion.
Supervisal by the central government, in what spirit soever
executed, is supervisal from a centre. By degrees the object
will become clearer, as it is at once made thereby universally
conspicuous. By degrees true vision of it will become
attainable, will be universally attained; whatsoever order
regarding it is just and wise, as grounded on the truth of it,
will then be capable of being taken. Let us welcome the
New Poor-Law as the harsh beginning of much, the harsh
ending of much! Most harsh and barren lies the new
ploughers' fallow-field, the crude subsoil all turned up, which
never saw the sun; which as yet grows no herb; which has
" out-door relief " for no one. Yet patience: innumerable
weeds and corruptions lie safely turned down and extinguished under it; this same crude subsoil is the first step
of all true husbandry; by Heaven's blessing and the skyey
influences, fruits that are good and blessed will yet come of it.

For, in truth, the claim of the poor labourer is something
quite other than that "Statute of the Forty-third of Elizabeth"

will ever fulfil for him. Not to be supported by roundsmen systems, by never so liberal parish doles, or lodged in free and easy workhouses when distress overtakes him; not for this, however in words he may clamour for it; not for this, but for something far different does the heart of him struggle. It is " for justice " that he struggles; for " just wages,"— not in money alone! An ever-toiling inferior, he would fain (though as yet he knows it not) find for himself a superior that should lovingly and wisely govern: is not that too the " just wages " of his service done? It is for a manlike place and relation, in this world where he sees himself a man, that he struggles. At bottom, may we not say, it is even for this, That guidance and government, which he cannot give himself, which in our so complex world he can no longer do without, might be afforded him? The thing he struggles for is one which no Forty-third of Elizabeth is in any condition to furnish him, to put him on the road towards getting. Let him quit the Forty-third of Elizabeth altogether; and rejoice that the Poor-Law Amendment Act has, even by harsh methods and against his own will, forced him away from it. That was a broken reed to lean on, if there ever was one; and did but run into his lamed right-hand. Let him cast it far from him, that broken reed, and look to quite the opposite point of the heavens for help. His unlamed right-hand, with the cunning industry that lies in it, is not this defined to be " the sceptre of our Planet"? He that can work is a born king of something; is in communion with Nature, is master of a thing or things, is a priest and king of Nature so far. He that can work at nothing is but a usurping king, be his trappings what they may; he is the born slave of all things. Let a man honour his craftmanship, his *can-do ;* and know that his rights of man have no concern at all with the Forty-third of Elizabeth.

CHAPTER IV

FINEST PEASANTRY IN THE WORLD

THE New Poor-Law is an announcement, sufficiently distinct, that whosoever will not work ought not to live. Can the poor man that is willing to work, always find work, and live by his work? Statistic Inquiry, as we say, has no answer to give. Legislation presupposes the answer—to be in the affirmative. A large postulate; which should have been made a proposition of; which should have been demonstrated, made indubitable to all persons! A man willing to work, and unable to find work, is perhaps the saddest sight that Fortune's inequality exhibits under this sun. Burns expresses feelingly what thoughts it gave him: a poor man seeking *work ;* seeking leave to toil that he might be fed and sheltered! That he might but be put on a level with the four-footed workers of the Planet which is his! There is not a horse willing to work but can get food and shelter in requital; a thing this two-footed worker has to seek for, to solicit occasionally in vain. He is nobody's two-footed worker; he is not even anybody's slave. And yet he is a *two*-footed worker; it is currently reported there is an immortal soul in him, sent down out of Heaven into the Earth; and one beholds him *seeking* for this!—Nay what will a wise Legislature say, if it turn out that he cannot find it; that the answer to their postulate proposition is not affirmative but negative?

There is one fact which Statistic Science has communicated, and a most astonishing one; the inference from which is pregnant as to this matter. Ireland has near seven millions of working people, the third unit of whom, it appears by Statistic Science, has not for thirty weeks each year as many third-rate potatoes as will suffice him. It is a fact perhaps the most eloquent that was ever written down in any language, at any date of the world's history. Was change and reformation needed in Ireland? Has Ireland been governed and guided in a " wise and loving " manner? A government and guidance of white European men which has issued in perennial hunger of potatoes to the third man extant,— ought to drop a veil over its face, and walk out of court under conduct of proper officers; saying no word; excepting now of a surety sentence either to change or die. All men, we must repeat, were made by God, and have immortal souls in them. The Sanspotato is of the selfsame stuff as the superfinest Lord Lieutenant. Not an individual Sanspotato human scarecrow but had a Life given him out of Heaven, with Eternities depending on it; for once and no second time. With Immensities in him, over him and round him; with feelings which a Shakspeare's speech would not utter; with desires illimitable as the Autocrat's of all the Russias!

Him various thrice-honoured persons, things and institutions have long been teaching, long been guiding, governing: and it is to perpetual scarcity of third-rate potatoes, and to what depends thereon, that he has been taught and guided. Figure thyself, O high-minded, clear-headed, clean-burnished reader, clapt by enchantment into the torn coat and waste hunger-lair of that same root-devouring brother man!—

Social anomalies are things to be defended, things to be amended; and in all places and things, short of the Pit itself, there is some admixture of worth and good. Room for extenuation, for pity, for patience! And yet when the general result has come to the length of perennial starvation, argument, extenuating logic, pity and patience on that subject may be considered as drawing to a close. It may be considered that such arrangement of things will have to terminate. That it has all just men for its natural enemies. That all just men, of what outward colour soever in Politics or otherwise, will say: This cannot last, Heaven disowns it, Earth is against it; Ireland will be burnt into a black unpeopled field of ashes rather than this should last.—The woes of Ireland, or "justice to Ireland," is not the chapter we have to write at present. It is a deep matter, an abysmal one, which no plummet of ours will sound. For the oppression has gone far farther than into the economics of Ireland; inwards to her very heart and soul. The Irish National character is degraded, disordered; till this recover itself, nothing is yet recovered. Immethodic, headlong, violent, mendacious: what can you make of the wretched Irishman? "A finer people never lived," as the Irish lady said to us; "only they have two faults, they do generally lie and steal: barring these"—! A people that knows not to speak the truth, and to act the truth, such people has departed from even the possibility of well-being. Such people works no longer on Nature and Reality; works now on Phantasm, Simulation, Nonentity; the result it arrives at is naturally not a thing but no-thing,—defect even of potatoes. Scarcity, futility, confusion, distraction must be perennial there. Such a people circulates not order but disorder, through every vein of it;—and the cure, if it is to be a cure, must begin at the heart: not in his condition only but in himself must the Patient be all changed. Poor Ireland! And yet let no true Irishman, who believes and sees all this, despair by reason of it. Cannot he too do something to withstand the unproductive falsehood, there as it lies accursed around him, and change it into truth, which is fruitful and blessed? Every mortal can and shall himself be a true man: it is a great thing, and the parent of great things;—as from a single acorn the whole earth might in the end be peopled with oaks! Every mortal can do something: this let him faithfully do, and leave with assured heart the issue to a Higher Power!

We English pay, even now, the bitter smart of long centuries of injustice to our neighbour Island. Injustice, doubt it not, abounds; or Ireland would not be miserable. The Earth is good, bountifully sends food and increase; if man's unwisdom did not intervene and forbid. It was an evil day when Strigul first meddled with that people. He could not extirpate them: could they but have agreed together, and extirpated him! Violent men there have been, and merciful; unjust rulers, and just; conflicting in a great element of violence, these five wild centuries now; and the violent and unjust have carried it, and we are come to *this*. England is guilty towards Ireland; and reaps at last, in full measure, the fruit of fifteen generations of wrong-doing.

But the thing we had to state here was our inference from that mournful fact of the third Sanspotato,—coupled with this other well-known fact that the Irish speak a partially intelligible dialect of English, and their fare across by steam is fourpence sterling! Crowds of miserable Irish darken all our towns. The wild Milesian features, looking false ingenuity, restlessness, unreason, misery and mockery, salute you on all highways and byways. The English coachman, as he whirls past, lashes the Milesian with his whip, curses him with his tongue; the Milesian is holding out his hat to beg. He is the sorest evil this country has to strive with. In his rags and laughing savagery, he is there to undertake all work that can be done by mere strength of hand and back; for wages that will purchase him potatoes. He needs only salt for condiment; he lodges to his mind in any pighutch or doghutch, roosts in outhouses; and wears a suit of tatters, the getting off and on of which is said to be a difficult operation, transacted only in festivals and the hightides of the calendar. The Saxon man if he cannot work on these terms, finds no work. He too may be ignorant; but he has not sunk from decent manhood to squalid apehood: he cannot continue there. American forests lie untilled across the ocean; the uncivilised Irishman, not by his strength, but by the opposite of strength, drives out the Saxon native, takes possession in his room. There abides he, in his squalor and unreason, in his falsity and drunken violence, as the ready-made nucleus of degradation and disorder. Whosoever struggles, swimming with difficulty, may now find an example how the human being can exist not swimming but sunk. Let him sink; he is not the worst of men; not worse than this man. We have quarantines against pestilence; but there is no pestilence like that; and against it what quarantine is possible? It is lamentable to look upon. This soil of Britain, these Saxon men have cleared it, made it arable, fertile and a home for them; they and their fathers have done that. Under the sky there exists no force of men who with arms in their hands could drive them out of it; all force of men with arms these Saxons would seize, in their grim way, and fling (Heaven's justice and their own Saxon humour aiding them) swiftly into the sea. But behold, a force of men armed only with rags, ignorance and nakedness; and the Saxon owners, paralysed by invisible magic of paper formula, have to fly far, and hide themselves in Transatlantic forests. "Irish repeal"? "Would to God," as Dutch William said, "*you* were King of Ireland, and could take yourself and it three thousand miles off,"—there to repeal it!

And yet these poor Celtiberian Irish brothers, what can *they* help it? They cannot stay at home, and starve. It is just and natural that they come hither as a curse to us. Alas, for them too it is not a luxury. It is not a straight or joyful way of avenging their sore wrongs this; but a most sad circuitous one. Yet a way it is, and an effectual way. The time has come when the Irish population must either be improved a little, or else exterminated. Plausible manage-ment, adapted to this hollow outcry or to that, will no longer do; it must be management grounded on sincerity and fact, to which the truth of things will respond—by an actual beginning of improvement to these wretched brother-men. In a state of perennial ultra-savage famine, in the midst of civilisation, they cannot continue. For that the Saxon British will ever submit to sink along with them to such a state, we assume as impossible. There is in these latter, thank God, an ingenuity which is not false; a methodic spirit, of insight, of perseverant well-doing; a rationality and veracity which Nature with her truth does *not* disown;—withal there is a " Berserkir rage " in the heart of them, which will prefer all things, including destruction and self-destruction, to that. Let no man awaken it, this same Berserkir rage! Deep-hidden it lies, far down in the centre, like genial central-fire, with stratum after stratum of arrangement, traditionary method, composed productiveness, all built above it, vivified and rendered fertile by it: justice, clearness, silence, perseverance, unhasting unresting diligence, hatred of disorder, hatred of injustice, which is the worst disorder, characterise this people; their inward fire we say, as all such fire should be, is hidden at the centre. Deep-hidden; but awakenable, but immeasurable;—let no man awaken it! With this strong silent people have the noisy vehement Irish now at length got common cause made. Ireland, now for the first time, in such strange circuitous way, does find itself embarked in the same boat with England, to sail together, or to sink together; the wretchedness of Ireland, slowly but inevitably, has crept over to us, and become our own wretchedness. The Irish population must get itself redressed and saved, for the sake of the English if for nothing else. Alas, that it should, on both sides, be poor toiling men that pay the smart for unruly Striguls, Henrys, Macdermots, and O'Donoghues! The strong have eaten sour grapes, and the teeth of the weak are set on edge. " Curses," says the Proverb, " are like chickens, they return always *home*."

But now, on the whole, it seems to us, English Statistic Science, with floods of the finest peasantry in the world streaming in on us daily, may fold up her Danaides reticulations on this matter of the Working Classes; and conclude, what every man who will take the statistic spectacles off his nose, and look, may discern in town or country: That the condition of the lower multitude of English labourers approximates more and more to that of the Irish competing with them in all markets; that whatsoever labour, to which mere strength with little skill will suffice, is to be done, will be done not at the English price, but at an approximation to the Irish price: at a price superior as yet to the Irish, that is, superior to scarcity of third-rate potatoes for thirty weeks yearly; superior, yet hourly, with the arrival of every new steamboat, sinking nearer to an equality with that. Half-a-million handloom weavers, working fifteen hours a-day, in perpetual inability to procure thereby enough of the coarsest food; English farm-labourers at nine shillings and at seven shillings a-week; Scotch farm-labourers who, " in districts the half of whose husbandry is that of cows, taste no milk, can procure no milk: " all these things are credible to us; several of them are known to us by the best evidence, by eyesight. With all this it is consistent that the wages of " skilled labour," as it is called, should in many cases be higher than they ever were: the giant Steamengine in a giant English Nation will here create violent demand for labour, and will there annihilate demand. But, alas, the great portion of labour is not skilled: the millions are and must be skilless, where strength alone is wanted; ploughers, delvers, borers; hewers of wood and drawers of water; menials of the Steamengine, only the *chief* menials and immediate *body*-servants of which require skill. English Commerce stretches its fibres over the whole earth; sensitive literally, nay quivering in convulsion, to the farthest influences of the earth. The huge demon of Mechanism smokes and thunders, panting at his great task, in all sections of English land; changing his *shape* like a very Proteus; and infallibly, at every change of shape, *oversetting* whole multitudes of workmen, and as if with the waving of his shadow from afar, hurling them asunder, this way and that, in their crowded march and course of work or traffic; so that the wisest no longer knows his whereabout. With an Ireland pouring daily in on us, in these circumstances; deluging us down to its own waste confusion, outward and inward, it seems a cruel mockery to tell poor drudges that *their* condition is improving.

New Poor-Law! *Laissez faire, laissez passer !* The master of horses, when the summer labour is done, has to feed his horses through the winter. If he said to his horses: " Quadrupeds, I have no longer work for you; but work exists abundantly over the world: are you ignorant (or must I read you Political-Economy Lectures) that the Steamengine always in the long-run creates additional work? Railways are forming in one quarter of this earth, canals in another, much cartage is wanted; somewhere in Europe, Asia, Africa or America, doubt it not, ye will find cartage: go and seek cartage, and good go with you! " They, with protrusive upper lip, snort dubious; signifying that Europe, Asia, Africa and America lie somewhat out of their beat; that what cartage may be wanted there is not too well known to them. *They* can find no cartage. They gallop distracted along highways, all fenced in to the right and to the left: finally, under pains of hunger, they take to leaping fences; eating foreign property, and—we know the rest. Ah, it is not a joyful mirth, it is sadder than tears, the laugh Humanity is forced to, at *Laissez-faire* applied to poor peasants, in a world like our Europe of the year 1839!

So much can observation altogether unstatistic, looking only at a Drogheda or Dublin steamboat, ascertain for itself. Another thing, likewise ascertainable on this vast obscure matter, excites a superficial surprise, but only a superficial one: That it is the best-paid workmen who, by Strikes, Trades-unions, Chartism, and the like, complain the most. No doubt of it! The best-paid workmen are they alone that *can* so complain! How shall he, the handloom weaver, who in the day that is passing over him has to find food for the day, strike work? If he strike work, he starves within the week. He is past complaint!—The fact itself, however, is one which, if we consider it, leads us into still deeper regions of the malady. Wages, it would appear, are no index of well-being to the working man: without proper wages there can be no well-being; but with them also there may be none. Wages of working men differ greatly in different quarters of this country; according to the researches or the guess of Mr. Symmons, an intelligent humane inquirer, they vary in the ratio of not less than three to one. Cotton-spinners, as we learn, are generally well paid, while employed; their wages, one week with another, wives and children all working, amount to sums which, if well laid out, were fully adequate to comfortable living. And yet, alas, there seems little question that comfort or reasonable well-being is as much a stranger in these households as in any. At the cold hearth of the ever-toiling ever-hungering weaver, dwells at least some equability, fixation as if in perennial ice: hope never comes; but also irregular impatience is absent. Of outward things these others have or might have enough, but of all inward things there is the fatalest lack. Economy does not exist among them; their trade now in plethoric prosperity, anon extenuated into inanition and "short time," is of the nature of gambling; they live by it like gamblers, now in luxurious superfluity, now in starvation. Black mutinous discontent devours them; simply the miserablest feeling that can inhabit the heart of man. English Commerce with its world-wide convulsive fluctuations, with its immeasurable Proteus Steam-demon, makes all paths uncertain for them, all life a bewilderment; sobriety, steadfastness, peaceable continuance, the first blessings of man, are not theirs.

It is in Glasgow among that class of operatives that "Number 60," in his dark room, pays down the price of blood. Be it with reason or with unreason, too surely they do in verity find the time all out of joint; this world for them no home, but a dingy prison-house, of reckless unthrift, rebellion, rancour, indignation against themselves and against all men. Is it a green flowery world, with azure everlasting sky stretched over it, the work and government of a God; or a murky-simmering Tophet, of copperas-fumes, cotton-fuzz, gin-riot, wrath and toil, created by a Demon, governed by a Demon? The sum of their wretchedness merited and unmerited welters, huge, dark and baleful, like a Dantean Hell, visible there in the statistics of Gin: Gin justly named the most authentic incarnation of the Infernal Principle in our times, too indisputable an incarnation; Gin the black throat into which wretchedness of every sort, consummating itself by calling on delirium to help it, whirls down; abdication of the power to think or resolve, as too painful now, on the part of men whose lot of all others would require thought and resolution; liquid Madness sold at ten-pence the quartern, all the products of which are and must be, like its origin, mad, miserable, ruinous, and that only! If from this black unluminous unheeded *Inferno*, and Prison-house of souls in pain, there do flash up from time to time, some dismal wide-spread glare of Chartism or the like, notable to all, claiming remedy from all,—are we to regard it as more baleful than the quiet state, or rather as not so baleful? Ireland is in chronic atrophy these five centuries; the disease of nobler England, identified now with that of Ireland, becomes acute, has crises, and will be cured or kill.

CHAPTER V

RIGHTS AND MIGHTS

It is not what a man outwardly has or wants that constitutes the happiness or misery of him. Nakedness, hunger, distress of all kinds, death itself have been cheerfully suffered, when the heart was right. It is the feeling of *injustice* that is insupportable to all men. The brutalest black African cannot bear that he should be used unjustly. No man can bear it, or ought to bear it. A deeper law than any parchment-law whatsoever, a law written direct by the hand of God in the inmost being of man, incessantly protests against it. What is injustice? Another name for *dis*order, for unveracity, unreality; a thing which veracious created Nature, even because it is not Chaos and a waste-whirling baseless Phantasm, rejects and disowns. It is not the outward pain of injustice; that, were it even the flaying of the back with knotted scourges, the severing of the head with guillotines, is comparatively a small matter. The real smart is the soul's pain and stigma, the hurt inflicted on the moral self. The rudest clown must draw himself up into attitude of battle, and resistance to the death, if such be offered him. He cannot live under it; his own soul aloud, and all the Universe with silent continual beckonings, says, It cannot be. He must revenge himself; *revancher* himself, make himself good again,—that so *meum* may be mine, *tuum* thine, and each party standing clear on his own basis, order be restored. There is something infinitely respectable in this, and we may say universally respected; it is the common stamp of manhood vindicating itself in all of us, the basis of whatever is worthy in all of us, and through superficial diversities, the same in all.

As *dis*order, insane by the nature of it, is the hatefulest of things to man, who lives by sanity and order, so injustice is the worst evil, some call it the only evil, in this world. All men submit to toil, to disappointment, to unhappiness; it is their lot here; but in all hearts, inextinguishable by sceptic logic, by sorrow, perversion or despair itself, there is a small still voice intimating that it is not the final lot; that wild, waste, incoherent as it looks, a God presides over it; that it is not an injustice, but a justice. Force itself, the hopelessness of resistance, has doubtless a composing effect;—against inanimate *Simooms*, and much other infliction of the like sort, we have found it suffice to produce complete composure. Yet one would say, a permanent Injustice even from an Infinite Power would prove unendurable by men. If men had lost belief in a God, their only resource against a blind No-God, of Necessity and Mechanism, that held them like a hideous Phalaris' Bull, imprisoned in its own iron belly, would be, with or without hope,—*revolt*. They could, as Novalis says, by a "simultaneous universal act of suicide," *depart* out of the World-Steamengine; and end, if not in victory, yet in invincibility, and unsubduable protest that such World-Steamengine was a failure and a stupidity.

Conquest, indeed, is a fact often witnessed; conquest, which seems mere wrong and force, everywhere asserts itself as a right among men. Yet if we examine, we shall find that, in this world, no conquest could ever become permanent, which did not withal show itself beneficial to the conquered as well as to conquerors. Mithridates King of Pontus, come now to extremity, "appealed to the patriotism of his people;" but, says the history, "he had squeezed them, and fleeced and plundered them for long years;" his requisitions, flying irregular, devastative, like the whirlwind, were less supportable than Roman strictness and method, regular though never so rigorous: he therefore appealed to their patriotism in vain. The Romans conquered Mithridates. The Romans, having conquered the world, held it conquered, *because* they could best govern the world; the mass of men found it nowise pressing to revolt; their fancy might be afflicted more or less, but in their solid interests they were better off than before.

So too in this England long ago, the old Saxon Nobles, disunited among themselves, and in power too nearly equal, could not have governed the country well; Harold being slain, their last chance of governing it, except in anarchy and civil war, was over: a new class of strong Norman Nobles, entering with a strong man, with a succession of strong men at the head of them, and not disunited, but united by many ties, by their very community of language and interest, had there been no other, *were* in a condition to govern it; and did govern it, we can believe, in some rather tolerable manner, or they would not have continued there. They acted, little conscious of such function on their part, as an immense volunteer Police Force, stationed everywhere, united, disciplined, feudally regimented, ready for action; strong Teutonic men; who, on the whole, proved effective men, and drilled this wild Teutonic people into unity and peaceable coöperation better than others could have done! How *can-do*, if we will well interpret it, unites itself with *shall-do* among mortals; how strength acts ever as the right-arm of justice; how might and right, so frightfully discrepant at first, are ever in the long-run one and the same,—is a cheering consideration, which always in the black tempestuous vortices of this world's history, will shine out on us, like an everlasting polar star.

Of conquest we may say that it never yet went by brute force and compulsion; conquest of that kind does not endure. Conquest, along with power of compulsion, an essential universally in human society, must bring benefit along with it, or men, of the ordinary strength of men, will fling it out. The strong man, what is he if we will consider? The wise man; the man with the gift of method, of faithfulness and valour, all of which are of the basis of wisdom; who has insight into what is what, into what will follow out of what, the eye to see and the hand to do; who is *fit* to administer, to direct, and guidingly command: he is the strong man. His muscles and bones are no stronger than ours; but his soul is stronger, his soul is wiser, clearer,—is better and nobler, for that is, has been and ever will be the root of all clearness worthy of such a name. Beautiful it is, and a gleam from the same eternal pole-star visible amid the destinies of men, that all talent, all intellect is in the first place mortal;—what a world were this otherwise! But it is the heart always that sees, before the head *can* see: let us know that; and know therefore that the Good alone is deathless and victorious, that Hope is sure and steadfast, in all phases of this "Place of Hope."—Shiftiness, quirk, attorney-cunning is a kind of thing that fancies itself, and is often fancied, to be talent; but it is luckily mistaken in that. Succeed truly it does, what is called succeeding; and even must in general succeed, if the dispensers of success be of due stupidity: men of due stupidity will needs say to it, "*Thou* art wisdom, rule thou!" Whereupon it rules. But Nature answers, "No, this ruling of thine is not according to *my* laws; thy wisdom was not wise enough! Dost thou take me too for a Quackery? For a Conventionality and Attorneyism? This chaff that thou sowest into my bosom, though it pass at the poll-booth and elsewhere for seed-corn, *I* will not grow wheat out of it, for it is chaff!"

But to return. Injustice, infidelity to truth and fact and Nature's order, being properly the one evil under the sun, and the feeling of injustice the one intolerable pain under the sun, our grand question as to the condition of these working men would be: Is it just? And first of all, What belief have they themselves formed about the justice of it? The words they promulgate are notable by way of answer; their actions are still more notable. Chartism with its pikes, Swing with his tinder-box, speak a most loud though inarticulate language. Glasgow Thuggery speaks aloud too, in a language we may well call infernal. What kind of " wild-justice " must it be in the hearts of these men that prompts them, with cold deliberation, in conclave assembled, to doom their brother workman, as the deserter of his order and his order's cause, to die as a traitor and deserter; and have him executed, since not by any public judge and hangman, then by a private one;—like your old Chivalry *Femgericht*, and Secret-Tribunal, suddenly in this strange guise become new; suddenly rising once more on the astonished eye, dressed now not in mail-shirts but in fustian jackets, meeting not in Westphalian forests but in the paved Gallowgate of Glasgow! Not loyal loving obedience to those placed over them, but a far other temper, must animate these men! It is frightful enough. Such temper must be widespread, virulent among the many, when even in its worst acme it can take such a form in a few. But indeed decay of loyalty in all senses, disobedience, decay of religious faith, has long been noticeable and lamentable in this largest class, as in other smaller ones. Revolt, sullen revengeful humour of revolt against the upper classes, decreasing respect for what their temporal superiors command, decreasing faith for what their spiritual superiors teach, is more and more the universal spirit of the lower classes. Such spirit may be blamed, may be vindicated; but all men must recognise it as extant there, all may know that it is mournful, that unless altered it will be fatal. Of lower classes so related to upper, happy nations are not made! To whatever other griefs the lower classes labour under, this bitterest and sorest grief now superadds itself: the unendurable conviction that they are unfairly dealt with, that their lot in this world is not founded on right, not even on necessity and might, and is neither what it should be, nor what it shall be.

Or why do we ask of Chartism, Glasgow Trades-unions, and suchlike? Has not broad Europe heard the question put, and answered, on the great scale; has not a FRENCH REVOLUTION been? Since the year 1789, there is now half a century complete; and a French Revolution not yet complete! Whosoever will look at that enormous Phenomenon may find many meanings in it, but this meaning as the ground of all: That it was a revolt of the oppressed lower classes against the oppressing or neglecting upper classes: not a French revolt only; no, a European one; full of stern monition to all countries of Europe. These Chartisms, Radicalisms, Reform Bill, Tithe Bill, and infinite other discrepancy, and acrid argument and jargon that there is yet to be, are *our* French Revolution: God grant that we, with our better methods, may be able to transact it by argument alone!

The French Revolution, now that we have sufficiently execrated its horrors and crimes, is found to have had withal a great meaning in it. As indeed, what great thing ever happened in this world, a world understood always to be made and governed by a Providence and Wisdom, not by an Unwisdom, without meaning somewhat? It was a tolerably audible voice of proclamation, and universal *oyez!* to all people, this of three-and-twenty years' close fighting, sieging, conflagrating, with a million or two of men shot dead: the world ought to know by this time that it was verily meant in earnest, that same Phenomenon, and had its own reasons for appearing there! Which accordingly the world begins now to do. The French Revolution is seen, or begins everywhere to be seen, " as the crowning phenomenon of our Modern time;" "the inevitable stern end of much; the fearful, but also wonderful, indispensable and sternly beneficent beginning of much." He who would understand the struggling convulsive unrest of European society, in any and every country, at this day, may read it in broad glaring lines there, in that the most convulsive phenomenon of the last thousand years. Europe lay pining, obstructed, moribund; quack-ridden, hag-ridden,—is there a hag, or spectre of the Pit, so baleful, hideous as your accredited quack, were he never so close-shaven, mild-spoken, plausible to himself and others? Quack-ridden: in that one word lies all misery whatsoever. Speciosity in all departments usurps the place of reality, thrusts reality away; instead of performance, there is appearance of performance. The quack is a Falsehood Incarnate; and speaks, and makes and does mere falsehoods, which Nature with her veracity has to disown. As chief priest, as chief governor, he stands there, intrusted with much. The husbandman of "Time's Seedfield;" he is the world's hired sower, hired and solemnly appointed to sow the kind true earth with wheat this year, that next year all men may have bread. He, miserable mortal, deceiving and self-deceiving, sows it, as we said, not with corn but with chaff; the world nothing doubting, harrows it in, pays him his wages, dismisses him with blessing, and—next year there has no corn sprung. Nature has disowned the chaff, declined growing chaff, and behold now there is no bread! It becomes necessary, in such case, to do several things; not soft things some of them, but hard.

Nay we will add that the very circumstance of quacks in unusual quantity getting domination, indicates that the heart of the world is *already* wrong. The impostor is false; but neither are his dupes altogether true: is not his first grand dupe the falsest of all,—himself namely? Sincere men, of never so limited intellect, have an instinct for discriminating sincerity. The cunningest Mephistopheles cannot deceive a simple Margaret of honest heart, "it stands written on his brow." Masses of people capable of being led away by quacks are themselves of partially untrue spirit. Alas, in such times it grows to be the universal belief, sole accredited knowingness, and the contrary of it accounted puerile enthusiasm, this sorrowfulest *dis*belief that there is properly speaking any truth in the world; that the world was, has been or ever can be guided, except by simulation, dissimulation, and the sufficiently dextrous practice of pretence. The faith of men is dead: in what has guineas in its pocket, beefeaters riding behind it, and cannons trundling before it, they can believe; in what has none of these things they cannot believe. Sense for the true and false is lost; there is properly no longer any true or false. It is the heyday of Imposture; of Semblance recognising itself, and getting itself recognised, for Substance. Gaping multitudes listen; unlistening multitudes see not but that it is all right, and in the order of Nature. Earnest men, one of a million, shut their lips; suppressing thoughts, which there are no words to utter. To them it is too visible that spiritual life has departed; that material life, in whatsoever figure of it, cannot long remain behind. To them it seems as if our Europe of the Eighteenth Century, long hag-ridden, vexed with foul enchanters, to the length now of gorgeous Domdaniel *Parcs-aux-cerfs* and " Peasants living on meal-husks and boiled grass," had verily sunk down to die and dissolve; and were now, with its French Philosophisms, Hume Scepticisms, Diderot Atheisms, maundering in the final deliration; writhing, with its Seven-years Silesian robber-wars, in the final agony. Glory to God, our Europe was not to die but to live! Our Europe rose like a frenzied giant; shook all that poisonous magician trumpery to right and left, trampling it stormfully under foot; and declared aloud that there was strength in him, not for life only, but for new and infinitely wider life. Antæus-like the giant had struck his foot once more upon Reality and the Earth; there only, if in this Universe at all, lay strength and healing for him. Heaven knows, it was not a gentle process; no wonder that it was a fearful process, this same " Phœnix fire-consummation!" But the alternative was it or death; the merciful Heavens, merciful in their severity, sent us it rather.

And so the " rights of man " were to be written down on paper; and experimentally wrought upon towards elaboration, in huge battle and wrestle, element conflicting with element, from side to side of this earth, for three-and-twenty years. Rights of man, wrongs of man? It is a question which has swallowed whole nations and generations; a question—on which we will not enter here. Far be it from us! Logic has small business with this question at present; logic has no plummet that will sound it at any time. But indeed the rights of man, as has been not unaptly remarked, are little worth ascertaining in comparison to the *mights* of man,—to what portion of his rights he has any chance of being able to make good! The accurate final rights of man lie in the far deeps of the Ideal, where " the Ideal weds itself to the Possible," as the Philosophers say. The ascertainable temporary rights of man vary not a little, according to place and time. They are known to depend much on what a man's convictions of them are. The Highland wife, with her husband at the foot of the gallows, patted him on the shoulder (if there be historical truth in Joseph Miller), and said amid her tears: "Go up, Donald, my man; the Laird bids ye." To her it seemed the rights of lairds were great, the rights of men small; and she acquiesced. Deputy Lapoule, in the *Salle des Menus* at Versailles, on the 4th of August 1789, demanded (he did actually "demand," and by unanimous vote obtain) that the "obsolete law" authorising a Seigneur, on his return from the chase or other needful fatigue, to slaughter not above two of his vassals, and refresh his feet in their warm blood and bowels, should be "abrogated." From such obsolete law, or mad tradition and phantasm of an obsolete law, down to any corn-law, game-law, rotten-borough law, or other law or practice clamoured of in this time of ours, the distance travelled over is great!

What are the rights of men? All men are justified in demanding and searching for their rights; moreover, justified or not, they will do it: by Chartisms, Radicalisms, French Revolutions, or whatsoever methods they have. Rights surely are right: on the other hand, this other saying is most true, "Use every man according to his *rights*, and who shall escape whipping?" These two things, we say, are both true; and both are essential to make up the whole truth. All good men know always and feel, each for himself, that the one is not less true than the other; and act accordingly. The contradiction is of the surface only; as in opposite sides of the same fact: universal in this *dualism* of a life we have. Between these two extremes, Society and all human things must fluctuatingly adjust themselves the best they can.

And yet that there is verily a "rights of man" let no mortal doubt. An ideal of right does dwell in all men, in all arrangements, pactions and procedures of men: it is to this ideal of right, more and more developing itself as it is more and more approximated to, that human Society forever tends and struggles. We say also that any given thing either *is* unjust or else just; however obscure the arguings and strugglings on it be, the thing in itself there as it lies, infallibly enough, *is* the one or the other. To which let us add only this, the first, last article of faith, the alpha and omega of all faith among men, That nothing which is unjust can hope to continue in this world. A faith true in all times, more or less forgotten in most, but altogether frightfully brought to remembrance again in ours! Lyons fusilladings, Nantes noyadings, reigns of terror, and such other universal battle-thunder and explosion; these, if we will understand them, were but a new irrefragable preaching abroad of that. It would appear that Speciosities which are not Realities cannot any longer inhabit this world. It would appear that the unjust thing has no friend in the Heaven, and a majority against it on the Earth; nay that *it* has at bottom all men for its enemies; that it may take shelter in this fallacy and then in that, but will be hunted from fallacy to fallacy till it find no fallacy to shelter-in any more, but must march and go elsewhither;—that, in a word, it ought to prepare incessantly for decent departure, before *in*decent departure, ignominious drumming out, nay savage smiting out and burning out, overtake it!

Alas, was that such new tidings? Is it not from of old indubitable, that Untruth, Injustice which is but acted untruth, has no power to continue in this true Universe of ours? The tidings was world-old, or older, as old as the Fall of Lucifer: and yet in that epoch unhappily it was new tidings, unexpected, incredible; and there had to be such earthquakes and shakings of the nations before it could be listened to, and laid to heart even slightly! Let us lay it to heart, let us know it well, that new shakings be not needed. Known and laid to heart it must everywhere be, before peace can pretend to come. This seems to us the secret of our convulsed era; this which is so easily written, which is and has been and will be so hard to bring to pass. All true men, high and low, each in his sphere, are consciously or unconsciously bringing it to pass; all false and half-true men are fruitlessly spending themselves to hinder it from coming to pass.

CHAPTER VI

LAISSEZ-FAIRE

FROM all which enormous events, with truths old and new embodied in them, what innumerable practical inferences are to be drawn! Events are written lessons, glaring in huge hieroglyphic picture-writing, that all may read and know them: the terror and horror they inspire is but the note of preparation for the truth they are to teach; a mere waste of terror if that be not learned. Inferences enough; most didactic, practically applicable in all departments of English things! One inference, but one inclusive of all, shall content us here; this namely: That *Laissez-faire* has as good as done its part in a great many provinces; that in the province of the Working Classes, *Laissez-faire* having passed its New Poor-Law, has reached the suicidal point, and now, as *felo-de-se*, lies dying there, in torchlight meetings and suchlike; that, in brief, a government of the under classes by the upper on a principle of *Let-alone* is no longer possible in England in these days. This is the one inference inclusive of all. For there can be no acting or doing of any kind, till it be recognised that there is a thing to be done; the thing once recognised, doing in a thousand shapes becomes possible. The Working Classes cannot any longer go on without government; without being *actually* guided and governed; England cannot subsist in peace till, by some means or other, some guidance and government for them is found.

For, alas, on us too the rude truth has come home. Wrappages and speciosities all worn off, the haggard naked fact speaks to us: Are these millions taught? Are these millions guided? We have a Church, the venerable embodiment of an idea which may well call itself divine; which our fathers for long ages, feeling it to be divine, have been embodying as we see: it is a Church well furnished with equipments and appurtenances; educated in universities; rich in money; set on high places that it may be conspicuous to all, honoured of all. We have an Aristocracy of landed wealth and commercial wealth, in whose hands lies the law-making and the law-administering; an Aristocracy rich, powerful, long secure in its place; an Aristocracy with more faculty put free into its hands than was ever before, in any country or time, put into the hands of any class of men. This Church answers: Yes, the people are taught. This Aristocracy, astonishment in every feature, answers: Yes, surely the people are guided! Do we not pass what Acts of Parliament are needful; as many as thirty-nine for the shooting of the partridges alone? Are there not treadmills, gibbets; even hospitals, poor-rates, New Poor-Law? So answers Church; so answers Aristocracy, astonishment in every feature.

Fact, in the mean while, takes his lucifer-box, sets fire to wheat-stacks; sheds an all-too dismal light on several things. Fact searches for his third-rate potato, not in the meekest humour, six-and-thirty weeks each year; and does not find it. Fact passionately joins Messiah Thom of Canterbury, and has himself shot for a new fifth-monarchy brought in by Bedlam. Fact holds his fustian-jacket *Femgericht* in Glasgow City. Fact carts his Petition over London streets, begging that you would simply have the goodness to grant him universal suffrage and " the five points," by way of remedy. These are not symptoms of teaching and guiding.

Nay, at bottom, is it not a singular thing this of *Laissez-faire*, from the first origin of it? As good as an *abdication* on the part of governors; an admission that they are henceforth incompetent to govern, that they are not there to govern at all, but to do—one knows not what! The universal demand of *Laissez-faire* by a people from its governors or upper classes, is a soft-sounding demand; but it is only one step removed from the fatalist. " *Laissez-faire*," exclaims a sardonic German writer, " What is this universal cry for *Laissez-faire* ? Does it mean that human affairs require no guidance; that wisdom and forethought cannot guide them better than folly and accident? Alas, does it not mean: ' *Such* guidance is worse than none! Leave us alone of *your* guidance; eat your wages, and sleep!'" And now if guidance have grown indispensable, and the sleep continue, what becomes of the sleep and its wages?—In those entirely surprising circumstances to which the Eighteenth Century had brought us, in the time of Adam Smith, *Laissez-faire* was a reasonable cry;—as indeed, in all circumstances, for a wise governor there will be meaning in the principle of it. To wise governors you will cry: " See what you will, and will not, let alone." To unwise governors, to hungry Greeks throttling down hungry Greeks on the floor of a St. Stephen's, you will cry: " Let *all* things alone; for Heaven's sake, meddle ye with nothing!"

How *Laissez-faire* may adjust itself in other provinces we say not: but we do venture to say, and ask whether events everywhere, in world - history and parish - history, in all manner of dialects are not saying it, That in regard to the lower orders of society, and their governance and guidance, the principle of *Laissez-faire* has terminated, and is no longer

applicable at all, in this Europe of ours, still less in this
England of ours. Not misgovernment, nor yet no-government; only government will now serve. What is the
meaning of the "five points," if we will understand them?
What are all popular commotions and maddest bellowings,
from Peterloo to the Place-de-Grève itself? Bellowings,
*in*articulate cries as of a dumb creature in rage and pain;
to the ear of wisdom they are inarticulate prayers: "Guide
me, govern me! I am mad and miserable, and cannot guide
myself!" Surely of all "rights of man," this right of the
ignorant man to be guided by the wiser, to be, gently or
forcibly, held in the true course by him, is the indisputablest.
Nature herself ordains it from the first; Society struggles
towards perfection by enforcing and accomplishing it more
and more. If Freedom have any meaning, it means enjoyment of this right, wherein all other rights are enjoyed. It
is a sacred right and duty, on both sides; and the summary
of all social duties whatsoever between the two. Why does
the one toil with his hands, if the other be not to toil, still
more unweariedly, with heart and head? The brawny
craftsman finds it no child's-play to mould his unpliant
rugged masses; neither is guidance of men a dilettantism:
what it becomes when treated as a dilettantism, we may see!
The wild horse bounds homeless through the wilderness, is
not led to stall and manger; but neither does he toil for you,
but for himself only.

Democracy, we are well aware, what is called "self-
government" of the multitude by the multitude, is in words
the thing everywhere passionately clamoured for at present.
Democracy makes rapid progress in these latter times, and
ever more rapid, in a perilous accelerative ratio; towards
democracy, and that only, the progress of things is everywhere tending as to the final goal and winning-post. So
think, so clamour the multitudes everywhere. And yet all
men may see, whose sight is good for much, that in democracy can lie no finality; that with the completest winning
of democracy there is nothing yet won,—except emptiness,
and the free chance to win! Democracy is, by the nature
of it, a self-cancelling business; and gives in the long-run
a net result of *zero*. Where no government is wanted, save
that of the parish-constable, as in America with its boundless
soil, every man being able to find work and recompense for

himself, democracy may subsist; not elsewhere, except briefly, as a swift transition towards something other and farther. Democracy never yet, that we heard of, was able to accomplish much work, beyond that same cancelling of itself. Rome and Athens are themes for the schools; unexceptionable for that purpose. In Rome and Athens, as elsewhere, if we look practically, we shall find that it was not by loud voting and debating of many, but by wise insight and ordering of a few that the work was done. So is it ever, so will it ever be.

The French Convention was a Parliament elected " by the five points," with ballot-boxes, universal suffrages, and what not, as perfectly as Parliament can hope to be in this world; and had indeed a pretty spell of work to do, and did it. The French Convention had to cease from being a free Parliament, and become more arbitrary than any Sultan Bajazet, before it could so much as subsist. It had to purge out its argumentative Girondins, elect its Supreme Committee of *Salut*, guillotine into silence and extinction all that gainsaid it, and rule and work literally by the sternest despotism ever seen in Europe, before it could rule at all. Napoleon was not president of a republic; Cromwell tried hard to rule in that way, but found that he could not. These, " the armed soldiers of democracy," had to chain democracy under their feet, and become despots over it, before they could work out the earnest obscure purpose of democracy itself!

Democracy, take it where you will in our Europe, is found but as a regulated method of rebellion and abrogation; it abrogates the old arrangement of things; and leaves, as we say, *zero* and vacuity for the institution of a new arrangement. It is the consummation of No-government and *Laissez-faire*. It may be natural for our Europe at present; but cannot be the ultimatum of it. Not towards the impossibility, " self-government " of a multitude by a multitude; but towards some possibility, government by the wisest, does bewildered Europe struggle. The blessedest possibility: not misgovernment, not *Laissez-faire*, but veritable government! Cannot one discern too, across all democratic turbulence, clattering of ballot-boxes and infinite sorrowful jangle, needful or not, that this at bottom is the wish and prayer of all human hearts, everywhere and at all times: " Give me a leader; a true leader, not a false sham-leader; a true leader, that he may guide me on the true way, that I may be loyal to him, that I may swear fealty to him and follow him, and feel that it is well with me!" The relation of the taught to the teacher, of the loyal subject to his guiding king, is, under one shape or another, the vital element of human Society; indispensable to it, perennial in it; without which, as a body reft of its soul, it falls down into death, and with horrid noisome dissolution passes away and disappears.

But verily in these times, with their new stern Evangel, that Speciosities which are not Realities can no longer be, all Aristocracies, Priesthoods, Persons in Authority, are called upon to consider. What is an Aristocracy? A corporation of the Best, of the Bravest. To this joyfully, with heart-loyalty, do men pay the half of their substance, to equip and decorate their Best, to lodge them in palaces, set them high over all. For it is of the nature of men, in every time, to honour and love their Best; to know no limit in honouring them. Whatsoever Aristocracy *is* still a corporation of the Best, is safe from all peril, and the land it rules is a safe and blessed land. Whatsoever Aristocracy does not even attempt to be that, but only to wear the clothes of that, is not safe; neither is the land it rules in safe! For this now is our sad lot, that we must find a *real* Aristocracy, that an apparent Aristocracy, how plausible soever, has become inadequate for us. One way or other, the world will absolutely need to be governed; if not by this class of men, then by that. One can predict, without gift of prophecy, that the era of routine is nearly ended. Wisdom and faculty alone, faithful, valiant, ever-zealous, not pleasant but painful, continual effort will suffice. Cost what it may, by one means or another, the toiling multitudes of this perplexed, over-crowded Europe must and will find governors. " *Laissez-faire*, Leave them to do "? The thing they will *do*, if so left, is too frightful to think of! It has been *done* once, in sight of the whole earth, in these generations: can it need to be done a second time?

For a Priesthood, in like manner, whatsoever its titles, possessions, professions, there is but one question: Does it teach and spiritually guide this people, yea or no? If yea, then is all well. But if no, then let it strive earnestly to alter, for as

yet there is nothing well! Nothing, we say: and indeed is
not this that we call spiritual guidance properly the soul of the
whole, the life and eyesight of the whole? The world asks of
its Church in these times, more passionately than of any other
Institution any question, " Canst thou teach us or not? "—A
Priesthood in France, when the world asked, " What canst
thou do for us? " answered only, aloud and ever louder,
" Are we not of God? Invested with all power? "—till at
length France cut short this controversy too, in what frightful
way we know. To all men who believed in the Church, to all
men who believed in God and the soul of man, there was no
issue of the French Revolution half so sorrowful as that.
France cast out its benighted blind Priesthood into destruction; yet with what a loss to France also! A solution of
continuity, what we may well call such; and this where continuity is so momentous: the New, whatever it may be,
cannot now *grow* out of the Old, but is severed sheer asunder
from the Old,—how much lies wasted in that gap! That one
whole generation of thinkers should be without a religion to
believe, or even to contradict; that Christianity, in thinking
France, should as it were fade away so long into a remote
extraneous tradition, was one of the saddest facts connected
with the future of that country. Look at such Political and
Moral Philosophies, St.-Simonisms, Robert-Macairisms, and
the " Literature of Desperation "! Kingship was perhaps
but a cheap waste, compared with this of the Priestship;
under which France still, all but unconsciously, labours;
and may long labour, remediless the while. Let others
consider it, and take warning by it! France is a pregnant
example in all ways. Aristocracies that do not govern,
Priesthoods that do not teach; the misery of that, and the
misery of altering that,—are written in Belshazzar fire-letters
on the history of France.

Or does the British reader, safe in the assurance that
" England is not France," call all this unpleasant doctrine
of ours ideology, perfectibility, and a vacant dream? Does
the British reader, resting on the faith that what has been
these two generations was from the beginning, and will be
to the end, assert to himself that things are already as they
can be, as they must be; that on the whole, no Upper Classes
did ever " govern " the Lower, in this sense of governing?
Believe it not, O British reader! Man is man everywhere;

dislikes to have "sensible species" and "ghosts of defunct bodies" foisted on him, in England even as in France.

How much the Upper Classes did actually, in any the most perfect Feudal time, return to the Under by way of recompense, in government, guidance, protection, we will not undertake to specify here. In Charity-Balls, Soup-Kitchens, in Quarter-Sessions, Prison-Discipline and Treadmills, we can well believe the old Feudal Aristocracy not to have surpassed the new. Yet we do say that the old Aristocracy were the governors of the Lower Classes, the guides of the Lower Classes; and even, at bottom, that they existed as an Aristocracy because they were found adequate for that. Not by Charity-Balls and Soup-Kitchens; not so; far otherwise! But it was their happiness that, in struggling for their own objects, they *had* to govern the Lower Classes, even in this sense of governing. For, in one word, *Cash Payment* had not then grown to be the universal sole nexus of man to man; it was something other than money that the high then expected from the low, and could not live without getting from the low. Not as buyer and seller alone, of land or what else it might be, but in many senses still as soldier and captain, as clansman and head, as loyal subject and guiding king, was the low related to the high. With the supreme triumph of Cash, a changed time has entered; there must a changed Aristocracy enter. We invite the British reader to meditate earnestly on these things.

Another thing, which the British reader often reads and hears in this time, is worth his meditating for a moment: That Society "exists for the protection of property." To which it is added, that the poor man also has property, namely, his "labour," and the fifteen-pence or three-and-sixpence a-day he can get for that. True enough, O friends, "for protecting *property* ;" most true: and indeed, if you will once sufficiently enforce that Eighth Commandment, the whole "rights of man" are well cared for; I know no better definition of the rights of man. *Thou shalt not steal, thou shalt not be stolen from :* what a Society were that; Plato's Republic, More's Utopia mere emblems of it! Give every man what is his, the accurate price of what he has done and been, no man shall any more complain, neither shall the earth suffer any more. For the protection of property, in very truth, and for that alone!

And now what is thy property? That parchment title-deed, that purse thou buttonest in thy breeches-pocket? Is that thy valuable property? Unhappy brother, most poor insolvent brother, I without parchment at all, with purse oftenest in the flaccid state, imponderous, which will not fling against the wind, have quite other property than that! I have the miraculous breath of Life in me, breathed into my nostrils by Almighty God. I have affections, thoughts, a god-given *capability* to be and do; rights, therefore,—the right for instance to thy love if I love thee, to thy guidance if I obey thee: the strangest rights, whereof in church-pulpits one still hears something, though almost unintelligible now; rights stretching high into Immensity, far into Eternity! Fifteen - pence a - day; three - and - sixpence a - day; eight hundred pounds and odd a-day, dost thou call that my property? I value that little; little all I could purchase with that. For truly, as is said, what matters it? In torn boots, in soft-hung carriages-and-four, a man gets always to his journey's end. Socrates walked barefoot, or in wooden shoes, and yet arrived happily. They never asked him, *What* shoes or conveyance? never, What wages hadst thou? but simply, What work didst thou?—Property, O brother? "Of my very body I have but a life-rent." As for this flaccid purse of mine, 'tis something, nothing; has been the slave of pickpockets, cutthroats, Jew-brokers, gold-dust robbers; 'twas his, 'tis mine;—'tis thine, if thou care much to steal it. But my soul, breathed into me by God, my *Me* and what capability is there; that is mine, and I will resist the stealing of it. I call that mine and not thine; I will keep that, and do what work I can with it: God has given it me, the Devil shall not take it away! Alas, my friends, Society exists and has existed for a great many purposes, not so easy to specify!

Society, it is understood, does not in any age prevent a man from being what he *can be*. A sooty African *can* become a Toussaint L'Ouverture, a murderous Three-fingered Jack, let the yellow West Indies say to it what they will. A Scottish Poet, "proud of his name and country," *can* apply fervently to "Gentlemen of the Caledonian Hunt," and become a gauger of beer-barrels, and tragic immortal broken-hearted Singer; the stifled echo of his melody audible through long centuries, one other note in "that sacred *Miserere*" that rises up to Heaven, out of all times and lands. What I *can be* thou decidedly wilt not hinder me from being. Nay even for being what I *could be*, I have the strangest claims on thee,—not convenient to adjust at present! Protection of breeches-pocket property? O reader, to what shifts is poor Society reduced, struggling to give still some account of herself, in epochs when Cash Payment has become the sole nexus of man to man! On the whole, we will advise Society not to talk at all about what she exists for; but rather with her whole industry to exist, to try how she can keep existing! That is her best plan. She may depend upon it, if she ever, by cruel chance, did come to exist only for protection of breeches-pocket property, she would lose very soon the gift of protecting even that, and find her career in our lower world on the point of terminating!—

For the rest, that in the most perfect Feudal Ages, the Ideal of Aristocracy nowhere lived in vacant serene purity as an Ideal, but always as a poor imperfect Actual, little heeding or not knowing at all that an Ideal lay in it,—this too we will cheerfully admit. Imperfection, it is known, cleaves to human things; far is the ideal departed from, in most times; very far! And yet so long as an Ideal (any soul of Truth) does, in never so confused a manner, exist and work within the Actual, it is a tolerable business. Not so, when the Ideal has entirely departed, and the Actual owns to itself that it has no Idea, no soul of Truth any longer: at that degree of imperfection human things cannot continue living; they are obliged to alter or expire, when they attain to that. Blotches and diseases exist on the skin and deeper, the heart continuing whole; but it is another matter when the heart itself becomes diseased; when there is no heart, but a monstrous gangrene pretending to exist there as heart!

On the whole, O reader, thou wilt find everywhere that things which have had an existence among men have first of all had to have a truth and worth in them, and were not semblances but realities. Nothing not a reality ever yet got men to pay bed and board to it for long. Look at Mahometanism itself! Dalai-Lamaism, even Dalai-Lamaism, one rejoices to discover, may be worth its victuals in this world; not a quackery but a sincerity; not a nothing but a something! The mistake of those who believe that fraud, force, injustice, whatsoever untrue thing, howsoever cloaked and decorated, was ever or can ever be the principle of man's relations to man, is great and the greatest. It is the error of the infidel; in whom the truth as yet is *not*. It is an error pregnant with mere errors and miseries; an error fatal, lamentable, to be abandoned by all men.

CHAPTER VII

NOT LAISSEZ-FAIRE

How an Aristocracy, in these present times and circumstances, could, if never so well disposed, set about governing the Under Class? What they should do; endeavour or attempt to do? That is even the question of questions:—the question which *they* have to solve; which it is our utmost function at present to tell them, lies there for solving, and must and will be solved.

Insoluble we cannot fancy it. One select class Society has furnished with wealth, intelligence, leisure, means outward and inward for governing; another huge class, furnished by Society with none of those things, declares that it must be governed: Negative stands fronting Positive; if Negative and Positive *cannot* unite,—it will be worse for both! Let the faculty and earnest constant effort of England combine round this matter; let it once be recognised as a vital matter. Innumerable things our Upper Classes and Lawgivers might " do; " but the preliminary of all things, we must repeat, is to know that a thing must needs be done. We lead them here to the shore of a boundless continent; ask them, Whether they do not with their own eyes see it, see strange symptoms of it, lying huge, dark, unexplored, inevitable; full of hope, but also full of difficulty, savagery, almost of despair? Let them enter; they must enter; Time and Necessity have brought them hither; where they are is no continuing! Let them enter; the first step once taken, the next will have become clearer, all future steps will become possible. It is a great problem for all of us; but for themselves, we may say, more than for any. On them chiefly, as the expected solvers of it, will the failure of a solution first fall. One way or other there must and will be a solution.

True, these matters lie far, very far indeed, from the " usual habits of Parliament," in late times; from the routine course of any Legislative or Administrative body of men that exists among us. Too true! And that is even the thing we complain of: had the mischief been looked into as it gradually rose, it would not have attained this magnitude. That self-cancelling Donothingism and *Laissez-faire* should have got so ingrained into our Practice, is the source of all these miseries. It is too true that Parliament, for the matter of near a century now, has been able to undertake the adjustment of almost one thing alone, of itself and its own interests; leaving other interests to rub along very much as they could and would. True, this was the practice of the whole Eighteenth Century; and struggles still to prolong itself into the Nineteenth,—which, however, is no longer the time for it!

Those Eighteenth-century Parliaments, one may hope, will become a curious object one day. Are not these same "*Memoirs*" of Horace Walpole, to an unparliamentary eye, already a curious object? One of the clearest-sighted men of the Eighteenth Century writes down his Parliamentary observation of it there; a determined despiser and merciless dissector of cant; a liberal withal, one who will go all lengths for the "glorious revolution," and resist Tory principles to the death: he writes, with an indignant elegiac feeling, how Mr. This, who had voted so and then voted so, and was the son of this and the brother of that, and had such claims to the fat appointment, was nevertheless scandalously postponed to Mr. That;—whereupon are not the affairs of this nation in a bad way? How hungry Greek meets hungry Greek on the floor of St. Stephen's, and wrestles him and throttles him till he has to cry, Hold! the office is thine!—of this does Horace write.—One must say, the destinies of nations do not always rest entirely on Parliament. One must say, it is a wonderful affair that science of "government," as practised in the Eighteenth Century of the Christian era, and still struggling to practise itself. One must say, it was a lucky century that could get it so practised: a century which had inherited richly from its predecessors; and also which did, not unnaturally, bequeath to its successors a French Revolution, general overturn, and reign of terror;—intimating, in most audible thunder, conflagration, guillotinement, cannonading and universal war and earthquake, that such century with its practices had *ended*.

Ended;—for decidedly that course of procedure will no longer serve. Parliament will absolutely, with whatever effort, have to lift itself out of those deep ruts of donothing routine; and learn to say, on all sides, something more edifying than *Laissez-faire*. If Parliament cannot learn it, what is to become of Parliament? The toiling millions of England ask of their English Parliament foremost of all, Canst thou govern us or not? Parliament with its privileges is strong; but Necessity and the Laws of Nature are stronger than it. If Parliament cannot do this thing, Parliament we prophesy will do some other thing and things which, in the strangest and not the happiest way, will forward its being done,—not much to the advantage of Parliament probably! Done, one way or other, the thing must be. In these complicated times, with Cash Payment as the sole nexus between man and man, the Toiling Classes of mankind declare, in their confused but must emphatic way, to the Untoiling, that they will be governed; that they must,—under penalty of Chartisms, Thuggeries, Rickburnings, and even blacker things than those. Vain also is it to think that the misery of one class, of the great universal under class, can be isolated, and kept apart and peculiar, down in that class. By infallible contagion, evident enough to reflection, evident even to Political Economy that will reflect, the misery of the lowest spreads upwards and upwards till it reaches the very highest; till all has grown miserable, palpably false and wrong; and poor drudges hungering " on meal-husks and boiled grass " do, by circuitous but sure methods, bring kings' heads to the block!

Cash Payment the sole nexus; and there are so many things which cash will not pay! Cash is a great miracle; yet it has not all power in Heaven, nor even on Earth. " Supply and demand " we will honour also; and yet how many " demands " are there, entirely indispensable, which have to go elsewhere than to the shops, and produce quite other than cash, before they can get their supply! On the whole, what astonishing payments does cash make in this world! Of your Samuel Johnson, furnished with " fourpence-halfpenny a-day," and solid lodging at nights on the paved streets, as his payment, we do not speak;—not in the way of complaint: it is a world-old business for the like of him, that same arrangement or a worse; perhaps the man, for his own uses, had need even of that, and of no better. Nay is not Society, busy with its Talfourd Copyright Bill and the like struggling to do something effectual for that man;—enacting with all industry that his own creation be accounted his own manufacture, and continue unstolen, on his own market-stand, for so long as sixty years? Perhaps Society is right there; for discrepancies on that side too may become excessive. All men are not patient docile Johnsons; some of them are half-mad inflammable Rousseaus. Such, in peculiar times, you may drive too far. Society in France, for example, was not destitute of cash: Society contrived to pay Philippe d'Orléans not yet Egalité three hundred thousand a-year and odd, for driving cabriolets through the streets of Paris and other work done; but in cash, encouragement, arrangement, recompense or recognition of any kind, it had nothing to give this same half-mad Rousseau for his work done; whose brain in consequence, *too* " much enforced " for a weak brain, uttered hasty sparks, *Contrat Social* and the like, which proved not so quenchable again! In regard to that species of men too, who knows whether *Laissez-faire* itself (which is Serjeant Talfourd's Copyright Bill continued to eternity instead of sixty years) will not turn out insufficient, and have to cease, one day?—

Alas, in regard to so very many things, *Laissez-faire* ought partly to endeavour to cease! But in regard to poor Sanspotato peasants, Trades-Union craftsmen, Chartist cotton-spinners, the time has come when it must either cease or a worse thing straightway begin,—a thing of tinder-boxes, vitriol-bottles, secondhand pistols, a visibly insupportable thing in the eyes of all.

CHAPTER VIII

NEW ERAS

FOR in very truth it is a " new Era; " a new Practice has become indispensable in it. One has heard so often of new eras, new and newest eras, that the word has grown rather empty of late. Yet new eras do come; there is no fact surer than that they have come more than once. And always with a change of era, with a change of intrinsic conditions, there has to be a change of practice and outward relations brought about,—if not peaceably, then by violence; for brought about it has to be, there could no rest come till then. How many eras and epochs, not noted at the moment;—which indeed is the blessedest condition of epochs, that they come quietly, making no proclamation of themselves, and are only visible long after: a Cromwell Rebellion, a French Revolution, "striking on the Horologe of Time," to tell all mortals what o'clock it has become, are too expensive, if one could help it!—

In a strange rhapsodic "History of the Teuton Kindred (*Geschichte der Teutschen Sippschaft*)," not yet translated into our language, we have found a Chapter on the Eras of England, which, were there room for it, would be instructive in this place. We shall crave leave to excerpt some pages; partly as a relief from the too near vexations of our own rather sorrowful Era; partly as calculated to throw, more or less obliquely, some degree of light on the meanings of that. The Author is anonymous: but we have heard him called the Herr Professor Sauerteig, and indeed think we know him under that name:

"Who shall say what work and works this England has yet to do? For what purpose this land of Britain was created, set like a jewel in the encircling blue of Ocean; and this Tribe of Saxons, fashioned in the depths of Time, 'on the shores of the Black Sea' or elsewhere, 'out of Harzgebirge rock' or whatever other material, was sent travelling hitherward? No man can say: it was for a work, and for works, incapable of announcement in words. Thou seest them there; part of them stand done, and visible to the eye; even these thou canst not *name :* how much less the others still matter of prophecy only!—They live and labour there, these twenty million Saxon men; they have been born into this mystery of life out of the darkness of Past Time:—how changed now since the first Father and first Mother of them set forth, quitting the tribe of *Theuth*, with passionate farewell, under questionable auspices; on scanty bullock-cart, if they had even bullocks and a cart; with axe and hunting-spear, to subdue a portion of our common Planet! This Nation now has cities and seedfields, has spring-vans, dray-wagons, Long-Acre carriages, nay railway trains; has coined-money, exchange-bills, laws, books, war-fleets, spinning-jennies, warehouses and West-India Docks: see what it has built and done, what it can and will yet build and do! These umbrageous pleasure-woods, green meadows, shaven stubblefields, smooth-sweeping roads; these high-domed cities, and what they hold and bear; this mild Good-morrow which the stranger bids thee, equitable, nay forbearant if need were, judicially calm and law-observing towards thee a stranger, what work has it not cost? How many brawny arms, generation after generation, sank down wearied; how many noble hearts, toiling while life lasted, and wise heads that wore themselves dim with scanning and discerning, before this waste *Whitecliff*, Albion so-called, with its other Cassiterides *Tin Islands*, became a BRITISH EMPIRE! The stream of World-History has altered its complexion; Romans are dead out, English are come in. The red broad mark of Romanhood, stamped ineffaceably on that Cart of Time, has disappeared from the present, and belongs only to the past. England plays its part; England too has a mark to leave, and we will hope none of the least significant. Of a truth, whosoever had, with the bodily eye, seen Hengst and Horsa mooring on the mud-beach of Thanet, on that spring morning of the Year 449; and then, with the spiritual eye, looked forward to New York, Calcutta, Sidney Cove, across the ages and the oceans; and thought what Wellingtons, Washingtons, Shakspeares, Miltons, Watts, Arkwrights, William Pitts and Davie Crocketts had to issue from that business, and do their several taskworks so,—he would have said, those leather-boats of Hengst's had a kind of cargo in them! A genealogic Mythus superior to any in the old Greek, to almost any in the old Hebrew itself; and not a Mythus either, but every fibre of it fact. An Epic Poem was there, and all manner of poems; except that the Poet has not yet made his appearance."

" Six centuries of obscure endeavour," continues Sauerteig, " which to read Historians, you would incline to call mere obscure slaughter, discord, and misendeavour; of which all that the human memory, after a thousand readings, can remember, is that it resembled, what Milton names it, the ' flocking and fighting of kites and crows:' this, in brief, is the history of the Heptarchy or Seven Kingdoms. Six centuries; a stormy springtime, if there ever was one, for a Nation. Obscure fighting of kites and crows, however, was not the History of it; but was only what the dim Historians of it saw good to record. Were not forests felled, bogs drained, fields made arable, towns built, laws made, and the Thought and Practice of men in many ways perfected? Venerable Bede had got a language which he could now not only speak, but spell and put on paper: think what lies in that. Bemurmured by the German sea-flood swinging slow with sullen roar against those hoarse Northumbrian rocks, the venerable man set down several things in a legible manner. Or was the smith idle, hammering only wartools? He had learned metallurgy, stithy-work in general; and made ploughshares withal, and adzes and mason-hammers. *Castra*, Caesters or Chesters, Dons, Tons (*Zauns*, Enclosures or *Towns*), not a few, did they not stand there; of burnt brick, of timber, of lath-and-clay; sending up the peaceable smoke of hearths? England had a History then too; though no Historian to write it. Those 'flockings and fightings,' sad inevitable necessities, were the expensive tentative steps towards some capability of living and working in concert: experiments they were, not always conclusive, to ascertain who had the might over whom, the right over whom."

" M. Thierry has written an ingenious Book, celebrating with considerable pathos the fate of the Saxons fallen under that fierce-hearted *Conquæstor*, Acquirer or Conqueror, as he is named. M. Thierry professes to have a turn for looking at that side of things: the fate of the Welsh too moves him; of the Celts generally, whom a fiercer race swept before them into the mountainous nooks of the West, whither they were not worth following. Noble deeds, according to M. Thierry, were done by these unsuccessful men, heroic sufferings undergone; which it is a pious duty to rescue from forgetfulness. True, surely! A tear at least is due to the unhappy: it is right and fit that there should be a man to assert that lost cause too, and see what can still be made of it. Most right: —and yet, on the whole, taking matters on that great scale, what can we say but that the cause which pleased the gods has in the end to please Cato also? Cato cannot alter it; Cato will find that he cannot at bottom wish to alter it.

" Might and Right do differ frightfully from hour to hour; but give them centuries to try it in, they are found to be identical. Whose land *was* this of Britain? God's who made it, His and no other's it was and is. Who of God's creatures had right to live in it? The wolves and bisons? Yes they, till one with a better right showed himself. The Celt, ' aboriginal savage of Europe,' as a snarling antiquary names him, arrived, pretending to have a better right; and did accordingly, not without pain to the bisons, make good the same. He had a better right to that piece of God's land; namely a better might to turn it to use;—a might to settle himself there, at least, and try what use he could turn it to. The bisons disappeared; the Celts took possession, and tilled. Forever, was it to be? Alas, *Forever* is not a category that can establish itself in this world of Time. A world of Time, by the very definition of it, is a world of mortality and mutability, of Beginning and Ending. No property is eternal but God the Maker's: whom Heaven permits to take possession, his is the right; Heaven's sanction *is* such permission,— while it lasts: nothing more can be said. Why does that hyssop grow there, in the chink of the wall? Because the whole Universe, sufficiently occupied otherwise, could not hitherto prevent its growing! It has the might and the right. By the same great law do Roman Empires establish themselves, Christian Religions promulgate themselves, and all extant Powers bear rule. The strong thing is the just thing: this thou wilt find throughout in our world;—as indeed was God and Truth the Maker of our world, or was Satan and Falsehood?

"One proposition widely current as to this Norman Conquest is of a Physiologic sort: That the conquerors and conquered here were of different races; nay that the Nobility of England is still, to this hour, of a somewhat different blood from the commonalty, their fine Norman features contrasting so pleasantly with the coarse Saxon ones of the others. God knows, there are coarse enough features to be seen among the commonalty of that country; but if the Nobility's be finer, it is not their Normanhood that can be the reason. Does the above Physiologist reflect who those same Normans, Northmen, originally were? Baltic Saxons, and what other miscellany of Lurdanes, Jutes and Deutsch Pirates from the East-sea marshes would join them in plunder of France! If living three centuries longer in Heathenism, sea-robbery, and the unlucrative fishing of amber could ennoble them beyond the others, then were they ennobled. The Normans were Saxons who had learned to speak French. No: by Thor and Wodan, the Saxons were all as noble as needful;—shaped, says the Mythus, 'from the rock of the Harzgebirge;' brother-tribes being made of clay, wood, water, or what other material might be going! A stubborn, taciturn, sulky, indomitable rock-made race of men; as the figure they cut in all quarters, in the cane-brake of Arkansas, in the Ghauts of the Himmalaya, no less than in London City, in Warwick or Lancaster County, does still abundantly manifest."

" To this English People in World-History, there have been, shall I prophesy, Two grand tasks assigned? Huge-looming through the dim tumult of the always incommensurable Present Time, outlines of two tasks disclose themselves: the grand Industrial task of conquering some half or more of this Terraqueous Planet for the use of man; then secondly, the grand Constitutional task of sharing, in some pacific endurable manner, the fruit of said conquest, and showing all people how it might be done. These I will call their two tasks, discernible hitherto in World-History: in both of these they have made respectable though unequal progress. Steam-engines, ploughshares, pickaxes; what is meant by conquering this Planet, they partly know. Elective franchise, ballot-box, representative assembly; how to accomplish sharing of that conquest, they do not so well know. Europe knows not; Europe vehemently asks in these days, but receives no answer, no credible answer. For as to the partial Delolmish, Benthamee, or other French or English answers, current in the proper quarters, and highly beneficial and indispensable there, thy disbelief in them as final answers, I take it, is complete."

" Succession of rebellions? Successive clippings away of the Supreme Authority; class after class rising in revolt to say, ' We will no more be governed so'? That is not the history of the English Constitution; not altogether that. Rebellion is the means, but it is not the motive cause. The motive cause, and true secret of the matter, were always this: The necessity there was for rebelling?

" Rights I will permit thee to call everywhere ' correctly-articulated *mights*.' A dreadful business to articulate correctly! Consider those Barons of Runnymede; consider all manner of successfully revolting men! Your Great Charter has to be experimented on, by battle and debate, for a hundred-and-fifty years; is then found to *be* correct; and stands as true *Magna Charta*,—nigh cut in pieces by a tailor, short of measure, in later generations. Mights, I say, are a dreadful business to articulate correctly! Yet articulated they have to be; the time comes for it, the need comes for it, and with enormous difficulty and experimenting it is got done. Call it not succession of rebellions; call it rather succession of expansions, of enlightenments, gift of articulate utterance descending ever lower. Class after class acquires faculty of utterance,—Necessity teaching and compelling; as the dumb man, seeing the knife at his father's throat, suddenly acquired speech! Consider too how class after class not only acquires faculty of articulating what its might is, but likewise grows in might, acquires might or loses might; so that always, after a space, there is not only new gift of articulating, but there is something new to articulate. Constitutional epochs will never cease among men."

" And so now, the Barons all settled and satisfied, a new class hitherto silent had begun to speak: the Middle Class, namely. In the time of James First, not only Knights of the Shire but Parliamentary Burgesses assemble, to assert, to complain and propose; a real House of Commons has come decisively into play,—much to the astonishment of James First. We call it a growth of mights, if also of necessities; a growth of power to articulate mights, and make rights of them.

" In those past silent centuries, among those silent classes, much had been going on. Not only had red-deer in the New and other Forests been got preserved and shot; and treacheries of Simon de Montfort, wars of Red and White Roses, Battles of Crecy, Battles of Bosworth, and many other battles been got transacted and adjusted; but England wholly, not without sore toil and aching bones to the millions of sires and the millions of sons these eighteen generations, had been got drained and tilled, covered with yellow harvests, beautiful and rich possessions; the mud-wooden Caesters and Chesters had become steepled tile-roofed compact Towns. Sheffield had taken to the manufacture of Sheffield whittles; Worstead could from wool spin yarn, and knit or weave the same into stockings or breeches for men. England had property valuable to the auctioneer; but the accumulate manufacturing, commercial, economic *skill* which lay impalpably warehoused in English hands and heads, what auctioneer could estimate?

" Hardly an Englishman to be met with but could *do* something; some cunninger thing than break his fellow-creature's head with battle-axes. The seven incorporated trades, with their million guild-brethren, with their hammers, their shuttles and tools, what an army;—fit to conquer that land of England, as we say, and to hold it conquered! Nay, strangest of all, the English people had acquired the faculty and habit of thinking,—even of believing: individual conscience had unfolded itself among them; Conscience, and Intelligence its handmaid. Ideas of innumerable kinds were circulating among these men: witness one Shakspeare, a woolcomber, poacher, or whatever else at Stratford in Warwickshire, who happened to write books! The finest human figure, as I apprehend, that Nature has hitherto seen fit to make of our widely diffused Teutonic clay. Saxon, Norman, Celt or Sarmat, I find no human soul so beautiful, these fifteen-hundred known years;—our supreme modern European man. Him England had contrived to realise: were there not ideas?

"Ideas poetic and also Puritanic,—that had to seek utterance in the notablest way! England had got her Shakspeare; but was now about to get her Milton and Oliver Cromwell. This too we will call a new expansion, hard as it might be to articulate and adjust; this, that a man could actually have a Conscience for his own behoof, and not for his Priest's only; that his Priest, be who he might, would henceforth have to take that fact along with him. One of the hardest things to adjust! It is not adjusted down to this hour. It lasts onwards to the time they call 'Glorious Revolution' before so much as a reasonable truce can be made, and the war proceed by logic mainly. And still it is war, and no peace, unless we call waste vacancy peace. But it needed to be adjusted, as the others had done, as still others will do. Nobility at Runnymede cannot endure foul-play grown palpable; no more can Gentry in Long Parliament; no more can Commonalty in Parliament they name Reformed. Prynne's bloody ears were as a testimony and question to all England: 'Englishmen, is this fair?' England no longer continent of herself, answered, bellowing as with the voice of lions: 'No, it is not fair!'"

"But now on the Industrial side, while this great Constitutional controversy, and revolt of the Middle Class had not ended, had yet but begun, what a shoot was that that England, carelessly, in quest of other objects, struck out across the Ocean, into the waste land which it named New England!

Hail to thee, poor little ship Mayflower, of Delft-Haven:
poor common-looking ship, hired by common charterparty
for coined dollars; caulked with mere oakum and tar; pro-
visioned with vulgarest biscuit and bacon;—yet what ship
Argo, or miraculous epic ship built by the Sea-Gods, was
other than a foolish bumbarge in comparison! Golden
fleeces or the like these sailed for, with or without effect;
thou little Mayflower hadst in thee a veritable Promethean
spark; life-spark of the largest Nation on our Earth,—so we
may already name the Transatlantic Saxon Nation. They
went seeking leave to hear sermon in their own method, these
Mayflower Puritans; a most honest indispensable search:
and yet like Saul the son of Kish, seeking a small thing, they
found this unexpected great thing! Honour to the brave
and true; they verily, we say, carry fire from Heaven, and
have a power that themselves dream not of. Let all men
honour Puritanism, since God has so honoured it. Islam
itself, with its wild heartfelt ' *Allah akbar*, God *is* great,'
was it not honoured? There is but one thing without honour;
smitten with eternal barrenness, inability to do or be:
Insincerity, Unbelief. He who believes no *thing*, who believes only the shows of things, is not in relation with Nature
and Fact at all. Nature denies him; orders him at his
earliest convenience to disappear. Let him disappear from
her domains,—into those of Chaos, Hypothesis and Simulacrum, or wherever else his parish may be."

" As to the Third Constitutional controversy, that of the
Working Classes, which now debates itself everywhere these
fifty years, in France specifically since 1789, in England too
since 1831, it is doubtless the hardest of all to get articulated:
finis of peace, or even reasonable truce on this, is a thing I
have little prospect of for several generations. Dark, wild-
weltering, dreary, boundless; nothing heard on it yet but
ballot-boxes, Parliamentary arguing; not to speak of much
far worse arguing, by steel and lead, from Valmy to Waterloo,
to Peterloo!"—

" And yet of Representative Assemblies may not this
good be said: That contending parties in a country do thereby
ascertain one another's strength? They fight there, since
fight they must, by petition, Parliamentary eloquence, not
by sword, bayonet and bursts of military cannon. Why

do men fight at all, if it be not that they are yet *un*acquainted with one another's strength, and must fight and ascertain it? Knowing that thou art stronger than I, that thou canst compel me, I will submit to thee: unless I chance to prefer extermination, and slightly circuitous suicide, there is no other course for me. That in England, by public meetings, by petitions, by elections, leading-articles, and other jangling hubbub and tongue-fence which perpetually goes on everywhere in that country, people ascertain one another's strength, and the most obdurate House of Lords has to yield and give-in before it come to cannonading and guillotinement: this is a saving characteristic of England. Nay, at bottom, is not this the celebrated English Constitution itself? This *un*-spoken Constitution whereof Privilege of Parliament, Money-Bill, Mutiny-Bill, and all that could be spoken and enacted hitherto, is not the essence and body, but only the shape and skin? Such Constitution is, in our times, verily invaluable."

" Long stormy spring-time, wet contentious April, winter chilling the lap of very May; but at length the season of summer does come. So long the tree stood naked; angry wiry naked boughs moaning and creaking in the wind: you would say, Cut it down, why cumbereth it the ground? Not so; we must wait; all things will have their time.—Of the man Shakspeare, and his Elizabethan Era, with its Sydneys, Raleighs, Bacons, what could we say? That it was a spiritual flower-time. Suddenly, as with the breath of June, your rude naked tree is touched; bursts into leaves and flowers, *such* leaves and flowers. The past long ages of nakedness, and wintry fermentation and elaboration, have done their part, though seeming to do nothing. The past silence has got a voice, all the more significant the longer it had continued silent. In trees, men, institutions, creeds, nations, in all things extant and growing in this Universe, we may note such vicissitudes and budding-times. Moreover there are spiritual budding-times; and then also there are physical, appointed to nations.

" Thus in the middle of that poor calumniated Eighteenth Century, see once more! Long winter again past, the dead-seeming tree proves to be living, to have been always living; after motionless times, every bough shoots forth on the sudden, very strangely:—it now turns out that this favoured England was not only to have had her Shakspeares, Bacons, Sydneys, but to have her Watts, Arkwrights, Brindleys! We will honour greatness in all kinds. The Prospero evoked the singing of Ariel, and took captive the world with those melodies: the same Prospero can send his Fire-demons panting across all oceans; shooting with the speed of meteors, on cunning highways, from end to end of kingdoms; and make Iron his missionary, preaching *its* evangel to the brute Primeval Powers, which listen and obey: neither is this small. Manchester, with its cotton-fuzz, its smoke and dust, its tumult and contentious squalor, is hideous to thee? Think not so: a precious substance, beautiful as magic dreams, and yet no dream but a reality, lies hidden in that noisome wrappage;—a wrappage struggling indeed (look at Chartisms and suchlike) to cast itself off, and leave the beauty free and visible there! Hast thou heard, with sound ears, the awakening of a Manchester, on Monday morning, at half-past five by the clock; the rushing-off of its thousand mills, like the boom of an Atlantic tide, ten-thousand times ten-thousand spools and spindles all set humming there,—it is perhaps, if thou knew it well, sublime as a Niagara, or more so. Cotton-spinning is the clothing of the naked in its result; the triumph of man over matter in its means. Soot and despair are not the essence of it; they are divisible from it,—at this hour, are they not crying fiercely to be divided? The great Goethe, looking at cotton Switzerland, declared it, I am told, to be of all things that he had seen in this world the most poetical. Whereat friend Kanzler von Müller, in search of the palpable picturesque, could not but stare wide-eyed. Nevertheless our World-Poet knew well what he was saying."

" Richard Arkwright, it would seem, was not a beautiful man; no romance-hero with haughty eyes, Apollo-lip, and gesture like the herald Mercury; a plain almost gross, bag-cheeked, potbellied Lancashire man, with an air of painful reflection, yet also of copious free digestion;—a man stationed by the community to shave certain dusty beards, in the Northern parts of England, at a halfpenny each. To such end, we say, by forethought, oversight, accident and arrangement, had Richard Arkwright been, by the community of England and his own consent, set apart. Nevertheless, in strapping of razors, in lathering of dusty beards, and the contradictions and confusions attendant thereon, the man had notions in that rough head of his; spindles, shuttles, wheels and contrivances plying ideally within the same: rather hopeless-looking; which, however, he did at last bring to bear. Not without difficulty! His townsfolk rose in mob round him, for threatening to shorten labour, to shorten wages; so that he had to fly, with broken wash-pots, scattered household, and seek refuge elsewhere. Nay his wife too, as I learn, rebelled; burnt his wooden model of his spinning-wheel; resolute that he should stick to his razors rather;—for which, however, he decisively, as thou wilt rejoice to understand, packed her out of doors. O reader, what a Historical Phenomenon is that bag-cheeked, potbellied, much-enduring, much-inventing barber! French Revolutions were a-brewing to resist the same in any measure, imperial Kaisers were impotent without the cotton and cloth of England; and it was this man that had to give England the power of cotton."

"Neither had Watt of the Steamengine a heroic origin, any kindred with the princes of this world. The princes of this world were shooting their partridges; noisily, in Parliament or elsewhere, solving the question, Head or tail? while this man with blackened fingers, with grim brow, was searching out, in his workshop, the Fire-secret; or, having found it, was painfully wending to and fro in quest of a "moneyed man," as indispensable man-midwife of the same. Reader, thou shalt admire what is admirable, not what is dressed in admirable; learn to know the British lion even when he is not throne-supporter, and also the British jackass in lion's skin even when he is. Ah, couldst thou always, what a world were it! But has the Berlin Royal Academy or any English Useful-Knowledge Society discovered, for instance, who it was that first scratched earth with a stick; and threw *corns*, the biggest he could find, into it; seedgrains of a certain grass, which he named *white* or *wheat?* Again, what is the whole Tees-water and other breeding-world to him who stole home from the forests the first bison-calf, and bred it up to be a tame bison, a milk-cow? No machine of all they showed me in Birmingham can be put in comparison for ingenuity with that figure of the wedge named *knife*, of the wedges named *saw*, of the lever named *hammer* :—nay is it not with the hammer-knife, named *sword*, that men fight, and maintain any semblance of constituted authority that yet survives among us? The steamengine I call fire-demon and great; but it is nothing to the invention of *fire*. Prometheus, Tubalcain, Triptolemus! Are not our greatest men as good as lost? The men that walk daily among us, clothing us, warming us, feeding us, walk shrouded in darkness, mere mythic men.

" It is said, ideas produce revolutions; and truly so they do; not spiritual ideas only, but even mechanical. In this clanging clashing universal Sword-dance that the European world now dances for the last half-century, Voltaire is but one choragus, where Richard Arkwright is another. Let it dance itself out. When Arkwright shall have become mythic like Arachne, we shall still spin in peaceable profit by him; and the Sword-dance, with all its sorrowful shufflings, Waterloo waltzes, Moscow gallopades, how forgotten will that be!"

" On the whole, were not all these things most unexpected, unforeseen? As indeed what thing is foreseen; especially what man, the parent of things! Robert Clive in that same time went out, with a developed gift of penmanship, as writer or superior book-keeper to a trading factory established in the distant East. With gift of penmanship developed; with other gifts not yet developed, which the calls of the case did by and by develop. Not fit for book-keeping alone, the man was found fit for conquering Nawaubs, founding kingdoms, Indian Empires! In a questionable manner, Indian Empire from the other hemisphere took up its abode in Leadenhall Street, in the City of London.

" Accidental all these things and persons look, unexpected every one of them to man. Yet inevitable every one of them; foreseen, not unexpected, by Supreme Power; prepared, appointed from afar. Advancing always through all centuries, in the middle of the eighteenth they *arrived*. The Saxon kindred burst forth into cotton - spinning, cloth-cropping, iron - forging, steamengineing, railwaying, commercing and careering towards all the winds of Heaven,— in this inexplicable noisy manner; the noise of which, in Power-mills, in progress-of-the-species Magazines, still deafens us somewhat. Most noisy, sudden! The Staffordshire coal-strata lay side by side with iron-strata, quiet since the creation of the world. Water flowed in Lancashire and Lanarkshire;

bituminous fire lay bedded in rocks there too,—over which how many fighting Stanleys, black Douglases, and other the like contentious persons, had fought out their bickerings and broils, not without result, we will hope! But God said, Let the iron missionaries be; and they were. Coal and iron, so long close unregardful neighbours, are wedded together; Birmingham and Wolverhampton, and the hundred Stygian forges, with their fire-throats and never-resting sledge-hammers, rose into day. Wet Manconium stretched out her hand towards Carolina and the torrid zone, and plucked cotton there; who could forbid her, that had the skill to weave it? Fish fled thereupon from the Mersey River, vexed with innumerable keels. England, I say, dug out her bitumen-fire, and bade it work: towns rose, and steeple-chimneys;—Chartisms also, and Parliaments they name Reformed."

Such, figuratively given, are some prominent points, chief mountain-summits, of our English History past and present, according to the Author of this strange untranslated Work, whom we think we recognise to be an old acquaintance.

CHAPTER IX

PARLIAMENTARY RADICALISM

To us, looking at these matters somewhat in the same light, Reform-Bills, French Revolutions, Louis-Philippes, Chartisms, Revolts of Three Days, and what not, are no longer inexplicable. Where the great mass of men is tolerably right, all is right; where they are not right, all is wrong. The speaking classes speak and debate, each for itself; the great dumb, deep-buried class lies like an Enceladus, who in his pain, if he will complain of it, has to produce earthquakes! Everywhere, in these countries, in these times, the central fact worthy of all consideration forces itself on us in this shape: the claim of the Free Working-man to be raised to a level, we may say, with the Working Slave; his anger and cureless discontent till that be done. Food, shelter, due guidance, in return for his labour: candidly interpreted, Chartism and all such *isms* mean that; and the madder they are, do they not the more emphatically mean, " See what guidance you have given us! What delirium we are brought to talk and project, guided by nobody!" *Laissez-faire* on the part of the Governing Classes, we repeat again and again, will, with whatever difficulty, have to cease; pacific mutual division of the spoil, and a world well let alone, will no longer suffice. A Do-nothing Guidance; and it is a Do-something World! Would to God our Ducal *Duces* would become Leaders indeed; our Aristocracies and Priesthoods discover in some suitable degree what the world expected of them, what the world could no longer do without getting of them! Nameless unmeasured confusions, misery to themselves and us, might so be spared. But that too will be as God has appointed. If they learn, it will be well and happy: if not they, then others instead of them will and must, and once more, though after a long sad circuit, it will be well and happy.

Neither is the history of Chartism mysterious in these times; especially if that of Radicalism be looked at. All along, for the last five-and-twenty years, it was curious to note how the internal discontent of England struggled to find vent for itself through *any* orifice: the poor patient, all sick from the centre to surface, complains now of this member, now of that;—corn-laws, currency-laws, free-trade, protection, want of free-trade: the poor patient tossing from side to side, seeking a sound side to lie on, finds none. This Doctor says, it is the liver; that other, it is the lungs, the head, the heart, defective transpiration in the skin. A thoroughgoing Doctor of eminence said, it was rotten boroughs; the want of extended suffrage to destroy rotten boroughs. From of old, the English patient himself had a continually recurring notion that this was it. The English people are used to suffrage; it is their panacea for all that goes wrong with them; they have a fixed-idea of suffrage. Singular enough: one's right to vote for a Member of Parliament, to send one's "twenty-thousandth part of a master of tongue-fence to National Palaver,"—the Doctors asserted that this was Freedom, this and no other. It seemed credible to many men, of high degree and of low. The persuasion of remedy grew, the evil was pressing; Swing's ricks were on fire. Some nine years ago, a State-surgeon rose, and in peculiar circumstances said: Let there be extension of the suffrage; let the great Doctor's nostrum, the patient's old passionate prayer be fulfilled!

Parliamentary Radicalism, while it gave articulate utter-

ance to the discontent of the English people, could not by its
worst enemy be said to be without a function. If it is in the
natural order of things that there must be discontent, no less
so is it that such discontent should have an outlet, a Parliamentary voice. Here the matter is debated of, demonstrated,
contradicted, qualified, reduced to feasibility;—can at least
solace itself with hope, and die gently, convinced of *un*feasibility. The New, Untried ascertains how it will fit itself
into the arrangements of the Old; whether the Old can be
compelled to admit it; how in that case it may, with the
minimum of violence, be admitted. Nor let us count it an
easy one, this function of Radicalism; it was one of the most
difficult. The pain-stricken patient does, indeed, without
effort groan and complain; but not without effort does the
physician ascertain what it is that has gone wrong with him,
how some remedy may be devised for him. And above all,
if your patient is not one sick man, but a whole sick nation!
Dingy dumb millions, grimed with dust and sweat, with
darkness, rage and sorrow, stood round these men, saying, or
struggling as they could to say: " Behold, our lot is unfair;
our life is not whole but sick; we cannot live under injustice;
go ye and get us justice!" For whether the poor operative
clamoured for Time-bill, Factory-bill, Corn-bill, for or against
whatever bill, this was what he meant. All bills plausibly
presented might have some look of hope in them, might get
some clamour of approval from him; as, for the man wholly
sick, there is no disease in the Nosology but he can trace in
himself some symptoms of it. Such was the mission of
Parliamentary Radicalism.

How Parliamentary Radicalism has fulfilled this mission,
intrusted to its management these eight years now, is known
to all men. The expectant millions have sat at a feast of
the Barmecide; been bidden fill themselves with the imagination of meat. What thing has Radicalism obtained for them;
what other than shadows of things has it so much as asked
for them? Cheap Justice, Justice to Ireland, Irish Appropria-
tion-Clause, Rate-paying Clause, Poor-Rate, Church-Rate,
Household Suffrage, Ballot - Question " open " or shut:
not things but shadows of things; Benthamee formulas;
barren as the east-wind! An Ultra-radical, not seemingly of
the Benthamee species, is forced to exclaim: " The people are
at last wearied. They say, Why should we be ruined in our

shops, thrown out of our farms, voting for these men? Ministerial majorities decline; this Ministry has become impotent, had it even the will to do good. They have called long to us, ' We are a Reform Ministry; will ye not support *us* ?' We have supported them; borne them forward indignantly on our shoulders, time after time, fall after fall, when they had been hurled out into the street; and lay prostrate, helpless, like dead luggage. It is the fact of a Reform Ministry, not the name of one that we would support! Languor, sickness of hope deferred pervades the public mind; the public mind says at last, Why all this struggle for the *name* of a Reform Ministry? Let the Tories be Ministry if they will; let at least some living reality be Ministry! A rearing horse that will only run backward, he is not the horse one would choose to travel on: yet of all conceivable horses the worst is the dead horse. Mounted on a rearing horse, you may back him, spur him, check him, make a little way even backwards: but seated astride of your dead horse, what chance is there for you in the chapter of possibilities? You sit motionless, hopeless, a spectacle to gods and men."

There is a class of revolutionists named *Girondins*, whose fate in history is remarkable enough! Men who rebel, and urge the Lower Classes to rebel, ought to have other than Formulas to go upon. Men who discern in the misery of the toiling complaining millions not misery, but only a raw-material which can be wrought upon and traded in, for one's own poor hidebound theories and egoisms; to whom millions of living fellow-creatures, with beating hearts in their bosoms, beating, suffering, hoping, are " masses," mere " explosive masses for blowing-down Bastilles with," for voting at hustings for *us :* such men are of the questionable species! No man is justified in resisting by word or deed the Authority he lives under, for a light cause, be such Authority what it may. Obedience, little as many may consider that side of the matter, is the primary duty of man. No man but is bound indefeasibly, with all force of obligation, to obey. Parents, teachers, superiors, leaders, these all creatures recognise as deserving obedience. Recognised or not recognised, a man *has* his superiors, a regular hierarchy above him; extending up, degree above degree, to Heaven itself and God the Maker, who made His world not for anarchy but for rule and order! It is not a light matter when the just man can recognise in the powers set over him no longer anything that is divine; when resistance against such becomes a deeper law of order than obedience to them; when the just man sees himself in the tragical position of a stirrer-up of strife! Rebel without due and most due cause, is the ugliest of words; the first rebel was Satan.—

But now in these circumstances shall we blame the unvoting disappointed millions that they turn away with horror from this name of a Reform Ministry, name of a Parliamentary Radicalism, and demand a fact and reality thereof? That they too, having still faith in what so many had faith in, still count " extension of the suffrage " the one thing needful; and say, in such manner as they can, Let the suffrage be still extended, *then* all will be well? It is the ancient British faith; promulgated in these ages by prophets and evangelists; preached forth from barrel-heads by all manner of men. He who is free and blessed has his twenty-thousandth part of a master of tongue-fence in National Palaver; whosoever is not blessed but unhappy, the ailment of him is that he has it not. Ought he not to have it, then? By the law of God and of men, yea;—and will have it withal! Chartism, with its " five points," borne aloft on pikeheads and torchlight meetings, is there. Chartism is one of the most natural phenomena in England. Not that Chartism now exists should provoke wonder; but that the invited hungry people should have sat eight years at such table of the Barmecide, patiently expecting somewhat from the Name of a Reform Ministry, and not till after eight years have grown hopeless, this is the respectable side of the miracle.

CHAPTER X

IMPOSSIBLE

" But what are we to do? " exclaims the practical man, impatiently on every side: " Descend from speculation and the safe pulpit, down into the rough market-place, and say what can be done! " — O practical man, there seem very many things which practice and true manlike effort, in Parliament and out of it, might actually avail to do. But the first of all things, as already said, is to gird thyself up for actual doing; to know that thou actually either must do, or, as the Irish say, " come out of that! ' "

It is not a lucky word this same *impossible :* no good comes of those that have it so often in their mouth. Who is he that says always, There is a lion in the way? Sluggard, thou must slay the lion, then; the way has to be travelled! In Art, in Practice, innumerable critics will demonstrate that most things are henceforth impossible; that we are got, once for all, into the region of perennial commonplace, and must contentedly continue there. Let such critics demonstrate; it is the nature of them: what harm is in it? Poetry once well demonstrated to be impossible, arises the Burns, arises the Goethe. Unheroic commonplace being now clearly all we have to look for, comes the Napoleon, comes the conquest of the world. It was proved by fluxionary calculus, that steamships could never get across the farthest point of Ireland to the nearest of Newfoundland: impelling force, resisting force, maximum here, minimum there; by law of Nature, and geometric demonstration:—what could be done? The Great Western could weigh anchor from Bristol Port; that could be done. The Great Western, bounding safe through the gullets of the Hudson, threw her cable out on the capstan of New York, and left our still moist paper-demonstration to dry itself at leisure. " Impossible? " cried Mirabeau to his secretary, " *Ne me dites jamais ce bête de mot,* Never name to me that blockhead of a word! "

There is a phenomenon which one might call Paralytic Radicalism, in these days; which gauges with Statistic measuring-reed, sounds with Philosophic Politico-Economic plummet the deep dark sea of troubles; and having taught us rightly what an infinite sea of troubles it is, sums-up with the practical inference, and use of consolation, That nothing whatever can be done in it by man, who has simply to sit still, and look wistfully to " time and general laws: " and thereupon, without so much as recommending suicide, coldly takes its leave of us. Most paralytic, uninstructive; unproductive of any comfort to one! They are an unreasonable class who cry, " Peace, peace," when there *is* no peace. But what kind of class are they who cry, " Peace, peace, have I not *told you* that there is no peace! " Paralytic Radicalism, frequent among those Statistic friends of ours, is one of the most afflictive phenomena the mind of man can be called to contemplate. One prays that *it* at least might cease. Let Paralysis retire into secret places, and dormitories proper for it; the public highways ought not to be occupied by people demonstrating that motion is impossible. Paralytic;—and also, thank Heaven, entirely false! Listen to a thinker of another sort: " All evil, and this evil too, is as a nightmare; the instant you begin to *stir* under it, the *evil* is, properly speaking, gone." Consider, O reader, whether it be not actually so? Evil, once manfully fronted, ceases to be evil; there is generous battle-hope in place of dead passive misery; the evil itself has become a kind of good.

To the practical man, therefore, we will repeat that he has, as the first thing he can " do," to gird himself up for actual doing; to know well that he is either there to do, or not there at all. Once rightly girded up, how many things will present themselves as doable which now are not attemptable! Two things, great things, dwell, for the last ten years, in all thinking heads in England; and are hovering, of late, even on the tongues of not a few. With a word on each of these, we will dismiss the practical man, and right gladly take ourselves into obscurity and silence again. Universal Education is the first great thing we mean; general Emigration is the second.

Who would suppose that Education were a thing which had to be advocated on the ground of local expediency, or indeed on any ground? As if it stood not on the basis of everlasting duty, as a prime necessity of man. It is a thing that should need no advocating; much as it does actually need. To impart the gift of thinking to those who cannot think, and yet who could in that case think: this, one would imagine, was the first function a government had to set about discharging. Were it not a cruel thing to see, in any province of an empire, the inhabitants living all mutilated in their limbs, each strong man with his right arm lamed? How much crueler to find the strong soul, with its eyes still sealed, its eyes extinct so that it sees not! Light has come into the world, but to this poor peasant it has come in vain. For six thousand years the Sons of Adam, in sleepless effort, have been devising, doing, discovering; in mysterious infinite indissoluble communion, warring, a little band of brothers, against the great black empire of Necessity and Night; they have accomplished such a conquest and conquests: and to

this man it is all as if it had not been. The four-and-twenty
letters of the Alphabet are still Runic enigmas to him. He
passes by on the other side; and that great Spiritual Kingdom, the toilworn conquest of his own brothers, all that his
brothers have conquered, is a thing non-extant for him. An
invisible empire; he knows it not, suspects it not. And is
it not his withal; the conquest of his own brothers, the
lawfully acquired possession of all men? Baleful enchantment lies over him, from generation to generation; he knows
not that such an empire is his, that such an empire is at all.
O, what are bills of rights, emancipations of black slaves into
black apprentices, lawsuits in chancery for some short usu-
fruct of a bit of land? The grand " seedfield of Time " is this
man's, and you give it him not. Time's seedfield, which
includes the Earth and all her seedfields and pearl-oceans,
nay her sowers too and pearl-divers, all that was wise and
heroic and victorious here below; of which the Earth's
centuries are but as furrows, for it stretches forth from the
Beginning onward even into this Day!

> " My inheritance, how lordly wide and fair;
> Time is my fair seedfield, to Time I'm heir! "—

Heavier wrong is not done under the sun. It lasts from
year to year, from century to century; the blinded sire slaves
himself out, and leaves a blinded son; and men, made in the
image of God, continue as two-legged beasts of labour;—and
in the largest empire of the world, it is a debate whether a
small fraction of the Revenue of one Day (£30,000 is but that)
shall, after Thirteen Centuries, be laid out on it, or not laid
out on it. Have we Governors, have we Teachers; have we
had a Church these thirteen hundred years? What is an
Overseer of souls, an Archoverseer, Archiepiscopus? Is he
something? If so, let him lay his hand on his heart, and say
what thing!

But quitting all that, of which the human soul cannot well
speak in terms of civility, let us observe now that Education
is not only an eternal duty, but has at length become even a
temporary and ephemeral one, which the necessities of the
hour will oblige us to look after. These Twenty-four million
labouring men, if their affairs remain unregulated, chaotic,
will burn ricks and mills; reduce us, themselves and the
world into ashes and ruin. Simply their affairs cannot

remain unregulated, chaotic; but must be regulated, brought into some kind of order. What intellect were able to regulate them? The intellect of a Bacon, the energy of a Luther, if left to their own strength, might pause in dismay before such a task; a Bacon and Luther added together, to be perpetual prime minister over us, could not do it. No one great and greatest intellect can do it. What can? Only Twenty-four million ordinary intellects, once awakened into action; these, well presided over, may. Intellect, insight, is the discernment of order in disorder; it is the discovery of the will of Nature, of God's will; the beginning of the capability to walk according to that. With perfect intellect, were such possible without perfect morality, the world would be perfect; its efforts unerringly correct, its results continually successful, its condition faultless. Intellect is like light; the Chaos becomes a World under it: *fiat lux*. These Twenty-four million intellects are but common intellects; but they are intellects; in earnest about the matter, instructed each about his own province of it; labouring each perpetually, with what partial light can be attained, to bring such province into rationality. From the partial determinations and their conflict springs the universal. Precisely what quantity of intellect was in the Twenty-four millions will be exhibited by the result they arrive at; that quantity and no more. According as there was intellect or no intellect in the individuals, will the general conclusion they make-out embody itself as a world-healing Truth and Wisdom, or as a baseless fateful Hallucination, a Chimæra breathing *not* fabulous fire!

Dissenters call for one scheme of Education, the Church objects; this party objects, and that; there is endless objection, by him and by her and by it: a subject encumbered with difficulties on every side! Pity that difficulties exist; that Religion, of all things, should occasion difficulties. We do not extenuate them: in their reality they are considerable; in their appearance and pretension, they are insuperable, heart-appalling to all Secretaries of the Home Department. For, in very truth, how can Religion be divorced from Education? An irreverent knowledge is no knowledge; may be a development of the logical or other handicraft faculty inward or outward; but is no culture of the soul of a man. A knowledge that ends in barren self-worship, comparative indifference or contempt for all God's Universe except one insignificant item thereof, what is it? Handicraft development, and even shallow as handicraft. Nevertheless is handicraft itself, and the habit of the merest logic, nothing? It is already something; it is the indispensable beginning of everything! Wise men know it to be an indispensable something; not yet much; and would so gladly superadd to it the element whereby it may become all. Wise men would not quarrel in attempting this; they would lovingly coöperate in attempting it.

"And now how teach religion?" so asks the indignant Ultra-radical, cited above; an Ultra-radical seemingly not of the Benthamee species, with whom, though his dialect is far different, there are sound Churchmen, we hope, who have some fellow-feeling: "How teach religion? By plying with liturgies, catechisms, credos; droning thirty-nine or other articles incessantly into the infant ear? Friends! In that case, why not apply to Birmingham, and have Machines made, and set-up at all street-corners, in highways and byways, to repeat and vociferate the same, not ceasing night or day? The genius of Birmingham is adequate to that. Albertus Magnus had a leather man that could articulate; not to speak of Martinus Scriblerus' Nürnberg man that could reason as well as we know who! Depend upon it, Birmingham can make machines to repeat liturgies and articles; to do whatsoever feat is mechanical. And what were all schoolmasters, nay all priests and churches, compared with this Birmingham Iron Church! Votes of two millions in aid of the Church were then something. You order, at so many pounds a-head, so many thousand iron parsons as your grant covers; and fix them by satisfactory masonry in all quarters wheresoever wanted, to preach there independent of the world. In loud thoroughfares, still more in unawakened districts, troubled with argumentative infidelity, you make the windpipes wider, strengthen the main steam-cylinder; your parson preaches, to the due pitch, while you give him coal; and fears no man or thing. Here *were* a 'Church-extension;' to which I, with my last penny, did I believe in it, would subscribe.——

"Ye blind leaders of the blind! Are we Calmucks, that pray by turning of a rotatory calabash with written prayers in it? Is Mammon and machinery the means of converting human souls, as of spinning cotton? Is God, as Jean Paul predicted it would be, become verily a Force; the Æther too a Gas! Alas, that Atheism should have got the length of putting on priests' vestments, and penetrating into the sanctuary itself! Can dronings of articles, repetitions of liturgies, and all the cash and contrivance of Birmingham and the Bank of England united bring ethereal fire into a human soul, quicken it out of earthly darkness into heavenly wisdom? Soul is kindled only by soul. To ' teach ' religion, the first thing needful, and also the last and the only thing, is finding of a man who *has* religion. All else follows from this, church-building, church-extension, whatever else is needful follows; without this nothing will follow.''

From which we for our part conclude that the method of teaching religion to the English people is still far behindhand; that the wise and pious may well ask themselves in silence wistfully, " How *is* that last priceless element, by which education becomes perfect, to be superadded? " and the unwise who think themselves pious, answering aloud, " By this method, By that method,'' long argue of it to small purpose.

But now, in the mean time, could not, by some fit official person, some fit announcement be made, in words well-weighed, in plan well-schemed, adequately representing the facts of the thing, That after thirteen centuries of waiting, he the official person, and England with him, was minded now to have the mystery of the Alphabetic Letters imparted to all human souls in this realm? Teaching of religion was a thing he could not undertake to settle this day; it would be work for a day after this; the work of this day was teaching of the alphabet to all people. The miraculous art of reading and writing, such seemed to him the needful preliminary of all teaching, the first corner-stone of what foundation soever could be laid for what edifice soever, in the teaching kind. Let pious Churchism make haste, let pious Dissenterism make haste, let all pious preachers and missionaries make haste, bestir themselves according to their zeal and skill: he the official person stood up for the Alphabet; and was even impatient for it, having waited thirteen centuries now. He insisted, and would take no denial, postponement, promise, excuse or subterfuge, That all English persons should be taught to read. He appealed to all rational Englishmen, of all creeds, classes and colours, Whether this was not a fair demand; nay whether it was not an indispensable one in these days, Swing and Chartism having risen? For a choice of inoffensive Hornbooks, and Schoolmasters able to teach reading, he trusted the mere secular sagacity of a National Collective Wisdom, in proper committee, might be found sufficient. He purposed to appoint such Schoolmasters, to venture on the choice of such Hornbooks; to send a School-master and Hornbook into every township, parish and hamlet of England; so that, in ten years hence, an English-man who could not read might be acknowledged as the monster, which he really is!

This official person's plan we do not give. The *thing* lies there, with the facts of it, and with the appearances or sham-facts of it; a plan adequately representing the facts of the thing could by human energy be struck out, does lie there for discovery and striking out. It is his, the official person's duty, not ours, to mature a plan. We can believe that Churchism and Dissenterism would clamour aloud; but yet that in the mere secular Wisdom of Parliament a perspicacity equal to the choice of Hornbooks might, in very deed, be found to reside. England we believe would, if consulted, resolve to that effect. Alas, grants of a half-day's revenue once in the thirteen centuries for such an object, do not call-out the voice of England, only the superficial clamour of England! Hornbooks unexceptionable to the candid portion of England, we will believe, might be selected. Nay, we can conceive that Schoolmasters fit to teach reading might, by a board of rational men, whether from Oxford or Hoxton, or from both or neither of these places, be pitched upon. We can conceive even, as in Prussia, that a penalty, civil dis-abilities, that penalties and disabilities till they were found effectual, might be by law inflicted on every parent who did not teach his children to read, on every man who had not been taught to read. We can conceive, in fine, such is the vigour of our imagination, there might be found in England, at a dead-lift, strength enough to perform this miracle, and produce it henceforth as a miracle done: the teaching of England to read! Harder things, we do know, have been performed by nations before now, not abler-looking than England.

Ah me! if by some beneficent chance, there should be an official man found in England who could and would, with deliberate courage, after ripe counsel, with candid insight, with patience, practical sense, knowing realities to be real, knowing clamours to be clamorous and to seem real, propose this thing, and the innumerable things springing from it,—woe to any Churchism or any Dissenterism that cast itself athwart the path of that man! Avaunt, ye gainsayers! is darkness and ignorance of the Alphabet necessary for you? Reconcile yourselves to the Alphabet, or depart elsewhither!—Would not all that has genuineness in England gradually rally round such a man; all that has strength in England? For realities alone have strength; wind-bags are wind; cant is cant, leave it alone there. Nor are all clamours momentous; among living creatures, we find, the loudest is the longest-eared; among lifeless things, the loudest is the drum, the emptiest. Alas, that official persons, and all of us, had not eyes to see what was real, what was merely chimerical, and thought or called itself real! How many dread minatory Castle-spectres should we leave there, with their admonishing right-hand and ghastly-burning saucer-eyes, to do simply whatsoever they might find themselves able to do! Alas, that we were not real ourselves; we should otherwise have surer vision for the real. Castle-spectres, in their utmost terror, are but poor mimicries of that real and most real terror which lies in the Life of every Man: that, thou coward, is the thing to be afraid of, if thou wilt live in fear. It is but the scratch of a bare bodkin; it is but the flight of a few days of time; and even thou, poor palpitating featherbrain, wilt find how real it is. ETERNITY: hast thou heard of that? Is that a fact, or is it no fact? Are Buckingham House and St. Stephen's *in* that, or not in that?

But now we have to speak of the second great thing: Emigration. It was said above, all new epochs, so convulsed and tumultuous to look upon, are " expansions," increase of faculty not yet organised. It is eminently true of the confusions of this time of ours. Disorganic Manchester afflicts us with its Chartisms; yet is not spinning of clothes for the naked intrinsically a most blessed thing? Manchester once organic will bless and not afflict. The confusions, if we would understand them, are at bottom mere increase which we know not yet how to manage; " new wealth which the old coffers will not hold." How true is this, above all, of the strange phenomenon called " over-population!" Over-population is the grand anomaly, which is bringing all other anomalies to a crisis. Now once more, as at the end of the Roman Empire, a most confused epoch and yet one of the greatest, the Teutonic Countries find themselves too full. On a certain western rim of our small Europe, there are more men than were expected. Heaped up against the western shore there, and for a couple of hundred miles inward, the "tide of population" swells too high, and confuses itself somewhat. Over-population? And yet, if this small western rim of Europe is overpeopled, does not everywhere else a whole vacant Earth, as it were, call to us, Come and till me, come and reap me! Can it be an evil that in an Earth such as ours there should be new Men? Considered as mercantile commodities, as working machines, is there in Birmingham or out of it a machine of such value? "Good Heavens! a white European Man, standing on his two legs, with his two five-fingered Hands at his shackle-bones, and miraculous Head on his shoulders, is worth something considerable, one would say!" The stupid black African man brings money in the market; the much stupider four-footed horse brings money;—it is we that have not yet learned the art of managing our white European man!

The controversies on Malthus and the "Population Principle," "Preventive check," and so forth, with which the public ear has been deafened for a long while, are indeed sufficiently mournful. Dreary, stolid, dismal, without hope for this world or the next, is all that of the preventive check and the denial of the preventive check. Anti-Malthusians quoting their Bible against palpable facts are not a pleasant spectacle. On the other hand, how often have we read in Malthusian benefactors of the species: "The working people have their condition in their own hands; let them diminish the supply of labourers, and of course the demand and the remuneration will increase!" Yes, let *them* diminish the supply: but who are they? They are twenty-four millions of human individuals, scattered over a hundred and eighteen thousand square miles of space and more; weaving, delving, hammering, joinering; each unknown to his neighbour; each distinct within his own skin. *They* are not a kind of character that can take a resolution, and act on it, very readily. Smart Sally in our alley proves all-too fascinating to brisk Tom in yours: can Tom be called on to make pause, and calculate the demand for labour in the British Empire first? Nay, if Tom did renounce his highest blessedness of life, and struggle and conquer like a Saint Francis of Assisi, what would it profit him or us? Seven millions of the finest peasantry do not renounce, but proceed all the more briskly; and with blue-visaged Hibernians instead of fair Saxon Tomsons and Sallysons, the latter end of that country is worse than the beginning. O wonderful Malthusian prophets! Millenniums are undoubtedly coming, must come one way or the other: but will it be, think you, by twenty millions of working people simultaneously striking work in that department; passing, in universal trades-union, a resolution not to beget any more till the labour-market become satisfactory? By Day and Night! they were indeed irresistible so; not to be compelled by law or war; might make their own terms with the richer classes, and defy the world!

A shade more rational is that of those other benefactors of the species, who counsel that in each parish, in some central locality, instead of the Parish Clergyman, there might be established some Parish Exterminator; or say a Reservoir of Arsenic, kept up at the public expense, free to all parishioners; for *which* Church the rates probably would not be grudged. —Ah, it is bitter jesting on such a subject. One's heart is sick to look at the dreary chaos, and valley of Jehosaphat, scattered with the limbs and souls of one's fellow-men; and no divine voice, only creaking of hungry vultures, inarticulate bodeful ravens, horn-eyed parrots that do articulate, proclaiming, Let these bones live!

Dante's *Divina Commedia* is called the mournfulest of books: transcendent mistemper of the noblest soul; utterance of a boundless, godlike, unspeakable, implacable sorrow and protest against the world. But in Holywell Street, not long ago, we bought, for three-pence, a book still mournfuler; the Pamphlet of one "Marcus," whom his poor Chartist editor and republisher calls the "Demon Author." This *Marcus* Pamphlet was the book alluded to by Stephens the Preacher Chartist, in one of his harangues: it proves to be no fable that such a book existed; here it lies, "Printed by John Hill, Black-horse Court, Fleet Street, and now reprinted for the instruction of the labourer, by William Dugdale, Holywell Street, Strand," the exasperated Chartist editor who sells it you for three-pence. We have read Marcus; but his sorrow is not divine. We hoped he would turn out to have been in sport: ah no, it is grim earnest with him; grim as very death. Marcus is not a demon author at all: he is a benefactor of the species in his own kind; has looked intensely on the world's woes, from a Benthamee-Malthusian watchtower, under a Heaven dead as iron; and does now, with much longwindedness, in a drawling, snuffling, circuitous, extremely dull, yet at bottom handfast and positive manner, recommend that all children of working people, after the third, be disposed of by " painless extinction." Charcoal-vapour and other methods exist. The mothers would consent, might be made to consent. Three children might be left living; or perhaps, for Marcus's calculations are not yet perfect, two and a half. There might be " beautiful cemeteries with colonnades and flower-plots," in which the patriot infanticide matrons might delight to take their evening walk of contemplation: and reflect what patriotesses they were, what a cheerful flowery world it was.

Such is the scheme of Marcus; this is what he, for his share, could devise to heal the world's woes. A benefactor of the species, clearly recognisable as such: the saddest scientific mortal we have ever in this world fallen in with; sadder even than poetic Dante. His is a *no*-godlike sorrow; sadder than the godlike. The Chartist editor, dull as he, calls him demon author, and a man set-on by the Poor-Law Commissioners. What a black, godless, waste-struggling world, in this once merry England of ours, do such pamphlets and such editors betoken! *Laissez-faire* and Malthus, Malthus and *Laissez-faire*: ought not *these* two at length to part company? Might we not hope that both of them had as good as delivered their message now, and were about to go their ways?

For all this of the " painless extinction," and the rest, is in a world where Canadian Forests stand unfelled, boundless Plains and Prairies unbroken with the plough; on the west and on the east green desert spaces never yet made white with corn; and to the overcrowded little western nook of Europe, our Terrestrial Planet, nine-tenths of it yet vacant or tenanted by nomades, is still crying, Come and till me, come and reap me! And in an England with wealth, and means for moving, such as no nation ever before had. With ships; with warships rotting idle, which, but bidden move and not rot, might bridge all oceans. With trained men, educated to pen and practise, to administer and act; briefless Barristers, charge-less Clergy, taskless Scholars, languishing in all court-houses, hiding in obscure garrets, besieging all antechambers, in passionate want of simply one thing, Work;—with as many Half-pay Officers of both Services, wearing themselves down in wretched tedium, as might lead an Emigrant host larger than Xerxes' was! *Laissez-faire* and Malthus positively must part company. Is it not as if this swelling, simmering, never-resting Europe of ours stood, once more, on the verge of an expansion without parallel; struggling, struggling like a mighty tree again about to burst in the embrace of summer, and shoot forth broad frondent boughs which would fill the whole earth? A disease; but the noblest of all,—as of her who is in pain and sore travail, but travails that she may be a mother, and say, Behold, there is a new Man born!

"True, thou Gold-Hofrath," exclaims an eloquent satiri-cal German of our acquaintance, in that strange Book of his,[1] "True, thou Gold-Hofrath: too crowded indeed! Meanwhile, what portion of this inconsiderable Terraqueous Globe have ye actually tilled and delved, till it will grow no more? How thick stands your population in the Pampas and Savannas of America; round ancient Carthage, and in the interior of Africa; on both slopes of the Altaic chain, in the central Platform of Asia; in Spain, Greece, Turkey, Crim Tartary, the Curragh of Kildare? One man, in one year, as I have understood it, if you lend him earth, will feed himself and nine others. Alas, where now are the Hengsts and Alarics of our still-glowing, still-expanding Europe; who, when their home is grown too narrow, will enlist and, like fire-pillars, guide onwards those superfluous masses of indomitable living Valour; equipped, not now with the battle-axe and war-chariot, but with the steam-engine and ploughshare? Where are they?—Preserving their Game!"

---

[1] *Sartor Resartus*, People's Edition, p. 159.

COUNT CAGLIOSTRO

IN TWO FLIGHTS[1]

[1833]

FLIGHT FIRST

"THE life of every man," says our friend Herr Sauerteig, "the life even of the meanest man, it were good to remember, is a Poem; perfect in all manner of Aristotelean requisites; with beginning, middle and end; with perplexities, and solutions; with its Will-strength (*Willenkraft*) and warfare against Fate, its elegy and battle-singing, courage marred by crime, everywhere the two tragic elements of Pity and Fear; above all, with supernatural machinery enough,—for was not the man *born* out of NONENTITY; did he not *die*, and miraculously vanishing return thither? The most indubitable Poem! Nay, whoso will, may he not name it a Prophecy, or whatever else is highest in his vocabulary; since only in Reality lies the essence and foundation of all that was ever fabled, visioned, sung, spoken, or babbled by the human species; and the actual Life of Man includes in it all Revelations, true and false, that have been, are, or are to be. Man! I say therefore, *reverence thy fellow-man*. He too issued from Above; is mystical and supernatural (as thou namest it): this know thou of a truth. Seeing also that we ourselves are of so high Authorship, is not that, in very deed, ' the highest Reverence,' and most needful for us: ' Reverence for oneself '?

"Thus, to my view, is every Life, more properly is every Man that has life to lead, a small strophe, or occasional verse, composed by the Supernal Powers; and published, in such type and shape, with such embellishments, emblematic head-piece and tail-piece as thou seest, to the thinking or unthinking Universe. Heroic strophes some few are; full of force and a sacred fire, so that to latest ages the hearts of

[1] *Fraser's Magazine*, Nos. 43, 44 (July and August).

those that read therein are made to tingle.   Jeremiads others seem; mere weeping laments, harmonious or disharmonious Remonstrances against Destiny; whereat we too may sometimes profitably weep.   Again, have we not flesh-and-blood strophes of the idyllic sort,—though in these days rarely, owing to Poor-Laws, Game-Laws, Population-Theories and the like!   Farther, of the comic laughter-loving sort; yet ever with an unfathomable earnestness, as is fit, lying underneath: for, bethink thee, what is the mirthfulest grinning face of any Grimaldi, but a transitory *mask*, behind which quite otherwise grins—the most indubitable *Death's-head!*   However, I say farther, there are strophes of the pastoral sort (as in Ettrick, Afghaunistan, and elsewhere); of the farcic-tragic, melodramatic, of all named and a thousand unnamable sorts there are poetic strophes, written, as was said, in Heaven, printed on Earth, and published (bound in woollen cloth, or *clothes*) for the use of the studious. Finally, a small number seem utter Pasquils, mere ribald libels on Humanity: these too, however, are at times worth reading.

" In this wise," continues our too obscure friend, " out of all imaginable elements, awakening all imaginable moods of heart and soul, ' barbarous enough to excite, tender enough to assuage,' ever contradictory yet ever coalescing, is that mighty world-old Rhapsodia of Existence page after page (generation after generation), and chapter (or epoch) after chapter, poetically put together!   This is what some one names ' the grand sacred Epos, or Bible of World-History; infinite in meaning as the Divine Mind it emblems; wherein he is wise that can read here a line, and there a line.'

" Remark too, under another aspect, whether it is not in this same Bible of World-History that all men, in all times, with or without clear consciousness, have been unwearied to read, what we may call *read;* and again to write, or rather to be *written!*   What is all History, and all Poesy, but a deciphering somewhat thereof, out of that mystic heaven-written Sanscrit; and rendering it into the speech of men? *Know thyself*, value thyself, is a moralist's commandment (which I only half approve of); but *Know others*, value others, is the hest of Nature herself.   Or again, *Work while it is called To-day :* is not that also the irreversible law of being for mortal man?   And now, what is all working, what is all knowing, but a faint interpreting and a faint showing-forth of that same *Mystery of Life*, which ever remains infinite,—heaven-written mystic Sanscrit? View it as we will, to him that lives, Life is a divine matter; felt to be of quite sacred significance. Consider the wretchedest 'straddling biped that wears breeches' of thy acquaintance; into whose wool-head, Thought, as thou rashly supposest, never entered; who, in froth-element of business, pleasure, or what else he names it, walks forever in a vain show; asking not Whence, or Why, or Whither; looking up to Heaven above as if some upholsterer had made it, and down to the Hell beneath as if *he* had neither part nor lot there: yet tell me, does not he too, over and above his five finite senses, acknowledge some sixth *infinite* sense, were it only that of Vanity? For, sate him in the other five as you may, will this sixth sense leave him rest? Does he not rise early and sit late, and study impromptus, and (in constitutional countries) parliamentary motions, and bursts of eloquence, and gird himself in whale-bone, and pad himself and perk himself, and in all ways painfully take heed to his goings; feeling (if we must admit it) that an altogether infinite endowment has been intrusted him also, namely, a Life to lead? Thus does he too, with his whole force, in his own way, proclaim that the world-old Rhapsodia of Existence is divine, and an inspired Bible; and, himself a wondrous *verse* therein (be it heroic, be it pasquillic), study with his whole soul, as we said, both to *read* and to *be written !*

"Here also I will observe, that the *manner* in which men read this same Bible is, like all else, proportionate to their stage of culture, to the circumstances of their environment. First, and among the earnest Oriental nations, it was read wholly like a Sacred Book; most clearly by the most earnest, those wondrous Hebrew Readers; whose reading accordingly was itself sacred, has meaning for all tribes of mortal men; since ever, to the latest generation of the world, a true utterance from the innermost of man's being will speak significantly to man. But, again, in how different a style was that other Oriental reading of the Magi; of Zerdusht, or whoever it was that first so opened the matter? Gorgeous semi-sensual Grandeurs and Splendours: on infinite darkness, brightest-glowing light and fire;—of which, all defaced by Time, and turned mostly into lies, a quite late reflex, in those Arabian Tales and the like, still leads captive every heart. Look, thirdly, at the earnest West, and that Consecration of the Flesh, which stept forth life-lusty, radiant, smiling-earnest, in immortal grace, from under the chisel and the stylus of old Greece. Here too was the Infinite intelligibly proclaimed as infinite: and the antique man walked between a Tartarus and an Elysium, his brilliant Paphos-islet of Existence embraced by boundless oceans of sadness and fateful gloom.—Of which three antique manners of reading, our modern manner, you will remark, has been little more than imitation: for always, indeed, the West has been rifer of doers than of speakers. The Hebrew manner has had its echo in our Pulpits and choral aisles; the Ethnic Greek and Arabian in numberless mountains of Fiction, rhymed, rhymeless, published by subscription, by puffery, in periodicals, or by money of your own (*durch eignes Geld*). Till now at last, by dint of iteration and reiteration through some ten centuries, all these manners have grown obsolete, wearisome, meaningless; listened to only as the monotonous moaning wind, while there is nothing else to listen to:—and so now, well-nigh in total oblivion of the Infinitude of Life (except what small *unconscious* recognition the ' straddling biped ' above argued of may have), we wait, in hope and patience, for some *fourth* manner of anew convincingly announcing it."

These singular sentences from the *Æsthetische Springwurzeln* we have thought right to translate and quote, by way of proem and apology. We are here about to give some critical account of what Herr Sauerteig would call a " flesh-and-blood Poem of the purest Pasquil sort; " in plain words, to examine the biography of the most perfect scoundrel that in these latter ages has marked the world's history. Pasquils too, says Sauerteig, " are at times worth reading." Or quitting that mystic dialect of his, may we not assert in our own way, that the history of an Original Man is always worth knowing? So magnificent a thing is Will incarnated in a creature of like fashion with ourselves, we run to witness *all* manifestations thereof: what man soever has marked out a peculiar path of life for himself, let it lead this way or that way, and successfully travelled the same, of him we specially inquire, How he travelled; What befell him on the journey? Though the man were a knave of the first water, this hinders not the question, How he managed his knavery? Nay it rather encourages such question; for nothing properly is wholly despicable, at once detestable and forgetable, but your half-knave, he who is neither true nor false; who never in his existence once spoke or did any true thing (for indeed his mind lives in twilight, with cat-vision, incapable of *discerning* truth); and yet had not the manfulness to speak or act any decided lie; but spent his whole life in plastering together the True and the False, and therefrom manufacturing the Plausible. Such a one our Transcendentals have defined as a Moral Hybrid and chimera; therefore, under the moral point of view, as an Impossibility, and mere deceptive Nonentity, — put together for commercial purposes. Of which sort, nevertheless, how many millions, through all manner of gradations, from the wielder of kings' sceptres to the vender of brimstone matches, at tea-tables, council-tables, behind shop-counters, in priests' pulpits, incessantly and everywhere, do now, in this world of ours, in this Isle of ours, offer themselves to view!

From such, at least from this intolerable over-proportion of such, might the merciful Heavens one day deliver us! Glorious, heroic, fruitful for his own Time, and for all Time and all Eternity, is the constant Speaker and Doer of Truth! If no such again, in the present generation, is to be vouchsafed us, let us have at least the melancholy pleasure of beholding a decided Liar. Wretched mortal, who with a single eye to be " respectable " forever sittest cobbling together two Inconsistencies, which stick not for an hour, but require ever new gluten and labour,—will it, by no length of experience, no bounty of Time or Chance, be revealed to thee that Truth is of Heaven, and Falsehood is of Hell; that if thou cast not from thee the one or the other, thy existence is wholly an Illusion and optical and tactual Phantasm; that properly thou existest not at all? Respectable! What, in the Devil's name, is the use of Respectability, with never so many gigs and silver spoons, if thou inwardly art the pitifulest of all men? I would thou wert either cold or hot.

One such desirable second-best, perhaps the chief of all such, we have here found in the Count Alessandro di Cagliostro, Pupil of the Sage Althotas, Foster-child of the Scherif of Mecca, probable Son of the last King of Trebisond; named also Acharat, and Unfortunate Child of Nature; by profession healer of diseases, abolisher of wrinkles, friend of the poor and impotent, grand-master of the Egyptian Mason-lodge of High Science, Spirit-summoner, Gold-cook, Grand Cophta, Prophet, Priest, and thaumaturgic moralist and swindler; really a Liar of the first magnitude, thorough-paced in all provinces of lying, what one may call the King of Liars. Mendez Pinto, Baron Münchausen and others are celebrated in this art, and not without some colour of justice; yet must it in candour remain doubtful whether any of these comparatively were much more than liars from the teeth onwards: a perfect character of the species in question, who lied not in word only, nor in act and word only, but continually, in thought, word and act; and, so to speak, lived wholly in an element of lying, and from birth to death did nothing but lie,—was still a desideratum. Of which desideratum Count Alessandro offers, we say, if not the fulfilment, perhaps as near an approach to it as the limited human faculties permit. Not in the modern ages, probably not in the ancient (though these had their Autolycus, their Apollonius, and enough else), did any completer figure of this sort issue out of Chaos and Old Night: a sublime kind of figure, presenting himself with " the air of calm strength," of sure perfection in his art; whom the heart opens itself to, with wonder and a sort of welcome. " The only vice I know," says one, " is Inconsistency." At lowest, answer we, he that *does* his work shall have his work judged of. Indeed, if Satan himself has in these days become a poetic hero, why should not Cagliostro, for some short hour, be a prose one? "One first question," says a great Philosopher, " I ask of every man: Has he an aim, which with undivided soul he follows, and advances towards? Whether his aim is a right one or a wrong one, forms but my second question." Here, then, is a small " human Pasquil," not without poetic interest.

However, be this as it may, we apprehend the eye of science at least cannot view him with indifference. Doubtful, false as much is in Cagliostro's manner of being, of this there is no doubt, that starting from the lowest point of Fortune's wheel, he rose to a height universally notable; that, without external furtherance, money, beauty, bravery, almost without common sense, or any discernible worth whatever, he sumptuously supported, for a long course of years, the wants and digestion of one of the greediest bodies, and one of the greediest minds; outwardly in his five senses, inwardly in his " sixth sense, that of vanity," nothing straitened. Clear enough it is, however much may be supposititious, that this japanned Chariot, rushing through the world, with dust-clouds and loud noise, at the speed of four swift horses, and topheavy with luggage, has an existence. The six Beef-eaters too, that ride prosperously heralding his advent, honourably escorting, menially waiting on him, are they not realities? Ever must the purse open, paying turnpikes, tavern-bills, drink-moneys, and the thousand-fold tear and wear of such a team; yet ever, like a horn-of-plenty, does it pour; and after brief rest, the chariot ceases not to roll. Whereupon rather pressingly arises the scientific question: How? Within that wonderful machinery, of horses, wheels, top-luggage, beef-eaters, sits only a gross, thickset Individual, evincing dulness enough; and by his side a Seraphina, with a look of doubtful reputation: how comes it that means still meet ends, that the whole Engine, like a steam-coach wanting fuel, does not stagnate, go silent, and fall to pieces in the ditch? Such question did the scientific curiosity of the present writer often put; and for many a day in vain.

Neither, indeed, as Book-readers know, was he peculiar herein. The great Schiller, for example, struck both with the poetic and the scientific phases of the matter, admitted the influences of the former to shape themselves anew within him; and strove with his usual impetuosity to burst (since unlocking was impossible) the secrets of the latter: and so his unfinished Novel, the *Geisterseher*, saw the light. Still more renowned is Goethe's Drama of the *Gross-Kophta ;* which, as himself informs us, delivered him from a state of mind that had become alarming to certain friends; so deep was the hold this business, at one of its epochs, had taken of him. A dramatic Fiction, that of his, based on the strictest possible historical study and inquiry; wherein perhaps the faithfulest image of the historical Fact, as yet extant in any shape, lies in artistic miniature curiously unfolded. Nay mere Newspaper-readers, of a certain age, can bethink them of our London Egyptian Lodges of High Science; of the Countess Seraphina's dazzling jewelries, nocturnal brilliancies, sibyllic ministrations and revelations; of Miss Fry and Milord Scott, and Messrs. Priddle and the other shark *bailiffs ;* and Lord Mansfield's judgment-seat; the Comte d'Adhémar, the Diamond Necklace, and Lord George Gordon. For Cagliostro, hovering through unknown space, twice (perhaps thrice) lighted on our London, and did business in the great chaos there.

Unparalleled Cagliostro! Looking at thy so attractively decorated private theatre, wherein thou actedst and livedst, what hand but itches to draw aside thy curtain; overhaul thy paste-boards, paintpots, paper-mantles, stage-lamps, and turning the whole inside out, find *thee* in the middle thereof! For there of a truth wert thou: though the rest was all foam and sham, there sattest *thou*, as large as life, and as esurient; warring against the world, and indeed conquering the world, for it remained thy tributary, and yielded daily rations. Innumerable Sheriff's-officers, Exempts, Sbirri, Alguazils, of every European climate, were prowling on thy traces, their intents hostile enough; thyself wert single against them all; in the whole earth thou hadst no friend. What say we, in the whole earth? In the whole universe thou hadst no friend! Heaven knew nothing of thee; *could* in charity know nothing of thee; and as for Beelzebub, *his* friendship, it is ascertained, cannot count for much.

But to proceed with business. The present inquirer, in obstinate investigation of a phenomenon so noteworthy, has searched through the whole not inconsiderable circle which his tether (of circumstances, geographical position, trade, health, extent of money-capital) enables him to describe: and, sad to say, with the most imperfect results. He has read Books in various languages and jargons; feared not to soil his fingers, hunting through ancient dusty Magazines, to sicken his heart in any labyrinth of iniquity and imbecility; nay he had not grudged to dive even into the infectious *Mémoires de Casanova*, for a hint or two,—could he have found that work, which, however, most Librarians make a point of denying that they possess. A painful search, as through some spiritual pest-house; and then with such issue! The quantity of discoverable printing about Cagliostro (so much being burnt) is now not great; nevertheless in frightful proportion to the quantity of information given. Except vague Newspaper rumours and surmises, the things found written of this Quack are little more than temporary Manifestos, by himself, by gulled or gulling disciples of his: not true therefore; at best only certain fractions of what he wished or expected the blinder Public to reckon true; misty, embroiled, for most part highly stupid; perplexing, even provoking; which can only be believed—to be, under such and such conditions, Lies. Of this sort emphatically is the English " *Life of the Count Cagliostro,* price three shillings and sixpence: " a Book indeed which one might hold (so fatuous, inane is it) to be some mere dream-vision and unreal eidolon, did it not now stand palpably there, as " Sold by T. Hookham, Bond Street, 1787; " and bear to be handled, spurned at and torn into pipe - matches. Some human creature doubtless was at the writing of it; but of what kind, country, trade, character or gender, you will in vain strive to fancy. Of like fabulous stamp are the *Mémoires pour le Comte de Cagliostro,* emitted, with *Requête à joindre,* from the Bastille, during that sorrowful business of the Diamond Necklace, in 1786; no less the *Lettre du Comte de Cagliostro au Peuple Anglais,* which followed shortly after, at London; from which two indeed, that fatuous inexplicable English *Life* has perhaps been mainly manufactured. Next come the *Mémoires authentiques pour servir à l'Histoire du Comte de Cagliostro,* twice printed in the same year 1786, at Strasburg and at Paris; a swaggering, lascivious Novelette, without talent, without truth or worth, happily of small size. So fares it with us: alas, all this is but the *outside* decorations of the private-theatre, or the sounding of catcalls and applauses from the stupid audience; nowise the interior bare walls and dress-room which we wanted to see! Almost our sole even half-genuine documents are a small barren pamphlet, *Cagliostro démasqué à Varsovie, en* 1780; and a small barren Volume purporting to be his *Life,* written at Rome, of which latter we have a French version, dated 1791. It is on this *Vie de Joseph Balsamo, connu sous le Nom de Comte Cagliostro,* that our main dependence must be placed; of which Work, meanwhile, whether it is wholly or only half-genuine, the reader may judge by one fact: that it comes to us through the medium of the Roman Inquisition, and the proofs to substantiate it lie in the Holy Office there. Alas, this reporting Familiar of the Inquisition was too probably something of a Liar; and he reports lying Confessions of one who was not so much a Liar as a Lie! In such enigmatic duskiness, and thrice-folded involution, after all inquiries, does the matter yet hang.

Nevertheless, by dint of meditation and comparison, light-points that stand fixed, and abide scrutiny, do here and there disclose themselves; diffusing a fainter light over what otherwise were dark, so that it is no longer invisible, but only dim. Nay after all, is there not in this same uncertainty a kind of fitness, of poetic congruity? Much that would offend the eye stands discreetly lapped in shade. Here too Destiny has cared for her favourite: that a powder-nimbus of astonishment, mystification and uncertainty should still encircle the Quack of Quacks, is right and suitable; such was by Nature and Art his chosen uniform and environment. Thus, as formerly in Life, so now in History, it is in huge fluctuating smoke-whirlwinds, partially illumed into a most brazen glory, yet united, coalescing with the region of everlasting Darkness, in miraculous clear-obscure, that he works and rides.

"Stern Accuracy in inquiring, bold Imagination in expounding and filling-up; these," says friend Sauerteig, "are the two pinions on which History soars,"—or flutters and wabbles. To which two pinions let us and the readers of this Magazine now daringly commit ourselves. Or chiefly indeed to the *latter* pinion, of Imagination; which, if it be the *larger*, will indeed make an unequal flight! Meanwhile, the style at least shall if possible be equal to the subject.

Know, then, that in the year 1743, in the city of Palermo, in Sicily, the family of Signor Pietro Balsamo, a shopkeeper, were exhilarated by the birth of a Boy. Such occurrences have now become so frequent, that, miraculous as they are, they occasion little astonishment: old Balsamo for a space, indeed, laid down his ellwands and unjust balances; but for the rest, met the event with equanimity. Of the possetings, junketings, gossipings, and other ceremonial rejoicings, transacted according to the custom of the country, for welcome to a New-comer, not the faintest tradition has survived; enough, that the small New-comer, hitherto a mere ethnic or heathen, is in a few days made a Christian of, or as we vulgarly say, christened; by the name Giuseppe. A fat, red, globular kind of fellow, not under nine pounds avoirdupois, the bold Imagination can figure him to be: if not proofs, there are indications that sufficiently betoken as much.

Of his teething and swaddling adventures, of his scaldings,

squallings, pukings, purgings, the strictest search into History can discover nothing; not so much as the epoch when he passed out of long-clothes stands noted in the fasti of Sicily. That same "larger pinion" of Imagination, nevertheless, conducts him from his native blind-alley, into the adjacent street *Casaro;* descries him, with certain contemporaries now unknown, essaying himself in small games of skill; watching what phenomena, of carriage-transits, dog-battles, street-music, or suchlike, the neighbourhood might offer (intent above all on any windfall of chance *provender*); now, with incipient scientific spirit, puddling in the gutters; now, as small poet (or maker), baking mud-pies. Thus does he tentatively coast along the outskirts of Existence, till once he shall be strong enough to land and make a footing there.

Neither does it seem doubtful that with the earliest exercise of speech, the gifts of simulation and dissimulation began to manifest themselves; Giuseppe, or Beppo as he was now called, could indeed speak the truth,—but only when he saw his advantage in it. Hungry also, as above hinted, he too-probably often was: a keen faculty of digestion, a meagre larder within doors; these two circumstances, so frequently conjoined in this world, reduced him to his inventions. As to the thing called Morals, and knowledge of Right and Wrong, it seems pretty certain that such knowledge, the sad fruit of Man's fall, had in great part been spared him; if he ever heard the commandment, *Thou shalt not steal*, he most probably could not believe in it, therefore could not obey it. For the rest, though of quick temper, and a ready striker where clear prospect of victory showed itself, we fancy him vociferous rather than bellicose, not prone to violence where stratagem will serve; almost pacific, indeed, had not his many wants necessitated him to many conquests. Above all things, a brazen impudence develops itself; the crowning gift of one born to scoundrelism. In a word, the fat thickset Beppo, as he skulks about there, plundering, playing dog's tricks, with his finger in every mischief, already gains character; shrill housewives of the neighbourhood, whose sausages he has filched, whose weaker sons maltreated, name him Beppo Maldetto, and indignantly prophesy that he will be hanged. A prediction which, as will be seen, the issue has signally falsified.

We hinted that the household larder was in a leanish state;

in fact, the outlook of the Balsamo family was getting troubled; old Balsamo had, during these things, been called away on his long journey. Poor man! The future eminence and preëminence of his Beppo he foresaw not, or what a world's-wonder he had thoughtlessly generated; as indeed, which of us, by much calculating, can sum-up the net-total (Utility, or Inutility) of any his most indifferent act,—a seed cast into the seedfield of TIME, to grow there, producing fruits or poisons, forever! Meanwhile Beppo himself gazed heavily into the matter; hung his thick lips while he saw his mother weeping; and, for the rest, eating what fat or sweet thing he could come at, let Destiny take its course.

The poor widow, ill-named *Felicità*, spinning out a painful livelihood by such means as only the poor and forsaken know, could not but many times cast an impatient eye on her brass-faced voracious Beppo; and ask him, If he never meant to turn himself to anything? A maternal uncle, of the moneyed sort (for he has uncles not without influence), has already placed him in the Seminary of St. Roch, to gain some tincture of schooling there: but Beppo feels himself misplaced in that sphere; "more than once runs away;" is flogged, snubbed, tyrannically checked on all sides; and finally, with such slender stock of schooling as had pleased to offer itself, returns to the street. The widow, as we said, urges him, the uncles urge: Beppo, wilt thou never turn thyself to anything? Beppo, with such speculative faculty, from such low watchtower as he commands, is in truth, being forced to it, from time to time, looking abroad into the world; surveying the conditions of mankind, therewith contrasting his own wishes and capabilities. Alas, his wishes are manifold; a most hot Hunger (in all kinds), as above hinted; but on the other hand, his leading capability seemed only the Power to Eat. What profession or condition, then? Choose; for it is time. Of all the terrestrial professions, that of Gentleman, it seemed to Beppo, had, under these circumstances, been most suited to his feelings: but then the outfit? the apprentice-fee? Failing which, he, with perhaps as much sagacity as one could expect, decides for the Ecclesiastical.

Behold him then, once more by the uncle's management, journeying, a chubby brass-faced boy of thirteen, beside the Reverend Father-General of the Benfratelli, to their neighbouring Convent of Cartegirone, with intent to enter himself novice there. He has donned the novice-habit; is "intrusted to the keeping of the Convent-Apothecary," on whose gallipots and crucibles he looks round with wonder. Were it by accident that he found himself Apothecary's Famulus, were it by choice of his own—nay was it not, in either case, by *design* of Destiny, intent on perfecting her work?—Enough, in this Cartegirone Laboratory there awaited him, though as yet he knew it not, life-guidance and determination; the great want of every genius, even of the scoundrel-genius. He himself confesses that he here learned some (or, as he calls it, *the*) "principles of chemistry and medicine." Natural enough: new books of the Chemists lay here, old books of the Alchemists; distillations, sublimations visibly went on; discussions there were, oral and written, of gold - making, salve - making, treasure - digging, divining-rods, projection, and the alcahest: besides, had he not among his fingers calxes, acids, Leyden-jars? Some first elements of medico-chemical conjurorship, so far as phosphorescent mixtures, aqua-toffana, ipecacuanha, cantharides tincture, and suchlike would go, were now attainable; sufficient when the hour came, to set-up any average Quack, much more the Quack of Quacks. It is here, in this unpromising environment, that the seeds, therapeutic, thaumaturgic, of the Grand Cophta's stupendous workings and renown were sown.

Meanwhile, as observed, the environment looked unpromising enough. Beppo with his two endowments of Hunger and of Power to Eat, had made the best choice he could; yet, as it soon proved, a rash and disappointing one. To his astonishment, he finds that even here he "is in a conditional world;" and, if he will employ his capability of eating or enjoying, must first, in some measure, work and suffer. Contention enough hereupon: but now dimly arises or reproduces itself, the question, Whether there were not a *shorter* road, that of stealing? Stealing—under which, generically taken, you may include the whole art of scoundrelism; for what is Lying itself but a *theft* of my belief? — stealing, we say, is properly the North-West Passage to Enjoyment: while common Navigators sail painfully along torrid shores, laboriously doubling this or the other Cape of Hope, your adroit Thief-Parry, drawn on smooth dog-sledges, is already there and back again. The misfortune is, that stealing requires a talent; and failure in that North-West voyage is more fatal than in any other. We hear that Beppo was " often punished: " painful experiences of the fate of genius; for all genius, by its nature, comes to disturb *somebody* in his ease, and your thief-genius more so than most!

Readers can now fancy the sensitive skin of Beppo mortified with prickly cilices, wealed by knotted thongs; his soul afflicted by vigils and forced fasts; no eye turned kindly on him; everywhere the bent of his genius rudely contravened. However, it is the first property of genius to grow in spite of contradiction, and even by means thereof;—as the vital germ pushes itself through the dull soil, and lives by what strove to bury it! Beppo, waxing into strength of bone and character, sets his face stiffly against persecution, and is not a whit disheartened. On *such* chastisements and chastisers he can look with a certain genial disdain. Beyond convent-wall, with their sour stupid shavelings, lies Palermo, lies the world; here too is he, still alive,—though worse off than he wished; and feels that the world is his oyster, which he (by chemical or other means) will one day open. Nay, we find there is a touch of grim Humour unfolds itself in the youth; the surest sign, as is often said, of a character naturally great. Witness, for example, how he acts on this to his ardent temperament so trying occasion. While the monks sit at meat, the impetuous voracious Beppo (that stupid Inquisition-Biographer records it as a thing of course) is set not to eat with them, not to pick up the crumbs that fall from them, but to stand "reading the Martyrology" for their pastime! The brave adjusts himself to the inevitable. Beppo reads that dullest Martyrology of theirs; but reads out of it not what is printed there, but what his own vivid brain on the spur of the moment devises: instead of the names of Saints, all heartily indifferent to him, he reads out the names of the most notable Palermo " unfortunate-females," now beginning to interest him a little. What a " deep world-irony," as the Germans call it, lies here! The Monks, of course, felled him to the earth, and flayed him with scourges; but what did it avail? This only became apparent, to himself and them, that he had now outgrown their monk-discipline; as the Psyche does its chrysalis-shell, and bursts it. Giuseppe Balsamo bids farewell to Cartegirone forever and a day.

So now, by consent or not of the ghostly Benfratelli (Friars of *Mercy*, as they were named!), our Beppo has again returned to the maternal uncle at Palermo. The uncle naturally asked him, What he next meant to do? Beppo, after stammering and hesitating for some length of weeks, makes answer: Try Painting. Well and good! So Beppo gets him colours, brushes, fit tackle, and addicts himself for some space of time to the study of what is innocently called *Design*. Alas, if we consider Beppo's great Hunger now that new senses were unfolding in him, how inadequate are the exiguous resources of Design; how necessary to attempt quite another deeper species of Design, of Designs! It is true, he lives with his uncle, has culinary meat; but where is the pocket-money for other costlier sorts of meats to come from? As the Kaiser Joseph was wont to say: From my head alone (*De ma tête seule*)!

The Roman Biographer, though a most wooden man, has incidentally thrown some light on Beppo's position at this juncture: both on his wants and his resources. As to the first, it appears (using the wooden man's phraseology) that he kept the " worst company," led the " loosest life; " was hand-in-glove with all the swindlers, gamblers, idle apprentices, unfortunate-females, of Palermo: in the study and practice of Scoundrelism diligent beyond most. The genius which has burst asunder convent-walls, and other rubbish of impediments, now flames upward towards its mature splendour. Wheresoever a stroke of mischief is to be done, a slush of so-called vicious enjoyment to be swallowed, there with hand and throat is Beppo Balsamo seen. He will be a Master, one day, in his profession. Not indeed that he has yet quitted Painting, or even purposes so much: for the present, it is useful, indispensable, as a stalking-horse to the maternal uncle and neighbours; nay to himself,—for with all the ebullient impulses of scoundrel-genius restlessly seething in him, irrepressibly bursting through, he has the noble unconsciousness of genius; guesses not, dare not guess, that he is a born scoundrel, much less a born world-scoundrel.

But as for the other question, of his resources, these we perceive were several-fold, and continually extending. Not to mention any pictorial exiguities, which indeed existed chiefly in expectance,—there had almost accidentally arisen for him, in the first place, the resource of Pandering. He has a fair cousin living in the house with him, and she again has

a lover; Beppo stations himself as go-between; delivers
letters; fails not to drop hints that a lady, to be won or kept,
must be generously treated; that such and such a pair of
earrings, watch, necklace, or even sum of money, would
work wonders; which valuables, adds the wooden Roman
Biographer, " he then appropriated furtively." Like enough!
Next, however, as another more lasting resource, he forges;
at first in a small way, and trying his apprentice-hand:
tickets for the theatre, and such trifles. Erelong, however,
we see him fly at higher quarry; by practice he has acquired
perfection in the great art of counterfeiting hands; and will
exercise it on the large or on the narrow scale, for a consideration. Among his relatives is a Notary, with whom he can
insinuate himself; for purpose of study, or even of practice.
In the presses of this Notary lies a Will, which Beppo contrives to come at, and falsify " for the benefit of a certain
Religious House." Much good may it do them! Many
years afterwards the fraud was detected; but Beppo's benefit
in it was spent and safe long before. Thus again the stolid
Biographer expresses horror or wonder that he should have
forged leave-of-absence for a monk, " counterfeiting the
signature of the Superior." Why not? A forger must forge
what is wanted of him: the Lion truly preys not on mice; yet
shall he refuse such, if they jump into his mouth? Enough,
the indefatigable Beppo has here opened a quite boundless
mine; wherein through his whole life he will, as occasion
calls, dig, at his convenience. Finally, he can predict fortunes and show visions,—by phosphorus and legerdemain.
This, however, only as a dilettantism; to take-up the earnest
profession of Magician does not yet enter into his views. Thus
perfecting himself in all branches of his art, does our Balsamo
live and grow. Stupid, pudding-faced as he looks and is,
there is a vulpine astucity in him; and then a wholeness, a
heartiness, a kind of blubbery impetuosity, an oiliness so
plausible-looking: give him only length of life, he will rise to
the top of his profession.

Consistent enough with such blubbery impetuosity in
Beppo is another fact we find recorded of him, that at this
time he was found " in most brawls," whether in street or
tavern. The way of his business led him into liability to
such; neither as yet had he learned prudence by age. Of
choleric temper, with all his obesity; a square-built, burly,

vociferous fellow; ever ready with his stroke (if victory seemed sure); nay, at bottom, not without a certain pig-like defensive - ferocity, perhaps even something more. Thus, when you find him making a point to attack, if possible, "*all* officers of justice," and deforce them; delivering the wretched from their talons: was not this, we say, a kind of dog-faithfulness, and public spirit, either of the mastiff or of the cur species? Perhaps too there was a touch of that old Humour and "world-irony" in it. One still more unquestionable feat he is recorded (we fear, on imperfect evidence) to have done: "assassinated a canon."

Remonstrances from growling maternal uncles could not fail; threats, disdains from ill-affected neighbours; tears from an expostulating widowed mother: these he shakes from him like dewdrops from the lion's mane. Still less could the Police neglect him; him the visibly rising Professor of Swindlery; the swashbuckler, to boot, and deforcer of bailiffs: he has often been captured, haled to their bar; yet hitherto, by defect of evidence, by good luck, intercession of friends, been dismissed with admonition. Two things, nevertheless, might now be growing clear: first, that the die was cast with Beppo, and he a scoundrel for life; second, that such a mixed, composite, crypto-scoundrel life could not endure, but must unfold itself into a pure, declared one. The Tree that is planted stands not still; *must* pass through all its stages and phases, from the state of acorn to that of green leafy oak, of withered leafless oak; to the state of felled timber, finally to that of firewood and ashes. Not less (though less visibly to dull eyes) the Act that is done, the condition that has realised itself; above all things, the Man, with his Fortunes, that has been born. Beppo, everyway in vigorous vitality, cannot continue half-painting half-swindling in Palermo; must develop himself into whole swindler; and, unless hanged there, seek his bread elsewhere. What the proximate cause, or signal, of such crisis and development might be, no man could say; yet most men would have confidently guessed, The Police. Nevertheless it proved otherwise; not by the flaming sword of Justice, but by the rusty dirk of a foolish private individual, is Beppo driven forth.

Walking one day in the fields (as the bold historic Imagination will figure) with a certain ninny of a "Goldsmith named

Marano," as they pass one of those rock-chasms frequent in the fair Island of Sicily, Beppo begins, in his oily, voluble way, to hint, That treasures often lay hid; that a Treasure lay hid *there*, as he knew by some pricking of his thumbs, divining-rod, or other talismanic monition: which Treasure might, by aid of science, courage, secrecy and a small judicious advance of money, be fortunately lifted. The gudgeon takes; advances, by degrees, to the length of " sixty gold Ounces;" [1] sees magic circles drawn in the wane or in the full of the moon, blue (phosphorus) flames arise, split twigs auspiciously quiver; and at length—demands peremptorily that the Treasure be dug. A night is fixed on: the ninny Goldsmith, trembling with rapture and terror, breaks ground; digs, with thick breath and cold sweat, fiercely down, down, Beppo relieving him: the work advances; when, ah! at a certain stage of it (*before* fruition) hideous yells arise, a jingle like the emptying of Birmingham; six Devils pounce upon the poor sheep Goldsmith, and beat him almost to *mutton ;* mercifully sparing Balsamo,—who indeed has himself summoned them thither, and as it were created them (with goatskins and burnt cork). Marano, though a ninny, now knew how it lay; and furthermore that he had a stiletto. One of the grand drawbacks of swindler-genius! You accomplish the Problem; and then—the Elementary Quantities, Algebraic Symbols you worked on, will fly in your face!

Hearing of stilettos, our Algebraist begins to look around him, and view his empire of Palermo in the concrete. An empire now much exhausted; much infested, too, with sorrows of all kinds, and every day the more; nigh ruinous, in short; not worth being stabbed for. There is a world elsewhere. In any case, the young Raven has now shed his pens, and got fledged for flying. Shall he not spurn the whole from him, and soar off? Resolved, performed! Our Beppo quits Palermo; and, as it proved, on a long voyage: or, as the Inquisition-Biographer has it, " he fled from Palermo, and overran the whole Earth."

Here, then, ends the First Act of Count Alessandro Cagliostro's Life-drama. Let the curtain drop; and hang unrent, before an audience of mixed feeling, till the First of August.

---

[1] The Sicilian Ounce (*Onza*) is worth about ten shillings sterling.

FLIGHT LAST

BEFORE entering on the second Section of Count Beppo's History, the Editor will indulge in a philosophical reflection.

This Beppic Hegira, or Flight from Palermo, we have now arrived at, brings us down, in European History, to somewhere about the epoch of the Peace of Paris. Old Feudal Europe, while Beppo flies forth into the whole Earth, has just finished the last of her " tavern-brawls," or wars; and lain down to doze, and yawn, and disconsolately wear-off the headaches, bruises, nervous prostration and flaccidity consequent thereon: for the brawl had been a long one, *Seven Years* long; and there had been many such, begotten, as is usual, of intoxication from Pride or other Devil's-drink, and foul humours in the constitution. Alas, it was not so much a disconsolate doze, after ebriety and quarrel, that poor old Feudal Europe had now to undergo, and then on awakening to drink anew, and quarrel anew: old Feudal Europe has fallen a-dozing to die! Her next awakening will be with no tavern-brawl, at the *King's Head* or *Prime Minister* tavern; but with the stern Avatar of DEMOCRACY, hymning its worldthrilling birth- and battle-song in the distant West;—therefrom to go out conquering and to conquer, till it have made a circuit of all the Earth, and old dead Feudal Europe is born again (after infinite pangs!) into a new Industrial one. At Beppo's Hegira, as we said, Europe was in the last languor and stertorous fever-sleep of Dissolution: alas, with us, and with our sons for a generation or two, it is almost still worse,— were it not that in Birth-throes there is ever hope, in Deaththroes the final departure of hope.

Now the philosophic reflection we were to indulge in, was no other than this, most germane to our subject: the portentous extent of Quackery, the multitudinous variety of Quacks that, along with our Beppo, and under him each in his degree, overran all Europe during that same period, the latter half of last century. It was the very age of impostors, cutpurses, swindlers, double-goers, enthusiasts, ambiguous persons; quacks simple, quacks compound; crackbrained, or with deceit prepense; quacks and quackeries of all colours and kinds. How many Mesmerists, Magicians, Cabalists,

Swedenborgians, Illuminati, Crucified Nuns, and Devils of Loudun! To which the Inquisition-Biographer adds Vampires, Sylphs, Rosicrucians, Freemasons, and an *Etcetera*. Consider your Schröpfers, Cagliostros, Casanovas, Saint-Germains, Dr. Grahams; the Chevalier d'Eon, Psalmanazar, Abbé Paris and the Ghost of Cock-lane! As if Bedlam had broken loose; as if, rather, in that " spiritual Twelfth-hour of the night," the everlasting Pit had opened itself, and from *its* still blacker bosom had issued Madness and all manner of shapeless Misbirths, to masquerade and chatter there.

But indeed, if we consider, how could it be otherwise? In that stertorous last fever-sleep of our European world, must not Phantasms enough, born of the Pit, as all such *are*, flit past, in ghastly masquerading and chattering? A low scarce-audible moan (in Parliamentary Petitions, Meal-mobs, Popish Riots, Treatises on Atheism) struggles from the moribund sleeper: frees him not from his hellish guests and saturnalia: Phantasms these " of a dying brain." So too, when the old Roman world, the measure of its iniquities being full, was to expire, and (in still bitterer agonies) be born again, had they not Veneficæ, Mathematici, Apolloniuses with the Golden Thigh, Apollonius' Asses, and False Christs enough,—before a REDEEMER arose!

For, in truth, and altogether apart from such half-figurative language, Putrescence is not more naturally the scene of unclean creatures in the world physical, than Social Decay is of quacks in the world moral. Nay, look at it with the eye of the mere Logician, of the Political Economist. In such periods of Social Decay, what is called an overflowing Population, that is a Population which, under the old Captains of Industry (named Higher Classes, *Ricos Hombres*, Aristocracies and the like), can no longer find work and wages, increases the number of Unprofessionals, Lackalls, Social Nondescripts; with appetite of utmost keenness, which there is no known method of satisfying. Nay more, and perversely enough, ever as Population augments, your Captains of Industry can and do dwindle more and more into Captains of Idleness; whereby the more and more overflowing Population is worse and worse governed (shown *what to do*, for that is the only government): thus is the candle lighted at both ends; and the number of social Nondescripts increases in *double*-quick ratio. Whoso is alive, it is said, "must live;" at all events, will live; a task which daily gets harder, reduces to stranger shifts.

And now furthermore, with general economic distress, in such a Period, there is usually conjoined the utmost decay of moral principle: indeed, so universal is this conjunction, many men have seen it to be a concatenation and causation; justly enough, except that such have very generally, ever since a certain religious-repentant feeling went out of date, committed one sore mistake: what is vulgarly called putting the cart before the horse. Politico-economical benefactor of the species! deceive not thyself with barren sophisms: National suffering *is*, if thou wilt understand the words, verily a " judgment of God;" has ever been preceded by national crime. "Be it here once more maintained before the world," cries Sauerteig, in one of his *Springwurzeln*, "that temporal Distress, that Misery of any kind, is not the *cause* of Immorality, but the effect thereof! Among individuals, it is true, so wide is the empire of Chance, poverty and wealth go all at hap-hazard; a St. Paul is making tents at Corinth, while a Kaiser Nero fiddles, in ivory palaces, over a burning Rome. Nevertheless here too, if nowise wealth and poverty, yet well-being and ill-being, even in the temporal economic sense, go commonly in respective partnership with Wisdom and with Folly: no man can, for a length of time, be wholly wretched, if there is not a disharmony (a folly and wickedness) within himself; neither can the richest Crœsus and never so eupeptic (for he too has his indigestions, and dies at last of surfeit), be other than discontented, perplexed, unhappy, if he be a Fool."—This we apprehend is true, O Sauerteig, yet not the whole truth: for there is more than day's-work and day's-wages in this world of ours: which, as thou knowest, is itself quite other than a " Workshop and Fancy-Bazaar," is also a " Mystic Temple and Hall of Doom." Thus we have heard of such things as good men struggling with adversity, and offering a spectacle for the very gods.

" But with a nation," continues he, " where the multitude of the chances covers, in great measure, the uncertainty of Chance, it may be said to hold always that general Suffering is the fruit of general Misbehaviour, general Dishonesty. Consider it well; had all men stood faithfully to their posts, the Evil, when it first arose, had been manfully fronted, and abolished, not lazily blinked, and left to grow, with the foul

sluggard's comfort: ' It will last my time.' Thou foul sluggard, and even thief (*Faulenzer, ja Dieb*)! For art thou not
a thief, to pocket thy day's-wages (be they counted in *groschen*
or in gold thousands) for this, if it be for anything, for watching
on thy special watch-tower that God's City (which this His
World is, where His children dwell) suffer no damage; and,
all the while, to watch only that thy own ease be not invaded,
—let otherwise hard come to hard as it will and can? Unhappy! It will last thy time: thy worthless sham of an
existence, wherein nothing but the Digestion was real, will
have evaporated in the interim; it will last thy time: but
will it last thy *Eternity?* Or what if it should *not* last thy
time (mark that also, for that also will be the fate of *some*
such lying sluggard), but take fire, and explode, and consume
thee like the moth!"

The sum of the matter, in any case, is, that national
Poverty and national Dishonesty go together; that continually increasing social Nondescripts get ever the hungrier,
ever the falser. Now say, have we not here the very making
of Quackery; raw-material, plastic-energy, both in full
action? Dishonesty the raw-material, Hunger the plastic-
energy: what will not the two realise? Nay observe farther
how Dishonesty is the raw-material not of Quacks only,
but also in great part of Dupes. In Goodness, were it never
so simple, there is the surest instinct for the Good; the
uneasiest unconquerable repulsion for the False and Bad.
The very Devil Mephistopheles cannot deceive poor guile-
less Margaret: " it stands written on his brow that he never
loved a living soul!" The like too has many a human
inferior Quack painfully experienced; the like lies in store for
our hero Beppo. But now with such abundant raw-material
not only to make Quacks of, but to feed and occupy them on,
if the plastic-energy of Hunger fail not, what a world shall
we have! The wonder is not that the eighteenth century had
very numerous Quacks, but rather that they were not
innumerable.

In that same French Revolution alone, which burnt-up
so much, what unmeasured masses of Quackism were set
fire to; nay, as foul mephitic fire-damp in that case, were
made to flame in a fierce, sublime *splendour ;* coruscating,
even illuminating! The Count Saint-Germain, some twenty
years later, had found a quite new element, of Fraternisation,

Sacred right of Insurrection, Oratorship of the Human
Species, wherefrom to body himself forth quite otherwise:
Schröpfer needed not now, as Blackguard undeterred, have
solemnly shot himself in the *Rosenthal ;* might have solemnly
sacrificed himself, as Jacobin half-heroic, in the *Place de la
Révolution.* For your quack-genius is indeed born, but also
made; circumstances shape him or stunt him. Beppo
Balsamo, born British in these new days, could have con-
jured fewer Spirits; yet had found a living and glory, as
Castlereagh Spy, Irish Associationist, Blacking-Manufacturer,
Book-Publisher, Able Editor. Withal too the reader will
observe that Quacks, in every time, are of two sorts: the
Declared Quack; and the Undeclared, who, if you question
him, will deny stormfully, both to others and to himself;
of which two quack-species the proportions vary with the
varying capacity of the age. If Beppo's was the age of the
Declared, therein, after all French Revolutions, we will grant,
lay one of its main distinctions from ours; which is it not
yet, and for a generation or two, the age of the Undeclared?
Alas, almost a still more detestable age;—yet now (by God's
grace), with Prophecy, with irreversible Enactment, registered
in Heaven's chancery,—where *thou* too, if thou wilt *look*,
mayst read and know, That its death-doom shall not linger.
Be it speedy, be it sure!—And so herewith were our philosophical reflection, on the nature, causes, prevalence, decline
and expected temporary destruction of Quackery, concluded;
and now the Beppic poetic Narrative can once more take
its course.

Beppo, then, like a Noah's Raven, is out upon that watery
waste of dissolute, beduped, distracted European Life, to see
if there is any carrion there. One unguided little Raven, in
the wide-weltering "Mother of Dead Dogs:" will he not
come to harm; will he not be snapt-up, drowned, starved
and washed to the Devil there? No fear of him,—for a time.
His eye (or scientific judgment), it is true, as yet takes-in only
a small section of it; but then his scent (instinct of genius) is
prodigious: several endowments, forgery and others, he has
unfolded into talents; the two sources of all quack-talent,
Cunning and Impudence, are his in richest measure.

As to his immediate course of action and adventure, the
foolish Inquisition-Biographer, it must be owned, shows

himself a fool, and can give us next to no insight. Like
enough, Beppo "fled to Messina;" simply as to the nearest
city, and to get across to the mainland: but as to this "certain
Althotas" whom he met there, and voyaged with to Alexan-
dria in Egypt, and how they made hemp into silk, and
realised much money, and came to Malta, and studied in
the Laboratory there, and then the certain Althotas died,—
of all this what shall be said? The foolish Inquisition-
Biographer is uncertain whether the certain Althotas was a
Greek or a Spaniard: but unhappily the prior question is not
settled, whether he *was* at all. Superfluous it seems to put
down Beppo's own account of his procedure; he gave multifarious accounts, as the exigencies of the case demanded: this
of the "certain Althotas," and hemp made into false silk,
is as verisimilar as that other of the "sage Althotas," the
heirship-apparent of Trebisond, and the Scherif of Mecca's
"Adieu, unfortunate Child of Nature." Nay the guesses of
the ignorant world; how Count Cagliostro had been travelling-
tutor to a Prince (name not given), whom he murdered and
took the money from; with others of the like,—were perhaps
still more absurd. Beppo, we can see, was out and away,—
the Devil knew whither. Far, variegated, painful might his
roamings be. A plausible-looking shadow of him shows
itself hovering over Naples and Calabria; thither, as to a
famed high-school of Laziness and Scoundrelism, he may
likely enough have gone to graduate. Of the Malta Laboratory, and Alexandrian hemp-silk, the less we say the better.
This only is clear: That Beppo dived deep down into the
lugubrious-obscure regions of Rascaldom; like a Knight to
the palace of his Fairy; remained unseen there, and returned
thence armed at all points.

If we fancy, meanwhile, that Beppo already meditated
becoming Grand Cophta, and riding at Strasburg in the Cardinal's carriage, we mistake much. Gift of Prophecy has been
wisely denied to man. Did a man *foresee* his life, and not
merely *hope* it, and grope it, and so, by Necessity and Freewill,
make and fabricate it into a reality, he were no *man*, but
some other kind of creature, superhuman or subterhuman.
No man sees far; the most see no farther than their noses.
From the quite dim uncertain mass of the future, "which
lies there," says a Scottish Humorist, "uncombed, uncarded,
like a mass of *tarry wool* proverbially *ill to spin*," they spin

out, better or worse, their rumply, infirm thread of Existence, and wind it up, up,—till the spool is *full ;* seeing but some little half-yard of it at once; exclaiming, as they look into the betarred entangled mass of Futurity, We *shall* see!

The first authentic fact with regard to Beppo is, that his swart squat figure becomes visible in the Corso and Campo Vaccino of Rome; that he "lodges at the Sign of the Sun in the Rotonda," and sells pen-drawings there. Properly they are not pen-drawings; but printed engravings or etchings, to which Beppo, with a pen and a little Indian ink, has added the degree of scratching to give them the air of such. Thereby mainly does he realise a thin livelihood. From which we infer that his transactions in Naples and Calabria, with Althotas and hemp-silk, or whatever else, had not turned to much.

Forged pen-drawings are no mine of wealth: neither was Beppo Balsamo anything of an Adonis; on the contrary, a most dusky, bull-necked, mastiff-faced, sinister-looking individual: nevertheless, on applying for the favour of the hand of Lorenza Feliciani, a beautiful Roman donzella, "dwelling near the Trinity of the Pilgrims," the unfortunate child of Nature prospers beyond our hopes. Authorities differ as to the rank and status of this fair Lorenza: one account says, she was the daughter of a Girdle-maker; but adds erroneously that it was in Calabria. The matter must remain suspended. Certain enough, she was a handsome buxom creature; "both pretty and ladylike," it is presumable; but having no offer, in a country too prone to celibacy, took-up with the bull-necked forger of pen-drawings, whose suit too was doubtless pressed with the most flowing rhetoric. She gave herself in marriage to him; and the parents admitted him to quarter in their house, till it should appear what was next to be done.

Two kitchen-fires, says the Proverb, burn not on one hearth: here, moreover, might be quite special causes of discord. Pen-drawing, at best a hungry concern, has now exhausted itself, and must be given up; but Beppo's household prospects brighten, on the other side: in the charms of his Lorenza he sees before him what the French call "a Future confused and immense." The hint was given; and, with reluctance, or without reluctance (for the evidence leans *both* ways), was taken and reduced to practice: Signor and Signora Balsamo are forth from the old Girdler's house, into the wide world, seeking and finding adventures.

The foolish Inquisition-Biographer, with painful scientific accuracy, furnishes a descriptive catalogue of all the successive Cullies (Italian Counts, French Envoys, Spanish Marquises, Dukes and Drakes) in various quarters of the known world, whom this accomplished pair took-in; with the sums each yielded, and the methods employed to bewitch him. Into which descriptive catalogue, why should we here so much as cast a glance? Cullies, the easy cushions on which knaves and knavesses repose and fatten, have at all times existed, in considerable profusion: neither can the fact of a clothed animal, Marquis or other, having acted in that capacity to never such lengths, entitle him to mention in History. We pass over these. Beppo, or as we must now learn to call him, the Count, appears at Venice, at Marseilles, at Madrid, Cadiz, Lisbon, Brussels; makes scientific pilgrimage to Quack Saint-Germain in Westphalia, religious-commercial to Saint Saint-James in Compostella, to Our Lady in Loretto: south, north, east, west, he shows himself; finds everywhere Lubricity and Stupidity (better or worse provided with cash), the two elements on which he thaumaturgically can work and live. Practice makes perfection; Beppo too was an apt scholar. By all methods he can awaken the stagnant imagination; cast maddening powder in the eyes.

Already in Rome he has cultivated whiskers, and put-on the uniform of a Prussian Colonel: dame Lorenza is fair to look upon; but how much fairer, if by the air of distance and dignity you lend enchantment to her! In other places, the Count appears as real Count; as Marquis Pellegrini (lately from foreign parts); as Count this and Count that, Count Proteus-Incognito; finally as Count Alessandro Cagliostro.[1] Figure him shooting through the world with utmost rapidity; ducking-under here, when the sword-fishes of Justice make a dart at him; ducking-up yonder in new shape, at the distance of a thousand miles; not unprovided with forged vouchers of respectability; above all, with that best voucher of respectability, a four-horse carriage, beef-eaters, and open

[1] Not altogether an *invention* this last; for his granduncle (a bell-founder at Messina?) was actually surnamed *Cagliostro*, as well as named *Giuseppe*.—O. Y.

purse, for Count Cagliostro has ready-money and pays his way. At some Hotel of the Sun, Hotel of the Angel, Gold Lion, or Green Goose, or whatever Hotel it is, in whatever world-famous capital City, his chariot-wheels have rested; sleep and food have refreshed his live-stock, chiefly the pearl and soul thereof, his indispensable Lorenza, now no longer Dame Lorenza, but Countess Seraphina, looking seraphic enough! Moneyed Donothings, whereof in this vexed Earth there are many, ever lounging about such places, scan and comment on the foreign coat-of-arms; ogle the fair foreign woman; who timidly recoils from their gaze, timidly responds to their reverences, as in halls and passages, they obsequiously throw themselves in her way: erelong one moneyed Donothing, from amid his tags and tassels, sword-belts, foptackle, frizzled hair without brains beneath it, is heard speaking to another: " Seen the Countess?—Divine creature that! "—and so the game is begun.

Let not the too sanguine reader, meanwhile, fancy that it is all holiday and heyday with his Lordship. The course of scoundrelism, any more than that of true love, never did run smooth. Seasons there may be when Count Proteus-Incognito has his epaulettes torn from his shoulders; his garment-skirts clipt close by the buttocks; and is bid sternly tarry at Jericho till his beard be grown. Harpies of Law defile his solemn feasts; his light burns languid; for a space seems utterly snuffed out, and dead in malodorous vapour. Dead only to blaze up the brighter! There is scoundrel-life in Beppo Cagliostro; cast him among the mud, tread him out of sight there, the miasmata do but stimulate and refresh him, he rises sneezing, is strong and young again.

Behold him, for example, again in Palermo, after having seen many men and many lands; and how he again escapes thence. Why did he return to Palermo? Perhaps to astonish old friends by new grandeur; or for temporary shelter, if the Continent were getting hot for him; or perhaps in the mere way of general trade. He is seized there, and clapt in prison, for those foolish old businesses of the treasure-digging Goldsmith, of the forged Will.

" The manner of his escape," says one, whose few words on this obscure matter are so many light-points for us, " deserves to be described. The Son of one of the first Sicilian Princes, and great landed Proprietors (who moreover had filled important stations at the Neapolitan Court), was a person that united with a strong body and ungovernable temper all the tyrannical caprice, which the rich and great, with cultivation, think themselves entitled to exhibit.

" Donna Lorenza had contrived to gain this man; and on him the fictitious Marchese Pellegrini founded his security. The Prince testified openly that he was the protector of this stranger pair: but what was his fury when Joseph Balsamo, at the instance of those whom he had cheated, was cast into prison! He tried various means to deliver him; and as these would not prosper, he publicly, in the President's ante-chamber, threatened the plaintiffs' Advocate with the frightfulest misusage if the suit were not dropt, and Balsamo forthwith set at liberty. As the Advocate declined such proposal, he clutched him, beat him, threw him on the floor, trampled him with his feet, and could hardly be restrained from still farther outrages, when the President himself came running out at the tumult, and commanded peace.

" This latter, a weak, dependent man, made no attempt to punish the injurer; the plaintiffs and their Advocate grew fainthearted; and Balsamo was let go; not so much as a registration in the Court-Books specifying his dismissal, who occasioned it, or how it took place." [1]

Thus sometimes, a friend in the court is better than a penny in the purse! Marchese Pellegrini " quickly thereafter left Palermo, and performed various travels, whereof my author could impart no clear information." Whether, or how far, the Game-chicken Prince went with him is not hinted.

So it might, at times, be quite otherwise than in coach-and-four that our Cagliostro journeyed. Occasionally we find him as outrider journeying on horseback; only Seraphina and her sop (whom she is to suck and eat) lolling on carriage-cushions; the hardy Count glad that hereby he can have the shot paid. Nay sometimes he looks utterly poverty-struck and has to journey one knows not how. Thus one briefest but authentic-looking glimpse of him presents itself in Eng-land, in the year 1772: no Count is he here, but mere Signor Balsamo again; engaged in house-painting, for which he has a most peculiar talent. Was it true that he painted the country-house of " a Doctor Benemore: " and having not painted, but only smeared it, was refused payment, and got

[1] Goethe's *Werke*, b. **xxviii**. 132.

a lawsuit with expenses instead? If Doctor Benemore have left any representatives in this Earth, they are desired to speak out. We add only, that if young Beppo had one of the prettiest wives, old Benemore had one of the ugliest daughters; and so, putting one thing to another, matters might not be so bad.

For it is to be observed, that the Count, on his own side, even in his days of highest splendour, is not idle. Faded dames of quality have many wants: the Count has not studied in the convent Laboratory, or pilgrimed to the Count Saint-Germain, in Westphalia, to no purpose. With loftiest condescension he stoops to impart somewhat of his supernatural secrets,—for a consideration. Rowland's Kalydor is valuable; but what to the Beautifying-water of Count Alessandro! He that will undertake to smooth wrinkles, and make withered green parchment into a fair carnation skin, is he not one whom faded dames of quality will delight to honour? Or again, let the Beautifying-water succeed or not, have not such dames, if calumny may be in aught believed, *another* want? This want, too, the indefatigable Cagliostro will supply,—for a consideration. For faded gentlemen of quality the Count likewise has help. Not a charming Countess alone; but a " Wine of Egypt " (cantharides not being unknown to him), sold in drops, more precious than nectar; which what faded gentleman of quality would not purchase with anything short of life? Consider now what may be done with potions, washes, charms, love-philtres, among a class of mortals, idle from the mother's womb; rejoicing to be taught the Ionic dances, and meditating of love from their tender nails!

Thus waxing, waning, broad-shining, or extinct, an inconstant but unwearied Moon, rides on its course the Cagliostric star. Thus are Count and Countess busy in their vocation; thus do they spend the golden season of their youth,—shall we say, " for the Greatest Happiness of the greatest number "? Happy enough, had there been no sumptuary or adultery or swindlery Law-acts; no Heaven above, no Hell beneath; no flight of Time, and gloomy land of Eld and Destitution and Desperation, towards which, by law of Fate, they see themselves, at all moments, with frightful regularity, unaidably drifting.

The prudent man provides against the inevitable. Already

Count Cagliostro, with his love-philtres, his cantharidic Wine of Egypt; nay far earlier, by his blue-flames and divining-rods, as with the poor sheep Goldsmith of Palermo; and ever since, by many a significant hint thrown out where the scene suited,—has dabbled in the Supernatural. As his seraphic Countess gives signs of withering, and one luxuriant branch of industry will die and drop off, others must be pushed into budding. Whether it was in England during what he called his " first visit " in the year 1776 (for the before-first, house-smearing visit was, reason or none, to go for nothing) that he first thought of Prophecy as a trade, is unknown: certain enough, he had begun to practise it then; and this indeed not without a glimpse of insight into the English national character. Various, truly, are the pursuits of mankind; whereon they would fain, unfolding the future, take Destiny by surprise: with us, however, as a nation of shopkeepers, they may be all said to centre in this one, *Put money in thy purse!* O for a Fortunatus'-Pocket, with its ever-new coined gold;—if, indeed, the true prayer were not rather: O for a Crassus'-Drink, of *liquid* gold, that so the accursed throat of Avarice might for once have enough and to spare! Meanwhile whoso should engage, keeping clear of the gallows, to teach men the secret of making money, were not he a Professor sure of audience? Strong were the general Scepticism; still stronger the general Need and Greed. Count Cagliostro, from his residence in Whitcombe Street, it is clear, had looked into the mysteries of the Little-go; by occult science knew the lucky number. Bish as yet was not; but Lotteries were; gulls also were. The Count has his Language-master, his Portuguese Jew, his nondescript Ex-Jesuits, whom he puts forth as antennæ, into coffee-houses, to stir-up the minds of men. "Lord" Scott (a swindler swindled), and Miss Fry, and many others, were they here, could tell what it cost them: nay, the very Lawbooks, and Lord Mansfield and Mr. Howarth speak of hundreds, and jewel-boxes, and quite handsome booties. Thus can the bustard pluck geese, and, if Law do get the carcass, live upon their giblets;—now and then, however, finds a vulture, too tough to pluck.

The attentive reader is no doubt curious to understand all the What and the How of Cagliostro's procedure while England was the scene. As we too are, and have been; but unhappily all in vain. To that English *Life* of uncertain gender none, as was said, need in their utmost extremity repair. Scarcely the very lodging of Cagliostro can be ascertained; except incidentally that it was once in Whitcombe Street; for a few days, in Warwick Court, Holborn; finally, for some space, in the King's Bench Jail. Vain were it, meanwhile, for any reverencer of genius to pilgrim thither, seeking memorials of a great man. Cagliostro is clean gone: on the strictest search, no token never so faint discloses itself. He went, and left nothing behind him;— except perhaps a few cast-clothes, and other inevitable exuviæ, long since, not indeed annihilated (this nothing can be), yet beaten into mud, and spread as new soil over the general surface of Middlesex and Surrey; floated by the Thames into old Ocean; or flitting, the gaseous parts of them, in the universal Atmosphere, borne thereby to remotest corners of the Earth, or beyond the limits of the Solar System! So fleeting is the track and habitation of man; so wondrous the stuff he builds of; his house, his very house of houses (what we call his *body*), were he the first of geniuses, will evaporate in the strangest manner, and vanish even whither we have said.

To us on our side, however, it is cheering to discover, for one thing, that Cagliostro found antagonists worthy of him: the bustard plucking geese, and living on their giblets, found not our whole Island peopled with geese, but here and there, as above hinted, with vultures, with hawks of still sharper quality than his. Priddle, Aylett, Saunders, O'Reilly: let these stand forth as the vindicators of English national character. By whom Count Alessandro Cagliostro, as in dim fluctuating outline indubitably appears, was bewritted, arrested, fleeced, hatchelled, bewildered and bedevilled, till the very Jail of King's Bench seemed a refuge from them. A wholly obscure contest, as was natural; wherein, however, to all candid eyes the vulturous and falconish character of our Isle fully asserts itself; and the foreign Quack of Quacks, with all his thaumaturgic Hemp-silks, Lottery-numbers, Beauty-waters, Seductions, Phosphorus-boxes, and Wines of Egypt, is seen matched, and nigh throttled, by the natural unassisted cunning of English Attorneys. Whereupon the bustard, feeling himself so pecked and plucked, takes wing, and flies to foreign parts.

One good thing he has carried with him, notwithstanding: initiation into some primary arcana of Freemasonry. The Quack of Quacks, with his primitive bias towards the super-natural-mystificatory, must long have had his eye on Masonry; which, with its blazonry and mummery, sashes, drawn sabres, brothers Terrible, brothers Venerable (the whole so imposing by candle-light), offered the choicest element for him. All men profit by *Union* with men; the quack as much as another; nay in these two words, *Sworn Secrecy*, alone has he not found a very talisman! Cagliostro, then, determines on Masonship. It was afterwards urged that the Lodge to which he and his Seraphina got admission, for she also was made a Mason, or Masoness, and had a riband-garter solemnly bound on, with order to sleep in it for a night,—was a Lodge of low rank in the social scale; numbering not a few of the pastrycook and hairdresser species. To which it could only be replied, that these alone spoke French; that a man and mason, though he cooked pastry, was still a man and mason. Be this as it might, the apt Recipiendary is rapidly promoted through the three grades of Apprentice, Companion, Master; at the cost of five guineas. That of his being first raised into the air, by means of a rope and pulley fixed in the ceiling, "during which the heavy mass of his body must assuredly have caused him a dolorous sensation;" and then being forced blindfold to shoot himself (though with privily *dis*-loaded pistol), in sign of courage and obedience: all this we can esteem an apocrypha,—palmed on the Roman Inquisition, otherwise prone to delusion. Five guineas, and some foolish froth-speeches, delivered over liquor and otherwise, was the cost. If you ask now, In *what* London Lodge was it? Alas, we know not, and shall never know. Certain only that Count Alessandro *is* a master-mason; that having once crossed the threshold, his plastic genius will not stop there. Behold, accordingly, he has bought from a "Bookseller" certain manuscripts belonging to "one George Cofton, a man absolutely unknown to him" and to us, which treat of the "Egyptian Masonry"! In other words, Count Alessandro will *blow* with his new five-guinea bellows; having always occasion to raise the wind.

With regard specially to that huge soap-bubble of an Egyptian Masonry which he blew, and as conjuror caught many flies with, it is our painful duty to say a little; not much. The Inquisition-Biographer, with deadly fear of heretical and democratical and black-magical Freemasons before his eyes, has gone into the matter to boundless depths; commenting, elucidating, even confuting: a certain expository masonic Order-Book of Cagliostro's which he has laid hand on, opens the whole mystery to him. The ideas he declares to be Cagliostro's; the composition all a disciple's, for the Count had no gift that way. What, then, does the disciple set forth,—or, at lowest, the Inquisition-Biographer say that he sets forth? Much, much that is not to the point.

Understand, however, that once inspired, by the absolutely unknown George Cofton, with the notion of Egyptian Masonry, wherein as yet lay much " magic and superstition," Count Alessandro resolves to free it of these impious ingredients, and make it a kind of Last Evangel, or Renovator of the Universe,—which so needed renovation. " As he did not believe anything in matter of Faith," says our wooden Familiar, " nothing could arrest him." True enough: how did he move along, then; to what length did he go?

" In his system he promises his followers to conduct them to *perfection*, by means of a *physical and moral regeneration ;* to enable them by the former (or physical) to find the *prime matter*, or Philosopher's Stone, and the *acacia* which consolidates in man the forces of the most vigorous youth, and renders him immortal; and by the latter (or moral) to procure them a Pentagon, which shall restore man to his primitive state of innocence, lost by original sin. The Founder supposes that this Egyptian Masonry was instituted by Enoch and Elias, who propagated it in different parts of the world: however, in time it lost much of its purity and splendour. And so, by degrees, the Masonry of men had been reduced to pure buffoonery; and that of women being almost entirely destroyed, having now for most part no place in common Masonry. Till at last, the zeal of the *Grand Cophta* (so are the High-priests of Egypt named) had signalised itself by restoring the Masonry of both sexes to its pristine lustre."

With regard to the great question of constructing this invaluable Pentagon, which is to abolish Original Sin: how you have to choose a solitary mountain, and call it Sinai; and build a Pavilion on it to be named Sion, with twelve sides, in every side a window, and three stories, one of which is named Ararat; and there, with Twelve Masters, each at a window, yourself in the middle of them, to go through unspeakable formalities, vigils, removals, fasts, toils, distresses, and hardly get your Pentagon after all,—with regard to this great question and construction, we shall say nothing. As little concerning the still grander and painfuller process of Physical Regeneration, or growing young again; a thing not to be accomplished without a forty-days' course of medicine, purgations, sweating-baths, fainting-fits, root-diet, phlebotomy, starvation and desperation, more perhaps than it is all worth. Leaving these interior solemnities, and many high moral precepts of union, virtue, wisdom, and doctrines of immortality and what not, will the reader care to cast an indifferent glance on certain esoteric ceremonial parts of this Egyptian Masonry,—as the Inquisition-Biographer, if we miscellaneously cull from him, may enable us?

" In all these ceremonial parts," huskily avers the wooden Biographer, " you find as much sacrilege, profanation, superstition and idolatry, as in common Masonry: invocations of the holy Name, prosternations, adorations lavished on the Venerable, or head of the Lodge; aspirations, insufflations, incense-burnings, fumigations, exorcisms of the Candidates and the garments they are to take; emblems of the sacrosanct Triad, of the Moon, of the Sun, of the Compass, Square, and a thousand-thousand other iniquities and ineptitudes, which are now well known in the world."

"We above made mention of the Grand Cophta. By this title has been designated the founder or restorer of Egyptian Masonry. Cagliostro made no difficulty in admitting " (to me the Inquisitor) " that under such name he was himself meant: now in this system the Grand Cophta is compared to the Highest: the most solemn acts of worship are paid him; he has authority over the Angels; he is invoked on all occasions; everything is done in virtue of his power; which you are assured he derives immediately from God. Nay more: among the various rites observed in this exercise of Masonry, you are ordered to recite the *Veni Creator spiritus*, the *Te Deum*, and some Psalms of David: to such an excess is impudence and audacity carried, that in the Psalm, *Memento, Domine, David et omnis mansuetudinis ejus*, every time the name David occurs, that of the Grand Cophta is to be substituted.

"No religion is excluded from the Egyptian Society: the Jew, the Calvinist, the Lutheran, can be admitted equally well with the Catholic, if so be they admit the existence of God and the immortality of the soul." "The men elevated to the rank of master take the names of the ancient Prophets; the women those of the Sibyls."

. . . "Then the grand Mistress blows on the face of the female Recipiendary, all along from brow to chin, and says: 'I give you this breath, to cause to germinate and become alive in your heart the Truth which we possess; to fortify in you the' etc. etc. 'Guardian of the new Knowledge which we prepare to make you partake of, by the sacred names of *Helios, Mene, Tetragrammaton.*'

"In the *Essai sur les Illuminés*, printed at Paris in 1789, I read that these latter words were suggested to Cagliostro as Arabic or Sacred ones by a Sleight-of-hand Man, who said that he was assisted by a spirit, and added that this spirit was the Soul of a Cabalist Jew, who by art-magic had killed his pig before the Christian Advent."

. . . "They take a young lad, or a girl who is in the state of innocence, such they call the *Pupil* or the *Columb;* the Venerable communicates to him the power he would have had before the Fall of Man; which power consists mainly in commanding the pure Spirits; these Spirits are to the number of seven: it is said they surround the throne; and that they govern the seven planets: their names are Anael, Michael, Raphael, Gabriel, Uriel, Zobiachel, Anachiel."

Or would the reader wish to see this *Columb* in action? She can act in two ways; either behind a curtain, behind a hieroglyphically-painted Screen with "table and three candles;" or as here "before the Caraffe," and showing face. If the miracle fail, it can only be because she is not "in the state of innocence,"—an accident much to be guarded against. This scene is at Mittau in Courland;—we find, indeed, that it is a *Pupil* affair, not a *Columb* one; but for the rest, that is perfectly indifferent:

"Cagliostro accordingly (it is his own story still) brought a little Boy into the Lodge; son of a nobleman there. He placed him on his knees before a table, whereon stood a Bottle of pure water, and behind this some lighted candles: he made an exorcism round the Boy, put his hand on his head:

and both, in this attitude, addressed their prayers to God for the happy accomplishment of the work. Having then bid the child look into the Bottle, directly the child cried that he saw a garden. Knowing hereby that Heaven assisted him, Cagliostro took courage, and bade the child ask of God the grace to see the Angel Michael. At first the child said: ' I see something white; I know not what it is.' Then he began jumping, stamping like a possessed creature, and cried: ' There now! I see a child, like myself, that seems to have something angelical.' All the assembly, and Cagliostro himself, remained speechless with emotion. . . . The child being anew exorcised, with the hands of the Venerable on his head, and the customary prayers addressed to Heaven, he looked into the Bottle, and said, he saw his Sister at that moment coming down stairs, and embracing one of her brothers. That appeared impossible, the brother in question being then hundreds of miles off: however, Cagliostro felt not disconcerted; said they might send to the country-house where the sister was, and see." [1]

Wonderful enough. Here, however, a fact rather suddenly transpires, which, as the Inquisition-Biographer well urges, must serve to undeceive all believers in Cagliostro; at least, call a blush into their cheeks. It seems: " The Grand Cophta, the restorer, the propagator of Egyptian Masonry, Count Cagliostro himself, testifies, in most part of his System, the profoundest respect for the Patriarch Moses: *and yet* this same Cagliostro affirmed before his judges that he had always felt the insurmountablest antipathy to Moses; and attributes this hatred to his constant opinion, that Moses was a thief for having carried-off the Egyptian vessels; which opinion, in spite of all the luminous arguments that were opposed to him to show how erroneous it was, he has continued to hold with an invincible obstinacy!" How reconcile these two inconsistencies? Ay, how?

But to finish-off this Egyptian Masonic business, and bring it all to a focus, we shall now, for the first and for the last time, peep one moment through the spyglass of Monsieur de Luchet, in that *Essai sur les Illuminés* of his. The whole matter being so much of a chimera, how can it be painted otherwise than chimerically? Of the following passage one

[1] *Vie de Joseph Balsamo, traduite d'après l'original Italien*, ch. ii. iii. (Paris, 1791.)

thing is true, that a creature of the seed of Adam believed it to be true. List, list, then; O list!

"The Recipiendary is led by a darksome path, into an immense hall, the ceiling, the walls, the floor of which are covered by a black cloth, sprinkled over with red flames and menacing serpents: three sepulchral lamps emit, from time to time, a dying glimmer; and the eye half distinguishes, in this lugubrious den, certain wrecks of mortality suspended by funereal crapes: a heap of skeletons forms in the centre a sort of altar; on both sides of it are piled books; some contain menaces against the perjured; others the deadly narrative of the vengeances which the Invisible Spirit has exacted; of the infernal evocations for a long time pronounced in vain.

"Eight hours elapse. Then Phantoms, trailing mortuary veils, slowly cross the hall, and sink in caverns, without audible noise of trap-doors or of falling. You notice only that they are gone, by a fetid odour exhaled from them.

"The novice remains four-and-twenty hours in this gloomy abode, in the midst of a freezing silence. A rigorous fast has already weakened his thinking faculties. Liquors, prepared for the purpose, first weary, and at length wear-out his senses. At his feet are placed three cups, filled with a drink of greenish colour. Necessity lifts them towards his lips; involuntary fear repels them.

"At last appear two men; looked upon as the ministers of death. These gird the pale brow of the Recipiendary with an auroral-coloured riband, dipt in blood, and full of silvered characters mixed with the figure of Our Lady of Loretto. He receives a copper crucifix, of two inches length; to his neck are hung a sort of amulets, wrapped in violet cloth. He is stript of his clothes; which two ministering brethren deposit on a funeral pile, erected at the other end of the hall. With blood, on his naked body, are traced crosses. In this state of suffering and humiliation, he sees approaching with large strides five Phantoms, armed with swords, and clad in garments dropping blood. Their faces are veiled: they spread a carpet on the floor; kneel there; pray; and remain with outstretched hands crossed on their breast, and face fixed on the ground, in deep silence. An hour passes in this painful attitude. After which fatiguing trial, plaintive cries are heard; the funeral pile takes fire, yet casts only a pale light; the garments are thrown on it and burnt. A colossal and almost transparent Figure rises from the very bosom of the pile. At sight of it, the five prostrated men fall into convulsions insupportable to look on; the too faithful image of those foaming struggles wherein a mortal, at handgrips with a sudden pain, ends by sinking under it.

" Then a trembling voice pierces the vault, and articulates the formula of those execrable oaths that are to be sworn: my pen falters; I think myself almost guilty to retrace them."

O Luchet, what a taking! Is there no hope left, thinkest thou? Thy brain is all gone to addled albumen; help seems none, if not in that last mother's-bosom of all the ruined: Brandy-and-water!—An unfeeling world may laugh; but ought to recollect that, forty years ago, these things were sad realities,—in the heads of many men.

As to the execrable oaths, this seems the main one: " Honour and respect *Aqua Toffana*, as a sure, prompt and necessary means of purging the Globe, by the death or the hebetation of such as endeavour to debase the Truth, or snatch it from our hands." And so the catastrophe ends by bathing our poor half-dead Recipiendary first in blood, then, after some genuflexions, in water; and " serving him a repast composed of roots,"—we grieve to say, mere potatoes-and-point!

Figure now all this boundless cunningly devised Agglomerate of royal-arches, death's-heads, hieroglyphically painted screens, *Columbs* in the state of innocence; with spacious masonic halls, dark, or in the favourablest theatrical light-and-dark; Kircher's magic-lantern, Belshazzar hand-writings, of phosphorus: " plaintive tones," gong-beatings; hoary beard of a supernatural Grand Cophta emerging from the gloom;—and how it acts, not only indirectly through the foolish senses of men, but directly on their Imagination; connecting itself with Enoch and Elias, with Philanthropy, Immortality, Eleutheromania, and Adam Weisshaupt's Illuminati, and so downwards to the infinite Deep: figure all this; and in the centre of it, sitting eager and alert, the skilfulest Panourgos, working the mighty chaos, into a creation—of ready-money. In such a wide plastic ocean of sham and foam had the Archquack now happily begun to envelop himself.

Accordingly he goes forth prospering and to prosper. Arrived in any City, he has but by masonic grip to accredit himself with the Venerable of the place; and, not by degrees as formerly, but in a single night, is introduced in Grand Lodge to all that is fattest and foolishest far or near; and in the fittest arena, a gilt-pasteboard Masonic hall. There between the two pillars of Jachin and Boaz, can the great Sheepstealer see his whole flock of Dupeables assembled in one penfold; affectionately blatant, licking the hand they are to bleed by. Victorious Acharat-Beppo! The genius of Amazement, moreover, has now shed her glory round him; he is radiant-headed, a supernatural by his very gait. Behold him everywhere welcomed with vivats, or in awestruck silence: gilt-pasteboard Freemasons receive him under the Steel-Arch of crossed sabres; he mounts to the Seat of the Venerable; holds high discourse hours long, on Masonry, Morality, Universal Science, Divinity, and Things in general, with " a sublimity, an emphasis and unction," proceeding, it appears, " from the special inspiration of the Holy Ghost." Then there are Egyptian Lodges to be founded, corresponded with, —a thing involving expense; elementary fractions of many a priceless arcanum, nay if the place will stand it, of the Pentagon itself, can be given to the purified in life: how gladly would he *give* them, but they have to be brought from the uttermost ends of the world, and cost money. Now too, with what tenfold impetuosity do all the old trades of Egyptian Drops, Beauty-waters, Secret-favours, expand themselves, and rise in price! Life-weary moneyed Do-nothing, this seraphic Countess is Grand Priestess of the Egyptian Female Lodges; has a touch of the supramundane Undine in her: among all thy intrigues, hadst thou ever yet Endymion-like an intrigue with the lunar Diana,—called also Hecate? And thou, O antique, much-loving faded Dowager, *this* Squire-of-dames can, it appears probable, command the Seven Angels, Uriel, Anachiel and Company; at lowest, has the eyes of all Europe fixed on him!—The dog pockets money enough, and can seem to despise money.

To us, much meditating on the matter, it seemed perhaps strangest of all, how Count Cagliostro, received under the Steel Arch, could hold Discourses, of from one to three hours long, on Universal Science, of such unction, we do not say as to seem inspired by the Holy Spirit, but as not to get him lugged out of doors directly after his first head of method, and drowned in whole oceans of salt-and-water. The man could not speak; only babble in long-winded diffusions, chaotic circumvolutions tending nowhither. He had no thought for speaking with; he had not even a language. His Sicilian Italian, and Laquais-de-place French, garnished with shreds from all European dialects, was wholly intelligible to no mortal; a Tower-of-Babel jargon, which made many think him a kind of Jew. But indeed, with the language of Greeks, or of Angels, what better were it? The man, once for all, has no articulate utterance; that tongue of his emits noises enough, but no speech. Let him begin the plainest story, his stream stagnates at the first stage; chafes, " ahem! ahem! " loses itself in the earth; or, bursting over, flies abroad without bank or channel,—into separate plashes. Not a stream, but a lake, a wide-spread indefinite marsh. His whole thought is confused, inextricable; what thought, what resemblance of thought he has, cannot deliver itself, except in gasps, blustering gushes, spasmodic refluences, which make bad worse. Bubble, bubble, toil and trouble: how thou bubblest, foolish " Bubblyjock"! Hear him once, and on a dead-lift occasion, as the Inquisition Gurney reports it:

" ' I mean and I wish to mean, that even as those who honour their father and mother, and respect the sovereign Pontiff, are blessed of God; even so all that I did, I did it by the order of God, with the power which he vouchsafed to me, and to the advantage of God and of Holy Church; and I mean to give the proofs of all that I have done and said, not only physically but morally, by showing that as I have served God for God and by the power of God, he has given me at last the counterpoison to confound and combat Hell; for I know no other enemies than those that are in Hell, and if I am wrong, the Holy Father will punish me; if I am right, he will reward me; and if the Holy Father could get into his hands to-night these answers of mine, I predict to all brethren, believers and unbelievers, that I should be at liberty to-morrow morning.' Being desired to give these proofs then, he answered: ' To prove that I have been chosen of God as an apostle to defend and propagate religion, I say that as the Holy Church has instituted pastors to demonstrate in face of the world that she is the true Catholic faith, even so, having operated with approbation and by the counsel of pastors of the Holy Church, I am, as I said, fully justified in regard to all my operations; and these pastors have assured me that my

Egyptian Order was divine, and deserved to be formed into an Order sanctioned by the Holy Father, as I said in another interrogatory.' "

How then, in the name of wonder, said we, could such a babbling, bubbling Turkey-cock speak " with unction "?

Two things here are to be taken into account. First, the difference between speaking and public speaking; a difference altogether generic. Secondly, the wonderful power of a certain audacity, often named impudence. Was it never thy hard fortune, good Reader, to attend any Meeting convened for Public purposes; any Bible-Society, Reform, Conservative, Thatched-Tavern, Hogg Dinner, or other such Meeting? Thou hast seen some full-fed Long-ear, by free determination or on sweet constraint, start to his legs, and give voice. Well aware wert thou that there was not, had not been, could not be, in that entire ass-cranium of his any fraction of an idea: nevertheless mark him. If at first an ominous haze flit round, and nothing, not even nonsense, dwell in his recollection,—heed it not; let him but plunge desperately on, the spell is broken. Commonplaces enough are at hand: " labour of love," " rights of suffering millions," " throne and altar," " divine gift of song," or what else it may be; the Meeting, by its very *name*, has environed itself in a given element of Commonplace. But anon, behold how his talking-organs get heated, and the friction vanishes; cheers, applauses, with the previous dinner and strong drink, raise him to height of noblest temper. And now, as for your vociferous Dullard, is easiest of all, let him keep on the soft, safe *parallel* course; parallel to the Truth, or nearly so; for Heaven's sake, not in *contact* with it: no obstacle will meet him; on the favouring given element of Commonplace he triumphantly careers.

He is as the ass, whom you took and cast headlong into the water: the water at first threatens to swallow him; but he finds, to his astonishment, that he can *swim* therein, that it is buoyant and bears him along. One sole condition is indispensable: audacity, vulgarly called impudence. Our ass must *commit* himself to his watery " element; " in free daring, strike-forth his four limbs from him: then shall he not drown and sink, but shoot gloriously forward, and swim, to the admiration of bystanders. The ass, safe landed on the other bank, shakes his rough hide, wonder-struck himself at the faculty that lay in him, and waves joyfully his long ears: so too the public speaker. Cagliostro, as we know him of old, is not without a certain blubbery oiliness of soul as of body, with vehemence lying under it; has the volublest, noisiest tongue; and in the audacity vulgarly called impudence is without a fellow. The Commonplaces of such Steel-Arch Meetings are soon at his finger-ends: that same blubbery oiliness and vehemence lying under it, once give them an element and stimulus, are the very gift of a fluent public speaker—to Dupeables.

Here too let us mention a circumstance, not insignificant, if true, which it may readily enough be. In younger years, Beppo Balsamo once, it is recorded, took some pains to procure, "from a country vicar," under quite false pretences, "a bit of cotton steeped in holy oils." What could such bit of cotton steeped in holy oils do for him? An Unbeliever from any basis of conviction the unbelieving Beppo could never be; but solely from stupidity and bad morals. Might there not lie in that chaotic blubbery nature of his, at the bottom of all, a certain musk-grain of real Superstitious Belief? How wonderfully such a musk-grain of Belief will flavour, and impregnate with seductive odour, a whole inward world of Quackery, so that every fibre thereof shall smell *musk*, is well known. No Quack can persuade like him who has himself some persuasion. Nay, so wondrous is the act of Believing, Deception and Self-Deception must, rigorously speaking, coexist in all Quacks; and he perhaps were definable as the best Quack, in whom the smallest musk-grain of the latter would sufficiently flavour the largest mass of the former.

But indeed, as we know otherwise, was there not in Cagliostro a certain pinchbeck counterfeit of all that is golden and good in man, of somewhat even that is best? Cheers, and illuminated hieroglyphs, and the ravishment of thronging audiences, can make him maudlin; his very wickedness of practice will render him louder in eloquence of theory; and "philanthropy," "divine science," "depth of unknown worlds," "finer feelings of the heart," and suchlike shall draw tears from most asses of sensibility. Neither, indeed, is it of moment how *few* his elementary Commonplaces are, how empty his head is, so he but agitate it well: thus a lead-drop or two, put into the emptiest dry-bladder, and jingled to and fro, will make noise enough; and even, if skilfully jingled, a kind of martial music.

Such is the Cagliostric palaver, that bewitches all manner of believing souls. If the ancient Father was named Chrysostom, or Mouth-of-Gold, be the modern Quack named Pinchbeckostom, or Mouth-of-Pinchbeck; in an Age of Bronze such metal finds elective affinities. On the whole, too, it is worth considering what element your Quack specially works in: the element of Wonder! The Genuine, be he artist or artisan, works in the finitude of the Known; the Quack in the infinitude of the Unknown. And then how, in rapidest progression, he grows and advances, once start him! Your name is up, says the adage; you may lie in bed. A nimbus of renown and preternatural astonishment envelops Cagliostro; enchants the general eye. The few reasoning mortals scattered here and there who see through him, deafened in the universal hubbub, shut their lips in sorrowful disdain; confident in the grand remedy, Time. The Enchanter meanwhile rolls on his way; what boundless materials of Deceptibility, what greediness and ignorance, especially what prurient brute-mindedness, exist over Europe in this the most deceivable of modern ages, are stirred up, fermenting in his behoof. He careers onward as a Comet; his nucleus, of paying and praising Dupes, embraces, in long radius, what city and province he rests over; his thinner tail, of wondering and curious Dupes, stretches into remotest lands. Good Lavater, from amid his Swiss Mountains, could say of him; "Cagliostro, a man; and a man such as few are; in whom, however, I am not a believer. O that he were simple of heart and humble, like a child; that he had feeling for the simplicity of the Gospel, and the majesty of the Lord (*Hoheit des Herrn*)! Who were so great as he? Cagliostro often tells what is not true, and promises what he does not perform. Yet do I nowise hold his operations as deception, though they are not what he calls them." [1] If good Lavater could so say of him, what must others have been saying!

Comet-wise, progressing with loud flourish of kettle-drums, everywhere under the Steel-Arch, evoking spirits, transmuting metals (to such as could stand it), the Archquack has traversed Saxony; at Leipzig has run athwart the hawser of a

---

[1] *Lettre du Comte Mirabeau sur Cagliostro et Lavater*, p. 42. (Berl. 1786.)

brother quack (poor Schröpfer, here scarcely recognisable as "*Scieffert*"), and wrecked him. Through Eastern Germany, Prussian Poland, he progresses; and so now at length, in the spring of 1780, has arrived at Petersburg. His pavilion is erected here, his flag prosperously hoisted: Mason-lodges have long ears; he is distributing, as has now become his wont, Spagiric Food, medicine for the poor; a train-oil Prince, Potemkin or something like him, for accounts are dubious, feels his chops water over a seraphic Seraphina: all goes merry, and promises the best. But in those despotic countries, the Police is so arbitrary! Cagliostro's thaumaturgy must be overhauled by the Empress's Physician (Mouncey, a hard Annandale Scot); is found nought, the Spagiric Food unfit for a dog: and so, the whole particulars of his Lordship's conduct being put together, the result is, that he must leave Petersburg, in a given brief term of hours. Happy for him that it was so brief: scarcely is he gone, till the Prussian Ambassador appears with a complaint, that he has falsely assumed the Prussian uniform at Rome; the Spanish Ambassador with a still graver complaint, that he has forged bills at Cadiz. However, he is safe over the marches: let them complain their fill.

In Courland, and in Poland, great things await him; yet not unalloyed by two small reverses. The famed Countess von der Recke, a born Fair Saint, what the Germans call *Schöne Seele*, as yet quite young in heart and experience, but broken down with grief for departed friends,—seeks to question the world-famous Spirit-summoner on the secrets of the Invisible Kingdoms; whither, with fond strained eyes, she is incessantly looking. The *galimathias* of Pinchbeckostom cannot impose on this pure-minded simple woman: she recognises the Quack in him, and in a printed Book makes known the same: Mephisto's mortifying experience with Margaret, as above foretold, renews itself for Cagliostro.[1] At Warsaw too, though he discourses on Egyptian Masonry, on Medical Philosophy, and the ignorance of Doctors, and performs successfully with *Pupil* and *Columb*, a certain "Count M." cherishes more than doubt; which ends in certainty, in a written *Cagliostro Unmasked*. The Archquack, triumphant, sumptuously feasted in the city, has retired with a chosen set of believers, with whom, however, was this un-

[1] *Zeitgenossen*, No. 15. § *Frau von der Recke.*

believing " M.," into the country; to transmute metals, to prepare perhaps the Pentagon itself. All that night, before leaving Warsaw, " our dear Master " had spent conversing with spirits. Spirits? cries " M.:" Not he; but melting ducats: he has a melted mass of them in this crucible, which now, by sleight of hand, he would fain substitute for that other, filled, as you all saw, with red-lead, carefully luted down, smelted, set to cool, smuggled from among our hands, and now (look at it, ye asses!)—found broken and hidden among these bushes!

Neither does the Pentagon, or Elixir of Life, or whatever it was, prosper better. " Our sweet Master enters into expostulation: " " swears by his great God, and his honour, that he will finish the work and make us happy. He carries his modesty so far as to propose that he shall work with chains on his feet; and consents to lose his life, by the hands of his disciples, if before the end of the *fourth passage*, his word be not made good. He lays his hand on the ground, and kisses it; holds it up to Heaven, and again takes God to witness that he speaks true; calls on Him to exterminate him if he lies." A vision of the hoary-bearded Grand Cophta himself makes night solemn. In vain! The sherds of that broken red-lead crucible, which pretends to stand here unbroken half-full of silver, lie *there*, before your eyes: that " resemblance of a sleeping child," grown visible in the magic cooking of our Elixir, proves to be an inserted rosemary-leaf; the Grand Cophta cannot be gone too soon.

Count " M.," balancing towards the opposite extreme, even thinks him inadequate as a Quack:

" Far from being modest," says this Unmasker, " he brags beyond expression, in anybody's presence, especially in women's, of the grand faculties he possesses. Every word is an exaggeration, or a statement you feel to be improbable. The smallest contradiction puts him in fury: his vanity breaks through on all sides; he lets you give him a festival that sets the whole city a-talking. Most impostors are supple, and endeavour to gain friends. This one, you might say, studies to appear arrogant, to make all men enemies, by his rude injurious speeches, by the squabbles and grudges he introduces among friends." " He quarrels with his coadjutors for trifles; fancies that a simple giving of the lie will persuade the public that they are liars." " Schröpfer at

Leipzig was far cleverer." " He should get some ventrilo-
quist for assistant: should read some Books of Chemistry;
study the Tricks of Philadelphia and Comus."[1]

Fair advices, good " M.; " but do not you yourself admit
that he has a " natural genius for deception; " above all
things " a forehead of brass (*front d'airain*), which nothing can
disconcert " ? To such a genius, and such a brow, Comus
and Philadelphia, and all the ventriloquists in Nature, can
add little. Give the Archquack his due. These arrogancies
of his prove only that he is mounted on his high horse, and has
now the world under him.

Such reverses, which will occur in the lot of every man, are,
for our Cagliostro, but as specks in the blaze of the meridian
Sun. With undimmed lustre, he is, as heretofore, handed-
over from this " Prince P." to that Prince Q.; among which
high believing potentates, what is an incredulous " Count
M." ? His pockets are distended with ducats and diamonds:
he is off to Vienna, to Frankfort, to Strasburg, by extra post;
and there also will work miracles. " The train he commonly
took with him," says the Inquisition-Biographer, " corresponded to the rest; he always travelled post, with a considerable suite: couriers, lackeys, body-servants, domestics of all
sorts, sumptuously dressed, gave an air of reality to the high
birth he vaunted. The very liveries he got made at Paris
cost twenty *louis* each. Apartments furnished in the height
of the mode; a magnificent table, open to numerous guests;
rich dresses for himself and his wife, corresponded to this
luxurious way of life. His feigned generosity likewise made
a great noise. Often he gratuitously doctored the poor, and
even gave them alms."[2]

In the inside of all this splendid travelling and lodging
economy are to be seen, as we know, two suspicious-looking
rouged or unrouged figures, of a Count and a Countess;
lolling on their cushions there, with a jaded, haggard kind of
aspect; they eye one another sullenly, in silence, with a scarce-
suppressed indignation; for each thinks the other does not
work enough and eats too much. Whether Dame Lorenza
followed her peculiar side of the business with reluctance or
with free alacrity, is a moot-point among Biographers: not
so that, with her choleric adipose Archquack, she had a sour

[1] *Cagliostro démasqué à Varsovie, en* 1780, pp. 35 *et seq.* (Paris, 1786.)
[2] *Vie de Joseph Balsamo*, p. 41.

life of it, and brawling abounded. If we look still farther inwards, and try to penetrate the inmost self-consciousness, what in another man would be called the conscience, of the Archquack himself, the view gets most uncertain; little or nothing to be seen but a thick fallacious haze. Which indeed *was* the main thing extant there. Much in the Count Front-d'airain remains dubious; yet hardly this: his want of clear insight into anything, most of all into his own inner man. Cunning in the supreme degree he has; intellect next to none. Nay, is not cunning (couple it with an esurient character) the natural consequence of *defective* intellect? It is properly the vehement exercise of a short, poor vision; of an intellect sunk, bemired; which can attain to no free vision, otherwise it would lead the esurient man to be honest.

Meanwhile gleams of muddy light will occasionally visit all mortals; every living creature (according to Milton, the very Devil) has some more or less faint resemblance to a Conscience; must make inwardly certain auricular confessions, absolutions, professions of faith,—were it only that he does not yet quite loathe, and so proceed to hang himself. What such a Porcus as Cagliostro might specially feel, and think, and *be*, were difficult in any case to say; much more when contradiction and mystification, designed and unavoidable, so involve the matter. One of the most authentic documents preserved of him is the Picture of his Visage. An Effigies once universally diffused; in oil-paint, aquatint, marble, stucco, and perhaps gingerbread, decorating millions of apartments: of which remarkable Effigies one copy, engraved in the line-manner, happily still lies here. Fittest of visages; worthy to be worn by the Quack of Quacks! A most portentous face of scoundrel-ism: a fat, snub, abominable face; dew-lapped, flat-nosed, greasy, full of greediness, sensuality, oxlike obstinacy; a fore-head impudent, refusing to be ashamed; and then two eyes turned up seraphically languishing, as in divine contemplation and adoration; a touch of quiz too; on the whole, perhaps the most perfect quack-face produced by the eighteenth century. There he sits, and seraphically languishes, with this epigraph:

> De l'Ami des Humains reconnaissez les traits :
> Tous ses jours sont marqués par de nouveaux bienfaits,
> Il prolonge la vie, il secourt l'indigence ;
> Le plaisir d'être utile est seul sa récompense.

A probable conjecture were, that this same Theosophy, Theophilanthropy, Solacement of the Poor, to which our Archquack now more and more betook himself, might serve not only as bird-lime for external game, but also half-unconsciously as salve for assuaging his own spiritual sores. Am not I a charitable man? could the Archquack say: if I have erred myself, have I not, by theosophic unctuous discourses, removed much cause of error? The lying, the quackery, what are these but the method of accommodating yourself to the temper of men; of getting their ear, their dull long ear, which Honesty had no chance to catch? Nay, at worst, is not this an unjust world; full of nothing but beasts of prey, four-footed or two-footed? Nature has commanded, saying: Man, help thyself. Ought not the man of my genius, since he was not born a Prince, since in these scandalous times he has not been elected a Prince, to make himself one? If not by open violence, for which he wants military force, then surely by superior science,—exercised in a private way. Heal the diseases of the Poor, the far deeper diseases of the Ignorant; in a word, found Egyptian Lodges, and get the means of founding them.—By such soliloquies can Count Front-of-brass Pinchbeckostom, in rare atrabiliar hours of self-questionings, compose himself. For the rest, such hours are rare: the Count is a man of action and digestion, not of self-questioning; usually the day brings its abundant task; there is no time for abstractions,—of the metaphysical sort.

Be this as it may, the Count has arrived at Strasburg; is working higher wonders than ever. At Strasburg, indeed, in the year 1783, occurs his apotheosis; what we can call the culmination and Fourth Act of his Life-drama. He was here for a number of months; in full blossom and radiance, the envy and admiration of the world. In large hired hospitals, he with open drug-box containing "Extract of Saturn," and even with open purse, relieves the suffering poor; unfolds himself lamb-like, angelic to a believing few, of the rich classes; turns a silent minatory lion-face to unbelievers, were they of the richest. Medical miracles have in all times been common: but what miracle is this of an Oriental or Occidental Serene-Excellence, who, "regardless of expense," employs himself not in preserving game, but in curing sickness, in illuminating ignorance? Behold how he dives, at noonday, into the infectious hovels of the mean; and on the equipages, haughtinesses, and even dinner-invitations of the great, turns only his negatory front-of-brass! The Prince Cardinal de Rohan, Archbishop of Strasburg, first-class peer of France, of the Blood-royal of Brittany, intimates a wish to see him! he answers: " If Monseigneur the Cardinal is sick, let him come, and I will cure him; if he is well, he has no need of me, I none of him." [1]

Heaven meanwhile has sent him a few disciples: by a nice tact, he knows his man; to one speaks only of Spagiric Medicine, Downfall of Tyranny, and the Egyptian Lodge; to another, of quite high matters, beyond this diurnal sphere, of visits from the Angel of Light, visits from him of Darkness; passing a Statue of Christ, he will pause with a wondrously accented plaintive " Ha ! " as of recognition, as of thousand-years remembrance; and when questioned, sink into mysterious silence. *Is* he the Wandering Jew, then? Heaven knows! At Strasburg, in a word, Fortune not only smiles but laughs upon him: as crowning favour, he finds here the richest, inflammablest, most open-handed Dupe ever yet vouchsafed him; no other than that same many-titled Louis de Rohan; strong in whose favour, he can laugh again at Fortune.

Let the curious reader look at him, for an instant or two, through the eyes of two eye-witnesses: the Abbé Georgel, Prince Louis's diplomatic Factotum, and Herr Meiners, the Göttingen Professor:

" Admitted at length," says our too-prosing Jesuit Abbé, " to the sanctuary of this Æsculapius, Prince Louis saw, according to his own account, in the incommunicative man's physiognomy, something so dignified, so imposing, that he felt penetrated with a religious awe, and reverence dictated his address. Their interview, which was brief, excited more keenly than ever his desire of farther acquaintance. He attained it at length: and the crafty empiric graduated so cunningly his words and procedure, that he gained, without appearing to court it, the Cardinal's entire confidence, and the greatest ascendency over his will. ' Your soul,' said he one day to the Prince, ' is worthy of mine; you deserve to be made participator of all my secrets.' Such an avowal captivated the whole faculties, intellectual and moral, of a

[1] *Mémoires de l'Abbé Georgel*, ii. 48.

man who at all times had hunted after secrets of alchymy and botany. From this moment their union became intimate and public: Cagliostro went and established himself at Saverne, while his Eminency was residing there; their solitary interviews were long and frequent." . . . "I remember once, having learnt, by a sure way, that Baron de Planta (his Eminency's man of affairs) had frequent, most expensive orgies, in the Archiepiscopal Palace, where Tokay wine ran like water, to regale Cagliostro and his pretended wife, I thought it my duty to inform the Cardinal: his answer was, 'I know it; I have even authorised him to commit abuses, if he judge fit.'" . . . "He came at last to have no other will than Cagliostro's: and to such a length had it gone, that this sham Egyptian, finding it good to quit Strasburg for a time, and retire into Switzerland, the Cardinal, apprised thereof, despatched his Secretary as well to attend him, as to obtain Predictions from him; such were transmitted in cipher to the Cardinal on every point he needed to consult of" [1]—

"Before ever I arrived in Strasburg" (hear now the as prosing Protestant Professor), "I knew almost to a certainty that I should not see Count Cagliostro; at least, not get to speak with him. From many persons I had heard that he, on no account, received visits from curious Travellers, in a state of health; that such as, without being sick, appeared in his audiences were sure to be treated by him, in the brutalest way, as spies." . . . "Nevertheless, though I saw not this new god of Physic near at hand and deliberately, but only for a moment as he rolled on in a rapid carriage, I fancy myself to be better acquainted with him than many that have lived in his society for months." "My unavoidable conviction is, that Count Cagliostro, from of old, has been more of a cheat than an enthusiast; and also that he continues a cheat to this day.

"As to his country I have ascertained nothing. Some make him a Spaniard, others a Jew, or an Italian, or a Ragusan; or even an Arab, who had persuaded some Asiatic Prince to send his son to travel in Europe, and then murdered the youth, and taken possession of his treasures. As the self-styled Count speaks badly all the languages you hear from him, and has most likely spent the greater part of his

[1] Georgel, *ubi supra*.

life under feigned names far from home, it is probable enough no sure trace of his origin may ever be discovered."

"On his first appearance in Strasburg he connected himself with the Freemasons; but only till he felt strong enough to stand on his own feet: he soon gained the favour of the Prætor and the Cardinal; and through these the favour of the Court, to such a degree that his adversaries cannot so much as think of overthrowing him. With the Prætor and Cardinal he is said to demean himself as with persons who were under boundless obligation to him, to whom he was under none: the equipage of the Cardinal he seems to use as freely as his own. He pretends that he can recognise Atheists or Blasphemers by the smell; that the vapour from such throws him into epileptic fits; into which sacred disorder he, like a true juggler, has the art of falling when he likes. In public he no longer vaunts of rule over spirits, or other magical arts; but I know, even as certainly, that he still pretends to evoke spirits, and by their help and apparition to heal diseases, as I know this other fact, that he understands no more of the human system, or the nature of its diseases, or the use of the commonest therapeutic methods, than any other quack."

"According to the crediblest accounts of persons who have long observed him, he is a man to an inconceivable degree choleric (*heftig*), heedless, inconstant; and therefore doubtless it was the happiest idea he ever in his whole life came upon, this of making himself inaccessible; of raising the most obstinate reserve as a bulwark round him; without which precaution he must long ago have been caught at fault.

"For his own labour he takes neither payment nor present: when presents are made him of such a sort as cannot without offence be refused, he forthwith returns some counter-present, of equal or still higher value. Nay he not only takes nothing from his patients, but frequently admits them, months long, to his house and his table, and will not consent to the smallest recompense. With all this disinterestedness (conspicuous enough, as you may suppose), he lives in an expensive way, plays deep, loses almost constantly to ladies; so that, according to the very lowest estimate, he must require at least 20,000 livres a-year. The darkness which Cagliostro has, on purpose, spread over the sources of his income and outlay, contributes even more than his munificence and miraculous cures to the notion that he is a divine extraordinary man, who has watched Nature in her deepest operations, and among other secrets stolen that of Gold-making from her." . . . "With a mixture of sorrow and indignation over our age, I have to record that this man has found acceptance, not only among the great, who from of old have been the easiest bewitched by such, but also with many of the learned, and even physicians and naturalists."[1]

Halcyon days; only too good to continue! All glory runs its course; has its culmination, and then its often precipitous decline. Eminency Rohan, with fervid temper and small instruction, perhaps of dissolute, certainly of dishonest manners, in whom the faculty of Wonder had attained such prodigious development, was indeed the very stranded whale for jackals to feed on: unhappily, however, no one jackal could long be left in solitary possession of him. A sharper-toothed she-jackal now strikes in; bites infinitely deeper; stranded whale and he-jackal both are like to become her prey. A young French Mantua-maker, "Countess de La Motte-Valois, descended from Henri II. by the bastard line," without Extract of Saturn, Egyptian Masonry, or any *verbal* conference with Dark Angels,—has genius enough to get her finger in the Archquack's rich Hermetic Projection, appropriate the golden proceeds, and even finally break the crucible. Prince Cardinal Louis de Rohan is off to Paris, under her guidance, to see the long-invisible Queen, or Queen's *Apparition*; to pick up the Rose in the Garden of Trianon, dropt by her fair sham-royal hand; and then—descend rapidly to the Devil, and drag Cagliostro along with him.

The intelligent reader observes, we have now arrived at that stupendous business of the *Diamond Necklace*: into the dark complexities of which we need not here do more than glance: who knows but, next month, our Historical Chapter, written specially on this subject, may itself see the light? Enough, for the present, if we fancy vividly the poor whale Cardinal, so deep in the adventure that Grand-Cophtic "predictions transmitted in cipher" will no longer illuminate him; but the Grand Cophta must leave all masonic or other business, happily begun in Naples, Bourdeaux, Lyons, and come personally to Paris with predictions at first hand.

[1] Meiners: *Briefe über die Schweiz* (as quoted in *Mirabeau*).

"The new Calchas," says poor Abbé Georgel, "must have read the entrails of his victim ill; for, on issuing from these communications with the Angel of Light and of Darkness, he prophesied to the Cardinal that this happy correspondence," with the Queen's Similitude, "would place him at the highest point of favour; that his influence in the Government would soon become paramount; that he would use it for the propagation of good principles, the glory of the Supreme Being, and the happiness of Frenchmen." The new Calchas was indeed at fault: but how could he be otherwise? Let these high Queen's-favours, and all terrestrial shiftings of the wind, turn as they will, *his* reign, he can well see, is appointed to be temporary; in the mean while, Tokay flows like water; prophecies of good, not of evil, are the method to keep it flowing. Thus if, for Circe de La Motte-Valois, the Egyptian Masonry is but a foolish enchanted cup wherewith to turn her fat Cardinal into a quadruped, she herself converse-wise, for the Grand Cophta, is one who must ever fodder said quadruped with Court hopes, and stall-feed him fatter and fatter, —it is expected, for the knife of *both* parties. They are mutually useful; live in peace, and Tokay festivity, though mutually suspicious, mutually contemptuous. So stand matters through the spring and summer months of the year 1785.

But fancy next that—while Tokay is flowing within doors, and abroad Egyptian Lodges are getting founded, and gold and glory, from Paris as from other cities, supernaturally coming in,—the latter end of August has arrived, and with it Commissary Chesnon, to lodge the whole unholy Brotherhood, from Cardinal down to Sham-queen, in separate cells of the Bastille! There, for nine long months, let them howl and wail, in bass or in treble; and emit the falsest of false *Mémoires;* among which that *Mémoire pour le Comte de Cagliostro, en présence des autres Co-Accusés,* with its Trebisond Acharats, Scherifs of Mecca, and Nature's unfortunate Child, all gravely printed with French types in the year 1786, may well bear the palm. Fancy that Necklace or Diamonds will nowhere unearth themselves; that the Tuileries Palace sits struck with astonishment and speechless chagrin; that Paris, that all Europe, is ringing with the wonder. That Count Front-of-Brass Pinchbeckostom, confronted, at the judgment-bar, with a shrill glib Circe de La Motte, has need of all his eloquence; that nevertheless the Front-of-brass prevails, and exasperated Circe "throws a candlestick at him." Finally, that on the 31st of May 1786, the assembled Parliament of Paris, "at nine in the evening, after a sitting of eighteen hours," has solemnly pronounced judgment: and now that Cardinal Louis is gone "to his estates;" Countess de La Motte is shaven on the head, branded, with red-hot iron, "V" (*Voleuse*) on both shoulders, and confined for life to the Salpêtrière; her Count wandering uncertain, with diamonds for sale, over the British Empire; that the Sieur de Villette, for handling a queen's pen, is banished forever; the too-queenlike Demoiselle Gay d'Oliva (with her unfathered infant) "put out of Court;"—and Grand Cophta Cagliostro liberated indeed, but pillaged, and ordered forthwith to take himself away. His disciples illuminate their windows; but what does that avail? Commissary Chesnon, Bastille-Governor De Launay cannot recollect the least particular of those priceless effects, those gold-rouleaus, repeating watches of his: he must even retire to Passy that very night; and two days afterwards, sees nothing for it but Boulogne and England. Thus does the miserable pickle - herring tragedy of the Diamond Necklace wind itself up, and wind Cagliostro once more to inhospitable shores.

Arrived here, and lodged tolerably in "Sloane Street, Knightsbridge," by the aid of a certain Mr. Swinton, whilom broken Wine-merchant, now Apothecary, to whom he carries introductions, he can drive a small trade in Egyptian pills, such as one "sells *in Paris* at thirty-shillings the dram;" in unctuously discoursing to Egyptian Lodges; in "giving public audiences as at Strasburg,"—if so be any one will bite. At all events, he can, by the aid of amanuensis-disciples, compose and publish his *Lettre au Peuple Anglais ;* setting forth his unheard - of generosities, unheard - of injustices suffered, in a world not worthy of him, at the hands of English Lawyers, Bastille-Governors, French Counts, and others; his *Lettre aux Français*, singing to the same tune, predicting too, what many inspired Editors had already boded, that "the Bastille would be destroyed," and "a King would come who should govern by States - General." But, alas, the shafts of Criticism are busy with him; so many hostile eyes look towards him; the world, in short, is getting too hot for him. Mark, nevertheless, how the brow of brass quails not;

nay a touch of his old poetic Humour, even in this sad crisis, unexpectedly unfolds itself.

One De Morande, Editor of a *Courrier de l'Europe* published here at that period, has for some time made it his distinction to be the foremost of Cagliostro's enemies. Cagliostro, enduring much in silence, happens once, in some "public audience," to mention a practice he had witnessed in Arabia the Stony: the people there, it seems, are in the habit of fattening a few pigs annually, on provender mixed with arsenic, whereby the whole pig-carcass by and by becomes, so to speak, arsenical; the arsenical pigs are then let loose in the woods; eaten by lions, leopards and other ferocious creatures; which latter naturally all die in consequence, and so the woods are cleared of them. This adroit practice the Sieur Morande thought a proper subject for banter; and accordingly, in his Seventeenth and two following Numbers, made merry enough with it. Whereupon Count Front-of-brass, whose patience has limits, writes as Advertisement (still to be read in old files of the *Public Advertiser*, under date September 3, 1786), a French Letter, not without causticity and aristocratic disdain; challenging the witty Sieur to breakfast with him, for the 9th of November next, in the face of the world, on an actual Sucking Pig, fattened by Cagliostro, but cooked, carved and selected from by the Sieur Morande,—under bet of Five Thousand Guineas sterling that, next morning thereafter, he the Sieur Morande shall be dead, and Count Cagliostro be alive! The poor Sieur durst not cry, Done; and backed-out of the transaction, making wry faces. Thus does a kind of red coppery splendour encircle our Archquack's decline; thus with brow of brass, grim smiling, does he meet his destiny.

But suppose we should now, from these foreign scenes turn homewards, for a moment, into the native alley in Palermo! Palermo, with its dinginess, its mud or dust, the old black Balsamo House, the very beds and chairs, all are still standing there; and Beppo has altered so strangely, has wandered so far away. Let us look; for happily we have the fairest opportunity.

In April 1787, Palermo contained a Traveller of a thousand; no other than the great Goethe from Weimar. At his Tabled'hôte he heard much of Cagliostro; at length also of a certain Palermo Lawyer, who had been engaged by the French Government to draw up an authentic genealogy and memoir of him. This Lawyer, and even the rude draft of his Memoir, he with little difficulty gets to see; inquires next whether it were not possible to see the actual Balsamo Family, whereof it appears the mother and a widowed sister still survive. For this matter, however, the Lawyer can do nothing; only refer him to his Clerk; who again starts difficulties: To get at those genealogic Documents he has been obliged to invent some story of a Government-Pension being in the wind for those poor Balsamos; and now that the whole matter is finished, and the Paper sent off to France, has nothing so much at heart as to keep out of their way:

" So said the Clerk. However, as I could not abandon my purpose, we after some study concerted that I should give myself out for an Englishman, and bring the family news of Cagliostro, who had lately got out of the Bastille, and gone to London.

" At the appointed hour, it might be three in the afternoon, we set forth. The house lay in the corner of an Alley, not far from the main street named *Il Casaro*. We ascended a miserable staircase, and came straight into the kitchen. A woman of middle stature, broad and stout, yet not corpulent, stood busy washing the kitchen-dishes. She was decently dressed; and, on our entrance, turned-up the one end of her apron, to hide the soiled side from us. She joyfully recognised my conductor, and said: ' Signor Giovanni, do you bring us good news? Have you made out anything? '

" He answered: ' In our affair, nothing yet; but here is a Stranger that brings a salutation from your Brother, and can tell you how he is at present.'

" The salutation I was to bring stood not in our agreement: meanwhile, one way or other, the introduction was accomplished. ' You know my Brother? ' inquired she.—' All Europe knows him,' answered I; ' and I fancied it would gratify you to hear that he is now in safety and well; as, of late, no doubt you have been anxious about him.'—' Step in,' said she; ' I will follow you directly; ' and with the Clerk I entered the room.

" It was large and high; and might, with us, have passed for a saloon; it seemed, indeed, to be almost the sole lodging of the family. A single window lighted the large walls, which had once had colour; and on which were black pictures of saints, in gilt frames, hanging round. Two large beds, with-

out curtains, stood at one wall; a brown press, in the form
of a writing-desk, at the other. Old rush-bottomed chairs,
the backs of which had once been gilt, stood by; and the tiles
of the floor were in many places worn deep into hollows. For
the rest, all was cleanly; and we approached the family,
which sat assembled at the one window, in the other end of
the apartment.

" Whilst my guide was explaining, to the old Widow
Balsamo, the purpose of our visit, and by reason of her deaf-
ness had to repeat his words several times aloud, I had time
to observe the chamber and the other persons in it. A girl
of about sixteen, well formed, whose features had become
uncertain by small-pox, stood at the window; beside her
a young man, whose disagreeable look, deformed by the
same disease, also struck me. In an easy-chair, right before
the window, sat or rather lay a sick, much misshapen person,
who appeared to labour under a sort of lethargy.

" My guide having made himself understood, we were
invited to take seats. The old woman put some questions
to me; which, however, I had to get interpreted before I
could answer them, the Sicilian dialect not being quite at
my command.

" Meanwhile I looked at the aged widow with satisfaction.
She was of middle stature, but well shaped; over her regular
features, which age had not deformed, lay that sort of peace
usual with people that have lost their hearing; the tone of
her voice was soft and agreeable.

" I answered her questions; and my answers also had
again to be interpreted for her.

" The slowness of our conversation gave me leisure to
measure my words. I told her that her son had been ac-
quitted in France, and was at present in England, where he
met with good reception. Her joy, which she testified at
these things, was mixed with expressions of a heartfelt piety;
and as she now spoke a little louder and slower, I could the
better understand her.

" In the mean time the daughter had entered; and taken
her seat beside my conductor, who repeated to her faithfully
what I had been narrating. She had put-on a clean apron;
had set her hair in order under the net-cap. The more I
looked at her, and compared her with her mother, the more
striking became the difference of the two figures. A viva-

cious healthy Sensualism (*Sinnlichkeit*) beamed forth from the whole structure of the daughter; she might be a woman of about forty. With brisk blue eyes she looked sharply round; yet in her look I could trace no suspicion. When she sat, her figure promised more height than it showed when she rose: her posture was determinate, she sat with her body leaned forwards, the hands resting on the knees. For the rest, her physiognomy, more of the snubby than the sharp sort, reminded me of her Brother's Portrait, familiar to us in engravings. She asked me several things about my journey, my purpose to see Sicily; and was sure I would come back, and celebrate the Feast of Saint Rosalia with them.

" As the grandmother, meanwhile, had again put some questions to me, and I was busy answering her, the daughter kept speaking to my companion half-aloud, yet so that I could take occasion to ask what it was. He answered: Signora Capitummino was telling him that her Brother owed her fourteen gold Ounces; on his sudden departure from Palermo, she had redeemed several things for him that were in pawn; but never since that day had either heard from him, or got money or any other help, though it was said he had great riches, and made a princely outlay. Now would not I perhaps undertake on my return, to remind him, in a handsome way, of the debt, and procure some assistance for her; nay would I not carry a Letter with me, or at all events get it carried? I offered to do so. She asked where I lodged, whither she must send the Letter to me? I avoided naming my abode, and offered to call next day towards night, and receive the Letter myself.

" She thereupon described to me her untoward situation: how she was a widow with three children, of whom the one girl was getting educated in a convent, the other was here present, and her son just gone out to his lesson. How, beside these three children, she had her mother to maintain; and moreover out of Christian love had taken the unhappy sick person there to her house, whereby the burden was heavier; how all her industry would scarcely suffice to get necessaries for herself and hers. She knew indeed that God did not leave good works unrewarded; yet must sigh very sore under the load she had long borne.

" The young people mixed in the dialogue, and our conversation grew livelier. While speaking with the others, I could hear the good old widow ask her daughter: If I belonged, then, to their holy Religion? I remarked also that the daughter strove, in a prudent way, to avoid an answer; signifying to her mother, so far as I could take it up: That the Stranger seemed to have a kind feeling towards them; and that it was not well-bred to question any one straightway on that point.

" As they heard that I was soon to leave Palermo, they became more pressing, and importuned me to come back; especially vaunting the paradisaic days of the Rosalia Festival, the like of which was not to be seen and tasted in all the world.

" My attendant, who had long been anxious to get off, at last put an end to the interview by his gestures; and I promised to return on the morrow evening, and take the Letter. My attendant expressed his joy that all had gone off so well, and we parted mutually content.

" You may fancy the impression this poor and pious, well-dispositioned family had made on me. My curiosity was satisfied; but their natural and worthy bearing had raised an interest in me, which reflection did but increase.

" Forthwith, however, there arose for me anxieties about the following day. It was natural that this appearance of mine, which, at the first moment, had taken them by surprise, should, after my departure, awaken many reflections. By the Genealogy I knew that several others of the family were in life: it was natural that they should call their friends together, and in the presence of all, get those things repeated which, the day before, they had heard from me with admiration. My object was attained; there remained nothing more than, in some good fashion, to end the adventure. I accordingly repaired next day, directly after dinner, alone to their house. They expressed surprise as I entered. The Letter was not ready yet, they said; and some of their relations wished to make my acquaintance, who towards night would be there.

" I answered, that having to set off to-morrow morning, and visits still to pay, and packing to transact, I had thought it better to come early than not at all.

" Meanwhile the son entered, whom yesterday I had not seen. He resembled his sister in size and figure. He brought the Letter they were to give me; he had, as is common in those parts, got it written out of doors, by one of their

Notaries that sit publicly to do such things. The young man had a still, melancholy and modest aspect; inquired after his Uncle, asked about his riches and outlays, and added sorrowfully, Why had he so forgotten his kindred? 'It were our greatest fortune,' continued he, 'should he once return hither, and take notice of us: but,' continued he, 'how came he to let you know that he had relatives in Palermo? It is said, he everywhere denies us, and gives himself out for a man of great birth.' I answered this question, which had now arisen by the imprudence of my Guide at our first entrance, in such sort as to make it seem that the Uncle, though he might have reason for concealing his birth from the public, did yet, towards his friends and acquaintance, keep it no secret.

"The sister, who had come up during this dialogue, and by the presence of her brother, perhaps also by the absence of her yesterday's friend, had got more courage, began also to speak with much grace and liveliness. They begged me earnestly to recommend them to their Uncle, if I wrote to him; and not less earnestly, when once I should have made this journey through the Island, to come back and pass the Rosalia Festival with them.

"The mother spoke in accordance with her children. 'Sir,' said she, 'though it is not seemly, as I have a grown daughter, to see stranger gentlemen in my house, and one has to guard against both danger and evil-speaking, yet shall you ever be welcome to us, when you return to this city.'

"'O yes,' answered the young ones, 'we will lead the Gentleman all round the Festival; we will show him everything, get a place on the scaffolds, where the grand sights are seen best. What will he say to the great Chariot, and more than all, to the glorious Illumination!'

"Meanwhile the Grandmother had read the Letter and again read it. Hearing that I was about to take leave, she arose, and gave me the folded sheet. 'Tell my son,' began she with a noble vivacity, nay with a sort of inspiration, 'Tell my son how happy the news have made me, which you brought from him! Tell him that I clasp him to my heart'—here she stretched out her arms asunder, and pressed them again together on her breast—'that I daily beseech God and our Holy Virgin for him in prayer; that I give him and his wife my blessing; and that I wish before my end to see him again with these eyes, which have shed so many tears for him.'

"The peculiar grace of the Italian tongue favoured the choice and noble arrangement of these words, which moreover were accompanied with lively gestures, wherewith that nation can add such a charm to spoken words.

"I took my leave, not without emotion. They all gave me their hands; the children showed me out; and as I went down stairs, they jumped to the balcony of the kitchenwindow, which projected over the street; called after me, threw me salutes, and repeated, that I must in no wise forget to come back. I saw them still on the balcony, when I turned the corner." [1]

Poor old Felicità, and must thy pious prayers, thy motherly blessings, and so many tears shed by those old eyes, be all in vain! To thyself, in any case, they were blessed.—As for the Signora Capitummino, with her three fatherless children, shall we not hope at least, that the fourteen gold Ounces were paid, by a sure hand, and so her heavy burden, for some space, lightened a little? Alas, no, it would seem; owing to accidents, not even that! [2]

Count Cagliostro, all this while, is rapidly proceeding with his Fifth Act; the red coppery splendour darkens more and more into final gloom. Some boiling muddleheads of a dupeable sort there still are in England: Popish-Riot Lord George, for instance, will walk with him to Count Barthélemy's or D'Adhémar's; and, in bad French and worse rhetoric, abuse the Queen of France: but what does it profit? Lord George must one day (after noise enough) revisit Newgate for it; and in the meanwhile, hard words pay no scores. Apothecary Swinton begins to get wearisome; French spies look ominously in; Egyptian Pills are slack of sale; the old vulturous Attorney-host anew scents carrion, is bestirring itself anew: Count Cagliostro, in the May of 1787, must once more leave England. But whither? Ah, whither! At Bâle, at Bienne, over Switzerland, the game is up. At Aix in Savoy, there are baths, but no gudgeons in them: at Turin, his Majesty of Sardinia meets you with an order to begone on the instant. A like fate from the Emperor Joseph at Roveredo;—before the *Liber memorialis de Caleostro dum esset Roboretti* could extend to many pages! Count Front-of-

brass begins confessing himself to priests: yet "at Trent
paints a new hieroglyphic Screen,"—touching last flicker of
a light that once burnt so high! He pawns diamond buckles;
wanders necessitous hither and thither; repents, unrepents;
knows not what to do. For Destiny has her nets round him;
they are straitening, straitening; too soon he will be *ginned!*

Driven out from Trent, what shall he make of the new
hieroglyphic Screen, what of himself? The wayworn Grand-
Cophtess has begun to blab family secrets; she longs to be
in Rome, by her mother's hearth, by her mother's grave; in
any nook, where so much as the shadow of refuge waits her.
To the desperate Count Front-of-brass all places are nearly
alike: urged by female babble, he will go to Rome, then;
why not? On a May-day, of the year 1789 (when such glorious work had just begun in France, to him all forbidden!),
he enters the Eternal City; it was his doom-summons that
called him thither. On the 29th of next December, the Holy
Inquisition, long watchful enough, detects him founding some
feeble moneyless ghost of an Egyptian Lodge; "picks him
off," as the military say, and locks him hard and fast in the
Castle of St. Angelo:

Lasciate ogni speranza, voi che 'ntrate !

Count Cagliostro did not lose all hope: nevertheless a few
words will now suffice for him. In vain, with his mouth of
pinchbeck and his front of brass, does he heap chimera on
chimera; demand religious Books (which are freely given
him); demand clean Linen, and an interview with his Wife
(which are refused him); assert now that the Egyptian
Masonry is a divine system, accommodated to erring and
gullible men, which the Holy Father, when he knows it, will
patronise; anon that there are some four millions of Freemasons, spread over Europe, all sworn to exterminate Priest
and King, wherever met with: in vain! they will not acquit
him, as misunderstood Theophilanthropist; will not emit
him, in Pope's pay, as renegade Masonic Spy: "he can't get
out." Donna Lorenza languishes, invisible to him, in a
neighbouring cell; begins at length to *confess!* Whereupon
he too, in torrents, will emit confessions and forestall her:
these the Inquisition pocket and sift (whence this *Life of
Balsamo*); but will not let him out. In fine, after some
eighteen months of the weariest hounding, doubling, worrying

and standing at bay, His Holiness gives sentence: The Manuscript of Egyptian Masonry is to be burnt by hand of the common Hangman, and all that intermeddle with such Masonry are accursed; Giuseppe Balsamo, justly forfeited of life for being a Freemason, shall nevertheless in mercy be forgiven; instructed in the duties of penitence, and even kept safe thenceforth and till death,—in ward of Holy Church. Ill-starred Acharat, must it so end with thee? This was in April 1791.

He addressed (how vainly!) an appeal to the French Constituent Assembly. As was said, in Heaven, in Earth, or in Hell there was no Assembly that could well take his part. For four years more, spent one knows not how,—most probably in the furor of edacity, with insufficient cookery, and the stupor of indigestion,—the curtain lazily falls. There rotted and gave way the cordage of a tough heart. One summer morning of the year 1795, the Body of Cagliostro is still found in the prison of St. Leo; but Cagliostro's Self has escaped,—*whither* no man yet knows. The brow of brass, behold how it has got all unlacquered; these pinchbeck lips can lie no more: Cagliostro's work is ended, and now only his *account* to present. As the Scherif of Mecca said, " Nature's unfortunate child, adieu! "

Such, according to our comprehension thereof, is the rise, progress, grandeur and decadence of the Quack of Quacks. Does the reader ask, What good was in it; Why occupy his time and ours with the biography of such a miscreant? We answer, It was stated on the very threshold of this matter, in the loftiest terms, by Herr Sauerteig, that the Lives of all Eminent Persons, miscreant or creant, ought to be written. Thus has not the very Devil his *Life*, deservedly written not by Daniel Defoe only, but by quite other hands than Daniel's? For the rest, the Thing represented on these pages is no Sham, but a Reality; thou hast it, O reader, as we have it: Nature was pleased to produce even such a man, even so, not otherwise; and the Editor of this Magazine is here mainly to record, in an adequate manner, what *she*, of her thousandfold mysterious richness and greatness, produces.

But the moral lesson? Where is the moral lesson? Foolish reader, in every Reality, nay in every genuine Shadow of a Reality (what we call Poem), there lie a hundred such, or a million such, according as thou hast the *eye* to read them! Of which hundred or million lying *here* in the present Reality, couldst not thou, for example, be advised to take this one, to thee worth all the rest: " Behold, I too have attained that immeasurable, mysterious glory of being *alive ;* to me also a Capability has been intrusted; shall I strive to work it out, manlike, into Faithfulness, and Doing; or, quacklike, into Eatableness, and Similitude of Doing? Or why not rather, gigman-like, and following the ' respectable ' countless multitude,—into *both ?* " The decision is of quite *infinite* moment; see thou make it aright.

But in fine, look at this matter of Cagliostro, as at all matters, with thy heart, with thy whole mind; no longer merely squint at it with the poor side-glance of thy calculative faculty. Look at it not *logically* only, but *mystically*. Thou shalt in sober truth see it (as Sauerteig asserted) to be a Pasquillant verse, of most inspired writing in its kind, in that same " Grand Bible of Universal History; " wondrously and even indispensably connected with the Heroic portions that stand there; even as the all-showing Light is with the Darkness wherein nothing can be seen; as the hideous taloned *roots* are with the fair *boughs*, and their leaves and flowers and fruit; both of which, and not one of which, make the Tree. Think also whether thou hast known no Public Quacks, on far higher scale than this, whom a Castle of St. Angelo never could get hold of; and how, as Emperors, Chancellors (having found much fitter machinery), they could run their Quack-career; and make whole kingdoms, whole continents, into one huge Egyptian Lodge, and squeeze supplies of money or of blood from it at discretion? Also, whether thou even now knowest not Private Quacks, innumerable as the sea-sands, toiling as mere *Half*-Cagliostros; imperfect, hybrid-quacks, of whom Cagliostro is as the unattainable ideal and type-specimen? Such is the world. Understand it, despise it, love it; cheerfully hold on thy way through it, with thy eye on higher load-stars!

THE NIGGER QUESTION

[*Precursor to Latter-day Pamphlets*]

[1849]

OCCASIONAL DISCOURSE ON THE NIGGER QUESTION [1]

THE following Occasional Discourse, delivered by we know not whom, and of date seemingly above a year back, may perhaps be welcome to here and there a speculative reader. It comes to us,—no speaker named, no time or place assigned, no commentary of any sort given,—in the handwriting of the so-called " Doctor," properly " Absconded Reporter," Dr. Phelim M'Quirk, whose singular powers of reporting, and also whose debts, extravagancies and sorrowful insidious finance-operations, now winded-up by a sudden disappearance, to the grief of many poor tradespeople, are making too much noise in the police-offices at present! Of M'Quirk's composition we by no means suppose it to be; but from M'Quirk, as the last traceable source, it comes to us;—offered, in fact, by his respectable unfortunate landlady, desirous to make-up part of her losses in this way.

To absconded reporters who bilk their lodgings, we have of course no account to give; but if the Speaker be of any eminence or substantiality, and feel himself aggrieved by the transaction, let him understand that such, and such only, is our connection with him or his affairs. As the Colonial and Negro Question is still alive, and likely to grow livelier for some time, we have accepted the Article, at a cheap market-rate; and give it publicity, without in the least committing ourselves to the strange doctrines and notions shadowed forth in it. Doctrines and notions which, we rather suspect, are pretty much in a " minority of one," in the present era of the world! Here, sure enough, are peculiar views of the Rights of Negroes; involving, it is probable, peculiar ditto of innumerable other rights, duties, expectations, wrongs and disappointments, much argued of, by logic and by grape-shot, in these emancipated epochs of the human mind!—Silence now, however; and let the Speaker himself enter.

My Philanthropic Friends,—It is my painful duty to address some words to you, this evening, on the Rights of Negroes.

[1] First printed in *Fraser's Magazine*, December 1849; reprinted in the form of a separate Pamphlet, London, 1853.

Taking, as we hope we do, an extensive survey of social affairs, which we find all in a state of the frightfulest embroilment, and as it were of inextricable final bankruptcy, just at present; and being desirous to adjust ourselves in that huge upbreak, and unutterable welter of tumbling ruins, and to see well that our grand proposed Association of Associations, the UNIVERSAL ABOLITION-OF-PAIN ASSOCIATION, which is meant to be the consummate golden flower and summary of modern Philanthropisms all in one, do *not* issue as a universal "Sluggard-and-Scoundrel Protection Society," —we have judged that, before constituting ourselves, it would be very proper to commune earnestly with one another, and discourse together on the leading elements of our great Problem, which surely is one of the greatest. With this view the Council has decided, both that the Negro Question, as lying at the bottom, was to be the first handled, and if possible the first settled; and then also, what was of much more questionable wisdom, that—that, in short, I was to be Speaker on the occasion. An honourable duty; yet, as I said, a painful one!—Well, you shall hear what I have to say on the matter; and probably you will not in the least like it.

West-Indian affairs, as we all know, and as some of us know to our cost, are in a rather troublous condition this good while. In regard to West-Indian affairs, however, Lord John Russell is able to comfort us with one fact, indisputable where so many are dubious, That the Negroes are all very happy and doing well. A fact very comfortable indeed. West-Indian Whites, it is admitted, are far enough from happy; West-Indian Colonies not unlike sinking wholly into ruin: at home too, the British Whites are rather badly off; several millions of them hanging on the verge of continual famine; and in single towns, many thousands of them very sore put to it, at this time, not to live "well" or as a man should, in any sense temporal or spiritual, but to live at all:—these, again, are uncomfortable facts; and they are extremely extensive and important ones. But, thank Heaven, our interesting Black population,—equalling almost in number of heads one of the Ridings of Yorkshire, and in *worth* (in quantity of intellect, faculty, docility, energy, and available human valour and value) perhaps one of the streets of Seven

Dials,—are all doing remarkably well. "Sweet blighted lilies,"—as the American epitaph on the Nigger child has it,—sweet blighted lilies, they are holding-up their heads again! How pleasant, in the universal bankruptcy abroad, and dim dreary stagnancy at home, as if for England too there remained nothing but to suppress Chartist riots, banish united Irishmen, vote the supplies, and *wait* with arms crossed till black Anarchy and Social Death devoured us also, as it has done the others; how pleasant to have always this fact to fall-back upon: Our beautiful Black darlings are at last happy; with little labour except to the teeth, *which* surely, in those excellent horse-jaws of theirs, will not fail!

Exeter Hall, my philanthropic friends, has had its way in this matter. The Twenty Millions, a mere trifle despatched with a single dash of the pen, are paid; and far over the sea, we have a few black persons rendered extremely "free" indeed. Sitting yonder with their beautiful muzzles up to the ears in pumpkins, imbibing sweet pulps and juices; the grinder and incisor teeth ready for ever new work, and the pumpkins cheap as grass in those rich climates: while the sugar-crops rot round them uncut, because labour cannot be hired, so cheap are the pumpkins;—and at home we are but required to rasp from the breakfast-loaves of our own English labourers some slight "differential sugar-duties," and lend a poor half-million or a few poor millions now and then, to keep that beautiful state of matters going on. A state of matters lovely to contemplate, in these emancipated epochs of the human mind; which has earned us not only the praises of Exeter Hall, and loud long-eared hallelujahs of laudatory psalmody from the Friends of Freedom everywhere, but lasting favour (it is hoped) from the Heavenly Powers themselves;—and which may, at least, justly appeal to the Heavenly Powers, and ask them, If ever in terrestrial procedure they saw the match of it? Certainly in the past history of the human species it has no parallel: nor, one hopes, will it have in the future. [*Some emotion in the audience: which the Chairman suppressed.*]

Sunk in deep froth-oceans of "Benevolence," "Fraternity," "Emancipation-principle," "Christian Philanthropy," and other most amiable-looking, but most baseless, and in the end baleful and all-bewildering jargon,—sad product of a sceptical Eighteenth Century, and of poor human hearts left *destitute* of any earnest guidance, and disbelieving that there ever was any, Christian or Heathen, and reduced to believe in rosepink Sentimentalism alone, and to cultivate the same under its Christian, Antichristian, Broad-brimmed, Brutus-headed, and other forms,—has not the human species gone strange roads, during that period? And poor Exeter Hall, cultivating the Broad-brimmed form of Christian Sentimentalism, and long talking and bleating and braying in that strain, has it not worked-out results? Our West-Indian Legislatings, with their spoutings, anti-spoutings, and interminable jangle and babble; our Twenty millions down on the nail for Blacks of our own; Thirty gradual millions more, and many brave British lives to boot, in watching Blacks of other people's; and now at last our ruined sugar-estates, differential sugar-duties, " immigration loan," and beautiful Blacks sitting there up to the ears in pumpkins, and doleful Whites sitting here without potatoes to eat: never till now, I think, did the sun look-down on such a jumble of human nonsenses;—of which, with the two hot nights of the Missing-Despatch Debate,[1] God grant that the measure might now at last be full! But no, it is not yet full; we have a long way to travel back, and terrible flounderings to make, and in fact an immense load of nonsense to dislodge from our poor heads, and manifold cobwebs to rend from our poor eyes, before we get into the road again, and can begin to act as serious men that have work to do in this Universe, and no longer as windy sentimentalists that merely have speeches to deliver and despatches to write. O Heaven, in West-Indian matters, and in all manner of matters, it is so with us: the more is the sorrow!—

The West Indies, it appears, are short of labour; as indeed is very conceivable in those circumstances. Where a Black man, by working about half-an-hour a-day (such is the calculation), can supply himself, by aid of sun and soil, with as much pumpkin as will suffice, he is likely to be a little stiff to raise into hard work! Supply and demand, which, science says, should be brought to bear on him, have an uphill task

[1] Does any reader now remember it? A cloudy reminiscence of some such thing, and of noise in the Newspapers upon it, remains with us,—fast hastening to abolition for everybody. (*Note of* 1849.)—This Missing-Despatch Debate, what on earth was it? (*Note of* 1853.)

of it with such a man. Strong sun supplies itself gratis, rich soil in those unpeopled or half-peopled regions almost gratis; these are *his* "supply;" and half-an-hour a-day, directed upon these, will produce pumpkin, which is his "demand." The fortunate Black man, very swiftly does he settle *his* account with supply and demand:—not so swiftly the less fortunate White man of those tropical localities. A bad case, his, just now. He himself cannot work; and his black neighbour, rich in pumpkin, is in no haste to help him. Sunk to the ears in pumpkin, imbibing saccharine juices, and much at his ease in the Creation, he can listen to the less fortunate white man's "demand" and take his own time in supplying it. Higher wages, massa; higher, for your cane-crop cannot wait; still higher,—till no conceivable opulence of cane-crop will cover such wages. In Demerara, as I read in the Blue-book of last year, the cane-crop, far and wide, stands rotting; the fortunate black gentlemen, strong in their pumpkins, having all struck till the "demand" rise a little. Sweet blighted lilies, now getting-up their heads again!

Science, however, has a remedy still. Since the demand is so pressing, and the supply so inadequate (equal in fact to *nothing* in some places, as appears), increase the supply; bring more Blacks into the labour-market, then will the rate fall, says science. Not the least surprising part of our West-Indian policy is this recipe of "immigration;" of keeping-down the labour-market in those islands by importing new Africans to labour and live there. If the Africans that are already there could be made to lay-down their pumpkins, and labour for their living, there are already Africans enough. If the new Africans, after labouring a little, take to pumpkins like the others, what remedy is there? To bring-in new and ever new Africans, say you, till pumpkins themselves grow dear; till the country is crowded with Africans; and black men there, like white men here, are forced by hunger to labour for their living? That will be a consummation. To have "emancipated" the West Indies into a *Black Ireland ;* "free" indeed, but an Ireland, and Black! The world may yet see prodigies; and reality be stranger than a nightmare dream.

Our own white or sallow Ireland, sluttishly starving from age to age on its act-of-parliament "freedom," was hitherto the flower of mismanagement among the nations: but what will this be to a Negro Ireland, with pumpkins themselves fallen scarce like potatoes! Imagination cannot fathom such an object; the belly of Chaos never held the like. The human mind, in its wide wanderings, has not dreamt yet of such a "freedom" as that will be. Towards that, if Exeter Hall and science of supply-and-demand are to continue our guides in the matter, we are daily travelling, and even struggling, with loans of half-a-million and suchlike, to accelerate ourselves.

Truly, my philanthropic friends, Exeter-Hall Philanthropy is wonderful. And the Social Science,—not a "gay science," but a rueful,—which finds the secret of this Universe in "supply and demand," and reduces the duty of human governors to that of letting men alone, is also wonderful. Not a "gay science," I should say, like some we have heard of; no, a dreary, desolate, and indeed quite abject and distressing one; what we might call, by way of eminence, the *dismal science*. These two, Exeter-Hall Philanthropy and the Dismal Science, led by any sacred cause of Black Emancipation, or the like, to fall in love and make a wedding of it,—will give birth to progenies and prodigies; dark extensive moon-calves, unnamable abortions, wide-coiled monstrosities, such as the world has not seen hitherto! [*Increased emotion, again suppressed by the Chairman.*]

In fact, it will behove us of this English nation to overhaul our West-Indian procedure from top to bottom, and ascertain a little better what it is that Fact and Nature demand of us, and what only Exeter Hall wedded to the Dismal Science demands. To the former set of demands we will endeavour, at our peril,—and worse peril than our purse's, at our soul's peril,—to give all obedience. To the latter we will very frequently demur, and try if we cannot stop short where they contradict the former,—and especially *before* arriving at the black throat of ruin, whither they appear to be leading us. Alas, in many other provinces besides the West Indian, that unhappy wedlock of Philanthropic Liberalism and the Dismal Science has engendered such all-enveloping delusions, of the moon-calf sort, and wrought huge woe for us, and for the poor civilised world, in these days! And sore will be the battle with said moon-calves; and terrible the struggle to return out of our delusions, floating rapidly on which, not the West

Indies alone, but Europe generally, is nearing the Niagara Falls. [*Here various persons, in an agitated manner, with an air of indignation, left the room ; especially one very tall gentleman in white trousers, whose boots creaked much. The President, in a resolved voice, with a look of official rigour, whatever his own private feelings might be, enjoined " Silence, Silence ! " The meeting again sat motionless.*]

My philanthropic friends, can you discern no fixed headlands in this wide-weltering deluge, of benevolent twaddle and revolutionary grape-shot, that has burst-forth on us; no sure bearings at all? Fact and Nature, it seems to me, say a few words to us, if happily we have still an ear for Fact and Nature. Let us listen a little and try.

And first, with regard to the West Indies, it may be laid-down as a principle, which no eloquence in Exeter Hall, or Westminster Hall, or elsewhere, can invalidate or hide, except for a short time only, That no Black man who will not work according to what ability the gods have given him for working, has the smallest right to eat pumpkin, or to any fraction of land that will grow pumpkin, however plentiful such land may be; but has an indisputable and perpetual *right* to be compelled, by the real proprietors of said land, to do competent work for his living. This is the everlasting duty of all men, black or white, who are born into this world. To do competent work, to labour honestly according to the ability given them; for that and for no other purpose was each one of us sent into this world; and woe is to every man who, by friend or by foe, is prevented from fulfilling this the end of his being. That is the " unhappy " lot: lot equally unhappy cannot otherwise be provided for man. Whatsoever prohibits or prevents a man from this his sacred appointment to labour while he lives on earth,—that, I say, is the man's deadliest enemy; and all men are called upon to do what is in their power or opportunity towards delivering him from that. If it be his own indolence that prevents and prohibits him, then his own indolence is the enemy he must be delivered from: and the first " right " he has,—poor indolent blockhead, black or white,—is, That every *un*prohibited man, whatsoever wiser, more industrious person may be passing that way, shall endeavour to " emancipate " him from his indolence, and by some wise means, as I said, compel him, since inducing will not serve, to do the work he is fit for.

Induce him, if you can: yes, sure enough, by all means try what inducement will do; and indeed every coachman and carman knows that secret, without our preaching, and applies it to his very horses as the true method:—but if your Nigger will not be induced? In that case, it is full certain, he must be compelled; should and must; and the tacit prayer he makes (unconsciously he, poor blockhead,) to you, and to me, and to all the world who are wiser than himself, is "Compel me!" For indeed he *must*, or else do and suffer worse,— he as well as we. It were better the work did come out of him! It was the meaning of the gods with him and with us, that his gift should turn to use in this Creation, and not lie poisoning the thoroughfares, as a rotten mass of idleness, agreeable to neither heaven nor earth. For idleness does, in all cases, inevitably *rot*, and become putrescent;—and I say deliberately, the very Devil is in *it*.

None of you, my friends, have been in Demerara lately, I apprehend? May none of you go till matters mend there a little! Under the sky there are uglier sights than perhaps were seen hitherto! Dead corpses, the rotting body of a brother man, whom fate or unjust men have killed, this is not a pleasant spectacle; but what say you to the dead soul of a man,—in a body which still pretends to be vigorously alive, and can drink rum? An idle White gentleman is not pleasant to me; though I confess the real work for him is not easy to find, in these our epochs; and perhaps he is seeking, poor soul, and may find at last. But what say you to an idle Black gentleman, with his rum-bottle in his hand (for a little additional pumpkin you can have red-herrings and rum, in Demerara),—rum-bottle in his hand, no breeches on his body, pumpkin at discretion, and the fruitfulest region of the earth going back to jungle round him? Such things the sun looks-down upon in our fine times; and I, for one, would rather have no hand in them.

Yes, this is the eternal law of Nature for a man, my bene-ficent Exeter-Hall friends; this, that he shall be permitted, encouraged, and if need be, compelled to do what work the Maker of him has intended by the making of him for this world! Not that he should eat pumpkin with never such felicity in the West-India Islands is, or can be, the blessedness of our Black friend; but that he should do useful work there, according as the gifts have been bestowed on him for that.

And his own happiness, and that of others round him, will alone be possible by his and their getting into such a relation that this can be permitted him, and in case of need, that this can be compelled him. I beg you to understand this; for you seem to have a little forgotten it, and there lie a thousand inferences in it, not quite useless for Exeter Hall, at present. The idle Black man in the West Indies had, not long since, the right, and will again under better form, if it please Heaven, have the right (actually the first "right of man" for an indolent person) to be *compelled* to work as he was fit, and to *do* the Maker's will who had constructed him with such and such capabilities, and prefigurements of capability. And I incessantly pray Heaven, all men, the whitest alike and the blackest, the richest and the poorest, in other regions of the world, had attained precisely the same right, the divine right of being compelled (if "permitted" will not answer) to do what work they are appointed for, and not to go idle another minute, in a life which is so short, and where idleness so soon runs to putrescence! Alas, we had then a perfect world; and the Millennium, and true "Organisation of Labour," and reign of complete blessedness, for all workers and men, had then arrived,—which in these our own poor districts of the Planet, as we all lament to know, it is very far from having yet done. [*More withdrawals ; but the rest sitting with increased attention.*]

Do I, then, hate the Negro? No; except when the soul is killed out of him, I decidedly like poor Quashee; and find him a pretty kind of man. With a pennyworth of oil, you can make a handsome glossy thing of Quashee, when the soul is not killed in him! A swift, supple fellow; a merry-hearted, grinning, dancing, singing, affectionate kind of creature, with a great deal of melody and amenability in his composition. This certainly is a notable fact: The black African, alone of wild-men, can live among men civilised. While all manner of Caribs and others pine into annihilation in presence of the pale faces, he contrives to continue; does not die of sullen irreconcilable rage, of rum, of brutish laziness and darkness, and fated incompatibility with his new place; but lives and multiplies, and evidently means to abide among us, if we can find the right regulation for him. We shall have to find it; we are now engaged in the search; and have at least discovered that of two methods, the old Demerara method, and the new Demerara method, neither will answer.

Alas, my friends, I understand well your rage against the poor Negro's slavery; what said rage proceeds from; and have a perfect sympathy with it, and even know it by experience. Can the oppressor of my black fellow-man be of any use to me, in particular? Am I gratified in my mind by the ill-usage of any two- or four-legged thing; of any horse or any dog? Not so, I assure you. In me too the natural sources of human rage exist more or less, and the capability of flying out into " fiery wrath against oppression," and of signing petitions; both of which things can be done very cheap. Good heavens, if signing petitions would do it, if hopping to Rome on one leg would do it, think you it were long undone!

Frightful things are continually told us of Negro slavery, of the hardships, bodily and spiritual, suffered by slaves. Much exaggerated, and mere exceptional cases, say the opponents. Exceptional cases, I answer; yes, and universal ones! On the whole, hardships, and even oppressions and injustices are not unknown in this world; I myself have suffered such, and have not you? It is said, Man, of whatever colour, is born to such, even as the sparks fly upwards. For in fact labour, and this is properly what we call hardship, misery, etc. (meaning mere ugly labour not yet done), labour is not joyous but grievous; and we have a good deal of it to do among us here. We have, simply, to carry the whole world and its businesses upon our backs, we poor united Human Species; to carry it, and shove it forward, from day to day, somehow or other, among us, or else be ground to powder under it, one and all. No light task, let me tell you, even if each did his part honestly, which each doesn't by any means. No, only the noble lift willingly with their whole strength, at the general burden; and in such a crowd, after all your drillings, regulatings, and attempts at equitable distribution, and compulsion, what deceptions are still practicable, what errors are inevitable! Many cunning ignoble fellows shirk the labour altogether; and instead of faithfully lifting at the immeasurable universal handbarrow with its thousand-million handles, contrive to get on some ledge of it, and be lifted!

What a story we have heard about all that, not from vague

rumour since yesterday, but from inspired prophets, speakers
and seers, ever since speech began! How the giant willing
spirit, among white masters, and in the best-regulated families,
is so often not loaded only but overloaded, crushed-down like
an Enceladus; and, all his life, has to have armies of pigmies
building tabernacles on his chest; marching composedly over
his neck, as if it were a highway; and much amazed if, when
they run their straw spear into his nostril, he is betrayed into
sudden sneezing, and oversets some of them. [*Some laughter,
the speaker himself looking terribly serious.*] My friends, I
have come to the sad conclusion that SLAVERY, whether
established by law, or by law abrogated, exists very extensively in this world, in and out of the West Indies; and, in
fact, that you cannot abolish slavery by act of parliament, but
can only abolish the *name* of it, which is very little!

In the West Indies itself, if you chance to abolish Slavery
to Men, and in return establish Slavery to the Devil (as we
see in Demerara), what good is it? To save men's bodies, and
fill them with pumpkins and rum, is a poor task for human
benevolence, if you have to kill their soul, what soul there
was, in the business! Slavery is not so easy to be abolished;
it will long continue, in spite of acts of parliament. And
shall I tell you which is the one intolerable sort of slavery;
the slavery over which the very gods weep? That sort is not
rifest in the West Indies; but, with all its sad fruits, prevails
in nobler countries. It is the slavery of the strong to the
weak; of the great and noble-minded to the small and mean!
The slavery of Wisdom to Folly. When Folly all " emancipated," and become supreme, armed with ballot-boxes,
universal suffrages, and appealing to what Dismal Sciences,
Statistics, Constitutional Philosophies, and other Fool
Gospels it has got devised for itself, can say to Wisdom: " Be
silent, or thou shalt repent it! Suppress thyself, I advise
thee; canst thou not contrive to cease, then? " That also,
in some anarchic-constitutional epochs, has been seen. When,
of high and noble objects, there remained, in the market-
place of human things, at length none; and he that could not
make guineas his pursuit, and the applause of flunkies his
reward, found himself in such a minority as seldom was before.

Minority, I know, there always was: but there are degrees
of it, down to minority of one,—down to suppression of the
unfortunate minority, and reducing it to zero, that the flunky

world may have peace from it henceforth. The flunky-world has peace; and descends, manipulating its ballot-boxes, Coppock suffrages, and divine constitutional apparatus; quoting its Dismal Sciences, Statistics, and other satisfactory Gospels and Talmuds,—into the throat of the Devil; not bothered by the importunate minority on the road. Did you never hear of "Crucify him! Crucify him!" That was a considerable feat in the suppressing of minorities; and is still talked-of on Sundays,—with very little understanding, when I last heard of it. My friends, my friends, I fear we are a stupid people; and stuffed with such delusions, above all with such immense hypocrisies and self-delusions, from our birth upwards, as no people were before; God help us! —Emancipated? Yes, indeed, we are emancipated out of several things, and into several things. No man, wise or foolish, any longer can control you for good or for evil. Foolish Tomkins, foolish Jobson, cannot now singly oppress you: but if the Universal Company of the Tomkinses and Jobsons, as by law established, can more than ever? If, on all highways and byways, that lead to other than a Tomkins-Jobson winning-post, you meet, at the second step, the big, dumb, universal genius of Chaos, and are so placidly yet peremptorily taught, "Halt here!" There is properly but one slavery in the world. One slavery, in which all other slaveries and miseries that afflict the earth are included; compared with which the worst West-Indian, white, or black, or yellow slaveries are a small matter. One slavery over which the very gods weep. Other slaveries, women and children and stump-orators weep over; but this is for men and gods! [*Sensation; some, however, took snuff.*]

If precisely the Wisest Man were at the top of society, and the next-wisest next, and so on till we reached the Demerara Nigger (from whom downwards, through the horse, etc., there is no question hitherto), then were this a perfect world, the extreme *maximum* of wisdom produced in it. That is how you might produce your maximum, would some god assist. And I can tell you also how the *minimum* were producible. Let no man in particular be put at the top; let all men be accounted equally wise and worthy, and the notion get abroad that anybody or nobody will do well enough at the top; that money (to which may be added success in stump-oratory) is the real symbol of wisdom, and supply-

and-demand the all-sufficient substitute for command and obedience among two-legged animals of the unfeathered class: accomplish all those remarkable convictions in your thinking department; and then in your practical, as is fit, decide by count of heads, the vote of a Demerara Nigger equal and no more to that of a Chancellor Bacon: this, I perceive, will (so soon as it is fairly under way, and *all* obstructions left behind) give the *minimum* of wisdom in your proceedings. Thus were your minimum producible,—with no God needed to assist, nor any Demon even, except the general Demon of *Ignavia* (Unvalour), lazy Indifference to the production or non-production of such things, which runs in our own blood. Were it beautiful, think you? Folly in such millionfold majority, at length peaceably supreme in this earth. Advancing on you as the huge buffalo-phalanx does in the Western Deserts; or as, on a smaller scale, those bristly creatures did in the Country of the Gadarenes. Rushing, namely, in wild *stampede* (the Devil being in them, some small fry having stung them), boundless,—one wing on that edge of your horizon, the other wing on that, and rearward whole tides and oceans of them:—so could Folly rush; the enlightened public one huge Gadarenes-swinery, tail cocked, snout in air, with joyful animating short squeak; fast and ever faster; down steep places,—to the sea of Tiberias, and the bottomless cloacas of Nature: quenched there, since nowhere sooner. My friends, such sight is *too* sublime, if you are out in it, and are not of it!—

Well, *except* by Mastership and Servantship, there is no conceivable deliverance from Tyranny and Slavery. Cosmos is not Chaos, simply by this one quality, That it is governed. Where wisdom, even approximately, can contrive to govern, all is right, or is ever striving to become so; where folly is "emancipated," and gets to govern, as it soon will, all is wrong. That is the sad fact; and in other places than Demerara, and in regard to other interests than those of sugar-making, we sorrowfully experience the same.

I have to complain that, in these days, the relation of master to servant, and of superior to inferior, in all stages of it, is fallen sadly out of joint. As may well be, when the very highest stage and form of it, which should be the summary of all and the keystone of all, is got to such a pass. Kings themselves are grown sham-kings; and their subjects very naturally are sham-subjects; with mere lip-homage, insincere to their sham-kings;—sincere chiefly when they get into the streets (as is now our desperate case generally in Europe) to shoot them down as nuisances. Royalty is terribly gone; and loyalty in consequence has had to go. No man reverences another; at the best, each man slaps the other good-humouredly on the shoulder, with, " Hail, fellow; well met: " —at the worst (which is sure enough to *follow* such unreasonable good-humour, in a world like ours) clutches him by the throat, with, " Tyrannous son of perdition, shall I endure thee, then, and thy injustices forever? " We are not yet got to the worst extreme, we here in these Isles; but we are well half-way towards it, I often think.

Certainly, by any ballot-box, Jesus Christ goes just as far as Judas Iscariot; and with reason, according to the New Gospels, Talmuds and Dismal Sciences of these days. Judas looks him in the face; asks proudly, " Am not I as good as thou? Better, perhaps! " slapping his breeches-pocket, in which is audible the cheerful jingle of thirty pieces of silver. " Thirty of them here, thou cowering pauper! " My philanthropic friends, if there be a state of matters under the stars which deserves the name of damnable and damned, this I perceive is it! Alas, I know well whence it came, and how it could not help coming;—and I continually pray the gods its errand were done, and it had begun to go its ways again. Vain hope, at least for a century to come! And there will be such a sediment of Egyptian mud to sweep away, and to fish all human things out of again, once this most sad though salutary deluge is well over, as the human species seldom had before. Patience, patience!—

In fact, without real masters you cannot have servants; and a master is not made by thirty pieces or thirty-million pieces of silver; only a sham-master is so made. The Dismal Science of this epoch defines him to be master good enough; but he is not such: you can see what kind of master he proves, what kind of servants he manages to have. Accordingly, the state of British servantship, of American helpship—I confess to you, my friends, if looking out for what was *least* human and heroic, least lovely to the Supreme Powers, I should not go to Carolina at this time; I should sorrowfully stay at home! Austere philosophers, possessed even of cash, have talked to me about the possibility of doing without servants; of trying somehow to serve yourself (boot-cleaning, etc., done by contract), and so escaping from a never-ending welter, dirtier for your mind than boot-cleaning itself. Of which the perpetual *fluctuation*, and change from month to month, is probably the most inhuman element; the fruitful parent of all else that is evil, unendurable and inhuman. A poor Negro overworked on the Cuba sugar-grounds, he is sad to look upon; yet he inspires me with sacred pity, and a kind of human respect is not denied him; him, the hapless brother mortal, performing something useful in his day, and only suffering inhumanity, not doing it or being it. But with what feelings can I look upon an over-fed White Flunky, if I know his ways? Disloyal, unheroic, this one; *in*human in his character, and his work, and his position; more so no creature ever was. Pity is not for him, or not a soft kind of it; nor is any remedy visible, except abolition at no distant date! He is the flower of *nomadic* servitude, proceeding by month's warning, and free supply-and-demand; if obedience is not in his heart, if chiefly gluttony and mutiny are in his heart, and he has to be bribed by high feeding to do the shows of obedience,—what can await him, or be prayed for him, among men, except even " abolition "?

The Duke of Trumps, who sometimes does me the honour of a little conversation, owned that the state of his domestic service was by no means satisfactory to the human mind. " Five-and-forty of them," said his Grace; " really, I suppose, the cleverest in the market, for there is no limit to the wages: I often think how many quiet families, all down to the basis of society, I have disturbed, in attracting gradually, by higher and higher offers, that set of fellows to me; and what the use of them is when here! I feed them like aldermen, pay them as if they were sages and heroes:—Samuel Johnson's wages, at the very last and best, as I have heard you say, were £300 or £500 a year; and Jellysnob, my butler, who indeed is clever, gets, I believe, more than the highest of these sums. And, shall I own it to you? In my young days, with one valet, I had more trouble saved me, more help afforded me to live,—actually more of my will accomplished,—than from these forty-five I now get, or ever shall. It is all a serious comedy; what you call a melancholy sham. Most civil, obsequious, and indeed expert fellows these; but

bid one of them step-out of his regulated sphere on your behalf! An iron law presses on us all here; on them and on
me. In my own house, how much of my will can I have
done, dare I propose to have done? Prudence, on my side,
is prescribed by a jealous and ridiculous point-of-honour
attitude on theirs. They lie here more like a troop of foreign
soldiers that had invaded me, than a body of servants I had
hired. At free quarters; we have strict laws of war established between us; they make their salutes, and do certain
bits of specified work, with many becks and scrapings; but
as to *service*, properly so called—!—I lead the life of a servant, sir; it is I that am a slave; and often I think of packing the whole brotherhood of them out of doors one good day,
and retiring to furnished lodgings; but have never done it
yet!"—Such was the confession of his Grace.

For, indeed, in the long run, it is not possible to buy *obedience* with money. You may buy work done with money: from
cleaning boots to building houses, and to far higher functions,
there is much work bought with money, and got done in a
supportable manner. But, mark withal, that is only from a
class of supportably wise human creatures: from a huge and
ever-increasing insupportably foolish class of human creatures
you cannot buy work in that way; and the attempt in London
itself, much more in Demerara, turns out a very "serious
comedy" indeed! Who has not heard of the Distressed
Needlewomen in these days? We have thirty-thousand
Distressed Needlewomen,—the most of whom cannot sew a
reasonable stitch; for they are, in fact, Mutinous Serving-
maids, who, instead of learning to work and to obey, learned
to give warning: "Then suit yourself, Ma'am!" Hapless
enfranchised White Women, who took the "freedom" to
serve the Devil with their faculties, instead of serving God
or man; hapless souls, they were "enfranchised" to a most
high degree, and had not the wisdom for so ticklish a predicament,—"Then suit yourself, Ma'am;"—and so have tumbled
from one stage of folly to the other stage; and at last are on
the street, with five hungry senses, and no available faculty
whatever. Having finger and thumb, they do procure a
needle, and call themselves Distressed Needlewomen, but
cannot sew at all. I have inquired in the proper places, and
find a quite passionate demand for women that can sew,—
such being unattainable just now. "As well call them

Distressed Astronomers as Distressed Needlewomen!" said a lady to me: " I myself will take three *sewing* Needlewomen, if you can get them for me to-day." Is not that a sight to set before the curious?

Distressed enough, God knows;—but it will require quite other remedies to get at the bottom of *their* complaint, I am afraid. O Brothers! O Sisters! It is for these White Women that my heart bleeds and my soul is heavy; it is for the sight of such mad notions and such unblessed doings now all-prevalent among mankind,—alas, it is for such life-theories and such life-practices, and ghastly clearstarched life-hypocrisies, playing their part under high Heaven, as render these inevitable and unaidable,—that the world of to-day looks black and vile to me, and with all its guineas, in the nostril smells badly! It is not to the West Indies that I run first of all; and not thither with " enfranchisement " first of all, when I discern what " enfranchisement " has led to in hopefuler localities. I tell you again and again, he or she that will not work, and in the anger of the gods cannot be compelled to work, shall die! And not he or she only: alas, alas, were it the guilty only! — But as yet we cannot help it; as yet, for a long while, we must be patient, and let the Exeter-Hallery and other tragic Tomfoolery rave itself out. [*Deep silence in the small remnant of audience ;—the gentleman in white trousers came in again, his creaking painfully audible in spite of efforts.*]

My friends, it is not good to be without a servant in this world; but to be without master, it appears, is a still fataler predicament for some. Without a master, in certain cases, you become a Distressed Needlewoman, and cannot so much as live. Happy he who has found his master, I will say; if not a good master, then some supportable approximation to a good one; for the worst, it appears, in some cases, is preferable to none!

Happy he who has found a master;—and now, farther I will say, having found, let him well keep him. In all human relations *permanency* is what I advocate; *nomadism*, continual change, is what I perceive to be prohibitory of any good whatsoever. Two men that have got to coöperate will do well not to quarrel at the first cause of offence, and throw-up the concern in disgust, hoping to suit themselves better elsewhere. For the most part such hope is fallacious; and they will, on the average, not suit themselves better, but only about as well,—and have to begin again *bare*, which loss often repeated becomes immense, and is finally the loss of everything, and of their joint enterprise itself. For no mutual relation while it continues " bare," is yet a human one, or can bring blessedness, but is only waiting to become such,—mere new-piled crags, which, if you leave them, *will* at last " gather moss," and yield some verdure and pasture. O my friends, what a remedy is this we have fallen upon, for everything that goes wrong between one man and another: " Go, then; I give you a month's warning! " What would you think of a sacrament of marriage constructed on such principles? Marriage by the month,—why this too has been tried, and is still extensively practised in spite of Law and Gospel; but it is not found to do! The legislator, the preacher, all rational mortals, answer, " No, no! " You must marry for longer than a month, and the contract not so easily revocable, even should mistakes occur, as they sometimes do.

I am prepared to maintain against all comers, That in every human relation, from that of husband and wife down to that of master and servant, *nomadism* is the bad plan, and continuance the good. A thousand times, since I first had servants, it has occurred to me, How much better had I servants that were bound to me, and to whom I were bound! Doubtless it were not easy; doubtless it is now impossible: but if it could be done! I say, if the Black gentleman is born to be a servant, and, in fact, is useful in God's creation only as a servant, then let him hire not by the month, but by a very much longer term. That he be " hired for life,"—really here is the essence of the position he now holds! Consider that matter. All else is abuse in it, and this only is essence;— and the abuses must be cleared away. They must and shall! Yes; and the thing itself seems to offer (its abuses once cleared away) a possibility of the most precious kind for the Black man and for us. Servants hired for life, or by a con- tract for a long period, and not easily dissoluble; so and not otherwise would all reasonable mortals, Black and White, wish to hire and to be hired! I invite you to reflect on that; for you will find it true. And if true, it is important for us, in reference to this Negro Question and some others. The Germans say, " You must empty-out the bathing-tub, but not the baby along with it." Fling-out your dirty water with all zeal, and set it careering down the kennels; but try if you can keep the little child!

How to abolish the abuses of slavery, and save the precious thing in it: alas, I do not pretend that this is easy, that it can be done in a day, or a single generation, or a single century: but I do surmise or perceive that it will, by straight methods or by circuitous, need to be done (not in the West-Indian regions alone); and that the one way of helping the Negro at present (Distressed Needlewomen, etc., being quite out of our reach) were, by piously and strenuously beginning it. Begun it must be, I perceive; and carried on in all regions where servants are born and masters; and are *not* prepared to become Distressed Needlewomen, or Demerara Niggers, but to live in some human manner with one another. And truly, my friends, with regard to this world-famous Nigger Question,—which perhaps is louder than it is big, after all,— I would advise you to attack it on that side. Try against the dirty water, with an eye to *save* the baby! That will be a quite new point of attack; where, it seems to me, some real benefit and victory for the poor Negro, might before long be accomplished; and something else than Demerara freedom (with its rum-bottle and no breeches,—" baby " quite *gone* down into the kennels!) or than American stump-oratory, with mutual exasperation fast rising to the desperate pitch, might be possible for philanthropic men and women of the Anglo-Saxon type. Try this; perhaps the very Carolina planter will coöperate with you; he will, if he has any wisdom left in this exasperation! If he do not, he will do worse; and go a strange road with those Niggers of his.

By one means or another these enormities we hear of from the Slave States,—though I think they are hardly so hideous, any of them, as the sight our own Demerara now offers,— must be heard of no more. Men will and must summon " indignation-meetings " about them; and simple persons,— like Wilhelm Meister's Felix flying at the cook's throat for plucking pigeons, yet himself seen shortly after pelting frogs to death with pebbles that lay handy,—will agitate their caucuses, ballot-boxes, dissever the Union, and, in short, play the very devil, if these things are not abated, and do not go on abating more and more towards perfect abolition. *Unjust* master over servant *hired for life* is, once for all, and

shall be, unendurable to human souls. To *cut* the tie, and
" fling Farmer Hodge's horses quite loose " upon the supply-
and-demand principle: that, I will believe, is not the method!
But by some method, by hundredfold restrictions, responsi-
bilities, laws, conditions, cunning methods, Hodge must be got
to treat his horses *justly*, for we cannot stand it longer. And
let Hodge think well of it,—I mean the American two-footed
Hodge,—for there is no other salvation for him. And if he
would avoid a consummation like our Demerara one, I would
advise him to know this secret; which our poor Hodge did not
know, or would not practise, and so is come to such a pass!—
Here is part of my answer to the Hon. Hickory Buckskin, a
senator in those Southern States, and man of really respectable
attainments and dimensions, who in his despair appears to
be entertaining very violent projects now and then, as to
uniting with our West Indies (under a *New Downing Street*),
forming a West-Indian empire, etc. etc.

" The *New Downing Street*, I take it, is at a great distance
here; and we shall wait yet awhile for it, and run good risk
of losing all our Colonies before we can discover the way of
managing them. On that side do not reckon upon help.
At the same time, I can well understand you should ' publicly
discuss the propriety of severing the Union,' and that the
resolution should be general ' you will rather die,' etc. A
man, having certified himself about his trade and post under
the sun, is actually called upon to ' die ' in vindication of it,
if needful; in defending the possibilities he has of carrying
it on, and eschewing with it the belly of Perdition, when
extraneous Insanity is pushing it thither. All this I pre-
suppose of you, of men born of your lineage; and have not a
word to say against it.

" Meanwhile suffer me to say this other thing. You will
not find Negro Slavery defensible by the mere resolution,
never so extensive, to defend it. No, there is another condition wanted: That your relation to the Negroes, in this
thing called Slavery (with such an emphasis upon the word)
be actually fair, just and according to the facts;—fair, I say,
not in the sight of New-England platforms, but of God
Almighty the Maker of both Negroes and you. That is the
one ground on which men can take their stand; in the long-
run all human causes, and this cause too, will come to be
settled *there*. Forgive me for saying that I do not think you

have yet got to that point of perfection with your Negro relations; that there is probably much in them *not* fair, nor agreeable to the Maker of us, and to the eternal laws of fact as written in the Negro's being and in ours.

" The advice of advices, therefore, to men so circumstanced were, With all diligence make them so! Otherwise than *so*, they are doomed by Earth and by Heaven. Demerara may be the maddest remedy, as I think it is a very mad one: but some remedy we must have; or if none, then destruction and annihilation, by the Demerara or a worse method. These things it would behove you of the Southern States, above all men, to be now thinking of. How to make the Negro's position among his White fellow-creatures a just one,—the real and genuine expression of what *commandment* the Maker has given to both of you, by making the one of you thus and the other so, and putting you in juxtaposition on this Earth of His? That you should *cut* the ligature, and say, ' He has made us equal,' would be saying a palpable falsity, big with hideous ruin for all concerned in it: I hope and believe, you, with our example before you, will say something much better than that. But something, very many things, do not hide from yourselves, will require to be said! And I do not pretend that it will be easy or soon done, to get a proper code of laws (and still more difficult, a proper system of habits, ways of thinking, for a basis to such ' code ') on the rights of Negroes and Whites. But that also, you may depend upon it, has fallen to White men as a duty;—to you now in the first place, after our sad failure. And unless you can do it, be certain, neither will you be able to keep your Negroes; your portion too will be the Demerara or a worse one. This seems to me indubitable.

" Or perhaps you have already begun? Persist diligently, if so; but at all events, begin! For example, ought there not to be in every Slave State, a fixed legal sum, on paying which, any Black man was entitled to demand his freedom? Settle a fair sum; and let it stand fixed by law. If the poor Black can, by forethought, industry, self-denial, accumulate this sum, has he not proved the actual ' freedom ' of his soul, to a fair extent: in God's name, why will you keep his body captive? It seems to me a well-considered law of this kind might do you invaluable service:—might it not be a real *safety-valve*, and ever-open *chimney*, for that downpressed Slave-world with whatever injustices are still in it; whereby all the stronger and really worthier elements would escape peaceably, as they arose, instead of accumulating there, and convulsing you, as now? Or again, look at the Serfs of the Middle Ages: they married and gave in marriage; nay, they could not even be *divorced* from their natal soil; had home, family, and a treatment that was human. Many laws, and gradually a whole code of laws, on this matter, could be made! And will have to be made; if you would avoid the ugly Demerara issue, or even uglier which may be in store. I can see no other road for you. This new question has arisen, million-voiced: 'What *are* the wages of a Black servant, hired for life by White men?' This question must be answered, in some not insupportably erroneous way: gods and men are warning you that you must answer it, if you would continue there!'—The Hon. Hickory never acknowledged my letter; but I hope he is getting on with the advice I gave him, all the same!

For the rest, I never thought the "rights of Negroes" worth much discussing, nor the rights of men in any form; the grand point, as I once said, is the *mights* of men,—what portion of their "rights" they have a chance of getting sorted out, and realised, in this confused world. We will not go deep into the question here about the Negro's rights. We will give a single glance into it, and see, for one thing, how complex it is.

West-India Islands, still full of waste fertility, produce abundant pumpkins: pumpkins, however, you will observe, are not the sole requisite for human well-being. No; for a pig they are the one thing needful; but for a man they are only the first of several things needful. The first is here; but the second and remaining, how are they to be got? The answer is wide as human society itself. Society at large, as instituted in each country of the world, is the answer such country has been able to give: Here, in this poor country, the rights of man and the mights of man are—such and such! An approximate answer to a question capable only of better and better solutions, never of any perfect, or absolutely good one. Nay, if we inquire, with much narrower scope, as to the right of chief management in cultivating those West-India lands: to the "right of property" so-called, and of doing what you like with your own? Even this question is abstruse enough. Who it may be that has a right to raise pumpkins and other produce on those Islands, perhaps none can, except temporarily, decide. The Islands are good withal for pepper, for sugar, for sago, arrow-root, for coffee, perhaps for cinnamon and precious spices; things far nobler than pumpkins; and leading towards Commerces, Arts, Politics and Social Developments, which alone are the noblest product, where men (and not pigs with pumpkins) are the parties concerned! Well, all this fruit too, fruit spicy and commercial, fruit spiritual and celestial, so far beyond the merely pumpkinish and grossly terrene, lies in the West-India lands: and the ultimate "proprietorship" of them,—why, I suppose, it will vest in him who can the *best* educe from them whatever of noble produce they were created fit for yielding. He, I compute, is the real "Vicegerent of the Maker" there; in him, better and better chosen, and not in another, is the "property" vested by decree of Heaven's chancery itself!

Up to this time it is the Saxon British mainly; they hitherto have cultivated with some manfulness: and when a manfuler class of cultivators, stronger, worthier to have such land, abler to bring fruit from it, shall make their appearance,—they, doubt it not, by fortune of war, and other confused negotiation and vicissitude, will be declared by Nature and Fact to *be* the worthier, and will become proprietors,—perhaps also only for a time. That is the law, I take it; ultimate, supreme, for all lands in all countries under this sky. The one perfect eternal proprietor is the Maker who created them: the temporary better or worse proprietor is he whom the Maker has sent on that mission; he who the best hitherto can educe from said lands the beneficent gifts the Maker endowed them with; or, which is but another definition of the same person, he who leads hitherto the manfulest life on that bit of soil, doing, better than another yet found can do, the Eternal Purpose and Supreme Will there.

And now observe, my friends, it was not Black Quashee, or those he represents, that made those West-India Islands what they are, or can, by any hypothesis, be considered to have the right of growing pumpkins there. For countless ages, since they first mounted oozy, on the back of earthquakes, from their dark bed in the Ocean deeps, and reeking saluted the tropical Sun, and ever onwards till the European

white man first saw them some three short centuries ago,
those Islands had produced mere jungle, savagery, poison-
reptiles and swamp-malaria: till the white European first
saw them, they were as if not yet created,—their noble
elements of cinnamon, sugar, coffee, pepper black and gray,
lying all asleep, waiting the white enchanter who should
say to them, Awake! Till the end of human history and the
sounding of the Trump of Doom, they might have lain so,
had Quashee and the like of him been the only artists in the
game. Swamps, fever-jungles, man-eating Caribs, rattlesnakes, and reeking waste and putrefaction, this has been the
produce of them under the incompetent Caribal (what we
call Cannibal) possessors, till that time; and Quashee knows,
himself, whether ever he could have introduced an improvement. Him, had he by a miraculous chance been wafted
thither, the Caribals would have eaten, rolling him as a fat
morsel under their tongue; for him, till the sounding of the
Trump of Doom, the rattlesnakes and savageries would have
held-on their way. It was not he, then; it was another than
he! Never by art of his could one pumpkin have grown there
to solace any human throat; nothing but savagery and
reeking putrefaction could have grown there. These plentiful
pumpkins, I say therefore, are not his: no, they are another's;
they are his only under conditions. Conditions which
Exeter Hall, for the present, has forgotten; but which Nature
and the Eternal Powers have by no manner of means forgotten,
but do at all moments keep in mind; and, at the right
moment, will, with the due impressiveness, perhaps in a
rather terrible manner, bring again to our mind also!

If Quashee will not honestly aid in bringing-out those
sugars, cinnamons and nobler products of the West-Indian
Islands, for the benefit of all mankind, then I say neither
will the Powers permit Quashee to continue growing pumpkins
there for his own lazy benefit; but will shear him out, by
and by, like a lazy gourd overshadowing rich ground; him
and all that partake with him,—perhaps in a very terrible
manner. For, under favour of Exeter Hall, the "terrible
manner" is not yet quite extinct with the Destinies in this
Universe; nor will it quite cease, I apprehend, for soft souw-
der or philanthropic stump-oratory now or henceforth. No;
the gods wish besides pumpkins, that spices and valuable
products be grown in their West Indies; thus much they have

declared in so making the West Indies:—infinitely more they wish, that manful industrious men occupy their West Indies, not indolent two-legged cattle, however "happy" over their abundant pumpkins! Both these things, we may be assured, the immortal gods have decided upon, passed their eternal Act of Parliament for: and both of them, though all terrestrial Parliaments and entities oppose it to the death, shall be done. Quashee, if he will not help in bringing-out the spices, will get himself made a slave again (which state will be a little less ugly than his present one), and with beneficent whip, since other methods avail not, will be compelled to work.

Or, alas, let him look across to Haiti, and trace a far sterner prophecy! Let him, by his ugliness, idleness, rebellion, banish all White men from the West Indies, and make it all one Haiti,—with little or no sugar growing, black Peter exterminating black Paul, and where a garden of the Hesperides might be, nothing but a tropical dog-kennel and pestiferous jungle,—does he think that will forever continue pleasant to gods and men? I see men, the rose-pink cant all peeled away from them, land one day on those black coasts; men *sent* by the Laws of this Universe, and inexorable Course of Things; men hungry for gold, remorseless, fierce as the old Buccaneers were;—and a doom for Quashee which I had rather not contemplate! The gods are long-suffering; but the law from the beginning was, He that will not work shall perish from the earth; and the patience of the gods has limits!

Before the West Indies could grow a pumpkin for any Negro, how much European heroism had to spend itself in obscure battle; to sink, in mortal agony, before the jungles, the putrescences and waste savageries could become arable, and the Devils be in some measure chained there! The West Indies grow pine-apples, and sweet fruits, and spices; we hope they will one day grow beautiful Heroic human lives too, which is surely the ultimate object they were made for; beautiful souls and brave; sages, poets, what not; making the Earth nobler round them, as their kindred from of old have been doing; true "splinters of the old Harz Rock;" heroic white men, worthy to be called old Saxons, browned with a mahogany tint in those new climates and conditions. But under the soil of Jamaica, before it could even produce spices or any pumpkin, the bones of many thousand British men had to be laid. Brave Colonel Fortescue, brave Colonel Sedgwick, brave Colonel Brayne,—the dust of many thousand strong old English hearts lies there; worn-down swiftly in frightful travail, chaining the Devils, which were manifold. Heroic Blake contributed a bit of his life to that Jamaica. A bit of the great Protector's own life lies there; beneath those pumpkins lies a bit of the life that was Oliver Cromwell's. How the great Protector would have rejoiced to think, that all this was to issue in growing pumpkins to keep Quashee in a comfortable idle condition! No; that is not the ultimate issue; not that.

The West-Indian Whites, so soon as this bewilderment of philanthropic and other jargon abates from them, and their poor eyes get to discern a little what the Facts are and what the Laws are, will strike into another course, I apprehend! I apprehend they will, as a preliminary, resolutely *refuse* to permit the Black man any privilege whatever of pumpkins till he agree for work in return. Not a square inch of soil in those fruitful Isles, purchased by British blood, shall any Black man hold to grow pumpkins for him, except on terms that are fair towards Britain. Fair; see that they be not unfair, not towards ourselves, and still more, not towards him. For injustice is *forever* accursed: and precisely our unfairness towards the enslaved Black man has,—by inevitable revulsion and fated turn of the wheel,—brought about these present confusions.

Fair towards Britain it will be, that Quashee give work for privilege to grow pumpkins. Not a pumpkin, Quashee, not a square yard of soil, till you agree to do the State so many days of service. Annually that soil will grow you pumpkins; but annually also, without fail, shall you, for the owner thereof, do your appointed days of labour. The State has plenty of waste soil; but the State will religiously give you none of it on other terms. The State wants sugar from these Islands, and means to have it; wants virtuous industry in these Islands, and must have it. The State demands of you such service as will bring these results, this latter result which includes all. Not a Black Ireland, by immigration, and boundless black supply for the demand; not that,—may the gods forbid!—but a regulated West Indies, with black working population in adequate numbers; all "happy," if they find it possible; and *not* entirely unbeautiful to gods and men, which latter result they *must* find possible! All "happy" enough; that is to say, all working according to the faculty they have got, making a little more divine this Earth which the gods have given them. Is there any other "happiness,"—if it be not that of pigs fattening daily to the slaughter? So will the State speak by and by.

Any poor idle Black man, any idle White man, rich or poor, is a mere eye-sorrow to the State; a perpetual blister on the skin of the State. The State is taking measures, some of them rather extensive, in Europe at this very time, and already, as in Paris, Berlin and elsewhere, rather tremendous measures, to *get* its rich white men set to work; for alas, they also have long sat Negro-like up to the ears in pumpkin, regardless of "work," and of a world all going to waste for their idleness! Extensive measures, I say; and already (as, in all European lands, this scandalous Year of street-barricades and fugitive sham - kings exhibits) *tremendous* measures; for the thing is urgent to be done.

The thing must be done everywhere; *must* is the word. Only it is so terribly difficult to do; and will take generations yet, this of getting our rich European white men "set to work"! But yours in the West Indies, my obscure Black friends, your work, and the getting of you set to it, is a simple affair; and by diligence, the West-Indian legislatures, and Royal governors, setting their faces fairly to the problem, will get it done. You are not "slaves" now; nor do I wish, if it can be avoided, to see you slaves again: but decidedly you will have to be servants to those that are born *wiser* than you, that are born lords of you; servants to the Whites, if they *are* (as what mortal can doubt they are?) born wiser than you. That, you may depend on it, my obscure Black friends, is and was always the Law of the World, for you and for all men: To *be* servants, the more foolish of us to the more wise; and only sorrow, futility and disappointment will betide both, till both in some approximate degree get to conform to the same. Heaven's laws are not repealable by Earth, however Earth may try,—and it has been trying hard, in some directions, of late! I say, no well-being, and in the end no being at all, will be possible for you or us, if the law of Heaven is not complied with. And if "slave" mean essentially "servant hired for life,"—for life, or by a contract of long continuance and not easily dissoluble,—I ask once more, Whether, in all human things, the "contract of long continuance" is not precisely the contract to be desired, were the right terms once found for it? Servant hired for life, were the right terms once found, which I do not pretend they are, seems to me much preferable to servant hired for the month, or by contract dissoluble in a day. What that amounts to, we have known, and our thirty-thousand Distressed Astronomers have known; and we don't want that! [*Some assent in the small remnant of an audience.* "*Silence!*" *from the Chair.*]

To state articulately, and put into practical Lawbooks, what on all sides is *fair* from the West-Indian White to the West-Indian Black; what relations the Eternal Maker *has* established between these two creatures of His; what He has written down with intricate but ineffaceable record, legible to candid human insight, in the respective qualities, strengths, necessities and capabilities of each of the two: this, as I told the Hon. Hickory my Carolina correspondent, will be a long problem; only to be solved by continuous human endeavour, and earnest effort gradually perfecting itself as experience successively yields new light to it. This will be to "*find* the right terms;" terms of a contract that will endure, and be sanctioned by Heaven, and obtain prosperity on Earth, between the two. A long problem, terribly neglected hitherto;—whence these West-Indian sorrows, and Exeter-Hall monstrosities, just now! But a problem which must be entered upon, and by degrees be completed. A problem which, I think, the English People also, if they mean to retain human Colonies, and not Black Irelands in addition to the White, cannot begin too soon. What are the true relations between Negro and White, their mutual duties under the sight of the Maker of them both; what human laws will assist both to comply more and more with these? The solution, only to be gained by earnest endeavour, and sincere reading of experience, such as have never yet been bestowed on it, is not yet here; the solution is perhaps still distant. But some approximation to it, various real approximations, could be made, and must be made:—this of declaring that Negro and White are *un*related, loose from one another, on a footing of perfect equality, and subject to no law but that of supply-and-demand according to the Dismal Science; this, which contradicts the palpablest facts, is clearly no solution, but a cutting of the knot asunder; and every hour we persist in this is leading us towards *dis*solution instead of solution!

What, then, is practically to be done by us poor English with our Demerara and other blacks? Well, in such a mess as we have made there, it is not easy saying what is first to be done! But all this of perfect equality, of cutting quite loose from one another; all this, with " immigration loan," " happiness of black peasantry," and the other melancholy stuff that has followed from it, will first of all require to be *un*done, and the ground cleared of it, by way of preliminary to " doing " ! After that there may several things be possible.

Already one hears of Black *Adscripti glebæ ;* which seems a promising arrangement, one of the first to suggest itself in such a complicacy. It appears the Dutch Blacks, in Java, are already a kind of *Adscripts,* after the manner of the old European serfs; bound, by royal authority, to give so many days of work a year. Is not this something like a real approximation; the first step towards all manner of such? Wherever, in British territory, there exists a Black man, and needful work to the just extent is not to be got out of him, such a law, in defect of better, should be brought to bear upon said Black man! How many laws of like purport, conceivable some of them, might be brought to bear upon the Black man and the White, with all despatch by way of solution instead of dissolution to their complicated case just now! On the whole, it ought to be rendered possible, ought it not, for White men to live beside Black men, and in some just manner to command Black men, and produce West-Indian fruitfulness by means of them? West-Indian fruitfulness will need to be produced. If the English cannot find the method for that, they may rest assured there will another come (Brother Jonathan or still another) who can. He it is whom the gods will bid continue in the West Indies; bidding us ignominiously, " Depart, ye quack-ridden, incompetent! "—

One other remark, as to the present Trade in Slaves, and to our suppression of the same. If buying of Black war-captives in Africa, and bringing them over to the Sugar Islands for sale again be, as I think it is, a contradiction of the Laws of this Universe, let us heartily pray Heaven to end the practice; let us ourselves help Heaven to end it, wherever the opportunity is given. If it be the most flagrant and alarming contradiction to the said Laws which is now witnessed on this Earth; so flagrant and alarming that a man cannot exist, and follow his affairs, in the same Planet with it; why, then indeed—— But is it, quite certainly, such? Alas, look at that group of *un*sold, unbought, unmarketable Irish " free " citizens, dying there in the ditch, whither my Lord of Rackrent and the constitutional sheriffs have evicted them; or at those " divine missionaries," of the same free country, now traversing, with rags on back, and child on each arm, the principal thoroughfares of London, to tell men what " freedom " really is;—and admit that there may be doubts on that point! But if it *is*, I say, the most alarming contradiction to the said Laws which is now witnessed on this earth; so flagrant a contradiction that a just man cannot exist, and follow his affairs, in the same Planet with it, then, sure enough, let us, in God's name, fling-aside all our affairs, and hasten out to put an end to it, as the first thing the Heavens want us to do. By all manner of means. This thing done, the Heavens will prosper all other things with us! Not a doubt of it,—provided your premiss be not doubtful.

But now, furthermore, give me leave to ask, Whether the way of doing it is this somewhat surprising one, of trying to blockade the continent of Africa itself, and to watch slave-ships along that extremely extensive and unwholesome coast? The enterprise is very gigantic; and proves hitherto as futile as any enterprise has lately done. Certain wise men once, before this, set about confining the cuckoo by a big circular wall; but they could not manage it!—Watch the coast of Africa? That is a very long Coast; good part of the Coast of the terraqueous Globe! And the living centres of this slave mischief, the live coals that produce all this world-wide smoke, it appears, lie simply in two points, Cuba and Brazil, which *are* perfectly accessible and manageable.

If the Laws of Heaven do authorise you to keep the whole world in a pother about this question; if you really can appeal to the Almighty God upon it, and set common interests, and terrestrial considerations, and common sense, at defiance in behalf of it,—why, in Heaven's name, not go to Cuba and Brazil with a sufficiency of Seventy-fours; and signify to those nefarious countries: " Nefarious countries, your procedure on the Negro Question is too bad; see, of all the solecisms now submitted to on Earth, it is the most alarming and transcendent, and, in fact, is such that a just man cannot follow his affairs any longer in the same Planet with it. You clearly will not, you nefarious populations, for love or fear, watching or entreaty, respect the rights of the Negro enough; —wherefore we here, with our Seventy-fours, are come to be King over you, and will on the spot henceforth see for ourselves that you do it!"

Why not, if Heaven do send us? The thing can be done; easily, if you are sure of that proviso. It can be done: it is the way to "suppress the Slave-trade;" and so far as yet appears, the one way.

Most thinking people,—if hen-stealing prevail to a plainly unendurable extent, will you station police-officers at every hen-roost; and keep them watching and cruising incessantly to and fro over the Parish, in the unwholesome dark, at enormous expense, with almost no effect? Or will you not try rather to discover where the fox's den is, and kill the fox! Which of those two things will you do? Most thinking people, you know the fox and his den; there he is,—kill him, and discharge your cruisers and police-watchers!—[*Laughter.*]

O my friends, I feel there is an immense fund of Human Stupidity circulating among us, and much clogging our affairs for some time past! A certain man has called us, "of all peoples the wisest in action;" but he added, "the stupidest in speech:"—and it is a sore thing, in these constitutional times, times mainly of universal Parliamentary and other Eloquence, that the "speakers" have all first to emit, in such tumultuous volumes, their human stupor, as the indispensable preliminary, and everywhere we must first see that and its results *out*, before beginning any business.— (*Explicit MS.*)

THE OPERA [1]

[" DEAR P.,—Not having anything of my own which I could contribute (as is my wish and duty) to this pious Adventure of yours, and not being able in these busy days to get anything ready, I decide to offer you a bit of an Excerpt from that singular *Conspectus of England*, lately written, not yet printed, by Professor Ezechiel Peasemeal, a distinguished American friend of mine. Dr. Peasemeal will excuse my printing it here. His *Conspectus*, a work of some extent, has already been crowned by the Phi Beta Kappa Society of Buncombe, which includes, as you know, the chief thinkers of the New World; and it will probably be printed entire in their ' Transactions ' one day. Meanwhile let your readers have the first taste of it; and much good may it do them and you! "—T. C.]

MUSIC is well said to be the speech of angels; in fact, nothing among the utterances allowed to man is felt to be so divine. It brings us near to the Infinite; we look for moments, across the cloudy elements, into the eternal Sea of Light, when song leads and inspires us. Serious nations, all nations that can still listen to the mandate of Nature, have prized song and music as the highest; as a vehicle for worship, for prophecy, and for whatsoever in them was divine. Their singer was a *vates*, admitted to the council of the universe, friend of the gods, and choicest benefactor to man.

Reader, it was actually so in Greek, in Roman, in Moslem, Christian, most of all in Old-Hebrew times; and if you look how it now is, you will find a change that should astonish you. Good Heavens, from a Psalm of Asaph to a seat at the London Opera in the Haymarket, what a road have men travelled! The waste that is made in music is probably among the saddest of all our squanderings of God's gifts. Music has, for a long time past, been avowedly mad, divorced from sense and the reality of things; and runs about now as an open Bedlamite, for a good many generations back, bragging that

---

[1] *Keepsake* for 1852.—The " dear P." there, I recollect, was my old friend Procter (Barry Cornwall); and his " pious Adventure " had reference to that same Publication, under touching human circumstances which had lately arisen.

she has nothing to do with sense and reality, but with fiction and delirium only; and stares with unaffected amazement, not able to suppress an elegant burst of witty laughter, at my suggesting the old fact to her.

Fact nevertheless it is, forgotten, and fallen ridiculous as it may be. Tyrtæus, who had a little music, did not sing Barbers of Seville, but the need of beating back one's country's enemies; a most *true* song, to which the hearts of men did burst responsive into fiery melody, followed by fiery strokes before long. Sophocles also sang, and showed in grand dramatic rhythm and melody, not a fable but a fact, the best he could interpret it; the judgments of Eternal Destiny upon the erring sons of men. Æschylus, Sophocles, all noble poets were priests as well; and sang the *truest* (which was also the divinest) they had been privileged to discover here below. To " sing the praise of God," that, you will find, if you can interpret old words, and see what new things they mean, was always, and will always be, the business of the singer. He who forsakes that business, and, wasting our divinest gifts, sings the praise of Chaos, what shall we say of him!

David, king of Judah, a soul inspired by divine music and much other heroism, was wont to pour himself in song; he, with seer's eye and heart, discerned the Godlike amid the Human; struck tones that were an echo of the sphere-harmonies, and are still felt to be such. Reader, art thou one of a thousand, able still to *read* a Psalm of David, and catch some echo of it through the old dim centuries; feeling far off, in thy own heart, what it once was to other hearts made as thine? To sing it attempt not, for it is impossible in this late time; only know that it once was sung. Then go to the Opera, and hear, with unspeakable reflections, what things men now sing! . . .

Of the Haymarket Opera my account, in fine, is this: Lustres, candelabras, painting, gilding at discretion; a hall as of the Caliph Alraschid, or him that commanded the slaves of the Lamp; a hall as if fitted-up by the genii, regardless of expense. Upholstery, and the outlay of human capital, could do no more. Artists, too, as they are called, have been got together from the ends of the world, regardless likewise of expense, to do dancing and singing, some of them even geniuses in their craft. One singer in particular, called Coletti or some such name, seemed to me, by the cast of his face, by the tones of his voice, by his general bearing, so far as I could read it, to be a man of deep and ardent sensibilities, of delicate intuitions, just sympathies; originally an almost poetic soul, or man of *genius*, as we term it; stamped by Nature as capable of far other work than squalling here, like a blind Samson, to make the Philistines sport!

Nay, all of them had aptitudes, perhaps of a distinguished kind; and must, by their own and other people's labour, have got a training equal or superior in toilsomeness, earnest assiduity and patient travail to what breeds men to the most arduous trades. I speak not of kings, grandees, or the like show-figures; but few soldiers, judges, men of letters, can have had such pains taken with them. The very ballet-girls, with their muslin saucers round them, were perhaps little short of miraculous; whirling and spinning there in strange mad vortexes, and then suddenly fixing themselves motionless, each upon her left or right great toe, with the other leg stretched out at an angle of ninety degrees,—as if you had suddenly pricked into the floor, by one of their points, a pair, or rather a multitudinous cohort, of mad restlessly jumping and clipping scissors, and so bidden them rest, with opened blades, and stand still, in the Devil's name! A truly notable motion; marvellous, almost miraculous, were not the people there so used to it. Motion peculiar to the Opera; perhaps the ugliest, and surely one of the most difficult, ever taught a female creature in this world. Nature abhors it; but Art does at least admit it to border on the impossible. One little Cerito, or Taglioni the Second, that night when I was there, went bounding from the floor as if she had been made of Indian-rubber, or filled with hydrogen gas, and inclined by positive levity to bolt through the ceiling; perhaps neither Semiramis nor Catherine the Second had bred herself so carefully.

Such talent, and such martyrdom of training, gathered from the four winds, was now here, to do its feat and be paid for it. Regardless of expense, indeed! The purse of Fortunatus seemed to have opened itself, and the divine art of Musical Sound and Rhythmic Motion was welcomed with an explosion of all the magnificences which the other arts, fine and coarse, could achieve. For you are to think of some

Rossini or Bellini in the rear of it, too: to say nothing of the Stanfields, and hosts of scene-painters, machinists, engineers, enterprisers;—fit to have taken Gibraltar, written the History of England, or reduced Ireland into Industrial Regiments, had they so set their minds to it!

Alas, and of all these notable or noticeable human talents, and excellent perseverances and energies, backed by mountains of wealth, and led by the divine art of Music and Rhythm vouchsafed by Heaven to them and us, what was to be the issue here this evening? An hour's amusement, not amusing either, but wearisome and dreary, to a high-dizened select populace of male and female persons, who seemed to me not much worth amusing! Could any one have pealed into their hearts once, one true thought, and glimpse of Self-vision: " High - dizened, most expensive persons, Aristocracy so-called, or *Best* of the World, beware, beware what proofs you are giving here of betterness and bestness!" And then the salutary pang of conscience in reply: " A select populace, with money in its purse, and drilled a little by the posture-master: good Heavens! if that were what, here and every-where in God's Creation, I *am?* And a world all dying because I am, and show myself to be, and to have long been, even that? John, the carriage, the carriage; swift! Let me go home in silence, to reflection, perhaps to sackcloth and ashes!" This, and not amusement, would have profited those high-dizened persons.

Amusement, at any rate, they did not get from Euterpe and Melpomene. These two Muses, sent-for regardless of expense, I could see, were but the vehicle of a kind of service which I judged to be Paphian rather. Young beauties of both sexes used their opera-glasses, you could notice, not entirely for looking at the stage. And, it must be owned, the light, in this explosion of all the upholsteries, and the human fine arts and coarse, was magical; and made your fair one an Armida, — if you liked her better so. Nay, certain old Improper Females (of quality), in their rouge and jewels, even these looked some *reminiscence* of enchantment; and I saw this and the other lean domestic Dandy, with icy smile on his old worn face; this and the other Marquis Chatabagues, Prince Mahogany, or the like foreign Dignitary, tripping into the boxes of said females, grinning there awhile, with dyed moustachios and macassar-oil graciosity, and then tripping-out again;—and, in fact, I perceived that Coletti and Cerito and the Rhythmic Arts were a mere accompaniment here.

Wonderful to see; and sad, if you had eyes! Do but think of it. Cleopatra threw pearls into her drink, in mere waste; which was reckoned foolish of her. But here had the Modern Aristocracy of men brought the divinest of its Arts, heavenly Music itself; and, piling all the upholsteries and ingenuities that other human art could do, had lighted them into a bonfire to illuminate an hour's flirtation of Chatabagues, Mahogany, and these improper persons! Never in Nature had I seen such waste before. O Coletti, you whose inborn melody, once of kindred, as I judged, to "the Melodies Eternal," might have valiantly weeded-out this and the other false thing from the ways of men, and made a bit of God's Creation more melodious,—they have purchased you away from that; chained you to the wheel of Prince Mahogany's chariot, and here you make sport for a macassar Chatabagues and his improper-females past the prime of life! Wretched spiritual Nigger, O, if you *had* some genius, and were not a born Nigger with mere appetite for pumpkin, should you have endured such a lot? I lament for you beyond all other expenses. Other expenses are light; you are the Cleopatra's pearl that should not have been flung into Mahogany's claret-cup. And Rossini, too, and Mozart and Bellini——O Heavens! when I think that Music too is condemned to be mad, and to burn herself, to this end, on such a funeral pile,— your celestial Opera-house grows dark and infernal to me! Behind its glitter stalks the shadow of Eternal Death; through it too, I look not "up into the divine eye," as Richter has it, "but down into the bottomless eyesocket"—not up towards God, Heaven, and the Throne of Truth, but too truly down towards Falsity, Vacuity, and the dwelling-place of Ever-lasting Despair. . . .

Good sirs, surely I by no means expect the Opera will abolish itself this year or the next. But if you ask me, Why heroes are not born now, why heroisms are not done now? I will answer you: It is a world all calculated for strangling of heroisms. At every ingress into life, the genius of the world lies in wait for heroisms, and by seduction or compulsion unweariedly does its utmost to pervert them or extinguish them. Yes; to its Hells of sweating tailors, distressed needlewomen and the like, this Opera of yours is the appropriate Heaven! Of a truth, if you will read a Psalm of Asaph till you understand it, and then come hither and hear the Rossini-and-Coletti Psalm, you will find the ages have altered a good deal. . . .

Nor do I wish all men to become Psalmist Asaphs and fanatic Hebrews. Far other is my wish; far other, and wider, is now my notion of this Universe. Populations of stern faces, stern as any Hebrew, but capable withal of bursting into inextinguishable laughter on occasion: — do you understand that new and better form of character? Laughter also, if it come from the heart, is a heavenly thing. But, at least and lowest, I would have you a Population abhorring phantasms;—abhorring *unveracity* in all things; and in your " amusements," which are voluntary and not compulsory things, abhorring it most impatiently of all. . . .

PETITION ON THE COPYRIGHT BILL [1]

[1839]

To the Honourable the Commons of England in Parliament assembled, the Petition of Thomas Carlyle, a Writer of Books,

Humbly showeth,

That your petitioner has written certain books, being incited thereto by various innocent or laudable considerations, chiefly by the thought that said books might in the end be found to be worth something.

That your petitioner had not the happiness to receive from Mr. Thomas Tegg, or any Publisher, Republisher, Printer, Bookseller, Bookbuyer, or other the like man or body of men, any encouragement or countenance in writing of said books, or to discern any chance of receiving such; but wrote them by efforts of his own and the favour of Heaven.

That all useful labour is worthy of recompense; that all honest labour is worthy of the chance of recompense; that the giving and assuring to each man what recompense his labour has actually merited, may be said to be the business of all Legislation, Polity, Government and Social Arrangement whatsoever among men;—a business indispensable to attempt, impossible to accomplish accurately, difficult to accomplish without inaccuracies that become enormous, insupportable, and the parent of Social Confusions which never altogether end.

That your petitioner does not undertake to say what recompense in money this labour of his may deserve; whether it deserves any recompense in money, or whether money in any quantity could hire him to do the like.

That this his labour has found hitherto, in money or money's worth, small recompense or none; that he is by no means sure of its ever finding recompense, but thinks that, if

[1] *The Examiner*, April 7, 1839.

so, it will be at a distant time, when he, the labourer, will probably no longer be in need of money, and those dear to him will still be in need of it.

That the law does at least protect all persons in selling the production of their labour at what they can get for it, in all market-places, to all lengths of time. Much more than this the law does to many, but so much it does to all, and less than this to none.

That your petitioner cannot discover himself to have done unlawfully in this his said labour of writing books, or to have become criminal, or have forfeited the law's protection thereby. Contrariwise your petitioner believes firmly that he is innocent in said labour; that if he be found in the long-run to have written a genuine enduring book, his merit therein, and desert towards England and English and other men, will be considerable, not easily estimable in money; that on the other hand, if his book proves false and ephemeral, he and it will be abolished and forgotten, and no harm done.

That, in this manner, your petitioner plays no unfair game against the world; his stake being life itself, so to speak (for the penalty is death by starvation), and the world's stake nothing till once it see the dice thrown; so that in any case the world cannot lose.

That in the happy and long-doubtful event of the game's going in his favour, your petitioner submits that the small winnings thereof do belong to him or his, and that no other mortal has justly either part or lot in them at all, now, henceforth or forever.

May it therefore please your Honourable House to protect him in said happy and long-doubtful event; and (by passing your Copyright Bill) forbid all Thomas Teggs and other extraneous persons, entirely unconcerned in this adventure of his, to steal from him his small winnings, for a space of sixty years at shortest. After sixty years, unless your Honourable House provide otherwise, they may begin to steal.

And your petitioner will ever pray.

THOMAS CARLYLE.